Hidde

Curtis Bollington lives and works in the North West of England. He has been a journalist and copywriter for more than 25 years, prior to which he worked through a variety of jobs including training as a motor mechanic, cleaning boilers in the last steam-operated colliery in Lancashire, and interviewing tenants on Manchester City Council's housing list. Hidden Gems is his first novel.

Reader reviews of *Hidden Gems*:

'Brilliant, the author manages to create visual imagery with cultural expression and the emotional intensity worthy of a great movie… This is not just a good read, it is a moving piece of work that deserves a huge audience following — a kind of a Kate Atkinson for boys (and tough women!). It made me cry, think and laugh out loud, what more is there? Loved loved loved it!' *PO*

'…only a handful of pages passed before I was hooked … *Hidden Gems* was simply unputdownable!' *Spenny*

'Chapter by chapter the reader is taken back and forth to view the drama unfolding in different sets of characters' lives. As the the book progresses the lives of the various characters become interwoven, paths cross unknowingly—all because of one unique, ugly but very much loved sportscar! Superbly written and well thought through. Highly recommended.' *Arnie Mawbs*

CURTIS
BOLLINGTON

Hidden Gems

mu media

This novel is a work of fiction.

First published in Great Britain by mu media 2011
mu media,
11 Parsonage Road, Heaton Moor, Stockport SK4 4JZ
Tel: 07880 535 615 email: curtis@mu-media.co.uk

ISBN: 978-0-9570476-0-0

Body text set in Adobe Caslon Pro by the author.
Cover design and artwork by the author.
Printed and bound in Great Britain.

For you, Dominic—our darling son.

Acknowledgements

You probably wouldn't be reading this on paper without the kind help if John and Karen Spencer. They enjoyed the ebook version of *Hidden Gems* so much, they insisted it needed to be read by more people, as a paperback—committing their own funds to get it printed. I did warn them they would probably never get their money back, but that didn't seem to make a difference.

I would never have considered writing, but for the love and support I've received from some wonderful people over the years: for example Fran and Mark Shaw helped my realise the world was much bigger than a Manchester overspill estate, and they will probably never be fully aware how much I owe to them; and Keith Elliott showed me how to string two words together, then edit one of them out—I'll always be grateful for that.

I am fortunate to have a long-established circle of friends and lots of family, now to be found in all directions, and often too distant. We have shared great and gentle adventures: some of which have seeped into *Hidden Gems*. Sadly, with the laws of odds and age, some lovely people have gone, so this is for them too.

And finally for Tania, for putting up with my hours of solitude, my occasional grumpiness, and the damned poverty of my chosen profession.

I dream that we'll all share a table one endless summer evening, probably in the countryside, about two-hours drive from Kiev.

This is a work of fiction. All the names and characters are either invented or used fictitiously. The events described are imaginary. Some events are imaginary versions of actual events, such as: the Cuban Missile Crisis, Khrushchev's passion for growing American corn, that the Soviets had few operable inter-continental nuclear missiles (the Americans weren't much better), and that most early Russian tractors were copied from American designs. Transdniester, or Transdnistria, is a real place, albeit an unrecognised state, and nothing like how it's portrayed here. The house with the maze exists, but not in Derbyshire. All Inuit food recipes are authentic. And one last point: I've had the great pleasure to work and be friends with people from the depths of Cornwall, across Ireland and Scotland, and from all over Western and Eastern Europe, so I make no apologies for their written accents, which were laid down with deep affection helped by the voices, I can still hear, of some wonderful characters—some much larger than fiction.

1: Booty

The sky is the usual colour for a Bank Holiday Monday—as grey as boiled meat. Nathaniel is trying to concentrate on watching cars, vans, motorcycles and caravans being driven onto the Dover to Calais ferry on which he is standing. He tries to focus on his task by tugging his worn, waxed-cotton jacket tighter around himself, attempting to fend off inevitable thoughts and keep out the chill wind, a gust of which catches a lock of his greying hair and blows it into his own mouth. He spits it out and brushes it back in place, pointlessly. The wind whips it down again. He squints at the line of traffic: the yellow Spider; the red Beetle; the blue Scorpion; the orange Bug; some ugly big black old sports thing that looks like a dung beetle trying to mount a centipede. He then closes his eyes tightly and mentally tries to shake out of cars-as-insects mode, but instead other distractions begin to buzz into his conscious mind: One tries to creep in from behind like an unwelcome visitor rattling the back-door lock, refusing to be convinced there's nobody at home. The other distraction is a skinny, shivering twenty-six-year-old, Icarus Smith, who is standing right next to him, cramming as much of a burger as he can into his mouth, his eyes first bulging open with the anticipation and the effort, then squeezed shut as he bites—there's something repulsively reptilian about it. Nathaniel can't watch, so instead checks the time again. It's seven-thirty.

'How can you eat that disgusting mess at this time of the morning?' He asked, irritated, trying to keep his attention on the load being swallowed by the ship.

'It's all relative…' Icarus replied while chewing—no more than six times before swallowing noisily with the lubrication of an unhealthy straw-suck of full-fat, full-fizz cola. He balanced the large paper cup on the wooden handrail, belched openly, then frowned as he picked out the remains of tomato, lettuce and gherkin from his burger; after licking off any ketchup, he casually tossed each item into a hub of silently circling seagulls: '…it's this time of the morning for you, but I didn't get to bed last night—well I didn't get to sleep anyway, so from a personal perspective, this is dinner. Anyway it's good for hangovers, which thank fuck I don't get.'

'I daren't guess what you were up to,' Nathaniel replied, with more than a hint of disapproval in his voice.

'You're just jealous; gorgeous Czech chick; works at the hotel as a chambermaid.'

'You'll catch something one of these days.'

'Naaah! I always take precautions—industrial-strength condoms and make sure their boyfriends aren't the romantic types who show up unannounced,' he grinned before taking another bite from the burger: six chews, slurp, swallow and belch.

'You're disgusting! I don't know what any girl sees in you.'

'Big knob,' said Icarus, shrugging matter-of-factly, 'Blessed upstairs, blessed downstairs.'

'I'm surprised anyone gets close enough to find out.'

'I can't help it if I've got too much natural charisma dude. Anyway, what's your problem? I'm just standing here enjoying me dinner, doing no harm to no-one. Why are you down, what's up?' Icarus didn't really expect an answer and neither did he get one. He scooped a finger-smear of smokey barbecue ketchup from his baggy, black, 'Lebowski is God!' tee-shirt and stuck it into his mouth.

Something caught Nathaniel's eye and his tense expression relaxed for a moment, 'There! That one!'

'Which one?' Icarus squinted, still licking his finger, as he scanned the traffic streaming onto the boat.

'That one! The white van.'

'Which? What? That one with black shit pouring out of the exhaust? It's fucked!'

'It's perfect.'

'It's your choice...' Icarus ended with a silent 'but'.

'What?'

'Nothing'

'What? Don't say nothing when there's obviously something...'

'Well, it's just that I've been thinking, and...well: What's the point?' Icarus looked questioningly at Nathaniel.

'What's the point of what?'

'Of doing it this way? I mean, it's such a hassle.'

Nathaniel tried to reply calmly, but his voice was at least two tones higher than usual: 'We've been over this how many times? The point is the risk—and not taking any. Not unnecessary ones anyway. Nobody is ever searched when they go onto a ferry, but all it takes is one casual spot-check on the way off, and bang! We lose everything: money, freedom, reputation. Only fools take unnecessary risks, and we're not fools. At least I'm not.'

'Come on! Get real, who's going to search us—I mean have you ever been searched at a ferry port?'

'No, but that's not the point.'

'Well if that's not the point, what is?'

'The point is the possibility. The chance of it happening—'

'Come to think of it dude, I have.' Icarus began loading fries into his mouth.

'Have what?' Nathaniel looked at Icarus quizzically.

Icarus swallowed: 'Been searched. But I think they were looking for drugs and stuff. Sniffer dog, black Labrador—started barking at me like I'd nicked its favourite ball or something; so they searched me.'

Nathaniel was finding it increasingly difficult to hide his irritation. He looked up to the grey blanket of sky, exasperated. 'Well there you go! That's exactly my point. We don't take risks when we can avoid them—that's how and why we've been so successful so far.' He shook his head. 'You know, for someone so brilliant, you can be a real dork sometimes, it must be your youth.'

'Dude! That's probably the nicest thing you've ever said about me, and there was me thinking you don't care any more.' Icarus grinned as he licked his salty fingers, the fries now finished. 'Anyway, I wasn't carrying drugs. It turns out the dog just took a dislike to me. Dogs have this thing about me. I told its handler—this really fit chick in a uniform—that if it had been a bitch it would have been different.'

'It was probably just objecting to another dog being on its territory.'

'What! Me a dog? I wish I was! Imagine what it'd be like to lick your own balls, suck your own—'

'You know what I mean.'

'Awe! Thanks for the compliment! That's two already today, so you really do love me! I'm like the son you never had. Go on, admit it.'

'You're like a sun that never sets—always in my face.'

'Now, there you go dude. You had to go and spoil it all!'

'Anyway, I do have a son as it happens.' Nathaniel's tone dropped as he spoke. When he realised what he'd said he immediately wished he hadn't.

'You slippery old Boot! You never told me that before! I thought you didn't have rugrats.'

'No, I said I don't have any regrets. See—you don't know everything, despite what you think.'

'Never said I did—just almost everything. So who was the donor then? Mrs Makeover?'

'Don't call her that! It's Sandra to you. Anyway, not that it's any of your business, but no. It was a long time ago, I was only twenty-six.'

'That's the same age as I am now. What happened?'

'Apart from the baby, not much. We split, she married

someone else, and … well, they're a family…'

'But, that's crazy, he's your son!'

'Well, believe it or not sometimes you have to be unselfish to make someone else happy. Bedsides, I couldn't do with all that meeting on Sundays stuff. You know—one of those sad dads who only see their kids over a happy-dinner, or sad-meal, or whatever they're called. Watching you eat that crap is bad enough! No, it had to be all or nothing. Anyway, it's all in the past. Another life.'

'Man you're a dark horse. How old are you now, fifty-two? That would make him twenty-six. The same age as me now! Now that's another coincidence. Hey dude! Twilight Zone! I could be…'

'Don't even go there! The thought of you being a chip off my block is more than I could bear! A chip on my shoulder is more than enough. Anyway—let's get to work. Have you got everything?'

'Yes dad,' Icarus grinned.

'You can quit that right here, and right now! Check to make sure.'

'OK! OK! Don't get your CKs in a twist!'

'M&Ss actually. God! I can't believe I'm standing on a ferry at half-seven in the morning tell a scruffy, twentysomething, drug-addled bigamist where I buy my underwear from!'

'Hey dude! Easy on the bigamist bit, they're all legal—sort of. I only actually married two of 'em—the one in the Philippines and the one in Thailand. The other one was pre-operative, and in Vegas, so it doesn't count. Legal's all kind of relative anyway: I mean, I don't make the rules dude.'

As he was talking, Icarus opened the cheap vinyl bag at his feet and rooted around in it; casually at first, but almost immediately his searching seemed to become increasingly frantic.

'What?' Nathaniel asked, with enough stress in his voice for Icarus to know he was on the hook.

'Oh shit! The box! It's gone! That chick last night…' Icarus looked up and saw the look of panic on Nathaniel's face, he grinned with satisfaction: 'Only kidding dude! Course I've got everything. Like you said: we're not fools!'

'Why you? Of all people I get lumbered with, why did it have to be you?'

'Well, I haven't got a clue. Could be the fact I'm brilliant, a modest genius who can hack into just about anything solid or virtual. Or maybe it's simply because you might be my dad!'

'No chance! Your genes are closer to a sloth's than they are to mine.'

Icarus's grin was bracketed by the ketchup at the corners of his mouth: 'Could be why you're such a miserable fucker then.' He lifted the bag and swung it over his shoulder: 'Right Mr Grumpy, I'll see you in the bar afterwards.' Icarus belched loudly, licked the corners of his mouth, and left Nathaniel watching the greedy gulls wheel and dive.

*

It is a little known fact that the word 'booty' comes from the Boot family. Nathaniel Boot is a smuggler, just like generations of Boots before him. Almost lost in time, the original definition of 'booty' was any kind of contraband safe enough to be put back into circulation: barrels of brandy, pieces of gold, lengths of silk, jars of spices, anything that wouldn't attract the attention of the authorities of the day—specifically 'the Revenue'. To a man and woman the Boot family were experts at procuring and managing such merchandise. Booty had considerably more value than 'swag'—which was generally the proceeds of any common burglary. Swag was hot and therefore risky to handle. Whereas anyone who handled contraband from the Boot family could be sure no questions would be raised. The difference between 'booty' and 'swag' was crucial in times when even a child could be hanged for stealing a loaf of bread. Indeed there is one obscure twig of etymological study that proposes the word 'swag' comes from the word 'sway'—as in swaying in the wind on the end of a rope. This is as yet unsubstantiated.

While taking risks was unavoidable, given the nature of their livelihood, the Boot family were always careful about taking unnecessary risks. Their ancient family motto translates from the Cornish language (western dialect) as: 'Them what holds it, owns it.' A more common interpretation could be: 'Finders, keepers'. And smuggling can be a subtle art: there are many ways of making things available to find. The Boot's involvement in their trade could, in theory, be traced back beyond Queen Elizabeth I. In theory because, as many a dogged Customs and Excise man had found to his cost, tracing any aspect of the Boot family soon became tangled with absurd complications, and could be downright dangerous. It was like trying to unravel a really complex knot only to find as you neared the end, that the rope—and the knot you had been busy on—were holding you safely suspended above a pit of vipers. The safest thing to do was to tie it back up again as carefully as possible and retreat to a safe distance. While noble and adventurous members of the first Elizabeth's court were exploring the possibilities of the potato, and stoking then choking on the unfamiliarity of tobacco, fishermen in distant Cornwall had for a long time since been enjoying fine, fresh, fish and fried potato suppers, with a good smoke to follow—in pipes made of Cornish clay. (It is nothing more than pure coincidence, and inconsequential, that in a particular Cornish coastal town there has for many years been an excellent fish and chip shop run by one of Nathaniel's distant relatives.)

The Boot family are a chapter of underworld folklore. Aristocrats of smuggling if you like. Throughout history, if someone had ever needed to get something in or out of the country without attracting attention, the Boot family were the ones who could be relied upon to do it. The expression 'Giving someone the boot,' used to mean that someone had been surreptitiously sent out of the country for their own well-being. Those who have been given the boot include everyone from petty thieves looking after their necks, to the very highest members of state looking after their interests. Of course you get what you pay for. Those who managed to return and take, or retake, their positions of influence generally gave generous rewards—one reason why over the centuries the Boot family had grown to become one of the richest in the country. Not that they or anyone else would ever have known this, because money or property were of little concern to them. Wealth attracted attention, especially from the Revenue and, unlike just about any other industry, attention was not good for smuggling. If the Boot family had smuggled for wealth, they could have slid into the silver-moonlit bay of comfortable retirement centuries ago. Of course they smuggled for the money, but it had long since stopped being their prime motivator. There's no altruism involved, it's just that smuggling is now, as it has been for a long time, deeply immersed in the Boot family's blood. It's an activity that scratches a fundamental itch in a way that wealth, art, music, nature—even love, cannot. Inevitably there were those who had tried to forsake their destiny—usually for love, but a Boot who didn't smuggle was like a gypsy living in a house or a sailor trying to forsake the sea: the caravan is always kept at the bottom of the garden; the ship in a bottle. Whenever oily clouds slithered across the moon—shining like a pearl in a black-velvet box, Boot moon-shadows slid quietly and with purpose.

Nathaniel Boot had tried to forsake his own destiny for the sake of his marriage, which in his case, was not the same as forsaking it for love. He'd managed perfectly well for the past ten years on the earnings of a three-star B&B masquerading as a 'boutique hotel' in Southend-on-Sea. It did steady and regular business. His wife Sandra also had an 'American Nail and Beauty' salon, which also seemed to do reliable business. The pair lived in a smart flat with a sea view. But at the middle-age of fifty-two, Nathaniel was troubled. His marriage was not only childless but somewhere along the way the wild red roses of love had been painted with silk vinyl emulsion—the colour of which was a hint of something bland. These days Sandra's only passion was making things over. It didn't matter what: the house, the salon, herself, other people. She watched every makeover programme on TV, and spent hours in obsessive research, speed-scanning the pages of style magazines that increased in number by the month, growing like a colourful rash across the walls of the local newsagent. Sandra bought every one, and contagious designs spilled from their pages and spread over the floor of the flat: then up the walls and across the ceiling before affecting all the soft furnishings. Nathaniel was the only thing Sandra never turned her attention to, which was a mixed blessing: he did not want making over, but he would have very much liked even the slightest acknowledgement that he was something more than a badly designed functional necessity. For some time Nathaniel had realised that Sandra was never going to see their relationship as anything more significant than an item of furniture that sort of suited the room, as long as it stayed exactly where it was—out of the way. He resigned himself to pottering around in what he hoped would be comfortable limbo: cooking breakfasts for guests; reading the latest trashy novels; walking on the beach; having semi-satisfactory routine sex with Sandra twice a month. He even tried his hand at watercolour painting. But he was only kidding one person if he had ever thought any of this was going to be enough. The watercolour painting was a dead giveaway—mainly midnight seascapes, usually with the moon dimmed by clouds, and silhouettes of twisted trees in the foreground.

Inevitably Nathaniel sought solace in smuggling. He

didn't slip back into it quickly: but boredom is a powerful motivator. He spotted several opportunities: which to his credit at first he managed to resist. But temptation dangled around aching to be satisfied, whispering sweet somethings until Nathaniel rationalised in a way that only an addict can: if he did a small, teeny, little job—just the one, it might quell the need and that would be that: 'Just get it out of my system,' he thought.

That first project in more than ten years delivered a thrill he couldn't have imagined. It rekindled something in him. It was a breath of fresh air that drew a flame from sleeping embers. Far from killing his appetite it only made him ravenous for more.

The excitement also managed to create a stark contrast to his marriage. One job became two which become one-too-many and soon Nathaniel was living a dual life. Boredom punctuated by pin-pricks of excitement became excitement punctuated by blunt boredom. He started to accept that he was being motivated by more than simply an adrenaline fix. Increasingly he felt he was only living in the real world when he was doing the contraband. And it was this that concerned him as he stood on the deck of the car ferry. These were the worries buzzing around inside his head like a fly banging against a closed window. Nathaniel was on a collision course with the point at which he would have to do something about his situation. Trying to avoid thinking about it was no longer an option.

Icarus was now on the car deck. He knew how to keep himself out of sight of the crew—who, thanks to staff cutbacks, dissipated to other duties almost as soon as they had closed the bow doors. He easily picked out the white van Nathaniel had targeted. He crouched down in front of it, unzipped the holdall and yanked out a pair of disposable overalls, which he quickly climbed into. He then snapped on a pair of yellow rubber household gloves. Next out was a rolled-up plastic tool bag containing a couple of spanners, sockets and a wrench. Finally out came a small metal cylinder covered in oil and rust. The cylinder had a small bracket attached to it. Icarus lay down on the greasy, wet, metal car deck and pulled himself under the van. 'Dirty bastard!' He said, as the van dripped a single splodge of dirty brown oil onto his forehead. He didn't want to spend any more time than necessary under the van. He quickly found what he was looking for—one of the bolts holding the gearbox to the engine would do fine. He grabbed a spanner to fit, undid the bolt, pushed it through the bracket on the box, then bolted it back into place. Icarus was satisfied. The box looked like it belonged where it now was. Just to make sure, he scooped up some gritty, dirty oil that coated the van's underside, and wiped it around the box to help it blend in even more. He pulled himself forwards, still under the van, reached up and slipped the bonnet catch before crawling out. He stood up and lifted the bonnet. The engine was a mess of oil and rust. It obviously already suffered with bad electrics—there were odd bits of wire and insulation tape here and there to cure something or other. More problems were definitely due as Icarus pulled hard at a couple of red and yellow wires, yanking them off and pushed them out of sight through a metal grille in the floor of the car deck. Satisfied, he gently closed the bonnet, removed the overalls and gloves and put them back into his holdall along with the tools, making sure he had every item. He then took some tissues and wiped the oily third-eye from his forehead, zipped up the bag and slipped quietly but confidently back to the passenger deck.

By the time the safety announcement had finished playing over the public address system the ship was out of the harbour and dragging a white line towards France. The shop was now open and squirming with idly curious purchasers comparing prices on bottles of gin, watches, digital cameras, boxes of fudge, key-rings, batteries, alarm clock radios, porcelain figurines, miniature teddy bears, ornamental chess sets, scarves, novelty musical-boxes, wine, perfume, earrings and a thousand other objects, many ending in '-esque' or '-ique' and guaranteed for life to be non-functional. It was comparatively quiet considering the number of people crowded into the shop. Voices suppressed by the deep vibrations from the ship's engine—a hypnotic hum that filled every cubic centimetre of this floating shopping channel. The atmosphere was more like a zombie shoplifters' convention than happy holiday shoppers. Minutes drifted by like hours as shopping's lost souls began to glide like sleepwalkers through air growing thick and sweet with sampled perfumes—oozing odour in syrupy curls around the engine's soporific drone. Icarus paid little attention to any of this as he passed it on his way to the bar, happy that his plastic holdall, tools, overall and rubber gloves were now safely stowed in Davey Jones's locker.

Nathaniel was already on a stool in the bar and

watching people. Thinking about his own life had made him more aware of those around him: A quiet, elderly couple sat holding hands tightly as they talked about how England had changed since the war—they were going to visit a battlefield and the graves of comrades—probably for the last time. Fourteen children of what looked like the same family group were being fussed over by happy, madly energetic parents, who furiously handed out packets of crisps, cans of fizzy drinks and processed-cheese rolls to eager hands that grabbed and snatched like the beaks of baby birds: 'Say 'Merci' – it means thank you in French!' The father said, before kissing his wife passionately:

'Je t'adore!' he said,

'Not in front of the kids Wilf!' She replied, blushing.

Around a nest of tables closest to the bar sat a large group, uniformed in white cotton tee-shirts stretched skin-tight over large beer-bellies. Expanded black lettering read: "Seventh Annual Booze Crooze—I'm not a tourist I drink here!" Additionally, the back of each shirt carried nicknames including: "Rhino", "Shagger", "Beano" and "Donkey". The men's nicknames were just as complimentary. They were all drinking beer of various kinds peeled from a diminishing stack of cans precariously piled onto a two-wheeled luggage trolley recently filled in the ship's shop. To a man and woman, they were laughing themselves to tears at each other's jokes and stories. Probably the same as those told last year, but nobody cared. The coach they were travelling on would be packed to bursting point with Euromarket booze and cigarettes as it lumbered back up the motorway to Wakefield or Warrington, or wherever, and to a person they would be sleeping like babies and snoring like buffalo when they arrived, shivering, at three the following morning.

Icarus found Nathaniel. 'All done dude. No problems. Jeez! Wassup? You look on a real downer.'

'I'm fine. I'm just a bit tired that's all.' Nathaniel was lying. He felt like he was wearing an overcoat with pockets full of bricks.

'What're you drinking? Is that water? You should be on something stronger man, we're celebrating!'

'I've told you, we don't celebrate, and if we did we'd wait until we had something to celebrate.'

'Chill and cheer up man! This is the third time now, and there haven't been any problems so far has there? Go-on dude, have a proper drink.'

'Problems or not, we don't celebrate. It's work, and it's not finished yet.'

'I dunno man, I don't understand you sometimes. But it's a free world—if you want to be a miserable bastard, go ahead. But while we're on the subject of celebrating, when do we, er… see the 'results' of all this?'

'Not for a while—the rewards come to he who waits, I think that's what they say.'

'Well whoever "they" are, better mean "to they who wait", otherwise I'm going to be really pissed off!'

'Stop being so obtuse. You know what I mean. If we wait a bit until any fuss dies down we'll get a better price. Also we've got to organise getting the 'results', as you put it, into an account somewhere without creating curiosity. I know what I'm doing, but now and here isn't the time and place to talk about it.'

'Well, it would be nice to see something for all the fuss we've created. Not that I need it, but it's always nice to get what's coming to you,' Icarus paused for a moment, frowned fleetingly, then added: 'Well almost always.'

'It will come, don't you worry. If there's one thing that life has taught me, it's that people always get what they deserve. Anyway, I'd love to sit here chatting to you all day, but I've got to make a phone call.' Nathaniel stood up and felt in his pocket for a mobile phone he'd bought especially for the occasion. He also pulled out a fifty-euro note and gave it to Icarus: 'Here, get yourself something.'

Icarus took the note. 'Thanks! I don't mind if I do. And, erm—send her my love,' Icarus said, before ordering a pint of lager. 'Yum! Brunch!'

Out on the deck, after making sure that there were no keen ears around, Nathaniel phoned a small garage in a Calais suburb.

'Allo!'

'It's me.'

'Aah! Uncle Nathan! I've bin waitin' foya call man. Is everythin' set?'

While the garage was close to the centre of Calais, the voice was from Cambois, which is not a small village near Paris or Clermont-Ferrand, but a small place not far from Newcastle-upon-Tyne. The voice belongs to Yvonne, known as 'Eve', or 'Yvie' depending which side of the Channel she was on. Fluent in French and Geordie, Eve was a brilliant mechanic; she was also one of Nathaniel's favourite nieces.

'It's a white van. You can't miss it. It's being held together by a prayer.'

'Aye! No problems man. I'll be there just like before.'

'Great! Icarus will sort things out, as usual.'

'Well get 'im to bath this time—he smells like a piss-head in a transport caff!'

Nathaniel couldn't help grinning. Talking to Eve always cheered him up. 'Wouldn't do any good. I'll see you soon. Take care OK?'

'Aye! I will that. And you take care too mind!'

Nathaniel dropped the phone into his pocket. It would be discarded later. There was now nothing for him to do other than make the return trip to England. He thought about getting off in France as he'd done before, and spending a couple of hours in Calais, maybe having lunch before heading back; but his heart wasn't in it. He had to work out what he was going to do about the irritations nibbling at his perimeters. He felt that he couldn't concentrate on anything; that there was always something just out of sight or earshot distracting him. He looked forward to the drive back to Southend: it would give him time to think.

2: A different age

It's four in the morning, which—like February, is neither here nor there. Which is exactly where Arthur is: retrospecting because in four weeks' time, he will be fifty. The void below the bedroom ceiling is being filled with a haze of memories, some more elusive than others. Arthur is thinking about his life. And the more he thinks, the more lives appear. He tries to think about being a child, but all he can remember are disjointed episodes: sitting on the floor reading comics, usually 'Superman', or the 'Beano'—which he preferred to the 'Dandy' (He wondered if there was any significance in preferring one over the other?); flicking through car magazines; building plastic model aeroplanes from kits and metal machines from Meccano. He remembers watching the tops of ships as they slid up the canal towards Manchester or Liverpool. He recalls how he and his mates used to climb more than fifty feet up to the railway bridge and walk precariously along the outside of it to cross the canal, just to save the tuppence ferry fare for sweets. It was too dangerous to walk inside the bridge because the line was then in use by billowing, oil-black steam trains. But bungling Beeching broke the branch and resigned an entire community to battered buses that stank of stale cigarette-smoke, vomit and diesel.

Arthur thought about his plans to leave home at the age of ten. He had kept a secret box under the bed in which to hoard useful things for his journey: a tin opener, a knife, and one of his granddad's tobacco tins transformed into a homemade first aid kit—which consisted of a plaster, an aspirin he'd found on the kitchen floor and a safety pin. It took him another seven years to finally leave. After a row with his mum, he kicked his Lambretta into life, and rode off with nothing more than a few clothes and a couple of cassette tapes in a single carrier bag gripped between his ankles. His mother told him many years later that she knew that once he'd left he would never go back. She also said she'd known about the box under the bed.

Arthur could hardly remember those initial wild years of independence: his first flat shared with two trainee accountants—a blur of hard drinking and casual sex. Nor could he remember much about his first encounter with the mob from the art school—a blur of soft drugs and casual sex.

Arthur's reverie broke and he opened his eyes without focussing. The only light was the monochrome grey-green of pre-dawn. He reached over to feel for his mobile, to confirm, rather than check, the time: his reliable body clock told him it was half-past-four. He knew sleep would soon find him again and he would then wake up at six-thirty, as usual.

He thought about work, and how, after many bad

labouring jobs, he managed to scrape into a bad art foundation course at the only college in Manchester that would accept his two insignificant qualifications: Physics, and Technical Drawing. The art course was a mish-mash of academic no-hopers, mostly grateful to be anywhere except working. Arthur smiled as he thought about the only saving grace of the college—the fact that half of it was given over to beauty therapists—gorgeous-looking women with mouths that would make a builder blush. There was a high dropout rate in that department, mainly because pregnancy and electrolysis weren't compatible.

Arthur's thoughts raced down the M6 and M1 to London, where he'd been drawn in pursuit of friends who were chasing their futures. With degrees in hand, his art-school mates managed to slot into jobs as designers with music or publishing companies, or were mastering their talents at Chelsea or the RCA. All of which was way out of Arthur's reach. Like most of the rest of the students from his own course—for some did actually fail—he left college with an insignificant certificate and no additional skills. He found a small college in Essex that ignored this, and on the strength of his portfolio trained him to be a photographer. Thankfully London was within reach, so weekends usually meant a train into London to party, followed by a slow recovery on a slow train back on Sunday evening. After completing the course it took him another two years of crap jobs before he finally managed to find a badly-paid position in a photographic studio situated in a small industrial unit in Paddington. His time in London became the flash of another life dashing through his memory.

Arthur's thoughts meandered backwards and forwards through a variety of episodes: Love unsuccessful, unrequited and unreciprocated; meaningless and meaningful sex; friendships that had cruised along the same course with fair winds in their sails, then parted on promises or rough seas; bed-sits, flats, houses and the floors sofas and beds he'd called home; restaurants; parties; journeys on planes, in cars and on foot; places—Southport, Paris, Whitby, New York, Rhyl, Marbella, Wigan, Nice, Orkney, Majorca, Edinburgh, Warsaw, Brighton, Rome, Manchester and Amsterdam; people's faces and names, or just faces—some polished by the years until they shone brighter than they probably deserved, others a sliver of memory—dim reflections in a dirty mirror.

Fifty used to mean slippers and cardigans, perhaps a pipe, a cloth cap, grey hair and an allotment. But Arthur had danced the twist at the age of eight with his mum to Chubby Checker on the radiogram; watched the Beatles metamorphose and split, and rocked to the Stones. He'd been a depressed hippy at fourteen, until Hendrix dragged him out of the blues. Then meandered into Led Zeppelin and Deep Purple, Lou Reed and Bowie. He'd punked, post-punked, new-romanticised and raved all-night in clubs and derelict warehouses while winding up to his thirtieth birthday. He'd smoked dope, 'experimented' with acid and speed, then acid and tequila, then magic mushrooms and tequila; even tried 'E' a couple of times. But had settled finally on red wine—plus the occasional tequila for old times' sake. Arthur was glad that being fifty now was a different age altogether.

He thought about health. He was comparatively fit for someone with a gym allergy. There was a bowel cancer scare for which he had been checked with what he affectionately called a 'rear-endoscope'. He hadn't been allowed to eat for a day beforehand. As they slid the camera in, Arthur's comment to the nurses present was: 'That's the first solid thing I've had in me for 24 hours'. He watched the colour screen with interest.

'We're 1.3 metres in now, and it's all clear,' the doctor had said.

'There can't be many people who've seen 1.3 metres up their own arse!' Arthur thought. The nurses couldn't, or wouldn't burn it to DVD. It was YouTube's loss.

Arthur kept fit by default rather than by design. He cycled to his studio as often as he could, and watched his weight: it rose gently. He thought about taking up yoga—realistically doubted that he would, but wondered whether thinking about taking up yoga constituted some kind of meditation.

Arthur's mind meandered to the possibility of having a mid-life crisis, wondering whether it was mandatory. There was that mild flip just after getting divorced more than ten years ago. But all that involved was some self-doubt and a bit of bondage and spanking of a deliciously round-arsed, very far-out hippy from Hebden Bridge. Arthur decided to untie the cosmic bond when she suggested joining a swingers' club in Rochdale: Arthur wasn't a club person. He left her an illustrated book of knots he'd picked up in a second-hand bookshop in Llandudno, and swept his then recent experiences, and the velvet-covered paddle, under the slightly frayed edge of the rich rug of life.

He did occasionally wonder whether he should have someone steady in his life. He had long since abandoned casual flings. He was sort of happy on his own, sort of. There was a lot to occupy him, including the convenience of occasional no-ties sex with Sara—who tended to call him whenever she was 'resting' between boyfriends, which averaged once a month. Although thinking about her made him realise he hadn't seen her, or had sex, for more than six months, which probably meant that she was seeing someone. 'Good for her,' Arthur thought. He liked Sara, she was bright company and good fun: very funny in that sharp way that Jewish Americans do best.

Arthur was sorted enough to know that a mid-life crisis happened when immortal youth clashed with the fear of death. But he wasn't afraid of death, even though he didn't want it to happen for a long time to come. His aim was to think—just before he died, that he couldn't have done anything more with the time he'd been given, however long or short that time was. Of course languishing on a deathbed with lucid thoughts was a luxury that not everybody could enjoy. Arthur thought about the saying that your whole life flashes before your eyes when you die. He hoped this wasn't true, otherwise his own dying might be slow going. How do you get a lifetime into a flash? Some fault in time maybe? Or maybe an explosion of memory as the last of life's energy leaves a useless carcass. But the basic laws of physics say that energy can't be destroyed, only transferred. So where does it go? As for that final moment—when and how would it be? He speculated on the possibilities: would he be hit by a bus; or would it be the end of an old heart in old-age in an old garden in the sun, just like old Marlon Brando in that old film 'The Godfather'. However it came, Arthur considered that he really couldn't have crammed much more into his time. But there were things he'd still like to do. There were things that he still had to do.

If Arthur could recognise one change as time passed, it was that he had grown less tolerant when dealing with stupidity, and there seemed to be a lot more of it about these days: maybe that in itself was something to do with age. 'Or maybe it's just me turning into a cantankerous old git!' He was thinking about the inexperienced young advertising executives who often thought they knew more than he did. He saw no reason to let them think otherwise. Arthur took photographs: Interesting shots of boring products for local ad agencies and PR firms. But his mainstay was weddings. He was reliable and experienced, which counted for a lot, especially in the wedding game. He found photography to be lucrative enough for a comfortable life, with the added bonus that generally no one told him what to do.

Arthur was happy taking photos. He knew what he was doing. He didn't have to work late into the evenings. He didn't work under stress, just the odd bit of pressure. He also didn't have to work every day if he didn't feel like it. He wasn't driven by money. He had ambled with good fortune up the property ladder, and was now mortgage-free in a smallish, but comfortable house that perfectly suited his needs. His business ticked over nicely. All he wanted to do was make a living and enjoy day-to-day life. He remembered, or just about remembered, being in a bar in Dublin. Inevitably he had struck up a conversation with a drunk-but-steady regular. Arthur could still hear the man's voice:

'How auld d'yer think I am? G'wan, guess', the man had asked.

Arthur had looked at him and, being generous, would have guessed sixty-five-ish. However, if being a photographer had taught him anything about dealing with the public, it was never to answer such questions, and if you have to, answer them as generally as possible: 'I haven't got a clue. But I'd guess old enough to know better and young enough to do it all again?'

The man wavered slightly, pivoting around one elbow: 'Bang on mister! Bang on! Yer one o' them psoichics, or oil be from Cardiff! Oim therty-foive, and d'yeknow whoi oiam this good fer me age?' The man paused, smiling proudly, holding his drink-heavy head as still as he could so that Arthur could take a good look at him.

Arthur didn't like to say.

'The reason whoi oi am dis good fer me age—an' oi does not mean ter offend yez—and you looks loik yer do, is because of the difference between the Oirish and the English. Do yer know the difference between the Oirish and the-English, moi frien'?'

Arthur shook his head diplomatically, although he suspected he could find a fair few reasons—most of which landed in favour of being Irish rather then English.

'The difference between the Oirish and the English is that yer Oirish works ter live, and yer English lives ter work. That! Moi frien', is all yer needs ter know about it.'

Arthur bought the man, and himself, yet another Guinness with a whiskey chaser, taking the time the Guinness was settling to ask the man why his arm was in plaster.

'Fell off a fuckin' roof.' Memories of the rest of the evening disappeared into deep, delicious, silky blackness.

Then there was his car. Arthur wondered why his thoughts about this seemed so separate from his thoughts about the rest of life: a totally different compartment altogether. His classic motor was one of the few things he felt he actually owned. He had a TV, an iPod, iBook, iPhone, furniture, a van for work, a house and a bicycle, but he didn't feel as if he actually possessed these things. They were just stuff. His car was so specialised, so rare, and in many ways so unique—nothing about it was of any concern to anyone else. It had always been his private 'obsession', which was not a word he was comfortable with when talking about it, but he had to admit it was probably the best word to use. In common with everyone else he had never understood why he had become quite so involved with it, and why that involvement had lasted as long as it did.

Arthur marvelled at the amount of stuff there was in his head. 'Maybe I could write a novel', he said, hoisting himself up onto his elbows before leaning over to check the time again, 'but I doubt if I could be arsed, or if anyone would be arsed reading it.' It was five-fifteen. He flopped back down onto the pillow. His eyelids were feeling increasingly heavy. 'Amazing, nearly fifty years of life and you can think it through in not much more than an hour. That's about ninety seconds for each year, and that doesn't count all the stuff I've forgotten about.' Sleep was stalking Arthur.

Memories started to fade except for one annoyingly persistent image: When he was at primary school he had gone to Derbyshire on his one and only field trip. His class had visited a rope-making works built partly into a hillside cave. Arthur remembered being mesmerised by the rope-making machine. It was pure mechanical magic the way the separate strands were spun together to make them thicker, before being combined by a larger rotating wheel to create a rope as thick as a man's arm; rope that would moor ships in ports around the world. In places an eight-year-old could, and did only dream about. Arthur saw the machine clearly in his mind's eye, ugly, elegant and mesmerising: its smaller bobbins spinning and rotating, the big wheels turning. He could smell the tar and damp hemp, or was it sisal? Or some other yarn? The arms of a snooze embraced Arthur and he relaxed into them.

*

It was a mystery to Arthur why he could wake up at four and be so clear-headed, then wake up at six-thirty and be so bleary-eyed. He had an erection—something else he'd never been able to work out: 'thing's got a mind of its own,' he said aloud, not for the first time, as he swung his legs out from the duvet and sat on the edge of the bed. Arthur stood and embraced the softening effect of the room's cool air.

There were some things about Arthur that were as regular as clockwork, including waking up at six-thirty, feeling very sleepy at about one o'clock in the afternoon—cured by a short catnap, and moving his bowels five minutes after finishing breakfast. It was exactly five minutes after breakfast, and Arthur was sitting comfortably, reading a newspaper supplement from several weeks ago: 'They should change the title of their restaurant reviews to 'London Restaurant Reviews', Arthur thought, 'the only time they review anything outside of London is when whoever's stuffing their face on expenses spends a weekend at their country gaff in Norfolk or Dorset or somewhere!' He realised that if he had spoken out loud, he would have sounded like a grumpy old git again, 'that's something I'm going to have to watch,' he thought. He wondered how much a restaurant review paid. 'How do people get jobs like that?' He thought, before being distracted in a most satisfying way while reading half of a regular column written by a London housewife—as usual about the supposed traumas of her four-year-old daughter. This week it was a gripping instalment about her refusal to eat steamed fennel despite the Michelin star recipe, and her continuing demands for a pony. The article had been too boring to finish. Job done, he flushed, showered, shaved, dressed and by eight-thirty was on his way to work, cycling along the banks of the Mersey, still flicking through dim corners for further fragments of memory about life so far. Legs and lungs exercised a steady rhythm. 'Friday!' He said, arriving at his studio.

3: A sharp lesson in automotive hydraulics

When the ferry docked, Eve was already waiting at the harbour, sitting relaxed in her pick-up. She put her mobile phone on the passenger seat and waited for the call from the traffic controller that would send her to collect a broken down vehicle. It wasn't unusual for her to hang around the port. She received first call on any breakdowns, which considering the number of vehicles that went through the port amounted to fairly lucrative business. Well worth the free labour on maintenance, servicing and repairs she offered to several members of the port authority.

The ferry doors opened. Within minutes it began regurgitating lines of trucks, coaches, caravans, cars, motorcycles and lots of white vans. Eve waited. From where she was parked, behind the port offices, she couldn't see the ship; but she could see the traffic as it drove by: dense at first, then a straggle that finally petered out. 'Any time now', she thought, and waited. Had she a clear view of the ship, she would have seen, after about ten minutes, the front of a tatty white van as it began to emerge slowly and silently from the car deck exit. At the wheel was a thick-necked, bald-headed man in his mid-twenties. He was gripping the steering wheel with both hands, gripping a burning cigarette between his lips, and bouncing up and down in the driver's seat for reasons known only to himself. As it rolled out of the ship it became clear that the van was being propelled by manpower rather than horsepower. That man being medium-built, unfit-looking, and of a similar age to the man at the wheel. The two may once have been friends. There was not much power in the pusher, who wheezed like the bellows of an old forge, his face glowed like burning coke. He still managed to find enough energy to swear. They're a tough lot, Scousers:

'Why... do... I... always... get... the... bleed'n... shite...!'

'Shut the fuck-up and push! We're nearly on the ramp! It'll bump start. Trust me! It's reliable as fuck this!'

'Why... do... I... always... get... the... bleed'n... shite...!'

'Keep goin' will yer!'

'Fuck off...!'

'I'm fuckin' tellin' yer!'

'An I'm fuck'n tellin' youz and your fuck'n shite ideas!' Manpower gave one last shove to get the van onto the ramp. He collapsed onto his knees—gasping for air. Wheezing with every inadequate intake of breath, he dug deep into his reserves: 'You're full of...' he paused to allow enough oxygen to be absorbed so that he could spit out his words: '...Shite! You Manc bastard! Full of fuckin' shite! If brains were made of fuckin' dynamite, you wouldn't have enough to blow off a fuckin' FART!' Manpower reached into his trouser pocket for a much needed ciggie.

'Fuck off you Scouse fu...! Oh... ...FUCK ME!' The driver's tone changed suddenly from anger to fear.

It's an interesting fact that seemingly ordinary, uninteresting things (and sometimes people) can suddenly become extraordinary and interesting. It's all to do with context. For example it is of little or no interest to the average person that there is an exit ramp from the Calais ferry that leads down into France via the Customs area. Indeed thousands of drivers negotiate this long, inconspicuous ramp every day without giving a second thought to specifications such as its length, or its angle of incline. The context of the ramp's ordinariness changes, however, if you find yourself descending it in a van with no power, no brakes and poor steering.

Here's another example of context adding interest: It concerns the workings of the brake servo, which is an hydraulic device that takes power from the engine, and uses it to boost the pressure supplied by the operator's foot when applied to the footbrake (of a van for example). Without a brake servo, the driver would need to apply a massive amount of pressure to the brake pedal in order to slow or stop the vehicle. Because the engine powers the brake servo, the brakes only work adequately when the engine is running. A very boring fact in itself. Indeed if you'd tried to explain the principles of brake hydraulics to the driver of the white van while he was lounging, casually drinking lager in the bar not twenty minutes ago, he would probably have told you to 'Fuck off. You boring bastard!' Of course if he'd listened, he might have gleaned some information that might have influenced his decision to try and bump-start the van by running it down the exit ramp. But at the time he didn't know it wasn't going to start. That's context for you.

If you were particularly persistent with that same gentleman and carried on to try and explain the principles of power steering, you may have attracted an altogether more pugilistic response. Had he listened, he might have understood why the van's steering was much heavier now than when he drove it onto the ferry. It's always easy to be wise after the event, they say. They also say that every cloud has a silver lining, so what do they know? The lack of steering control at first had probably helped, because repeated impacts with the crash barriers either side of the ramp had prevented the van from accelerating to an even higher speed than the considerable pace it had achieved as it left the ramp and headed towards the distant line of cars, trucks, caravans and vans moving steadily and slowly towards the green channel of French Customs. Luckily the speed helped lighten the steering slightly, enabling the driver to veer the van away from the line of traffic...one split-second before something, somewhere, snapped, and the steering wheel became completely free to rotate in the 'driver's' hands with no effect on the direction of the van.

While knowledge can be useful, there is also an argument for the blissfulness of ignorance. Sometimes what you don't know can be a blessing. If, before his trip to France, anyone had asked the driver of the rusty white van what a capstan was, he would have answered that it was a brand of full-strength ciggies his granddad had smoked. It did the driver no harm to remain blissfully ignorant of the fact that a capstan is also a usually massive, often solid metal device for winding ships' cables. Sometimes it's not what you know that counts, but how you come to know it.

A van especially one weakened by rust, is not designed to be stopped dead by a capstan, but by servo-assisted brakes. Power steering is another excellent way of avoiding all kinds of objects, such as hedgehogs, lamp-posts, and capstans.

None of these facts were being fully appreciated by the stunned, but otherwise miraculously fairly unharmed driver of the so rudely-stopped white van. He managed to say only 'Fuck…' before slipping into a short but not uncomfortable unconsciousness. The entire scene had been watched, as if in slow motion, by a solitary figure standing framed by the cavernous mouth of the exit from the car deck: 'Fuckin' shite!' He said, as he threw his just-lit cigarette overboard, before turning and stomping back into the ship—like some kind of angry Jonah who had been given the chance to leave, but realised that world outside contained more bile than a whale's stomach.

Eve wasn't surprised when she received the call asking her to proceed to recover a vehicle. She was surprised, however, when a gendarme diverted her away from her usual route towards the ferry's ramp. Her eyes tracked his pointing hand towards a white van. Of which not a door or window was in place. There was a green and white-striped paramedic's car nearby with lights flashing. As she drew close she could see a couple of luminous-green jacketed figures standing in front of a large, thick-set man holding a blood-stained dressing to his very bright, shiny, shaved head.

Eve drove round and parked next to the ambulance. It didn't take an expert eye to see that there was no way this van was going anywhere under its own power ever again. The area around the capstan and the front of the van was strewn with pieces of rusty metal, lumps of plastic, shattered glass and twisted chrome. Both headlights now glared at each other from either side of a crumpled grille. A growing pool of iridescent oil and water was spreading slowly around the feet of the dazed driver, who seemed fine, despite the fact that he kept repeating the same four-letter word over and over again like some kind of mantra.

It took some time to unfold the van from the capstan and yet more time to hoist up the front, via a complicated rigging of chains and ropes, to such a degree that it could be towed away. The ground underneath where the van had been was coated with water, oil and powdered rust, and littered with assorted items such as the exhaust, odd nuts and bolts, and other unrecognisable bits and pieces. A couple of gendarmes helped gather the debris, throwing it either onto the back of the pickup truck, or into the cab of the van now dangling from it. One picked up a small metal box that had been laying with other scraps and pieces. He looked at it, idly curious. He shook it close to his ear to see if it rattled. It didn't. He shrugged, walked over to the pick-up and casually tossed it in the back, smiling at Eve as he did so. He didn't realise that he had just unwittingly playing a tiny part in smuggling into France diamonds with a black market value of at least £3million. Eve smiled back.

As she drove from the port with the metal canister by her side, and the rattling wreck of a van hitched to the back of her pick-up, she made a mental note to tell Uncle Nathan to pay a little more attention to the state of the vehicle and its driver next time. Apart from everything else, extracting two hundred euros from the driver as payment to tow the van away had been far from easy—especially on her ears.

4: Scooter boy (i)

The opportunity was too good to miss. Tadeuz packed a small canvas bag with a few clothes, a dried sausage, cheese, some of his mother's dark bread and a litre bottle of beer. He emptied his savings from the tin he kept in his secret place in the barn. He was proud at how much he had managed to collect using nothing more than his own hands: a few Hrivna's here for fixing someone's tractor, a few there from selling a wide variety of contraband, mainly bottles of Scotch from Albania and cigarettes smuggled into Ukraine across the Black Sea from Turkey. He tied the bag to the back of his scooter. His mother had been tearful for all of today and most of yesterday. He felt sorry for her. Of course he would miss her, but an ambitious boy had to do what an ambitions boy had to do, and he had to do it now. Besides, he would send her money when he got work. He wanted to help her so that she didn't have to work every day in their fields. He wanted her to relax instead of standing around the market in all weathers trying to sell their fruit and vegetables. He couldn't spend all his life on a small farm. He wanted to see the world that was constantly teasing him from the TV. With Poland next door, Europe was now right on his doorstep. He had often driven to the border to see it, but now he wanted to touch it—to be in it. He had ambitions. He was a handsome nineteen-year old. Maybe he could be an actor. He had a good voice. Maybe he could be a pop star. He would make his mother proud one day—she would be able to relax, enjoy her old age. One thing Tadeuz knew for sure was there was only one place to be, and that was London, England. Well there was also New York, USA, which to be honest he would have preferred, but London was much easier to get to on a scooter.

5: The hounds of the sea

Arthur was having a fine day and the sun was shining after a grey, drizzly week. Such changes are usual for Manchester, where they say: 'If you don't like the weather, wait a minute.' Arthur only had one job today, a wedding, which had been organised, unusually, via a single phone call. Usually the bride, at the request of her mother, would demand a visit to sift through Arthur's wedding portfolio. This also gave Arthur the opportunity to present details of the various packages he could offer—the main difference being the album the photos were delivered in. 'Silver Stars' was an embossed silver leather album with silver corners and leaves of tissue between each page. 'Glorious Gold' was a Gold cornered version of the same album in white leather. While 'Diamond Delight' was leather-covered and studded with diamanté in the name of the bride and groom. Arthur also threw in an extra print to send to the local newspaper with the 'Diamond Delight' package. He did have one other version that was only brought out on demand, this was a stitched black leather cover decorated with silver studs—very popular in certain quarters of central Manchester.

Today's job had been booked a couple of months ago. A man with a strong Irish accent had phoned and asked for 'the best'; agreed the cost; provided the venue and date; and that was that. The deposit arrived in the post the following day: cash in a registered envelope. Arthur had learnt always to take a deposit, and cash was always a bonus. It wasn't unusual for couples to not make it up the altar—some had planned their wedding up to two years in advance. Sometimes the planning lasted longer than the marriage. Photographing weddings for several decades had made Arthur something of an expert on spotting those most likely to run the course, and those that would barely survive the honeymoon. Experience had taught him those that survived usually understood the difference between a marriage and a wedding.

Arthur loaded up the van with his gear. He didn't need much, but always took his emergency pack with him—which consisted of a spare camera, flash and some good old-fashioned film. He used a good digital camera, but the last thing he needed was a technological breakdown with nothing to fall back on. Fully loaded, he locked up his studio—a handy, cheap place he rented above a shop in a trendy south Manchester suburb—and set off for the church, sifting through a pile of CDs as he drove. He thought about Led Zeppelin, or perhaps Nirvana, then picked up a disk of twentieth century string music, before settling on Bob Marley's 'Natty Dread', 'Old, but timeless, and perfect for a sunny day' he said aloud, as he slid the CD into the slot.

The church was down a rutted road, lined with trees

and littered with potholes. Arthur thought about parking up and walking the short distance to the church, which he could see ahead of him on the other side of a large unkempt green; but with a little concentration, he managed to weave around the potholes, half-bricks and large, loose stones. He parked up and got out.

He was leaning over, head in the back of his van, retrieving his gear, when a great gust of alcohol-heavy breeze wafted over his shoulder, propelled by an enormous Irish voice which Arthur vaguely recognised from the phone booking.

'So! You'd be the pho-tographer then!' Arthur jumped and banged his head on the inside of the van's roof. He winced slightly and stood up.

'Yes, I'm Arthur. Arthur Pod, at your service!' He turned around as he spoke. In front of him stood the reddest face he had ever seen, topped with sandy coloured hair, which—despite being plastered down with something wet and shiny—was already beginning to spring free. Arthur had never seen anyone literally smiling from ear to ear, but this man seemed to be doing exactly that. He looked like a large, grinning, ginger tom. He was dressed in a tweed jacket and a yellow waistcoat, which was obviously not designed as a corset, but was stretched to its limits fulfilling that very function.

'At your service! At your service! Ha! Ha! That's a good 'un, without a shred of a doubt! An me not the one that's gettin' married and all! Well Mr. Arthur Pod the pho-tographer, I am Cedric MacNamara, as of the original Mac Conmara's, which—I will tell you this Mr. Arthur

Pod—means 'the hounds of the sea'. And to a man and woman, every one of us hates the fekkin water! Now how do you make account of that, Mr. Arthur Pod? How do you make account of that!' He laughed out loud as he handed a green paper bag to Arthur, a bottle neck poking out of the top: 'will you join me Mr. Arthur Pod? In a small toast to me dearly beloved niece Geraldine, the broid herself. And I hope you're going to do a foin job for me darlin' niece on this—most wonderful of days!' Cedric never stopped smiling, but Arthur detected a hint of something in the man that he wouldn't want to cross. But a lion with claws safely retracted is just a pussycat. He was about to politely decline the bottle, he didn't like drinking while working, but Cedric was not the kind of man to take no for an answer

'G'wan! Tis past midday after all, and we're celebrat'n'! It won't hurt you, we've been making this stuff fur generations!' He pushed the bottle insistently towards Arthur, who tentatively took it, lifted it to his mouth and took a polite sip before handing the bag back to Cedric. Arthur had braced himself for the worst. Never having tasted poteen before, he didn't know what to expect. He was pleasantly surprised: it was almost tasteless, like thick water. He swallowed the tiny sip he'd taken. The liquid went down smoothly enough. But almost immediately his teeth went numb and something grabbed his throat, holding it in a spasm. He couldn't breathe, swallow or choke. Some kind of fire whipped rapidly up his alimentary canal, and then extinguished itself just as quickly. Something started to run up the outside of his spine—under his skin. Arthur could feel it as clearly as if it was an alien insect. Not that he'd ever experienced an alien insect, but he'd seen films. Every hair on his body prickled as it ran up through his neck and into his head. His skin took on the texture of a bald chicken in a snowstorm. The alien spread out across his brain and did something that reduced its density, weight and operating power by around fifty per cent. Arthur took his first breath in what felt like a week. An involuntary gasp, followed by a fit of coughing.

'Aye! It always does that the ferst toim! We've been making it for generations—but we've never managed to make it any better!' Cedric laughed as he slammed Arthur repeatedly on the back with a hand that felt like a sledgehammer, an action that didn't help Arthur's predicament one bit.

As Arthur's condition returned from critical to stable, he heard the growing growl of a car with an inadequate exhaust coming up the road. It careered into view: a battered old Volvo estate that made no attempt to negotiate its way around the obstacles. It bounced and battered straight across bricks, boulders and potholes. The engine note grew louder, roaring and resonated off the perimeter of large, mostly dilapidated, Victorian houses that surrounded the green. The driver took no notice of the road that encircled the green, but continued straight across the middle, narrowly missing several large trees before sliding to a halt leaving at least a metre of ploughed mud on the grass. Every door flew open. From the back spilled a pile of children of various sizes, sexes and ages. The unfortunate ones who had been sitting closest to the doors were ejected onto the damp grass by the force of those in the middle. It wasn't immediately obvious how many bodies were crammed inside, certainly not less than half-a-dozen just on the back seat. A large woman struggled out of the passenger door, holding a baby in one arm and a copious bag looped over the other. She stood, dropped the bag onto the car's bonnet, put a hand onto the small of her back and stretched backwards in an arc of obvious relief.

'Sweet Jesus! That's better! Me back was bleed'n killin' me! It's them seats Marjorie. I swear it's them seats!'

A broad and loud Scouse voice came from the other side of the car 'It's not the bloody seats! It's yer fat arse! If there's a spring left in them seats it's a bleed'n miracle!' A door slammed. Arthur could hear the driver's voice but couldn't see her until she turned the corner at the back of the car. Marjorie, as far as Arthur could see, was less then five feet tall and stick-thin, with a pretty face and long, blonde hair. She opened the tailgate, struggling to lift it up over her head. Three more children fell out, followed by a frenzied medium-sized black dog of no particular breed. The dog immediately did a U-turn and peed up one of the car tyres, span waggy-tailed around, then chased the gang of children now attempting to clamber over a laughing Cedric, who had picked up the smallest with one hand, and was handing out fifty-pence pieces with the other, the bottle of poteen now stuffed safely into his jacket pocket.

Marjorie was standing by the open tailgate, a concerned look on her face as she counted, finger-wagging in the air. 'Ten? Will, Seamus, Holly, Gabriel, Rufus, Kylie, Peter, Roy, Poppy, Annie…' she counted again from one to ten, then looked over to the large woman still standing by the passenger door, 'Jesus Siobhan! We must have left John at the bleed'n petrol station again! I'll kill him! I told him not to wander off!'

'That's John! Just like his dad!' She was walking over towards Marjorie. 'You go back for him. I'll stay here with the kids!'

'I'll kill him!'

'Calm down Marj, the sooner you get there, the sooner you'll get back! Anyway you can't kill him on Geri's wedding day!'

'Watch me! I told him last time! I told him! Seventy miles I had to drive. Seventy miles! That time we went to Bridlington, remember? I told you?'

'Yes! Look, it'll be fine, It's only about fifteen miles... you'll be back in no time.'

'I'll kill him!'

'Well if you're going to kill him, there's no point in going. Just leave him there!'

'That's not the point. I want the satisfaction of killing him!' Marj slammed the tailgate shut. She turned around, furious. As she did so a small hand pressed into the condensation from the inside of the tailgate window, then a face appeared, pushed contorted against it—mouth wide open, and a small tongue started to lick away at the condensation.

'That'll be John then,' said Siobhan, nodding her head towards the tailgate, grinning.

Marj was relieved, which made her even more angry. She opened the tailgate and dragged John out by his collar, then slammed the tailgate again.

'Get out of there! You little bugger, hiding from me were you! I'll kill you!'

'But you told me to get in before!' Protested John.

'Well now I'm telling you to get out! Don't argue with me! Get in that church and thank the Lord Jesus our Blessed Saviour for your bleed'n life!' The two women walked towards Cedric and Arthur. The children and the dog had already scampered off into the churchyard; barking and excited yelping provided a rough location.

'Mr. Arthur Pod, I would like you to meet two of my dearest nieces, and sisters of the broid. This gorgeous woman is the verluptious Siobhan, a goddess amongst women and a she-devil amongst men! And this is Marjorie the bountiful! Gerls, would you be havin' a sip?' Cedric handed them the bottle.

'Just a sip Cedric, I'm driving,' replied Marj, after kissing Cedric fondly on his crimson cheeks.

'To be sure we've got time for no more than that anyway. Is that not the broid's car coming up the road?'

Arthur looked down the road, sure enough, a white Volvo estate was bouncing across the potholes, green ribbons stretched between the front of the bonnet to either side of the windscreen. A splurge of pink flowers could be seen stuffed in the middle of the dashboard. 'Strange choice of car for a wedding!' Arthur thought to himself.

'We'd better be going inside,' Cedric said 'Come on, gather your clan Marjorie!' They turned towards the church.

'You go ahead; I'll just get the rest of my stuff out. I

need to take a picture of the bride and her father,' Arthur said. He walked towards the van.

Cedric turned around and looked at him, 'We'll be seeing you in a minute then!' He waved at Arthur before turning and heading through the gates to the church.

His attention released, Arthur noticed the line of cars parked up against the hawthorn hedge that ran along the front of the church. It wasn't the number that caught Arthur's attention—he estimated there were more than thirty. What was unusual was that every one of them was a Volvo Estate—in every condition, from brand new to those so bad they looked as though they were being held together by Hail Marys and repair tape. He didn't have time to draw any conclusions. He took a camera from a flight case in the back of the van and hurried over to the church gates just in time as the bridal car bounced to a halt.

First out was a small man wearing a grey suit, white shirt and a green tie. He had the build and energy of a jockey. His sandy-hair was combed and plastered down like the ripples of wet sand where the beach meets the sea. His red face was peppered with jewels of perspiration as he ran around the back of the car and opened the door. Geraldine emerged. She was even smaller than her father, smaller, even than her sister Marjorie. Arthur thought she looked like a china doll. Her features were small and fine, her skin almost white, cheeks flushed, her lips deep red. Her hair was so black it was as iridescent as the feathers of a raven. But by far her most striking feature were her eyes. They were the colour of pale emeralds. Arthur took several pictures by the car then, while walking backwards, took a couple of less formal shots as the beaming father and shining bride walked up to the church doors.

As he worked, Arthur had been vaguely aware of the growing murmur of a crowd. He left father and bride outside to collect themselves, turned around and pushed opened the heavy wooden doors. The full force of the congregation hit him like the exhaust of an airliner taking off. It flashed through Arthur's mind that he was pushing the doors against the weight of the noise. The church was heaving.

Just about every pew was taken, and everyone was enjoying this opportunity of reunion. People waved to each other and mimed exaggerated greetings. Or talked with tight intensity as they caught up with each others' lives. There were the ancient, there were babies, and every age in-between. But the children had it: Running and screaming along the aisles, climbing on the statues and anything that gave a vertical grip. They were splashing each other from the font, hiding under pews, trying to open locked doors, some were building a castle out of prayer and hymn books. Arthur saw Marjorie dragging a wriggling John out from a small hatch on the side of the church's massive pipe organ, he was covered in dust and cobwebs and clutching something that Arthur couldn't quite see from where he was standing, but strongly suspected was a dead rodent. The air was filled with laughter, talk, shouts, giggles, screams, whines and crying. It was impossible to determine an individual thread of conversation, or make out anything other then the odd word or phrase as the noise reverberated and resonated around the holy cavern.

'Not human books! Hymn books!'

'You'll have to wait!'

'...four months you say...'

'...I ask you! On top of the washing machine...'

'Maaaaaaaaaaaaam!'

'...if only I'd got that last number...'

'Michael! Stop playing with your willie!'

'...and she said...'

'...four to one...'

'...eighteen months...'

'...shaman...'

'You'll have to wait! I've told you already!'

'No dear, God's name isn't Harold, it's 'hallowed' be thy name...'

'Maaaaaaaaaaaaam!'

A subsonic boom echoed around the cavern as the organ struck up its first imposing notes, its heavy cloak smothering the congregation's conversations. It was the first time many of the younger children had been confronted with the voice of such a monster. Some screamed in fear and ran back to their parents. Others stood in wide-eyed, wide-mouthed awe as their tiny tummies rumbled with the noise. At the keyboard was the desiccated remains of someone's once-great, great grandmother, perched like an ancient parrot, her small round glasses hooked on a beak-shaped nose, wispy remnants of white hair feathered across her head. Her arthritic hands worked like sinuous claws as they stabbed at the ivory and ebony. Her head turned slowly sideways, and she looked over her glasses at the stilled throng. She smiled with the smallest movement that did nothing but tighten the wrinkles at the corners of her pursed lips. Satisfied with her impact, she turned back to her sheet music and closed her eyes, as 'here comes the bride'.

The bride cruised up the aisle, sending ripples of approval down the pews on either side. She was pure happiness. The groom looked over his shoulder and smiled broadly in pure relief. He had the whitest teeth that Arthur had ever seen. His dark, almond-shaped eyes shone with pride. The bride arrived at his side, slipped a hand under his arm, and he placed his hand over hers as they looked into each other's eyes.

As the last tone of the organ's tune finished falling from the stone walls of the church, the priest began his address. He looked young enough to have been nothing more than a choirboy, and admitted to the congregation, with a mixture of flushed embarrassment and pride, that this was his first wedding ceremony.

'...however I'm delighted that it is this ceremony, the coming together of Geraldine and Kaujajuk...'

Throughout the ceremony there was hardly a dry-eye in the house, women and men. Only the children didn't see what all the fuss was about. At the end of the ceremony, as the bride and groom walked to sign the wedding certificate, young John was shoved into the aisle by mother Marjorie. 'G'wan!' She rasped.

'Aaaaw mam! Do I 'aff ter!' He whined.

'Don't argue. Just do it!' She ordered.

'But maaaam...!' He begged.

'We made a deal...' She reminded him, sternly.

John turned around defeated. He shuffled reluctantly to the front of the church, dragged his feet up three ornately carpeted steps, and turned to face the congregation. He was still covered in dust and cobwebs from his earlier expedition into the organ. His hands were thrust into the pockets of his trousers, one of which contained the dehydrated remains of a long-dead church mouse. Madam Parrot held, for much longer than was required, the last note of the refrain she'd being playing to accompany the bride and groom's slow walk to sign the register, before slumping back onto her stool as if what remained of her life had been sucked out of her body and blown dustily through the organ pipes.

John began to sing. From his first note there was no other sound to be heard in the church. From its beginning to its end Arthur didn't remember breathing. He couldn't remember how long the song went on for, or how many verses there were. He didn't understand the language, but he recognised it was Gaelic. He had never heard anything so ethereal. Each note seemed to carry its own life—powerful yet gentle, each painting the air a different texture. It reminded Arthur of something, but he couldn't remember what. He tried hard to focus, but it was too elusive—just out of reach, like having a wonderful dream and trying to remember it later in the day.

As the song ended, there was silence.

'Can I 'ave that video game now mam?'

A proud Marjory nodded through her smile and tears. John walked unmoved back towards his mother as the whole congregation applauded, smiling, laughing and nodding in approval.

Arthur enjoyed taking the photos. Some weddings were a trial where it was almost impossible to organise the families into anything resembling a harmonious group—and where Arthur almost had to wipe the frost from the lens between each shot. He could even recall one occasion when a fight worthy of the Wild West broke out before the two families had even left the church. Today's wedding couldn't have been more different: The groom's family consisted of his mother and father, two brothers, and an elderly woman who Arthur discovered was his mother's aunt. There was no formality and no order, but no one seemed to care one iota. Outside the church it was joyous chaos. Cedric had already said to Arthur that all he needed to do was to make sure that everyone was in the picture, or at the very least to make sure he had got a picture of everyone: 'You'll never get the lot of 'em to stand still for long enough for one o' them formal shots! Which to be sure is not a bad thing, without a shred of a doubt: We should be as our nature makes of us. Talking of shots, would you like a wee sup?' Arthur declined—verbally on the basis of professionalism, mentally on the instinct of survival. Of course 'no' was never going to be the right answer.

Arthur reckoned he'd got some good photos, but it was exhausting trying to rein everyone's energy into a two-dimensional, four-sided frame. He'd had never seen so many children in one place outside of a school assembly. But their happiness, and that of the adults, was infectious. After some time spent shepherding children while simultaneously tactfully de-animating catch-up conversations between the adults, Arthur managed to get the final, albeit chaotic, group shot he needed. 'Thank you everybody!' He shouted. They all applauded him, which surprised him as it had never happened before. He grinned and his ears went hot.

Arthur was standing disassembling his camera and tripod, when Cedric wandered over from the dispersing group that had started to drift towards the church gate in the wake of the bride and groom. 'Well Arthur! How did it go? I thought it went well meself! Without a shred of a doubt!'

Arthur agreed 'Yes I think we got some good shots there. I think Geraldine and Kua… Kua…'

'Kuajajuk! 'Jack' to us all.'

'Yes, I think they'll be pleased.' Arthur said. 'Kuajajuk? That's unusual, I've never heard a name like that before, where's he from?'

Cedric laughed, 'Well, they live in Chorlton-cum-Hardy, in fact in that house over there,' Cedric pointed to a large semi-detached Victorian house over the way. 'He's Inuit!'

'In what?' Arthur asked, in all innocence.

Cedric laughed, 'In-u-it'.

'Inuit? What, like an Eskimo you mean?'

'Yes, but that's not polite! They're properly called Inuit. Geraldine met him while she was over on Baffin Island doin' research—she's a clever 'un our Geraldine, got one o' them PhDs—somethin' to do with social ant'ropology or whatever!'

Arthur shrugged, saying he had a vague idea, but it wasn't something he'd ever looked into.

'Nor me! Course I've asked her, an' she says it's somethin' to do with the study o' ethnicity and culture. I told her she could stay at home for that! Ha! Aye, but he's a foine feller! A foine feller indeed! An his family too… I will tell you this Art'ur—you seem like an honest feller, so I'm sure you won't mind if I'm honest widjer?' Arthur nodded. '… In fact, answer me this Arthur: How far is Ireland from England?'

Arthur confessed that he didn't actually know.

'Well, ter tell you the truth Art'ur, I don't actually know meself. But let's just say, that it's not that far! Are we agreed on that?' Arthur nodded again. 'Good, an' how far would you say it is between Ireland and Baffin Island?'

Arthur shrugged his lack of knowledge,

'…well ter be absolutely honest, I don't actually know meself how far it is to Baffin Island either! But I don't think I'd be too presumptious if I said we agreed on the fact that the distance between Baffin Island and Ireland, is a bloody sight furder than the distance between Ireland and England—do we agree on that?'

They did.

'Well… an' don't take this the wrong way Art'ur, because you're a good man, but there's more in common between the Inuit and the Irish, than there ever was between the Irish and the English, now is that not the strangest thing? How do you account for somethin' like that?'

Arthur thought about it for a second or two, but had to admit that he couldn't account for it.

'Anyway, the thing is, Art'ur, you've been invited to the reception this evening—we'd be pleased to have you along.'

Arthur was a little taken aback. He had hardly spoken to anyone apart from guiding them into position. It crossed his mind that the might want him to take photos…

'Aunty Meek—she's the old aunt of Jack's mother, she insists you come along this evenin'. She's a fascinatin' woman, an …oh what's that word now…'Angat- something or other'—some kind of shaman or priest or whatever', but don't let that put you off, she hasn't sacrificed anyone. Well not yet anyways! Ha! Anyhow we'd all like you to come, you'll enjoy yerself. The fiddle and drum; dancing all night; great food—it'll be a foin craic! Without a shred-of-a-doubt! And you're not allowed to say no!'

'Well I'm really grateful. I mean, I'd love too, but I've…'

'Good! Well that's settled then!' Cedric was resolute.

'No! You see I have this…' Arthur tried to explain.

'Don't worry Art'ur! It'll be a foin craic! We'd all love you to be there! Anyway, Aunty Meek has invited you, and, well—she had these dreams. She said she'd seen a man with a third eye and a woman with two dogs. I think you're the man with the third eye…'

Arthur looked puzzled.

'Camera?'

'Oh, of course!'

'I'm not sure about the woman with the two dogs though. Is there a Mrs Art'ur?'

'There's no Mrs Arthur, I mean, I'm not married.'

'Yer not one 'o them 'omusexuals? Well, no matter! Whatever takes yer fancy is foin by us…'

'No, I'm not! It's just that… Well…' Truth was Arthur was getting confused, he couldn't think of a reason not to go, but answered, 'single, er, divorced…' he tailed off, lost.

'Great! That's great! Trust me—you can't argue with fate. Now here's where we'll be.' Cedric handed a piece of paper to Arthur, a printout from a website map finder, 'We had 'em printed for everyone, it's cousin Joe's place up in Derbyshire—a bit remote, but special. See you there.' Cedric was already walking off, carrying his last words with him. He stepped into a metallic blue Volvo Estate that had pulled up on the other side of the green, slammed the door and the car lurched forward, then stopped. Cedric wound down the window and shouted across to Arthur: 'And you'll not be needing your camera. See you later Mr Arthur Pod the pho-tographer!' Cedric wound the window up and the car lurched forward again, and then stopped. He stuck his head out of the window again and shouted, '… and don't dress fancy! Wear warm!' He wound the window up as the car lurched off again and down the rutted and potholed road, joining a caravan of Volvo estates.

6: A twist of fate

As Arthur sat in his studio downloading the wedding photos from his camera, one phrase kept popping up in his head: 'You can't argue with fate'. He was clicking through the pictures on his computer, making minor changes here and there, cropping to get better compositions, altering the contrast—all automatic tasks for him. Maybe it was because he had been thinking about his life that this phrase stuck in his mind. He was thinking about the course of his life. It was natural to think that he had been in control of it all. But out of idle curiosity he began to explore the possibility of it instead being controlled by fate. The more he thought about it, the more curious he became. At first it was easy to dismiss the fact that everything happened for reasons that he understood, and had control over. For example… (and he searched around for an example) …his car.

He had been in the dentist's waiting room when he was twelve years old. All he had done was casually picked up a magazine; he could remember the incident as clearly as if it had happened yesterday. Like all magazines in all dentists' waiting rooms it was out of date by at least a year. He had searched through the pile hoping to find a comic—a vain hope. The car magazine was the best option, and better than the alternatives: Woman's Realm or the Reader's Digest. As he was flicking idly through pages, he came across a spread about a Russian sports car, complete with a reproduction of its ad of the period—the early sixties. There was something about the car, something that hit him instantly. It was the ugliest, most beautiful thing he had ever seen. He rolled up the magazine and slipped it into his school bag. And he still had it, safely archived with all his other collected material.

But what if he hadn't been late for that appointment? He might not have had to wait, and might not have seen the magazine. But he'd been late because the French teacher wouldn't let him out until the class had finished. Which meant he'd have to cycle like mad to get back home in time to dump his bike before getting the bus with his mum. If the French teacher had let him out of class when he'd asked to go, maybe he would have cycled more slowly, and maybe he would have seen the brick that buckled his front wheel, which is why he had to push his bike the rest of the way home. When he got home his mum was furious. They had to wait for the next bus down to the shopping centre where the dentist had his practice, which is why they were late for the appointment. And why they had to sit and wait until the dentist could fit him in between the rest of the patients. That had given him the opportunity to search for something to read, which is when he found the magazine article that had started an obsession that must surely have changed at least some parts of his life.

He now owned one of the few cars of its type in existence. Even today, few people had heard or knew anything about them. But Arthur had spent years researching its story. He had seen much more of the world than otherwise he might have, learnt a great deal about modern history, and ruined a few relationships, all because of his French teacher.

But the more he thought about it, the more he realised that the story went back even further. He had the misfortune to have been to a good grammar school. There were only about thirty kids from his council estate who went to this school, which was in a posh village a couple of miles away. In those days the teachers were much more socially conscious—and not in a good way. In common with many of the other teachers, the French teacher hated the kids from the estate, whom she thought were dirty, ill-mannered, rough and not worth educating. Not all of which was true because manners played an important part in Arthur's home life.

In the classroom, the estate kids were victimised at any opportunity. If it had been a kid from a posher part of the county who'd had a dental appointment, Arthur was in no doubt that he or she would have been allowed to leave on time. So it was really because he was from the council estate that he was late for the dentist. Then he realised that the only reason that they lived on the council estate was because his step-dad had got a job in the factory over the canal. Otherwise they'd be living somewhere else and he would probably have gone to a different school. Then there was the fact that Arthur's own father had died of lung-cancer just before Arthur was born. If his father hadn't died, his mother wouldn't have had to marry his stepfather, who wouldn't have had to get the job at the factory over the canal, or move to the new council estate, which meant that Arthur wouldn't have gone to the grammar school where the French teacher hated him enough not to let him out for the dentists. And so on.

It was all very frustrating and began to twist Arthur's brain into knots. He thought about other incidents in his life, and realised that however he thought about them, the same process applied. Everything depended upon something else, and that in turn had its own dependencies. Arthur was beginning to think that he had no control at all. He realised that the ability to make decisions was based purely on the opportunities or options available. He had long held the opinion that freedom is choice. A fundamental for all levels of moral politics: personal, religious and national. It's the ability to make a choice that's the key to a sense of freedom, but to choose from what? If all choices have dependencies, then where does freedom come into it at all?

Arthur wasn't prepared to believe that everything was so preordained. It was too boring, too frightening. Nevertheless, if it was, if things were mapped out, then seeing into the future wasn't too far beyond the boundaries of possibility for those with the ability to tune into particular chains of dependencies. Then Arthur had one more frightening thought, that if everything depended upon something else, then there could be no accidents, because every thread was also dependent upon every other thread, this meant that nothing could be changed away from its preordained path. Any attempt at change was simply fulfilling fate, because choices had to be made within a limited number of options. It was all too much for a man to think about, it was a good job he was only passing time.

It was easy sorting out the pictures from that day's wedding. He still had a couple of hours to kill so, as he wouldn't be able to print them until he got back from his trip in a week, he decided to spend a couple of hours doing it now and mounting up the album. He realised that he had more-or-less decided to go to the reception that evening. Or had fate decided it for him?

7: Reluctant relaxation

Arthur had decided to celebrate his birthday by taking a trip to France for a week, as a kind of warm-up to his birthday. He loved France and loved driving, so it would be the perfect way for him to enjoy his fiftieth. He also had some friends, Lytton and Nancy, who spearheaded the invasion of France by London inhabitants in search of weekend retreats. Arthur had been with them one sub-zero Christmas holiday more than fifteen years ago, when they drove into the local town under cover of darkness to sign for their crumbling 'fermette'. Arthur had met Lyt and Nancy at a party in London almost twenty years ago and stayed friends, and partied, ever since. Lyt and Nancy spent almost every weekend fermetting, usually with a crowd of close friends and friends of friends also seeking retreat from people, noise, traffic and stress. Although escaping noise was something of a moot point, because there was always dance music blasting into the otherwise quiet French air. A weekend away was one thing. A weekend away from noise was, apparently, something else. The noise provided the sound track for renovation work. There was no escape from either for visitors. Inexperience counted for nothing. Ineptitude was tolerated. Consequently, after a decade and a half, the place was finally warm, dry and comfortable, but still needed lots of work. It was also the setting for some monumental parties, alternative Jubilee celebrations for liberals and republicans for example, fuelled by fabulous food, an excess of drink and a medicine chest of imported social drugs. The combination of DIY and LSD generated interesting results.

Arthur would stay with Lyt and Nancy for a few days—accepting whatever social arrangements, and tools, that were thrust upon him. He'd then head off for a couple of days driving and exploring. He loved the freedom of waking up each morning, making loose plans about where to go, then just sitting and enjoying the passing countryside. Lunch in one village, dinner in another. A cute hotel. Lots of good food and wine. He was looking forward to a week of abandoning healthy eating; bring on the cream and butter sauces, endless cheeses, crispy fresh bread and croissants, delicious fish—maybe even a succulent steak, with frites of course, and loads of wine. He had also decided to buy fifty bottles of champagne for his birthday celebrations. Buying them in France would save almost enough money to pay for the ferry fare.

By mid-afternoon Arthur had locked the studio for the week; locked the van in the garage behind the shop; and cycled home via the supermarket, where he picked up a bottle of rioja, and a bottle of champagne as an afterthought—it was a good one and it was on offer.

Because he was leaving for France in the morning,

Arthur didn't want to get too out of it this evening. He was looking forward to a quiet drink and a takeaway at home with Ronnie, his oldest friend. Ronnie had never left Manchester except to go to Blackpool once, but that didn't count as it was just Manchester by the sea: the equivalent to London's Brighton. Ron had married Vicki, his childhood sweetheart, and they begat three children—the first when Ron was only eighteen and Vix sixteen. The 'kids' were now well into adulthood. Despite this, they still haunted his life: The youngest still lived at home, stubbornly refusing to leave his mother's apron; except at the weekend when he disappeared to spend his wages on as much alcohol as he could squeeze out of Manchester's many bars. The one in the middle had two children of her own by different fathers; she had used Vicki as a daily babysitter almost since the day the first one was born. Their eldest rarely visited except when he'd been thrown out yet again by his own wife—usually because he was drunk, or she was drunk.

Ronnie had passed his fifty mark three years ago. Arthur met him in a pub in south Manchester on his own twenty-first birthday, so they had a lot of history, particularly in their love of music. Friday nights were usually spent with a stack of CDs, a takeaway and a couple of bottles of something.

Arthur wondered whether Sara was around. She would know it was his birthday soon. Maybe he'd phone her. As for wandering off to an Inuit/Irish wedding reception in deepest Derbyshire, he was cooling off the idea. It was just far too strange, and he wouldn't be able to drink at all if he planned on driving back in time to leave for his ferry the following morning. Besides, he wouldn't know anyone. No, it would be more comfortable to spend this evening at home with Ron and get stuck into a bottle, an Indian takeaway and some good music—maybe even get the guitars out. Like many of his generation, Arthur was a competent strummer, and like many he'd wanted to be a rock star when he was too old to stand any chance of success—thirty. He'd tried to join a band that year, but despite protestations that he was younger than Mick Jagger, he wasn't accepted on the grounds that 'everyone's younger than Mick Jagger'.

At home, the champagne went into the fridge. Arthur checked the freezer compartment for ice. There was plenty next to a couple of frozen pizzas for emergencies. He'd plucked a handful of envelopes from the hall floor, they included a premature birthday card from his mother—he could tell from the stamp. She was getting better as time progressed, because for years she was convinced that his birthday was a month earlier than it actually was. He'd raised the issue with her ages ago, and she admitted that she may have been a bit confused, but nothing changed.

He showered, and slipped into a pair of loose-fit jeans, a too-old tee shirt and an even older baggy fleece top. All clothes he felt most comfortable in. He then opened the red wine, poured himself a glass, settled into his sofa, and flicked the TV on to a news channel to catch up on the world while he opened the birthday card from his mum. The answer to the question as to whether Sara was around was in the second letter: a birthday card she'd sent—also prematurely. 'What is it with people? Oh well, it's the thought that counts, no matter what day it's on,' Arthur said, as he read the letter that slipped from Sara's card. It turned out that the reason he hadn't seen Sara was because she was living in Spain with the eldest son of a Hollywood film producer: 'Whose name I can't POSSIBLY give you Arty in case it gets into the tabloids but he's a darling and his father's just sooo famous but he's trying to make it as a film-maker on his own and he's got SUCH talent and he's walked out on his wife who was SUCH a bitch I can't tell you but I hope you have an excellent birthday and we'll be thinking about you and if the press calls don't tell them a thing and…'

'Like anyone would care,' Arthur thought, while seriously considering looking into the envelope to see whether her punctuation had slid off the page while the letter was in the post. He raised his glass in a toast to her 'Well at least you've found your nice Jewish man! Here's to your happiness…'

8: Beneath the streets of London town

As Arthur enjoyed his wine and watched the news, a small inflatable dinghy with three figures on-board slid silently into the mouth of a tunnel just off a little known tributary of the Thames not far from St Katherine's Dock. Subterranean London is like a Swiss cheese. Over centuries, engineers have tunnelled for all kinds of reasons: treason, transport, sewage, mail and war being just a few. Many are well documented and unused—ghosts of underground stations for example; some are long forgotten and unused. Some are long forgotten by almost everyone but still used by some.

Across the country, in several of our larger cities and in certain parts of the countryside, warrens such as these formed an infrastructure for the movement of all sorts of traffic of a less than usual kind. These tunnels are not unique to Britain; many cities in other countries are similarly structured, the most famous and notorious being Paris and Rome.

The tunnel along which the dinghy now floated gently was part of a network that provided access to many parts of the City of London. It was partly flooded, death-black and lined with dripping stones. A sour smell hung in the chilly air. Now and then, scurrying rats could be heard as they flitted along rusted pipes, chains and rotting rope. Like the hounds of the sea, rats will do just about anything to avoid water. Nathaniel Boot and Bob the Dog paddled steadily, Icarus—not the paddling kind, was sitting quietly, holding a torch in the direction they were moving, shifting the light according to Nathan's instructions: 'OK, now left.' More paddling until 'Left here.' Then a pause and 'Now take a right'. As they paddled, Nathaniel hummed a song quietly to himself, punctuating it with his instructions:

'Hear my tale of Johnny Porter,
Lost his one and only daughter,
Slid away, upon the water,
Beneath the streets of London Town.
That's right my boys, that's right, that's right,
She left for love that fateful night,
With the moon to port a-shining bright,
She stole away with Billy Brown.
But Billy was nowt but a thief -
A fox that worked the Hampstead Heath,
A rat that charmed John's lass beneath
The streets of London Town.
That's right my boys, she left, she left,
She left her father so bereft,
John swore that he would never rest,
'til he'd hunted Billy down..."

The Boot family had always been a poetic and musical family. No special occasion was considered a celebration unless everyone had performed their favourite rhyme or shanty—a song for their supper. They even wrote their own ditties. One or two were even composed purely for entertainment, rather than to act as an aide-memoir or a lyrical legacy.

The dinghy stopped at the mouth of a smaller tunnel, the floor of which was just above water level. They stepped out of the rocking craft, then lifted it and carried it along before dropping it back into the slow, satin-black water oozing through another tunnel. Icarus was amazed at how Nathaniel could tell which way was where. He was also terrified at the prospect of accidentally losing touch with the others, doubting whether he'd ever find his way out alone. After almost an hour in this labyrinth they reached a set of stone steps that rose up into darkness.

'This will do nicely!' Nathaniel said, as he placed his paddle on the floor of the dinghy, picked up a bag, which he slung over his shoulder, and stepped sure-footedly out of the rocking boat.

'Come on boys, come on. Follow me.' Nathaniel was in his element as he urged the others on, following the skinny beam of his torch-light into the darkness. Icarus and Bob were more tentative as they two climbed out of the boat and carefully searched for footing on the slippery steps. Neither wanted to fall into this ominous, and—they had both decided—poisonous soup. Relieved at having solid ground beneath them, they scrambled to catch up with Nathaniel.

The trio walked for some time, through gently descending stone-lined tunnels, eventually arriving at a spot which might have looked no different than any other, if someone hadn't obviously been hard at work, building a pile of loose stones.

'Where are we?' Icarus asked

'We are directly under the floor of the vault of a very famous firm of jewellers, who have occupied these premises for more than two hundred years.' Nathaniel replied. 'They pride themselves on their security, or at least they have done up until now!' Nathaniel was beaming almost brighter than his torch. This was the first that Icarus had heard about their target, but he'd suspected it was diamonds—which did nothing for him, but a challenge was a challenge.

Nathaniel and Bob had already paid several visits to the tunnel, preparing the ground, or more accurately, the ceiling. Icarus didn't particularly like Bob, otherwise known as 'Bob the Dog', which Icarus thought was just a bad name, something that might have come straight out of some stupid 'B' movie. Icarus was aware that he himself was not the cleanest of people, and had a few bad habits, didn't everyone? But Bob the Dog was disgusting, a weasel of a man who always wore a heavy overcoat, protesting to be cold even on the hottest days of the hottest summer. A more unpleasant person it would be difficult to imagine. He was married to a twenty-six stone woman with generous body hair, both features of which were a total turn-on to Bob. In fact life was a total turn on to Bob, to the extent of which he sported an almost permanent erection—part of the reason for the overcoat. When not having sex with his wife, which happened in multiple figures each day, he masturbated whenever the occasion permitted. His overcoat provided many hidden opportunities. He worked in the parks department for the council, driving a Land Rover and trailer which transported grass cutters, small earth movers, and similar machinery around the borough, a job which gave Bob ample time to nip back home each day for impromptu sex, and many peaceful moments in the quiet corner of a park with a magazine—which he had an uncanny knack of sniffing out of park waste bins or ferreting out of recycling skips.

The Dog possessed a particular talent with explosives, which brought in extra income for his ample wife and fifteen children (the sixteenth was on its way). To be fair to Bob, it has to be said that not all the children were his—when he met the now Mrs Prawngetter, she already had one child from a previous relationship. Bob The Dog Prawngetter's explosive talent was picked up during a brief stint in the Royal Engineers. He was not so much an explosives expert, as an artiste. He could blow up anything that was required, exactly as required. During his booming career he had blown cars, safes, vaults, doors, security vans, sheds, houses, a working-men's club and, just the once—a very vicious, very annoying bull terrier that had belonged to a troublesome petty crook and minor thug who lived two doors away on the Peckham council estate they lived on. To his extra-curricular curriculum vitae, Bob the Dog could soon add blowing away several feet of concrete and stone from the ceiling of the tunnel in which he was standing.

'Right, everything's set. All we have to do is to connect these two wires to this battery, and we're in!' Bob demonstrated, holding the battery in one hand and the wires in another. The demonstration made Icarus nervous: they were standing right under the explosives, and the wire and battery were being held far to close to each other for Icarus's comfort. Bob needed to check the circuit one last time, so he handed the battery to Nathaniel who put it in his bag for safe-keeping. 'It's going to make a right old box of toys down here, but there'll be no sound up-top.' Bob added knowledgeably.

Nathaniel nodded to Bob that he understood, then turned to Icarus: 'There's a strong-box inside—you'll recognise the type, it won't give you any problems. Very old firm—make a thing about the vault being impenetrable "the deepest and safest in London". The shop's alarmed, but down here—nothing. The only way in and out is by one set of narrow stairs, and a dumb waiter to carry boxes up and down. Nobody seems to have thought about how the vault got built thirty feet underground though, especially how its door was put in place—it's a monster!'

'How?' Icarus asked.

'Honestly...I don't know, but I'd guess the builders probably brought everything along these tunnels—then blocked it off for security. OK, everything ready?'

Bob nodded.

Icarus was concerned, 'But are you sure about them not having an alarm? I mean, it seems a bit stupid to say the least?'

Nathaniel nodded, 'Very stupid, but I'm positive.'

'What are we after? Anything special?' Icarus asked.

'Aha! Something very special this time, you wait and

see!' Nathaniel looked at Bob, and they grinned. 'Come-on, let's pull back a bit.' They all walked back down the tunnel, following a wire for about twenty yards. Nathaniel knelt down, lifted the battery out of his bag and handed it to Bob. He then pulled out some industrial ear protectors, dust masks and goggles, which he told the pair to put on. 'Have you got a white rabbit and some doves in there as well?' Icarus asked, as he pulled the goggles over his head. Nathaniel grinned, reached into the bag, and drew out a telescopic ladder, which was almost three metres fully extended.

'As if by magic! And for my next trick, ladies and gentlemen, my beautiful assistant will climb the ladder, completely unaided, as if defying the very laws of gravity itself.'

'Not 'til I've blown the bleeder open. And if you don't get yer loaf down, you'll be pulling that out of your bag an' all.' Bob said, dryly.

Bob wrapped a wire around one terminal of the battery. After checking everything and everyone was set—and after a thumbs up from Nathaniel, he placed the remaining wire on the second terminal. Icarus winced in expectation.

There was a second's delay before the muffled blast. After a further second or two a wall of dust flew down the tunnel and immersed the trio like a sudden desert sandstorm. It seemed to take an age for the dust to settle enough to enable Nathaniel to see anything. As the dust thinned, Icarus could be seen staggering—arms outstretched, trying to feel for something in his blindness. Nathaniel wiped his goggles for him. Icarus nodded his gratitude as he bashed the dust out of his overalls, pointlessly.

Nathaniel passed the ladder to Icarus. They followed Bob back through the swirling dust and over a pile of rubble to the point of the explosion. The three peered up into the blackness. Nathaniel shone his torch into the hole, dust danced in the shaft of light. Above them, gradually coming into view as the dust thinned, was the ancient painted ceiling of a stone vault. 'Fucking A-plus, dude!' Icarus exclaimed.

'I couldn't have put it better myself,' Nathaniel said, 'but come on, we've got to be quick!' Icarus stuck the ladder up through the hole. 'Good job, Bob!' Nathaniel climbed, followed closely by the other two.

Icarus took stock of the vault almost immediately. It was lined with metal deposit boxes, each painted a municipal green, and bearing a brass handle above which was a small label carrying a code number. He slid one out of its rack and inspected the lock: 'Jeeez! Are you seriously telling me this is all they use! I could open this with my penknife!' Which he duly did in a matter of seconds, helped by the fact that his penknife had been specially made in a tiny workshop in a Bangkok backstreet to a Swiss design augmented to his own specifications. It didn't take him long to get a rhythm going as he deftly unlocked the boxes, row by row. Most contained the shop's normal stock-in-trade jewellery. It was valuable, but of no interest. Mere swag.

Nathaniel was paying no attention to Icarus. He was instead paying close attention to a particular row, moving along reading numbers until he found the box he was looking for. He slid it out and placed it on the floor: 'Open this one.' Icarus obliged with a twist of the wrist.

Nathaniel lifted the lid, removed a velvet pouch and tipped the contents into his palm—a selection of large lumps of what looked like rough glass.

'Looks like big lumps of crystallised sugar!' Icarus said.

'Not sugar, but sweet. Oh, so sweet!' Nathaniel held the uncut diamonds in the palm of his hand. Icarus picked up one and held it in the light:

'Doesn't look like anything special. Like something you might pick up on the beach. What's it worth?' He asked.

'That one? I'm not exactly sure, but all together, approximately seven mill, less commission.'

Even though he had little interest in diamonds, and wasn't that interested in money, on hearing the value of the stones, Icarus stepped back in astonishment and trod on a small rubber mat in front of the door. Instantly bells started sounding a long way off. A red light flashed above their heads. 'Oh Shit!' Icarus said.

'Shit indeed! Out! Fast' Nathaniel commanded. Bob held a bag open while Nathaniel emptied the contents of the box into it. Within seconds the three were back down in the tunnel, the ladder was dropped, and they headed back to the dinghy. Bob the Dog stopped roughly at the spot where they had waited for the first explosion. 'Keep going! Keep going! Get a bleedin' move on! I'll be along in a minute!' Nathaniel grabbed Icarus's sleeve and yanked him along: 'Come on! Come on! He'll come. Trust me, you wouldn't want to be here in a minute!' Icarus stumbled, then found his footing and followed Nathaniel around a corner, leaving Bob out of sight. Bob knelt down and swept the ground with his hands until he found a small spool of wire beneath the dust. He picked it up and ran, following the other two, unravelling the wire until the spool was empty. He then stuck his hand inside his overcoat, delved deep and drew out a battery, which he placed on the floor then connected the wires to it. He immediately ran as fast as he could, as the explosion behind him blasted a thick cloud of dust down the tunnel. Icarus dropped his torch with the shock of it, but instinct warned him that it wasn't safe to stop and pick it up. He ran into the pitch black, feeling the walls as he went. He could feel the blast of air and dust on his back, small stones hit the back of his head—one cutting he ear slightly. He pulled the goggles back over his eyes and tried to protect himself even further by covering his mouth with one sleeve of his overall as he felt his way with his other hand, scraping his fingers along the tunnel walls as he went. Finally a torchlight beam bounced out of the dust behind him as Bob caught up. The two ran around a corner and into the comforting lamp-light that lit the dinghy, which Nathaniel had quickly prepared for embarkation.

'What the fuck was that!' Icarus asked, as he sat down in the rocking craft, slightly pissed off that he hadn't been warned.

'Insurance, courtesy of Mr Prawngetter here! We've blown the tunnel. It will take ages to dig through from the other side, and I don't think there's any chance of them ever finding this way in. Besides these places don't belong to anyone other than those who know they're here, and we want to keep it that way, eh Bob? Now let's get out of here.'

The destiny of the diamonds was unknown to Nathaniel; he was only responsible for their delivery as far as a smallholding run by a Portuguese family who lived next to a cemetery in Brussels. He didn't know that from there they would make their way eastwards, ending up in a variety of destinations, mainly Moscow and Kiev. For now the stones were expertly encased in a rusty metal box in Mr Bob Prawngetter's workshop-cum-garage, then thrown in a holdall in the back of a dirty, anonymous-grey, old-but-sound Fiat Tipo acquired specifically for the job. Nathaniel carried the stones, and the Fiat carried Nathaniel and Icarus to Dover, where they checked into a 'Sleep-Tite' budget hotel—which was as anonymous as the car and only marginally cleaner. As for Bob the dog, he had personal things to attend to. He found blowing up things exceptionally stimulating, and Mrs Prawngetter was poised.

9: Home alone

Arthur was finding it difficult to relax. It was getting on for eight o'clock and there was no word from Ronnie. A telephone call delivered no reply. Arthur tried Ronnie's mobile. At first, nothing. But eventually a loudly whispering voice answered:

'Hullo! It's Ron?'

'It's me!'

'I know, I can see your name on me mobi. Happy birthday!'

'Ronnie! Not you as well! It's not my bloody birthday yet! What's up with everyone? Where are you?'

'Didn't you get my email?'

'What email?'

'You didn't get it! Bugger! I'm sure I sent it. Have you checked your email today?'

'Yes, as soon as I got in from work, but I didn't see anything from you. All I got were the usual penis enlargements, which I forwarded to you, and some sad news about a couple of distant relatives who have died in Nigeria in a car crash leaving me a fortune.'

‘Sorry to hear that, on your birthday too! How much did they leave you?’

‘Are you deaf or just stupid! It’s not my birthday Ronnie. Anyway, you’re a hard-hearted bastard! Apparently I’m the sole surviving relative and they’ve left me about $15million I think.’

‘Forget it, it’s too much. Who would want that kind of responsibility?’

‘Yeah! That’s what I thought. Not worth the bother.’

‘Good man!’

‘Anyway, enough of this fooling around. As you’re not here, I gather you’re standing me up?’

‘Aaaw, look, I’m sorry mate. I emailed you to tell you that I couldn’t make it this evening. There’s this play that Vix wanted to see but it ends this evening and I promised to take her to see it earlier this week, but it was sold out, anyway—so you remember Mickey? He used to work here—at the theatre? Well I called him and he said he might be able to get us a couple of comps, but he wasn’t sure for what night. Well he did and they’re for tonight. Did that make sense? I confuse myself sometimes…’

‘Perfect sense. Why are you whispering, by the way, and what’s that hissing noise? Is your phone on the blink?’

‘No mate, like I said, I’m here—in the theatre, that’s a couple of miserable bastards shushing me… Ouch!’

‘Are you alright? What was that?’

‘Vix just slapped my arm for saying ‘bastards’. Bloody hurt as well! Ow! Stop hitting me! Look, I’d better go, there’s a bloke coming down the aisle with a torch and he doesn’t look like he’s selling ice cream. Happy birthday!

See you soon…'

'It's not my birth….' Arthur started to protest, but Ronnie had already hung up, '…day yet!' He made a mental note to check his birth certificate, just to make sure he wasn't going doolally.

*

'So, this is it then. Alone!' Arthur thought about finishing the bottle of wine he'd just started and watching a DVD. But that was such a miserable, clichéd thing to do. Besides which he was restless. He thought about going to the bar down the road, but it would be full of twentysomethings. He decided it would be less lonely staying in.

He thought about the wedding reception invitation from earlier that day—a trek out to Derbyshire? He looked at the time. 'Nah! It's too late and too far, and I'm going to France tomorrow,' he thought. Normally that would have been that. But today was not a normal day. It was the beginning of his holiday; the first bit of the languorous build-up to his birthday celebrations, and he felt that he had to make some sort of effort—if only to prove to himself that he still had a sense of adventure despite approaching fifty. He dug around and found the printout of the map Cedric had given him at the wedding earlier that day. He unfolded it, turned it the right way up and studied it.

'That's not so bad. Can't be more than, oooh, forty minutes. I can do that easily. If it's crap I'll just turn around and come back! Nothing to lose!' With which he stood up, pushed the cork back into the bottle of red wine and went to his wardrobe to find something suitable for a wedding party, heeding Cedric's advice on dress code. Fifteen minutes later and—warmly dressed, with the wedding album, an extra fleece under one arm, and clutching a carrier bag containing the bottle of champagne—he was standing in front of the garage door, now slowly whirring open in response to the encrypted signal from a sophisticated key fob. A light flickered into life inside and a steady beeping could be heard as the garage's independent alarm began its warning. Arthur keyed in the code to disarm it. All was silent. His eyes adjusted to the light and he gazed at the object in front of him. How many times had he looked at it, stared at it, dreamed of it, caressed it with his eyes and hands. There was something about this car that stirred Arthur deeply, like an emotion that hadn't yet been given a name. He knew every cubic centimetre and each square millimetre of this car. He should do—he'd painstakingly restored it totally from the heartbreakingly sorry state in which he'd found it. The Russian engineers who originally built it would have been proud of him.

10: Blip

Conceptually, communism had a lot going for it. But in the USSR the powers that be realised there was a major flaw: it was a massive country and it was skint. Lenin was too busy to do anything about it, besides, he had acquired some inheritance in the treasures from the Tsars which—auctioned off discreetly in Paris, New York, Florence and London—brought in a comfortable amount of foreign currency for a while. Stalin at first bluntly refused to accept the fact that there was no money. Finally, he had to face up to finding a solution for something that was blatantly obvious to just about everyone else in the country, especially those who were starving. After several months of brain bashing, including his own, he came up with what he considered to be a masterstroke of creative thinking. He decided to reduce spending by reducing the population. It was radical perhaps, but he didn't think anyone would argue. At first he didn't realise the scale of the task he'd created. It was exhausting. He was relieved when war finally arrived on his doorstep—help had arrived.

It fell to Nikita Khrushchev to face up to the problem

that had dogged the country for almost half a century. It was the late fifties and countries all over the world seemed to be prospering. In particular those that had lost wars. On one side Germany had rebuilt itself and was exporting its industrial production worldwide. On the other side was Japan, which had rebuilt itself and was exporting its industrial production worldwide. Khrushchev felt frustrated at being stuck in the middle. And America! America really annoyed him—it seemed to have so much of everything, much more than it needed.

Khrushchev loved foreign magazines—he liked to keep himself up to date with what was going on in the world. He was particularly fond of browsing through those that showed America in all its fifties' glory. Images such as fresh-faced teenagers—the boys in jeans and shirts, the girls in wide skirts and tight sweaters—sitting in long, open-top cars with high tail fins and white-walled tyres. There were glossy features on sprawling suburban detached homes with drives and pools, and advertisements: for toothpaste, cars, real estate, fashion, kitchens, food mixers, furniture, holidays, bicycles, candy and toilet paper. Another American dream that really annoyed Khrushchev was Hollywood. To his mind, Hollywood was a sordid city making movies that were shown in cinemas all over the world. Movies that spread the script about how great America was. 'Glossy propaganda!' He thought, deeply envious every time he watched one, and gently guilty for enjoying them. If Khrushchev loved three things, it was Russia, American movies and American cars, and not necessarily in that order.

It's 1957 and Khrushchev is not a happy bunny. He had promised reforms the previous year at the 20th Party Congress, and he needed to deliver.

'We need to export!' He said with determination, banging his clenched fist down for effect. An action that failed to impress the meeting of his closest advisers because the table was at least five inches thick and twenty feet long, and made of wood so hard and old that it failed to resonate. 'We need to bring in foreign currency. That's the only way we're going to get out of this mess! We need to advertise what a great country this is! We need to make people interested in the USSR! We need marketing! We need to make people take notice of us! We need glamour!'

'We've got nuclear weapons…' one adviser nervously suggested.

'Nuclear weapons aren't sexy! And they're crap! Anyway the Americans have nuclear weapons; and with their security being the way it is the whole damned world will have them before long! No, we need to do something big! Something different! Anyone got any ideas?' Khrushchev rubbed his aching hand.

There was silence around the table. Khrushchev glared at each adviser in turn. Outwardly they bore the expressions of thinking men; inwardly their stomachs churned like nervous children. Panic nibbled at their bones and sucked the juices from any creativity.

Boris Baranovsky, a small, bald-headed man with a goatee beard and tiny round glasses, leaned over and whispered into the ear of the colleague to his right—a stick-thin, white-faced man with slicked-back hair:

'I told you, he's insane, his head's up his arse…'

'What was that?' Shouted Khrushchev, 'if you have an idea, share it with the whole table!'

'Oh, er, I was just saying, that, erm. well… erm….' Baranovsky dried up, shifting in his seat uneasily. A long train ride to winters of –58C was a mere sentence away.

'He said that he had an insane idea to send a man to Mars,' said Silentov the stick man, dryly, while glaring at Baranovsky. There was silence—two minutes that seemed like an hour. Khrushchev was thinking.

'Alexei Voloshyn, how many ballistic missiles do we have?'

'Exactly? I'm not sure, favoured leader. Many.'

'Stop being such a creep! How many of them actually work?'

'It depends what you mean by work? As in take off, travel somewhere, hit a target, or actually explode?'

'I mean, Voloshyn, how many could actually take off?'

'I think there's quite a few that could manage it. But surely leader, you're not planning to…' The man looked anxiously around the table, but all he saw were anxious faces looking back at him. One person shrugged indifferently.

'Do I look stupid Voloshyn? I'm not thinking of launching a war or anything like that, I like America; I might even retire there one day. Florida is an up and coming place I hear, and conveniently close to Cuba. How are we getting on with our friends in Havana?' He asked of the group, before checking himself: 'Forgive me, I'm getting distracted. Tell me Alexei Voloshyn, how long would it take to build a really big missile, a rocket? One capable of reaching space?'

'Space?' Answered Alexei, as if someone had asked him to grow wings.

'Yes, you know—stars, planets, black stuff! Space!'

'As in just straight up and down again? Or as in going around a bit?'.

'Whatever! And stop answering my questions with questions!' Khrushchev realised that if he was going to survive in this job for any length of time he'd need more tolerance for idiots.

Alexei Voloshyn had been in politics long enough to be a politician, he thought he'd better be optimistic and halve his estimate: 'Well, given the money, maybe five years…'

'No! No! No! No! No!' Khrushchev looked towards the ceiling and shook his head firmly from side to side. Then he paced to and fro across the floor, hands behind his back, seemingly lost in some distant meditative state. After ten minutes he stopped, turned and leaned forward, hands upon the table. He stared into Alexei Voloshyn.

'Three years?' Alexei said, shrugging in despair as he looked at his leader pleadingly and then in turn to the various blank faces around him. He received no help: '… maybe two?'

Khrushchev stepped back, and in a calm voice asked: 'How difficult can it be Alexei, we've got the technology already. Just strap a couple of missiles together or something.'

'It's not as simple as that Nikita. There's gravity and all sorts of other stuff to overcome…' There was a hint of despair in Alexei's voice.

'Fuck gravity! Overcome that, and whatever the other stuff is, and get something into space by September!'

'What! This year?' Alexei looked around the table and laughed nervously at what he thought was his own joke.

'Of course this year! That's plenty of time. We need to show the world what we can do. Just get something into orbit. Anything. We'll think about Mars or the Moon another time.'

Alexei's imminent protest was silenced by a gesture from across the table—a finger to the lip and a frown from Boris Baranovsky. Alexei glared back.

'OK! OK! I don't want to be seen to be a difficult man. Voloshyn, you have until October. Now! On to other matters!' Khrushchev continued: 'I have ideas…' His head ducked down out of sight behind the table. Drawers could be heard opening and closing. He reappeared with a pile of American magazines, which he dropped heavily onto the table. '…Luxury goods!'

'Luxury goods?' Someone around the table questioned.

'Luxury goods! That's how we're going to make money; we're going to make luxury goods. Not for our own people of course. No! No! They will all be for export—to those bourgeois countries whose decadent people need to spend as much as they can on things they don't need. So that's what we'll make: cameras, watches, telescopes, cars, radios, and so-on, and so-on. Supply and demand! I'm initiating a luxury goods programme!'

'But leader, it will take time to build factories. We need materials, resources, and what about designers?' said a tall, athletic-looking man—a young, but talented engineer.

'I've been thinking about all that, Sergei Zadinsky and, as it happens we already have the resources. I'm putting you in charge of the car programme.'

'Thank you leader,' Zadinsky said, without conviction, 'but what resources?'

'OK, take your programme—we have tractor plants to make the bodywork and engines. It's all the same materials, just made into different shapes. We have that factory that's been stockpiling leather trench coats since the war. Use it to make the seats and interior stuff. And we can get the carpets from Afghanistan—pay them in small arms: but no ammunition! Get the glass from that optical factory near Leningrad.'

'If you don't mind me saying leader, but what about the Wartburg factory in Zwickau, or the Trabant?' The question came from a uniformed officer sitting at the far end of the table.

'East Germany, that's what about! They think they have the monopoly on engineering. Anyway there was all that fuss with BMW a couple of years back: EMW, BMW—as if it mattered! No…there's nothing romantic about the Soviet Union—but 'Russia' is much more evocative. No, it has to be something purely Russian. Something completely new! Something we can be proud of! Something the world will desire and more importantly, pay for! That's what it's all about you see—desire! Well that and dollars of course; we don't have enough of either here. Where's the Russian Marilyn Monroe? The Russian Charlie Chaplin? The Russian Alfred Hitchcock. Where's the Russian Chevrolet? The Russian Hollywood?—I mean mention

Soviet films and what does the rest of the world think of: 'The Battleship Potempkin'. OK, I admit it's a good film, but it's more than 30 years' old now, and it's not exactly 'The African Queen', is it? Colour! Romance. Look—even our national drink has no colour! Desire! Zadinsky, that's what I want you to create.

Here's a few ideas for you…' Khrushchev slid the magazines down the table towards Sergei; they were helped along their way by a column of hands. 'As you'll see, I've circled a few pictures to give you a starting point.'

He disappeared below the table again, and again followed sound of drawers opening and closing. 'Here's an envelope for each of you which gives you an outline of your tasks. Read them carefully and get back to me if you have any queries, which I'm sure you won't.' As he was talking the envelopes were passed around the table, opened and read. Silence for a few seconds. Then shuffling from one side of the table, and heavy sighs.

'What's the matter Professor Zenit?' Khrushchev asked, mildly irritated, 'out with it, is there a problem?'

'I, erm, forgive me leader, but I don't fully understand…'

'Understand what?'

'Well, it says here, that I'm in charge of the toilet paper programme?' There was a snigger from across the table.

'Is something funny Andrei Andreksovich?'

'No leader! Nothing!' But he couldn't swallow his mirth.

'I believe you are in charge of the camera programme?'

'Yes leader?' the mirth was fading fast.

'You may exchange envelopes with the Professor...' The exchange took place, Andreksovich sheepishly and slowly handing his to Professor Zenit, who was very careful not to smile.

'I trust you will succeed, Andrei, in this most important task. Soft toilet paper is the cornerstone of a civilised society. I want you to develop soft toilet paper for the people of Russia—succeed and they will thank you for it, maybe even write folk songs about you. Toilet paper, soft and strong—that's your task. Make sure you succeed. I will personally test your developments, and any shit on my hands will be shit on yours!'

*

The programme began in earnest. And there were some successes. Alexei Voloshyn miraculously managed to get a rocket into space by October. It even put a small satellite into orbit. TV and radio stations worldwide reported Russia's great achievement. Khrushchev stood in the control room, obviously delighted: 'OK Voloshyn, now it's up, and we have the eyes and ears of the world, let's show them all what it can do!'

'Yes leader. If you would like to do the honours.' Alexei pointed to a small, black switch on a panel of similar small, black switches.

Khrushchev made a proud, but short speech to the room full of technicians, journalists, and the world, before flicking the switch. The sound of a regular 'blip', 'blip', blip', began to emit from a small round speaker screwed to a wall. Khrushchev looked at Alexei questioningly. Alexei looked at Khrushchev, smiled and shrugged. Khrushchev leaned over to Alexei and whispered through gritted teeth:

'What's that?'

'That's it.'

'That's what?'

'It.'

'That's it?'

'Well, I guess technically that's a they rather than an it.'

'That's it? Blip! Blip! Blip?'

'Not just Blip! Blip! Blip! Leader—Blip! Blip! Blip! From space!'

'It doesn't matter whether it's from space or the next room; it's still Blip, Blip, Blip! Is that the best you could do? Do you know how much this mission has cost?'

'Yes leader, four hundre…'

'I already know, you idiot! And given the results, I wish I didn't! The first time in the history of the Earth that a man-made object has ever been put into orbit. The ears of the entire world are on us, and what do they get? Blip! Blip! Blip! See me later! And pack some warm clothes! And get that dog out of here! Furious, Khrushchev headed for the door.

'Yes leader. Laika! Laika! Come here! Who's a good…'

'Wait!' Khrushchev stopped in his tracks and spun around. Unpack. 'I've had an idea…'

*

The space programme proved to be a major distraction for Khrushchev, and his mind temporarily slipped away from the rest of the 'Profit Programme'. But Sergei Zadinsky knew he was on borrowed time. The design and build process for the automotive project had been stretched out over almost five years. But he was running out of excuses. Zadinsky and his team had spent many hours looking at the American magazines, wondering what to do. Superficially it was simple, he had the brief from Khrushchev: "Come up with a luxury car the likes of which Russia and the world has never seen". The team had tried, and tried, and tried without success. One young designer summed up the general attitude as he threw down his pencil after the latest failed attempt by the team, 'How can we design something new, when we don't even know what it looks like?'

By 1961, Zadinsky was desperate. It was the Bay of Pigs that gave him an idea that might turn the project around. But he didn't have the courage to pursue it until after the American's mock invasion of a Caribbean Island in 1962—the purpose of the invasion was to overthrow a fictitious leader named 'Ortsac'. Zadinsky made a call to Castro, who was furious at this act of theatre and convinced that the Americans were still planning to invade Cuba. Castro listened to Zadinsky's request, went silent for a few moments, then said he'd get back to him.

He got back several hours later. Castro said he'd talked it over and he was prepared to do a deal. Giving approval for it, however, was way out of Zadinsky's authority. He needed to speak to Khrushchev.

Khrushchev was in a sombre mood and looked dark around the eyes. 'Ah Sergei Zadinsky, sit down! Take some tea.'

'Thank you Nikita. What's the matter, are you not feeling so good?'

'Haven't you heard?'

'About the American exercise? Yes I heard,' Sergei replied, thankful that Khrushchev seemed to be preoccupied.

'What did they hope to achieve? Look at that Bay of Pigs fiasco last year. They're so stupid. They couldn't even be bothered getting involved themselves! Fancy sending in a bunch of Cuban exiles! How lazy can you get? And now this! But it's not this invasion that bothers me so much as the fact that Kennedy did it. I mean the Bay of Pigs—you'd expect that from Eisenhower, and Kennedy was just the new kid. But this? Now he's acting just like a spoilt brat, just because he didn't get his own way in Vienna last year! Tell me Sergei, is it me? What's happening to the kids of today? I mean, what kind of President would say, "We've got more missiles than you!" It's so juvenile. He really pisses me off.'

'Quite so. Understandable.'

'Anyway, enough of my problems, what can I do for you? What are you doing at the moment?'

'The automotive programme.'

'The what?'

'Automotive—you know, the Profit Programme?' Sergei could see that he had only half of Nikita's attention.

'Oh yes! I remember. Is that still going?'

'I'm sorry?' Sergei thought he'd misheard.

'How's it going? Do you have something yet?'

'That's why I'm here Nikita. You see we need to get hold of a couple of American cars.'

'Impossible! After what's just happened! I don't want anything to do with them.'

'Aah well! Yes, I understand. But, the thing is, the ones

we'd like are in Cuba, a '58 Chevy Convertible, and a '59 Cadillac Coupe de Ville.'

'Cuba? How come? When was it Castro kicked out Batista?'

' Fifty-six'

'So how come they've got a '58 Chevy and a '59 Cadillac?'

'I'm not sure; it's something to do with the mafia needing to get back in to ship drugs. I think the automobiles were part of a failed business package. The thing is that we feel these two cars have some essential technology we need for our project.'

'Essential?'

'Essential.'

Khrushchev stroked his chin. 'Well Sergei, if they're essential then it's essential... but please don't bore me with the technical details. What does Cuba say?'

'Aah well! It's not so much what they've said as what they, or more specifically he, wants.'

'Who? Castro?'

'Yes.'

'Well! Come on! What does he want?'

There was no way Sergei could beat about the bush: 'A couple of missiles.'

Khrushchev threw up his arms and stormed around the room. 'Missiles! Is he crazy?! Why does he want missiles? Don't answer that! It's obvious why he wants them! Bloody Americans! Why do they insist on pissing people off!' He stopped and turned to Sergei: 'Tell me he doesn't want nuclear?'

Sergei took a strategic sip from his tea, looking down into the dark liquid.

'What! You are seriously asking me to swap nuclear missiles for two old American cars?'

'They're not that old, anyway they're modern classics, or at least they will be,' Sergei emphasised.

Khrushchev was just about to fly off the handle completely, but stopped himself. Thoughts were entering his head. 'Give me a minute to think about this,' he said. He walked to a desk piled with papers and sat down in a deep leather chair. He leaned forward with his head in his hands, and didn't move for almost twenty minutes.

Sergei sat, staring around the room, picking fluff from his trousers, idly checking the condition of his nails, thinking about the weather in Siberia at this time of year, and about his pregnant wife.

Eventually Khrushchev raised his head. He was smiling. 'You know Zadinsky, it might actually work. It's ironic that we can get a rocket into space, but we haven't got enough power to reach the US from here. Of course we could seriously damage Alaska, but who gives a shit about a few bears and a bit of salmon. But Cuba... now that's a different bowl of caviar. What is it... ninety miles from Florida? Think about all those retired voters! How happy do you think they would be to find out that Soviet nuclear missiles were less than a hundred miles away!' Khrushchev was grinning like a Chechnyan cat. 'The Americans will be furious! Kennedy will be furious! I like that! I like that a lot!'

Sergei was having second thoughts. 'But is it safe to give nuclear missiles to Cuba?'

'Safe? Well it's safe for us, because we'll be way out of range. But that's not the point. We don't need to send anything that actually works. I mean, what we say we'll send, and what we actually send doesn't necessarily need to be the same. It's not as if the Cubans are actually going to use them. The important thing is that they think they're getting the real thing. Or more importantly the Americans think Cuba's getting the real thing. In fact most importantly that Kennedy thinks Cuba's getting the real thing. You see Sergei Zadinsky, this is politics, it's all theatre, and these are just the props. And between you and me, most of our missiles are just props anyway—we used the guts of most of them in the space programme.'

So a deal was struck. A Soviet ship sailed to Cuba, which, in anticipation of its arrival, set hastily about constructing 'secret' missile bases. A few weeks later, several toothless SS-4 missiles were delivered—much to the delight of Castro, who happily handed over the Chevy and the Cadillac—the trunk of the Chevy contained several boxes of cigars for Khrushchev.

Everyone was happy except President Kennedy, who nearly choked on his breakfast as an advisor explained what the pictures taken of Cuba from a U-2 spy plane actually showed. His initial reaction, to blow Cuba out of the Caribbean, was tempered by the more moderate members of his staff. Eventually he decided to 'quarantine' Cuba with his navy to prevent anything going in or coming out. He initially wanted a blockade, but was told that would have been illegal. A furious Castro told Khrushchev that he'd use the missiles if America invaded.

'Feel free!' Khrushchev told him, puffing a cigar with great satisfaction. Everything was going according to plan.

Khrushchev's advisors were urging him to do something. It seemed that the whole world was waiting on tenterhooks as the crisis unfolded. But Khrushchev remained calm; it was as if he wasn't acknowledging that a crisis existed. Kennedy called several times, but was told that Khrushchev was on the other line.

'He's in denial,' said one advisor.

'He doesn't seem to listen,' said another.

'Maybe he going slightly Stalin,' someone added.

'Don't even think about it,' replied the first.

Eventually, after seven days—which seemed to Khrushchev like the optimum time, he picked up the ringing red phone.

'Hello, Kennedy here. Who's that?'

'Khrushchev—who were you expecting?'

'OK Niki. Here's how it is. We've got you surrounded,'

'…And you want me to come out with my hands up?'

'Well, not exactly, but in a manner of speaking, I guess you could say that. Just take your missiles back and get the hell out of Cuba! It's not your business.'

'But it's not your business either!'

'No, but you make it our business. Cuba is only sixty miles from Florida!'

'Ninety.'

'Ninety? Are you sure? Hang on…' Kennedy put his hands over the phone; his muffled voice could be heard talking to advisors. 'OK ninety miles, you must see how difficult you're making it for me?'

'Now you know how it feels—you've got missiles in Turkey—just 150 miles from us.'

'Have we? Hang on…' Again Kennedy's hand was over the receiver.

'OK! OK! I accept that we need to sort things out a little.'

The World's two most powerful leaders talked: Khrushchev said he'd take back all his missiles if Kennedy gave reassurance that he wouldn't invade Cuba. Kennedy was happy to agree in principle—he hadn't planned to invade Cuba anyway—it was never his idea, but an Eisenhower legacy he had found it difficult to get out of. Even if he did invade Cuba and succeed, it would become another US state, which would mean they'd have to make Cubans American nationals, and the first thing they'd do is leave for the mainland. So he was happy when Khrushchev asked him to 'ease off Castro a bit' and be 'a bit more open-minded about the whole nuclear weapons thing'. Of course neither leader could make the decisions there and then—there were formal avenues that needed to be negotiated—a route filled with people who specialise in getting from A to B via as many letters as possible. They agreed to get back to each other later that day.

Khrushchev spoke to Castro, who reluctantly agreed to let Russia have the missiles back, but pride demanded that the two automobiles were returned. This was impossible. They had been stripped, analysed and distributed across the USSR. The Chevy's V8 engine now powered a luxury speedboat on the Black Sea. The electrically adjustable leather seats had pride of place in a dacha south of Moscow. The only items Nikita Khrushchev could be sure about were the Cadillac wheels, which were on his own limousine, and were staying on his limousine—not least for the reason that there was no other part of the Cadillac left to attach them to.

A day of tough meetings ended. Finally everything was agreed. The missiles were pulled out of Cuba. America lifted its 'quarantine'. Russian ships left for home, and promises were made to start some kind of negotiation to ease the Cold War situation. There were a few sub-clauses necessary: one was that Kennedy organised the delivery of a 1959 Cadillac Coupe de Ville and a 1957 Chevrolet Convertible to a remote Caribbean island. Another was the 'allocation' of a single-storey detached house, with pool, on a retirement complex in Fort Lauderdale. Yet another ensured that a supply of Cuban cigars would somehow regularly find its way to a house near Lake Tahoe.

It was a tired but relaxed Khrushchev who sat down to watch TV that evening. 'A week is a long time in politics', he said, as he poured himself a bourbon.

*

The Chevy and the Cadillac were a revelation to Zadinsky's design team, but not the inspiration he'd hoped for. There were some similarities to an early ZIL, which was one avenue Sergei tried to pursue. But attempts to find a half-decent example of the particular model of ZIL he had in mind proved fruitless. In the end, Sergei came up with a desperate solution for a desperate situation. He took photos of all the individual body parts of the American cars, and then he took pictures of parts of the most popular Russian cars. He piled them up according to which part of the car they were from. Took the first pile—pictures of radiator grilles, and put them into a fur hat. He then passed the hat to a young designer.

'Pick a photo.'

Although puzzled, the young man did as he was told.

'The first of a particular piece out of the hat is the one we use!' Said Sergei.

'I don't understand.' Said one of the team.

'I mean that the first picture of a radiator is the one we use, the first roof, the first tail fin, the first wheel. OK?'

'Ah ha!'

The photos were carefully laid out. After a little shuffling around, and a bit of trimming here and there, the result was a car. It was recognisably American, but not recognisable as any known make. As far as Sergei was concerned, it was what Khrushchev had asked for, and didn't Khrushchev know better than anyone?

'Fine!' Sergei concluded. 'Just make it look a little less… a little less American: smooth the edges a bit and it will be perfect!' Sergei tried to sound as convincing as possible.

On paper the vehicle began to take shape. Or rather shapes. The big circular chrome nose-cum-radiator grille was a nice touch. The long bulging bonnet had a certain elegance. The front wheel arches were fulsome and framed the white-walled tyres well. While the straight run of panels over the rear wheel kept the line going. The large tail fins had a dramatic sweep about them that adequately counterbalanced the protruding rear lamps, which were modelled on a movie poster displaying Jane Mansfield.

In all fairness, the design did contain many of the elements that had made several classic American cars classics. The clash occurred in bringing them all together. Not that anyone working on it saw this. Because by the time the team had put the design together, they had all been working on it for too long and far too closely to notice. It did have a certain charm though, so Sergei took an executive decision and approved the design and work began in earnest on the prototypes. Meanwhile, an understandably clueless marketing team was assembled from prominent artists and writers to promote Russia's new strategy to the world.

'Advertising is easy,' explained Sergei at the briefing, having just read a book on it by an American advertising guru, 'all you have to do is explain how wonderful things are. Think of yourselves as the tailors of the emperor's new clothes. Come up with a name that creates desire in the minds of people. There's not enough desire in Russia. Where are our hot dogs! Where is Marilyn Monroe? Where is the South Pacific!' None of the team had a clue what Sergei was on about, especially as it was common knowledge that Marilyn Monroe had died earlier that year. At least two members of the team looked towards the door wistfully.

Despite not having a clue about what they were supposed to do, they spent many hours discussing the philosophy of Russian desire. They were allowed as much vodka as was necessary to lubricate the process. Finally, they began to agree on some essential elements:

'Sex and religion are the only two things that create desire,' said one prominent artist.

'Alcohol.' Added a writer. At which an attendant topped up his glass again. 'Sex, religion and alcohol!'

'And money!' Said another artist.

'Sex, religion, alcohol and money.' Slurred the same writer.

'Power,' said one of the other writers.

'Sex, religion, alcohol and power,' the first writer continued.

'You forgot money, said the second artist.

'I told you. I'll pay you back on Tuesday!' Rasped the first writer

'No not that money! Money! You forgot Money!' Insisted the second artist.

'Aaah, yes. Money! Sex, religion, alcohol, money, and power', the first writer said, counting on his fingers…is that it? Anyone got anything else to add?'

'You already said money,' someone said.

'Well you can never have enough,' someone else replied.

There was silence for a while. Then someone said: 'Politics?' This was dismissed instantly

'I don't think so, politics is not desire, it is a device. A device fuelled by desire, sex, religion, alcohol, money and power.' There was sombre agreement on this from around the table.

'Right, now how can we apply that to this?' Said the first writer, who had become a natural spokesman for the group. He was pointing to a board, on which was pinned an artist's impression of the car, several prototypes of which were now being assembled in a tractor plant somewhere. In silence, they all looked at the picture—they had been looking at it for hours, and no matter how much they looked at it, it still it didn't grow any more desirable. The silence continued. Until someone commented:

'I think we should ignore the physical manifestation of our project. Instead we should concentrate on the conceptual aspects and 'focus' our thoughts and our discussions into the, erm, neuro-construction of the proto-conceptualisation of a physical entity that is, by its very nature, an archetypical object expressing desirability from a capitalist, and materialist perspective, even if, or more accurately specifically for, that conceptualisation—'

'Proto-conceptualisation.'

'Thank you comrade—for that protoconceptualisation to offer an extended, but acceptable parameter of accuracy.'

There were a few puzzled frowns and glances around the room.

'He means we should pretend it's better than it is—bloody scientists, worse than poets!' Sergei said. 'So lets go over what we've got so far. Any thoughts on 'Power'?'

'Well power is behind the desire to own such a car, surely that, in itself, is an expression of, how can I put it…' The artist making this contribution stood up, and grabbed his crotch with both hands, before sitting down again '… Power! The engine in the machine. Man's motor!'

'Good, good, and I think we can also assume that the same can be said of money, yes?' Asked the first writer. There was a few seconds intense thinking around the table, during which everyone looked at each other, shrugged or raised eyebrows and agreed that this was probably true. 'And I think we can dismiss alcohol on this occasion—although before we do, pour me another vodka; and sex—well that's always a sticky subject. This is Russia, so religion has to go out of the window also, all agreed?' The same gestures of agreement rippled around the table. 'So what we need are words that conjure up money and power. Let's make a list.'

This process went on for several hours. The band of intellectuals argued their way around most of the world's consumeristic tendencies, talked about sex long into the night, and consumed vast amounts of vodka. By first light, most were asleep or semi-conscious. One figure stirred: An old writer called Vladimir Pavluk—a large man with long grey hair, a full white beard and a deep frown of concentration—moved as if emerging from hibernation. He inhaled as though it was the first breath he had taken in days. He lifted his pen, and wrote a word slowly on his pad in large letters. He sat back in his chair and held the pad up in front of himself. He scrutinised it for several minutes.

'Comrades!' He said, in a deep voice, which, although not loud, echoed around the room, crawled into the fuzzy fibre of dozing and exhausted brains and beckoned the semi-consciousness. 'Comrades!' He repeated.

Slowly, attention was drawn out of heads heavy with the extra weight of sleep, dreams and memories. Eyes blinked, or were wiped into focus. One by one, the members of the team looked at the pad being held up in front of them.

And gradually they all read the same word.

'Munter.'

There was total silence from around the table. The word immersed itself deeply into the nonverbal consciousness of each person around the table like a bee drowning in honey. Someone wiped away a tear, and uttered what would be the only other word heard in the room before sunrise: 'Brilliant!'

And so the Munter took shape. The team worked on advertisements and a marketing strategy, soon settling comfortably into the new process—making almost exact copies of ads from American magazines and billboards. Copies of the former and photographs of the latter of which had been gathered from spies working in America, who were under the impression they were passing coded messages hidden in the pictures. Although they were not half as baffled as CIA cryptologists.

Finally, more than four years after the project started, six prototype Munter Dropheads were displayed, along with the marketing campaign: designs for billboards, magazine and TV advertisements, complemented with a glossy brochure that sold the Munter lifestyle—healthy looking men and women in traditional dress laughing gaily against a panoramic background of factories and fields.

Khrushchev was delighted. He ordered five of the prototypes to be given to foreign diplomats, so that 'the glory of the New Soviet strategy might begin to spread worldwide immediately'. One inevitably went to Kennedy, who felt obliged to call and thank Khrushchev, even though the Munter was immediately re-boxed in its original wooden case and dispatched swiftly to a large storage facility under a desert in New Mexico.

'He's a good man I suppose,' Khrushchev said, as he put the phone down after Kennedy's thank you call. 'But how long can a good man last in politics these days?'

11: Into the mystery

Arthur was glad he'd decided to get out. He was winding his Munter Drophead around gently curving roads, climbing up the backbone of England. The Moon was up in a clear sky. He supposed there was a great view of the stars from up here, but he was concentrating on his driving too much to find out. He glanced at the map print-out as he drove, taking turnings off turnings down increasingly narrow roads. Finally he pulled off to the left and down a steep and bumpy track. There were no lights apart from his own headlights. As the track levelled out, his lights shone across a line of parked Volvo estates. 'This'll be the place then!' He thought to himself.

Arthur steered the Munter gently into a space, up against a high hedge. He reached into the back seat again and pulled out his spare fleece jacket, careful not to drop the cold champagne that was wrapped in it. He stepped out of the car into the cool evening air. He looked up; the sky was prickled with stars, more than he had ever seen from the suburbs of Manchester. There was a faint glow to his right, which filtered through a gap further along hedge against which he had parked. He walked towards it; it seemed the most sensible thing to do. As he turned the corner he stopped in amazement as he came face-to-face with the heavy silhouette of an enormous house against the moonlit sky.

'Now that's what I call imposing,' said Arthur, eyebrows raised. There were no lights on in the house, but there was a path defined by a small jars of tea-lights which Arthur followed around the side of the house. The path wound away from the house, through some trees and down to a river. Here the jars changed to paper lanterns, which led the path through a Japanese-style garden. Arthur walked over a small wooden bridge, and continued to follow the lights along the riverbank. The river seemed to come to an end in a large pool. Arthur realised that the river wasn't a river at all, but a cleverly designed man-made pond. Small jars of light led up through several open terraced patios, on which stood sculptures—carved whales and seals, totems depicting salmon and eagles. On the wall of one terrace a naked female figure reclined, its bronze arm dipped into a silver shaft of moonlight. Arthur paused momentarily, captivated by this magical scene. Ahead, the lanterns disappeared into what looked like a wall of bushes. He could hear the faint sound of a violin and guitar, and the beating of a drum—the lilt of Irish music carried through the liquorice darkness. The music seemed to be coming from the middle of the shrubbery, so he continued to follow the lamps through a gap in the hedge, as he stepped through he saw that the lights dispersed in three directions. The hedge was ragged but the route clear. It took Arthur only a few footsteps to understand that he was in a maze and the candles lit each path. It was obvious that if he wanted to get to the party he had no choice but to find the way, he decided to go straight then followed a path to the right. He was trying to memorise each turning: 'right, second right, left, left, right, straight, right…' but soon forgot his sequence. Every time he hit a dead end, there was some feature as a reward: here a wooden carving of a fearsome face, there a bronze figure in a dancing pose, somewhere else a hunched stone gargoyle or the trickle of water from an elegant fountain. Even when Arthur tried to retrace his steps he met a dead end—which he suspected he might have hit before, until he saw for the first time a white marble unicorn glowing in the moonlight.

Although he probably wouldn't have admitted it, he was panicking just a little. He recalled his words before leaving home, about being able to turn back and go home if he wasn't enjoying himself. 'Easier said than done!' He said aloud to himself.

'Hello?'

Arthur nearly jumped out of his skin on hearing the voice, which seemed to come from the other side of a nearby hedge.

'Hello?' Arthur replied.

'I was going to ask if anyone was there, but I guess there is?' It was a woman's voice.

'There is. It's me. But I'm not sure where 'here' is,' Arthur craned his neck to try and find a gap so that he could see who he was talking to.

'Aah! I thought it was you.' There was a gentle mocking

tone in the voice. 'Are you lost?'

'Lost? Not in a manner of speaking. I mean, I used a map to get here. Not here as in 'here', I mean here as in here. I mean—I'm sure I'll find my way in a minute, if I can just find out where I've been...'

'So you're not exactly lost then, you just can't find your way?'

The more he heard the voice, the more it enchanted him. 'I suppose you could put it like that. If I could just find my way I'd be fine. I, erm... Do I... I was just wondering—but do I know you? Only there's something very familiar about your voice.'

'Well! That question presents me with something of a problem...' The voice from the other side of the hedge said.

'A problem? Why?' Arthur gave up trying to find a gap—the hedge was impenetrable.

'Well, you see I don't know who you are yet, so I don't know whether you know me or not.'

Arthur grimaced at his own stupidity. 'Oh god! Sorry I'm a bit of an idiot!'

'Why? Have you forgotten who you are?'

'No I mean... I mean, I know who I am, I mean. My name's Arthur. Arthur Pod.'

'Arthur Pod! Is that your real name?' There was a giggle from the other side of the hedge. 'I'm sorry, I didn't mean to...'

'Oh don't worry. I don't mind. What about you?'

'What about me?'

'Your name.'

'Aaah! Yes. Well you see I can't go around giving my name to complete strangers.'

'Maybe I'm not a complete stranger.'

'Maybe not. But all I know is your name. So I know I don't know you. And what do I know about you? How do I know you're not completely strange?'

'I see your point. But I'm not. But I guess I'd say that even if I was. So what is your name?'

'Maybe I don't have one.'

'Everyone has a name.'

'How do you know I'm someone. You can't see me. Maybe I'm a spirit of the night. A ghost. Maybe I don't exist.'

'You sound as though you exist. Anyway, I don't believe in ghosts and spirits.'

'Aah, so where's your magic.'

'In my hat.'

'You're not wearing a hat!'

'How do you know that?'

'I can tell from your voice. Or maybe I can see you. Anyway, just because you say you don't have magic, doesn't mean you don't have it. Everybody has magic. You have magic Arthur Pod. I would guess you have more than you know.'

'I don't know about that. Look, are you sure I don't know you?' Arthur was trying to remember the voice, but it was like trying to examine the tip of your tongue without a mirror.

'Oh, I'm sure you don't know me. Maybe I'm just a voice in your head. Maybe I'll just disappear…'

'OK—if you're a voice in my head, tell me what I'm thinking?' Arthur waited for a reply. There was nothing. 'Hello?' He waited, but nothing. He tried to jump up to see if he could see over the hedge. But nothing. 'Hello! Are you there? Look that's very funny, but I'd like to get out of here this evening. Maybe, if you know the way…' Still nothing.

'You wouldn't leave a poor defenceless man to find his way out of this place would you?' After a few seconds, Arthur answered his own question: 'You would!' Truth is, he would have stayed in the maze all evening just to carry on listening to that voice. There was something about it that gave him butterflies. 'Can't be butterflies, it's night-time, they must be moths.' He thought. 'Never had moths before.'

With his encounter loud in his mind, Arthur followed a path that led to a dead end, at which stood a beautiful stone sculpture of a man's head on a pedestal. It was grinning mischievously. 'Hmm? Not this way then!' Arthur said. He turned round and followed another path, trying to count how many times he had turned left or right. Again he came to a dead end, occupied by a sheltered seat beneath Gothic-style trelliswork, around which roses wound, thickly scenting the night air. The buds and flowers looked black against the night. The scent was so beautiful that Arthur sat down to enjoy the moment.

He leaned back to watch the moon, which hung lazily and soft edged. How many minutes are there in a second? How many hours in a minute? How many days in an hour? For a second he was in touch with infinity.

Moonlight painted the edges of trees, bushes and the few inconsequential clouds. The air was cool enough to turn breath into mist, and moist enough to feel against the skin. Music melted through the perfume of roses. Arthur thought about that voice and its familiarity unnerved him. Yet he sort of knew that he hadn't heard it before. There was so much in it. It was so—Arthur searched for the word—but couldn't find one. He tried to picture the face that might go with such a voice, but couldn't. He sighed and stood. Amazing as everything was, he had to try and get to where he was supposed to be going and it hit him that the best way to succeed was probably not to try—just go for a walk and see what happens. He turned towards the music and followed the path. He ended up back where he had started, his exit and his entrance into the maze.

'This might get frustrating,' Arthur thought, but at least he now had the option of getting back into the car and going home. He looked at the maze again. To go back in there would be madness. He tried waking around the outside of it, but there was no way round, and apparently no other way in. The music was definitely coming from the centre. He hesitated for a second, but really had no choice. He had moths. He stepped in again, following the lanterns. He stopped at a junction and looked to his left: 'It can't be that way,' he thought, but on a stroke of inspiration, decided to take it anyway. 'The problem is that I'm trying to think this out logically, and there's no logic to it.' He stopped, shook his arms loosely to try to relax and let his body take over. After a few false steps, he got into it. He stopped worrying about whether he was going the right way or not and instead started singing to the jiggy fiddle in a funky kind of James Brown way. 'Get on down! Get in-to the groove! Get on up! Get in-to the groove!' He started moving to his own rhythm. He was feeling more confident.

The music changed from a lively reel to the lament of a single fiddle, which allowed the silence of the night to weave through it. Arthur was enjoying the stroll. The hedges either side created a certain cosiness. The music seemed to be close. Arthur searched for a gap in the thick foliage that he was sure would lead him to its source. He found one, but was faced with yet another path, and another hedge in front of him.

With the music now even closer, he followed the path's course around the high shrubbery in an enormous circle, but the music didn't get any louder, neither quieter. After two circumnavigations of the same path, he realised the music was definitely coming from the other side of this high hedge somewhere, so there must be a way through.

'This place is very, very weird!' he said to himself. He put the champagne bottle down—a risky strategy, but one he felt he had to pursue—and walked again around the circular path. He was relieved and even more curious when he found the bottle a few moments later. So he was definitely on a circular path, but there was no gap? Yet quite clearly the music was coming from the other side of the hedge? He stepped back and peered at the dark shape of the bushes in front of him. His eyes followed its curves upwards into the darkness. He realised that it wasn't a hedge like the others, but a massive bush, or maybe a dome. This was the centre.

The music was definitely coming from inside. 'Very, very strange!' With curiosity kindled, he began to walk slowly around again, following the nightlights in painted glass pots laid out on the ground. About two-thirds of the way round, he noticed that the gap between two of the lamps was slightly wider than the rest.'

He crouched down and tried to adjust to the dark. He found a small gap and pushed his hand through, finding what felt like a woven carpet. Arthur pushed the heavy fabric. It gave way under the pressure of his hand, light appeared at one edge and the fiddler's lament slipped clearly through. He poked his head in, blinking to adjust to the light.

'Come in! Come in! Whoever you are!' A man's voice called. Someone pulled back the heavy rug; Arthur was still trying to adjust to what he was seeing as he crawled through the entrance. As his eyes adjusted to the new light, he looked around in amazement.

*

The bush was indeed a dome, a giant metal-worked hemispherical matrix around which shrubs and ivy had been trained to climb over many years until they formed a dense mass of vegetation growing from twisted stems as thick as thighs. Inside it was roughly ten metres across and half as high. A fire burned in the middle, its smoke drifted up and through a single hole in the apex. Candles glowed golden in lanterns hanging from hooks around the walls: these and the fire were the only sourced of light. Rugs covered the floor and lined the walls. There were patterns from North America, India, Turkey, Mexico, Afghanistan,

China, Iran and others. There were also carvings, either hanging between the rugs or freestanding: strange masks and totems; a suspended winged figure—a naked angel carved from wood—glowed like bronze in the firelight.

The dome was full of people. Most were sitting on cushions scattered about low wooden tables situated around the fire. Musicians were seated on short stools—instruments resting as they listened to a fiddler's tune of mist and moor. The air smelt of smoke and incense, grass and earth, hot food and damp wool. Arthur stood stunned.

'Art'ur! Art'ur! Art'ur! I'm so glad you could make it to our humble gatherin' Come in! Come in! It's a pleasure to be sure. Without a shred of a doubt a pleasure! Sit yerself down and join the merry throng. Will ye be havin' a drink?'

Arthur handed the bottle of bubbly he was carrying to Cedric, then held up the gift-wrapped album he had brought: 'What should I do with this?'

'Well I think you should give it to those it's intended for, follow me…' Cedric led Arthur towards the other side of the dome, where the bride and groom were nestled in a pile of cushions, in front of them was a wide table strewn with food, drink, rose petals and cards. The couple formed the centre of a small group, which included an elderly woman Arthur recognised from the afternoon. He tried, but couldn't remember her name, getting as far as 'Mee-something-or-other'. He also recognised one or two faces from the church, but there were others whom he was sure hadn't been there. As he walked across the room he searched around the dome, trying to take in as many faces as he could, looking for the possible owner of the voice in the maze. But there were lots of small groups, and the light was low, so polite glances weren't enough and he didn't want to appear rudely distracted by looking for longer.

Cedric was making the introductions: 'Geraldine, Jack, you remember Art'ur from this afternoon, the photographer? They both started to stand. 'Please! Don't get up!' Arthur gestured for them to stay seated, but they stood anyway. Jack took Arthur's hand mid-gesture, and shook it warmly.

'We're delighted you could make it!' Jack pulled Arthur towards him, hugged him warmly and kissed him on both cheeks. Geraldine then pulled him down so that she could reach his cheeks and kiss him likewise.

'I'm delighted to be here! Thanks for inviting me. This is for you both.' Arthur handed the album to Geraldine.

'That's so sweet of you Arthur! And such a surprise!' Geraldine recognised what was in the package and started to tear off the wrapping paper. 'We didn't expect to see these for a while. You really didn't have to do it especially, but I'm glad you did!'

'Oh it was no problem, really. Besides, I'm on holiday for this next week, so…' Arthur smiled, he felt a little embarrassed that he hadn't brought a more personal gift as well, '… I thought I'd print them out today, so I could give them to you if I came this evening.'

'Oh Arthur, these are wonderful!' Geraldine carefully turned each page, stroking each image and showing them to Jack, who smiled affectionately at his wife's appreciation.

'The wonders of modern technology,' Arthur replied, feeling his ears burn with a blush. He couldn't help but smile as he watched how delighted Geraldine was.

'This has made our day extra-special. Please sit down, Arthur. Sit down!' Jack beckoned.

Arthur wondered what to do, he felt awkward at being asked to join the bride and groom—after all he wasn't friend or family. 'I don't want to disturb—'

'No excuses Arthur, please sit down, come on, chill out.' Jack interrupted.

'We insist Arthur! Come on—we don't stand on ceremony here! Look, this nice comfy cushion is just waiting for you, don't disappoint it!' Geraldine plumped it up and looked up at Arthur.

Arthur, capitulation in hand, sighed away his hesitance and relaxed. 'This is a fantastic place by the way. That maze is really…er, something.' Arthur said, as he made himself comfortable.

'The whole place is really something,' Geraldine said.

'But you obviously made it through!' Jack was grinning as he spoke.

'Just about!' Arthur laughed nervously. 'I haven't got any idea how long it took me though. Is it late?'

'I don't know, time's not allowed in here.'

'So, do you live here? Not here in this, er, bush, I mean in the house!'

Jack laughed: 'No! No! But we'd love to—who wouldn't! It's a wonderful place, it belongs to one of Jez's uncles—Joe, Cedric's older brother.'

Arthur took 'Jez' to be Geraldine.

'You should see it in daylight Arthur, it's fabulous', Geraldine said.

'I can imagine.' Arthur replied.

'Joe used to travel a lot—still does a bit, brings stuff back from everywhere,' Jack explained, his gaze travelled around the dome crossing all the rugs and artefacts, 'He might be down later, he's up at the house sorting out the children.'

Geraldine looked up from browsing through the album, holding a page mid-turn: 'Probably telling them some scary story about magic and spirits! I don't know how they're going to sleep tonight, but I suppose it doesn't matter.'

'Well, I don't know that much about kids, but I know they love a scary story,' Arthur added.

Geraldine smiled and nodded: 'Yes, you're right. I loved anything with witches and goblins. As long as the princess married the prince in the end, of course. But please call me Jez, everyone does! Except Cedric, who insists on calling everyone by their full and proper name.'

Cedric was crouched behind Geraldine, looking over her shoulder approvingly at the photos. He laughed, 'You are, everything that you are, none-the-less, as we all are!'

'You'll have to excuse him, he talks in riddles, especially when he's been putting his energies into celebrating!' Jez looked up at Cedric lovingly 'He's an old rogue, but I love him.'

'I do not talk in riddles!' Cedric feigned that he'd been insulted, but loved the affection from his niece, whom he loved dearly. 'There's never been anyone talks straighter than me good self! And as for celebratin'—isn't life itself worth celebratin' at every opportunity for the miracle that it is!' He leaned forward, kissed Geraldine on the cheek and hugged her with the arm that wasn't still holding the bottle of champagne, then stood up. 'If you don't mind now, I'll go and put this somewhere, and leave you to it. I'll sort you a drop and some food,' Cedric winked at Arthur and wandered off towards a laden table on the other side of the dome. Geraldine turned to Arthur: 'He's always been like that, ever since I was a baby. Do you know he's never been any younger, and he never seems to get any older. He says it's the poteen. And the gods know that he sips enough of it! But I wouldn't change him for the world!'

Soon they were all chatting warmly, exchanging stories about each other's lives and life in general. Arthur fell into talking to Jack, while Geraldine had been drawn into a small group of women, including the elderly aunty Meek. They were all sharing the album and a lot of good humour. As they were talking, someone slipped a tray of food onto the table in front of Arthur.

'Eat!' Jack said to Arthur, 'try some traditional food. My aunt made it.' In the dimmed light of the dome it was difficult to see exactly what was on the plates, but Arthur dipped into what looked like pâté, and tasted it.

'Mmmm, this is good, very unusual. A bit like black pudding! What is it?' He mumbled through the meaty flavour, and texture that melted in his mouth. Jack looked at the plate,

'Oh yes! That's good isn't it? That's a pudding my aunt makes by putting hot stones inside a Caribou stomach filled with blood. It's really easy to make.'

Arthur laughed nervously, and overcame his gut reaction to retch by decided that it was in fact delicious, and helped himself to another morsel. There was a pile of meat strips on another plate and a couple of bowls of dips. Following Jack's lead, Arthur took a strip of meat and dipped it into a bowl. 'Mmm! Now this is unusual! Not quite as good as the pudding, but very nice. Venison?'

Jack laughed, 'Sort of. It's Caribou again, but the dip's interesting, it's made from melted fat, seal meat, blood and something called 'uruniq'—which is ptarmigan intestine; it's all mixed together then frothed up with the fingers—it's very popular.'

Arthur smiled, the idea of ptarmigan intestine was much worse than the taste. Even so, he decided it might be prudent to ask before tasting anything else. He pointed at another bowl containing a clear liquid, 'What's that one?'

'Oh, the Misiraq! You've got to try that, it's delicious.'

'What's in it?' Arthur thought it sounded like some Middle Eastern delicacy, like falafel, or something.

'Its made from blubber,' Jack said, matter-of-factly.

'What! Like whale fat?'

'Yes, this is seal, but whale will do. You put it into a container with holes in the top, and let it age, keeping it cool all the time. You can tell when it's ready because it turns clear—give it a go!' Jack took another strip of meat and dipped it into the clear liquid, 'this is a particularly good one.' Jack encouraged Arthur, who politely declined on the basis that the psychological struggle to swallow old seal fat might lead to him throw up regardless of how good it tasted. Jack took a strip of flat bread and dipped it into a bowl containing a pile of a beige-coloured creamy substance with small lumps in it, 'probably some kind of mashed seal brain' Arthur thought to himself.

'You should try this though, it's one of Jez's specialities,' he popped the morsel into his mouth. He seemed to really enjoy it.

'What is it? Penguin?' Arthur joked. Jack had his mouth full, but laughed as he talked; all Arthur caught was what sounded like 'Moose'. 'Moose?' Arthur asked, his imagination running loose on what part of a Moose was beige, thick and creamy. The possible answers he could come up with didn't bear thinking about. Needless to say he had already decided to draw the line at tasting whatever bit of a Moose it was.

'Hummus,' Jack said, after swallowing. 'Home made. Very garlicky. Delicious!'

Arthur smiled nervously, he could feel a blush building up again, and hoped that no one would notice in the low light. Low light or high light, nobody would have cared even if they had noticed.

As Arthur helped himself to the hummus, the heavy carpet covering the entrance moved to one side and a face appeared. Arthur had seen many faces, paid closer attention to them than most people, particularly those faces that demanded a certain attention of light and shade in order to produce a picture to sit suitably upon a mantelpiece, grace a boardroom wall without causing offence, or live comfortably upon a piano. A brief thought flashed through his mind that achieving that for this face would be—at least a challenge, at most nigh on impossible. It was red.

Red from alcohol maybe, or heat, or exertion, or the sun and wind, or many years of being on the sea, or on the mountains and moors, or even a combination of them all, but it was red. It was also scarred. Old scars that his natural creases and wrinkles worked around. And a nose that had been broken who knows how many times. His eyes were the colour of blue skies that only occurs on bright, sunny, frosty mornings. This was an old face painted on a head the shape of a baby's, and with as little hair. Here was the face of a person to whom age didn't matter, he could have been fifty-five, he could have been a-hundred-and-five.

'Well that's the children settled! Now we can get on with some serious caper!' he said, grinning as he pushed the rest of his enormous body through the carpet doorway.

'Uncle Joe! I hope you haven't frightened the living wits out of them all with your tales,' Geraldine said, with mock concern and genuine delight at seeing him. She knew the children loved his stories, especially because they were always a little bit scary. She also knew they'd now be fast asleep after a comfortable ending, because Uncle Joe used to tell her tales when she was the same age as her own children now were.

'Now my darling, would I do a thing like that! Why I can scarcely remember two words to string together.' His eyes scanned the dim light, and settle on Arthur. 'But what have we here! You didn't tell me that a new friend has arrived. Welcome! Welcome! Welcome, to you. If I remember with my senile brain, you're the talented photographer, Mr Arthur Pod! I'm Joe. Not Joseph, nor Josiah, nor Mr-this-nor-that-nor-anything-else, just plain old Joe, and it is a pleasure to meet you, for pleasure is in meeting and knowing. And surely the world exists for us to know, so welcome to this company of family and friends; we are only what we are, and we know only what we know, so let our pleasure be your pleasure.'

Arthur could hardly make head nor tail out of what Joe was saying, but he got the gist of it, and instantly felt comfortable. Whereas previously he had wondered why he'd been invited, he now felt as though he belonged exactly where he was.

'Uncle Joe, we think it's time you played for us,' Jack said, half asking, half good-humoured demand.

'Yes, Uncle Joe. Please play!' Added Geraldine, a request that prompted encouraging whoops and whistles from amongst the gathering.

'Well, my fingers are worn and the arthritis has got me, and the years have taken the edge off me ears, but if you'll forgive me this I might try and string together a tune or two for you; especially as we're celebrating the poetic union of the descendents of St Brendan!' There was laughter and affirmation from everyone.

Joe moved slowly across to where the musicians were sitting. The fiddler gradually drew the last bow over a lively ditty before shifting sideways and seating himself comfortably on a cushion.

Joe took his seat, leant forward and opened a violin case, a case so old there was hardly any fabric left on it, just plywood darkened and polished by wear. Arthur noticed Joe's hands, gnarled by the arthritis he had mentioned. There didn't seem to be any way that he could pick up a violin, never mind play one. Nevertheless he picked the violin carefully out of its case, handling it as delicately as if he was picking a butterfly's wing out of snow. The instrument didn't look like anything special, a cheap fiddle battered and worn. Joe settled down on a low chair, tucked the violin under his chin and closed his eyes.

Beauty may be in the eye of the beholder. But it is driven from within. A true quality—beauty flows whenever destiny and nature meet. A child playing. An artist painting. A builder building. Within us all there is a destiny. Some are fortunate enough to live it. Others, often through circumstance, sometimes through neglect, either push or pull it around like a weight, or try to swat it away like an annoying fly that buzzes constantly around their lives. The beauty of nature and destiny is another world: real and ethereal, body and spirit, yin and yang, motivation and equilibrium. It can exist in the smallest gesture or the grandest design. When Joe and his fiddle came together a mystery was resolved somewhere between substance and the subconscious. Arthur, like everyone else in the room was awestruck by Joe as he played. His face was transformed into what Arthur could only later think of as the face of an ancient angel. It seemed as though time had no place in Joe's countenance. As he began to play, a gentle smile appeared, his eyebrows raised and occasionally twitching to a rhythm. The scars and wrinkles seemed to disappear behind a glow as his face reddened even more. His eyes never opened. His hands never stopped. His fingers hardly seemed to move as he played: And what music. One tune seemed to melt into another, from complex melodies that danced through to the tips of the fingers and taps of the feet, to aching melancholy that tapped into the ancient tragedies of lovers, loss and dormant emotions. There were tunes with the romanticism of Mozart, the rich lilt of Stravinsky, the natural beauty of Sibelius. There was music from the hills and the valleys, the city and the field. Joe made magic as he played, magic that changed the air the mind and the flesh. As it took hold, people began talking again, or dancing, or laughing, or simply listened in reverie—travelling to private places. Time passed, and time stood still. Gradually, other instruments began to pick up, but only where they could help a texture, or underline a melody: a guitar, flute, whistle or bohdrun, even another fiddle. Jack sang an ancient song in Inuktitut which, when translated, told the tale of how King Ptolemy acquired a Polar Bear for his private zoo.

Sometimes, as naturally as it was, Joe played alone. And so it was that the only time that existed belonged to the music, which wove its rhythms and melodies around the seconds, minutes and hours with romance and mischief, with melancholy and joy. And finally, at the first light of dawn—and still holding the violin in his hands, Joe gave himself up completely to his world of dreams. Sleeping. Smiling. Silence. Slumped. Still sitting.

Arthur wasn't sure when or how he himself had fallen asleep. At first he wasn't sure where he was. He could smell wood-smoke mixed with incense, alcohol and the distinct smell of very good, fresh, coffee. Dust and smoke danced in the cone of light dropped into the dome from a disc of daylight above. Outside, birds were singing. Inside, the only sounds were the breathing of people in various states of sleeping and waking, the occasional crackle of the fire and a stirring spoon. Arthur's own breath was quiet and steady. He felt good. He was snuggled into large cushions and was covered in a soft woven blanket. How and where it came from, he wasn't sure. He lay for a moment, trying to remember details of the previous evening, but they were elusive. His dreams seemed to be more accessible.

Gradually he stretched—hoisted himself up onto his elbows and looked around. A few people were sitting around the slow fire, some were staring into the red flames, some were holding mugs out of which steam curled. Someone held up a mug in Arthur's direction and smiled, he smiled back, nodded affirmation and the coffee was poured. He pushed the blanket back, knelt, stretched again, and—crouching as if it made his walking quieter, went to collect the mug, nodding his thanks. Whatever the time, it was too early for words. Still in a semi-dream state, he took a seat by the fire, staring into the dull heart of it. He was thinking about the magic voice and moths as he sipped the dark, hot, slightly bitter and completely delicious coffee. He shivered a little in the morning air, holding the mug tightly to make sure no warmth was lost. He looked around at the few mounds of blankets covering still-sleeping bodies; he couldn't make out who was who. He wondered what time it was, but didn't have a clue. He wasn't sure what time he fell asleep, or how, but it must have been late. It was obviously now early, yet he felt awake and relaxed, even though he could tell that he hadn't had enough sleep. The coffee began tugging at his consciousness. Dreams began drifting away, and would soon sail out of sight but not completely out of mind. Throughout the day they would hover tantalisingly just over his horizon.

Arthur remembered he was due to go to France today and had a six-hour drive ahead of him down to Dover. He drained the last drop from his mug and placed it on the floor between him and the fire. He stood up, careful to be quiet, raised a hand in a half-wave and smiled at the few people around the fire—by way of 'goodbye'. They smiled back. As quietly as he could, Arthur left the dome.

He had forgotten that he'd have to renegotiate the maze. As he wandered through it, he hoped to hear a voice. But all he could hear were birds singing. As he wound his way out, he was dragged further away from the dreamlike atmosphere of the previous night. By the time he reached the house, he was awake and using both halves of his brain again. The air was chilly and he was chilly. He decided to go to the house to see if there was anyone around who he could ask about the voice. Although in reality he was hoping to hear it.

The house was enormous, brick-built and well-kept. Arthur smiled at a large trampoline, which looked like a permanent feature on the immaculate lawn. He was tempted. The lawn was scattered with brightly coloured plastic toys. He walked to the front door, but it was closed and a casual glance through an adjacent window did not reveal any activity. He decided not to knock or ring the bell, thinking that—as it was early, the kitchen was the usual place to be. He walked around the back, through a small arch-topped wooden doorway set into a walled garden that was breathtakingly beautiful—an exotic delight. Arthur wasn't a gardener, but there were some strange plants here, as well as some more familiar to him, mainly in the well-stocked vegetable plot.

'Bet this family never goes to the supermarket', Arthur thought to himself. He found the back door, but it was locked, he looked through a window but the kitchen was empty.

After a few more glances of admiration he left the garden and wandered back to his car, which was a less chilly place to sit and work out what he should do. It seemed that there had been quite a few early risers, judging by the number of cars that weren't here compared to the previous evening.

He felt around his pocket for his car keys, then noticed the slip of paper under the windscreen wiper. He picked it off before unlocking the door and settling into the driver's seat. The hands on the dashboard clock sat at five-thirty as Arthur unfolded the note.

"Dear Arthur,

We can know, without knowing.

Will you keep your faith for me?

X"

*

By six-thirty, Arthur was already at home, stepping into a deliciously hot bath. It was the place he always did his best thinking. He started to mull over the events of the previous day, trying to make some sense of it all. But the more he thought about it, the less sense it seemed to make. This time yesterday he was thinking about life and how it had chugged along in a meandering, but vaguely interesting way. And even his thoughts about fate and cause and effect, although initially frustrating, were somehow also reassuring, with their seemingly inevitable effect on events. But now he felt something had turned everything upside down—ripped away the comfort layer and rearranged his insides with a blender. Arthur began to feel a little dizzy from a combination of slightly too much alcohol, too little sleep, and strong coffee.

He was holding the note in one hand—carefully keeping it clear of the water. He had read it over and over, but couldn't fully fathom it. 'OK. She remembered my name. But as for the rest of it? It's all a bit weird.' He thought to himself. "Will you keep your faith for me?' seems a strange thing to ask. What faith? I mean I've never actually met her before.' In the back of his mind he caught the snippet of a poem, something about 'keeping the faith', but he didn't know what the poem was called, who wrote it, or any other lines, so he dismissed it. He might also have dismissed the note as the workings of someone obsessive, fanatical, psychotic or just plain strange—but all such dark thoughts washed away when he thought of that voice. He could still hear every word. It was like music. Music so familiar—its rhythm, pitch and lilt. Its melody. Its magic. He wanted to hear it again. To discover who it belonged to. The note was proof that it didn't belong to a spirit of the night—which he had vaguely started to consider as a possibility. The voice was real. But how could he find out whose voice it was?

An hour or so later he had other things on his mind. The bath had relaxed him; he was now dry, dressed and packing for his trip. He crammed everything he needed into a single, small rucksack—a change of clothes, passport, money and keys, plus his wash bag, and that was it; he always travelled light. In the past he'd taken more, but realised that he only ever wore the same two sets of clothes—the rest of his holiday suitcase never got used. After several trials and errors over the years, he arrived at the perfect bag for his various journeys: a compact but spacious backpack. Another advantage of travelling light was that he would be able to cram more booze into the car for the return journey. Luggage space had not figured highly on the list of the car's design features.

Soon Arthur was on the road, and for him this was one of the best feelings in the world—driving, with almost a whole week ahead of him to go where he pleased.

When he was younger he'd hitched everywhere—right around Europe. Not a summer of his youth passed without him exercising those itchy feet on hot, sandy roadsides. The travel bug had never left him. He'd often had the feeling when walking of just wanting to carry on, never turning round. He still wondered whether it would happen one day. He envied adventurers, such as Laurie Lee—who walked out one summer's morning—and kept on going.

Now here was Arthur driving south down the M6. 'Not very romantic, calling it the M6,' he thought, 'why don't they give them more romantic-sounding names like the used to, such as 'The Great North Road'. You'd really want to travel down the Great North Road; its very name makes it an adventure. Maybe it could be 'The Great North West Passage', or 'The Midlands to Scotland Trunk Road', but the M6? It's just so boring!'

Arthur tried to think where all the motorways were, the sort of idle-minded game it was possible to play while driving. There were many he couldn't place, which didn't matter much, but the one that bothered him most was the location of the M13. Maybe out of consideration for the superstitions it was called the 'M12b'—wherever it was. Then he remembered.

This Saturday morning proved to be a good time to travel. The sun was shining and he had a few compilations organised on his iPod that kept him occupied for the six hours of the trip down to Dover: 'Classical', 'Reggae', 'Blues', 'Jazz', 'Latin', 'Dance' and 'Odd bits'. The 'Latin' stuff, kept him going for most of the journey. With just one stop for fuel, and with Faithless now playing in the background he arrived at Dover in perfect time for the early afternoon ferry. He'd already bought his ticket on the Internet, so all he had to do was drive through the checks and wait to board. He was feeling very relaxed as he pulled up behind a Land Rover in aisle 193. He turned off the engine, and settled into the silence for a short snooze.

12: The sorry tale of Rupert Smithereen, esq.

The Munter was not a success—either commercially or as a design icon. It never made the production line. While attention, skills and money were heavily invested in the Russian space programme, most of the rest of the 'profit programme' resulted in nothing more than cobwebs on telephones in rarely-visited offices. There were one or two minor successes: the cameras, for example, did moderately well abroad; but the Japanese did better. By the time the under-funded Munter project reached any state of completion its design and technology were already way out of date. More so even than when the project started.

Of the half-dozen prototypes, some never got past the parts stage; there was Kennedy's of course; and one was sent as a gift to Castro, who after one look at it, ordered it to be put to some kind of use—anything as long as he didn't have to see it again. The bodywork was removed and large wheels were fitted to the rear of the chassis, this, plus a bit of mechanical tinkering, turned it with relative ease into a tractor that is still doing good service to this day. More amazing to the mechanic who undertook the task, was the fact that the various body panels turned out to be perfect replacements for those on several of the old American cars which still run on the streets of Cuba.

Yet another Munter was given as a gift to Rupert Smithereen, a minor British Diplomat, on the day of his involuntary voluntary departure from the British Embassy in Moscow. It was a parting gift from some grateful friends.

Rupert Smithereen was from a semi-aristocratic, fiercely religious family whose home was a dilapidated mansion on the Isle of Man. A feud had smouldered between two sides of the family for three generations; it started when the paternal side converted to some obscure branch of Roman Catholicism that insisted on all services being in Latin. The maternal side refused to subscribe, and adhered to the English version in the family's private chapel. The rift proved irreparable. Divorce was out of the question. So the family divided and decamped to different parts of the house. As time dribbled on, the rift became a valley, which soon became a canyon with crumbling walls. Lack of communication and denial of responsibility meant that the once beautiful house became virtually derelict. Yet both halves of the family refused to budge; adapting instead to the increasing ingress of rainwater and wind. The house was permanently cold. Most of the larger rooms had been divided up using whatever materials were to hand; the aim being to create smaller spaces that kept out the weather and which might be easier to heat. Hanging from rusty nails in drift-wood frames and scavenged scaffolding were beautiful Persian carpets damp and rotted to tatters, faded velvet curtains, bits of beach-scavenged plywood—and sheets of skin-thin polythene that constantly moved and whispered. Inside these contraptions single bar electric fires or rusting gas heaters glowed day and night, winter and summer, failing to remove any chill from the two halves of the family.

The Smithereens were supreme masters at trading on their alleged-aristocratic heritage. Despite being totally broke—and having been that way for almost a century, all had been to recognised public schools, cruised through decent or at least half-decent universities, and waltzed into positions with good firms in the City, or into some government department. This was achieved through shrewd networking and an extraordinarily developed sense of cunning, mixed with a total indifference to emotional consequences. They were as cold as the home they came from. The family feud had been going on for much longer than the ages of the youngest generation of children, which made the cause of their creation a mystery. Rupert, the middle one of three children had developed a sixth sense for finding girlfriends with wealthy parents. In university he had moved in with Ffiona, the daughter of a prominent surgeon who, in the late fifties, had turned his hand to the emerging art of plastic surgery. Rupert and Ffiona lived a typically unhealthy student life of parties, alcohol and soft drugs. During the holidays they took off to the Riviera, courtesy of a cheque account constantly topped up by Ffiona's parents. On finishing university, Rupert moved to London and took up with Jemma, the daughter of a well-connected property developer who was also a resident of the Isle-of-Man. Through Jemma's father Marty, Rupert was not only provided with contacts which gained him a well paid job in the Home Office, but also managed to hitch a lift back to the Isle almost every weekend with Jemma in Marty's private plane. With Marty's help Rupert bought a crumbling six-bedroomed house in Maida Vale, which he converted into twenty bedsits using the cheapest labour and materials he could find. The property market was booming as London began to swing, Marty was doing extremely well building multi-storey tower blocks in the suburbs. So well in fact, that he had invested in holiday homes in the Caribbean and Portugal. Jemma was an only child, so—blinded by money, Rupert proposed and—blinded by love, she accepted.

Everything would have been fine, except that Rupert was a Smithereen, and Smithereens are terriers when it comes to an opportunity. He couldn't resist the one that presented itself when he heard that the parents of an old friend of his sister's had been killed in a car crash near their winter home in Antibes. The girl, Andrea, 'a handsome woman with a love of nature' he recalled, had been left everything—which amounted to several million and a large house by the sea.

Several months after this sad incident, by way of consolation, Rupert whisked Andrea off to Tanzania for a safari holiday. He bought her airline ticket. She paid for everything else. He wined, dined and wooed her using her own money, fully aware—via a network of intelligence provided by his sister—that Andrea had always carried a torch for him. Not wanting to put all his eggs in one basket, he told Jemma that he had to go to Tanzania on a diplomatic mission. What Rupert didn't know, was that extremely diligent trustees administered Andrea's estate, and one of them was a member of the same golf club as Rupert's prospective father-in-law, Marty.

A powerful machine is a wonderful thing when it's working for you: the Titanic, for example. When Rupert returned from Africa even the maximum execution of his considerable charms couldn't divert the iceberg that threatened to sink him. Jemma was devastated and dumped him. As she flew to the Caribbean to recuperate, her father watched concrete being poured into the foundations of a new multi-storey in New Cross and thought about the cause of his little girl's tears. Andrea, already fragile from the loss of her parents, was even more devastated and immersed herself and a large part of her fortune into caring for abandoned mules. Fortunately she met and fell in love with the mechanic who came to her rescue when her car broke down one sunny summer evening. He polished her spark plugs, got her motor running, and then drove her home. From that point on the two never parted. They married, settled into a small harbour-side house, had several children and lived a modest, but comfortable and happy life, mainly on the income from her husband's garage.

Rupert accepted the offer he couldn't refuse almost as soon as it landed on his desk: a minor consular post in Moscow. The offer was in an envelope that also contained the necessary train tickets. The Smithereens are not stupid. As hints go this was as subtle as being hit in the privates with a sock-full of ball bearings, which was probably a mild sample of what he could expect if he stuck around London. Moscow could guarantee him the longevity and the continuing potential to father children that London could no longer promise if Rupert's last conversation with Marty was anything to go by. Rupert thought that Marty's anger was a little over the top—it wasn't as if he had been actually married to Jemma after all.

Rupert arrived in Moscow at just about the time that London was beginning to swing like a pendulum. He was thoroughly pissed off. He had been so close to his ultimate dream of a life of unfettered, debauched leisure, and now it was all so many miles away.

Rupert had found an inexpensive property agent to collect rent and manage his house in London while he was away, but—according to the monthly statements he received—there always seemed to be repairs that needed doing and fees to pay, and never a penny left to boost Rupert's bank account. Not that there was anything to spend money on in Moscow. He searched around for opportunities, but there were none. He boosted his income a little by selling minor secrets to the KGB—he had been approached soon after arriving. But he was aware that he was making nowhere near enough to keep him in the style to which he was striving to become accustomed when he could eventually return to London.

There was little in Moscow that interested him. He even looked forward to going to work—at least it was something to do. He spent a few days tramping the tourist thing, but thought most of it was dull. Rupert decided fairly quickly that the brightest thing about communism was the flag—the rest of it was pretty drab. The only obvious benefits he could find were that champagne was cheap and just about palatable—especially when washing down copious amounts of caviar. Rupert tried everything to kill his spare time and prevent his mind dwelling on almosts. The ballet was OK, but he wasn't really into it enough to go unless he was invited. The opera was good—if you liked that kind of thing. He didn't speak Russian and didn't see the point in learning, so the theatre and cinema were as tedious as each other. He enjoyed the odd classical music concert though, and of course there were various receptions and soirees that he was obliged to attend—but these were generally sedate affairs. The other distraction he discovered came in the shape of young women in the oldest profession. Hanging around the few clubs and the hotel bars that existed was an abundance of beautiful women who were very eager to earn a few dollars for an evening's work. With Rupert it could be a hard-earned dollar.

Wandering aimlessly and bored around the streets one balmy summer evening, Rupert came across some freshly-pasted posters for the Travelling National Circus. He had never been to a circus before so, with nothing better to do, he decided to give it a whirl. Besides which, this was the last night of a week-long run; the final performance before it uprooted and moved to another city. Although he didn't speak Russian, he had mastered the Cyrillic alphabet, and recognised the park were the circus was being performed. Rupert lived just inside Moscow's central ring road and the park wasn't too far away on the same side of the city.

It was a pleasant evening and he had plenty of time, so he decided to walk there, ambling casually through side streets.

Everything was fine and Rupert was relaxed, until he found himself walking down one seemingly deserted street of anonymously grey buildings with heavy, closed, decaying doors. He became aware of someone stepping out—he heard their footsteps behind him. He didn't turn around, but continued to walk at the same pace. Across the road, a small boy, who Rupert hadn't noticed had been leaning against the wall of a building, watched as Rupert walked. As he drew parallel, the boy pushed his weight off the wall and started to walk at the same pace and in the same direction. Rupert turned left into a street containing a variety of shops, mostly closed. He noticed that another set of footsteps had joined those already behind him. The high buildings echoed the footsteps, making it difficult to hear how many there were. In the distance he heard the sound of a car. There weren't many cars in Moscow. Most were Trabants, or 'TBs' as Rupert called them because of the wheezing and coughing of their small two-stroke engines. This was no Trabant, but the rumble of something larger coming up behind, 'possibly a ZIL'. Rupert thought, as he neared the corner of the street. His heart began to beat faster, but he knew that at the next corner all he had to do was turn right and it was then only twenty yards to the busier main avenue. He tried to move faster by lengthening his stride rather than quickening it: he didn't want to seem panicked. He reached the corner about the same time as the car, which paused beside him at the junction: a large, black Mercedes. Rupert turned right and continued to walk. The Mercedes turned right and slowly rolled along. Rupert was about five steps from the junction of the main avenue, when he realised that if he carried on his intended course to the circus, he would have to turn left, which would mean crossing the road. He couldn't do this without stopping at exactly the time the Mercedes reached the same junction. He decided to turn right instead, so that he could stay on the same pavement.

Rupert had been too distracted by the seemingly ominous presence of the car to pay attention to what was happening ahead. But now his attention was captured. The street ahead was a solid mass of people travelling across the junction from right to left. Never had Rupert seen so many people heading in a single direction. It made Oxford Street look like a walk on the beach. Rupert forgot all about the car and immersed himself into the flow. In the distance he could see the colourful canvas twin-peaked roof of the big top, on which red flags hung expectantly in the still evening air. Everyone was going to the circus.

As he drew closer, the smell hit him. It was like nothing he had ever experienced: the mustiness of animals—the sharpness of their urine and fermenting shit, the duth of old canvas mixed with the turpentine odour of fresh cut pine and oily paint. These were embraced by a contradiction of acrid cooking fat and burning sugar from savouries and sweets—spread on paper on the ground, or on the many small barrows that lined the route to the entrance and seemed to sell just about anything—from bottles of beer kept cool in buckets of water, to cigarettes, painted wooden carvings, trinkets—junk of every description, much of which seemed to Rupert to be nothing more than rubbish or stuff searching for a last home before becoming rubbish. Slithering its way around everything was the scent of ubiquitous chai—heavy, hot, sweet tea—which slid like black snakes from the spouts of enormous samovars and into rapidly rinsed and reused glasses.

The intensity of odours gripped Rupert so much; it initially overpowered the noise that was now working its way through. Everybody seemed to be shouting—either arguing about their position in some disorganised, unboundaried queue, or recounting small tales, which would probably contain some element of boasting—a Russian national past-time. Rupert didn't understand a word of course, but he had been in Moscow long enough to taste a conversation from its tone.

Opportunists need to focus their intelligence on opportunities. They need to spot finger-holds, foot-holds, unlocked doors, cracks and nooks to grab, climb, enter, widen and hide. Rupert was intelligent enough to have discovered that Russians were fairly similar to himself. The main difference being not so much the poverty, but the way that status was used. Rupert knew from his own experience that in the clear-cut class system of England, status could be simply inherited, and its influence used to benefit one's self. Here in Moscow however, status was gained by claiming to have influence. If one actually had influence, it was not etiquette to use this directly to improve one's own station: nothing so simple. This was communism, where everyone was meant to be on a level. It was not done to openly stand yourself above your comrades. But politics doesn't stop the march of genes. And survival of the fittest was not a rule that could be applied to a society fuelled by vodka. Fit didn't come into it, to survive you needed influence. Influence gave you status. Status was achieved by claiming that you had influential contacts that might help a friend, a neighbour or a family member. Even knowing someone who had influence with local officials was cause enough for a small rise in status. Best of all though, was proof of influence. A photo taken with an official was social currency. A son or daughter moving to America or England meant automatic elevation within the community—it opened a portal through which wealth might flow one day, although more often it only dribbled through: the odd parcel containing fresh coffee or a box of chocolates were good, and pop singles were particularly beneficial in the status stakes. The latest Beatles single meant that friends and neighbours would call, bearing the customary small gift of a cake, vodka or flowers, and gather around the record player to listen and comment with greater intensity than was ever given to one of the classical masterpieces that filtered from the radiogram. 'Everyone owns a little bit of land, but no one has a brass farthing to rub together, almost like the bloody aristocracy in England! There's not much difference between us at all!' was Rupert's wry observation, as he watched a solitary man, dressed in a patched and frayed jacket, woollen sweater and baggy trousers belted pinch-tight at the waist. The man danced in his own world, a bottle of some spirit in one hand, the other hand slowly caressing shapes out of the air; tracing the beauty of his own imagination. Uncommonly, Rupert slipped a couple of roubles into the man's pocket. They fell through holes and rolled off, to be snatched by a small child who ran off into the crowd before Rupert could shout after him. The drunk dancer noticed nothing.

Over the top of the sound of the crowd the stall holders shouted, urging people to buy their victuals or chattels in a tone that suggested refusal would cause deep offence. There was also music of all kinds: a lone violinist, probably a student at the conservatoire, playing furiously but beautifully for small coins; an accordionist, lost in the tune of a perpetually repetitive folk dance which had passers-by nodding in approval; a guitarist played accompaniment behind the voice of an as-short-as-broad and very pretty woman dressed in colourfully embroidered clothes. She sang long, slow songs that had tears streaming down the faces of one old man who had stopped to listen. Rupert drifted deeper into the circus city: lions roared, bears growled, horses snorted and stamped, dogs barked and yelped. A massive diesel-powered generator drummed and hummed, thick smoke sat on top of its exhaust pipe like a giant black ostrich feather. An orchestra tuned.

Steeped in all this, Rupert didn't hear an individual sound, pick out an individual smell or see an individual colour. Each sound blended into a single meditative hum, not white noise but orange. Colours merged and blurred and swam and shone. All the smells combined to become an overpowering incense. Rupert was transported to a state he could never have imagined. He was floating above himself, he felt totally singular, becalmed. His being was exactly what and where it should be at that precise point in time. It was as if every physical and metaphysical condition had merged to create an absolute, and it was being channelled into Rupert through a now achingly erect part of his own body. Rupert was firmly at the centre of his own universe.

Like an opiate, the circus claimed Rupert. And he willingly lost himself to it. He laughed and giggled and gasped and gaped and awed—and gripped and clapped his own hands together so hard that they hurt—as wide-eyed as a child and barely blinking he watched the clowns and the trapeze artists, the bareback riders and the elephants, the tiger tamers and the contortionists, the jugglers and the strong-men, the knife-throwers and the dancing bears, the gymnasts and the ringmaster; they all soaked his senses throughout the entire performance. But when it ended, he felt as though it hadn't yet started. Rupert wanted it back. He didn't realise any of this until he recovered himself walking down the street back to his apartment, when reality returned with such force that he was deeply depressed for days. So inconsolable was he, that his colleagues exchanged speculative whispers that he must have either found or lost love. They were wrong, not least because he was incapable of feeling love. But they were on the right track, because for the first time in his life, he had found something that was as close to love as he was ever going to experience.

It would be a year before the same circus returned, even though Rupert didn't know that at the time. But almost every month a new one arrived in the city from some distant place. There was also the Moscow Circus, which had its permanent home in the city. Rupert saw them all. He taught himself to indulge his new obsession with diligence and relish. He had been buying sexual favours since he first arrived in Moscow. All of the women he 'employed' were eager and beautiful, the KGB obviously already simultaneously employed some of them, but Rupert had neither conscience nor patriotism. After the circus, 'normal' sex flew out of the window, carrying with it the usual variety of blowjobs, doggy style, missionary positions—even the enthusiastic spankings essential to a certain class of Englishman. Enter stage left: sparkling leotards, feather headdresses and clown costumes, greasepaint and glitter. As time progressed—and as with any fetish—Rupert's routines became ever more elaborate in increasingly desperate attempts to recreate the excitement he felt during his first time under the big top. He had trouble finding canvas to drape in his bedroom, but he did manage to find a couple of old silk parachutes, which were shaped to his design by an ancient wardrobe mistress from the Taganka Theatre. Rupert also paid her to create all his costumes to his own designs. He felt marvellous when he was dressed up in his Ring Master's outfit, top hat in one hand, whip in the other, and a keen, well-paid performer at his feet. But 'marvellous' wasn't the feeling he was searching for.

The Muscovite grapevine of gossip is wide and strong and rich in fruit, some ripe for picking, some not quite ready, and some just plain rotten. Speculation began to sprout about Rupert's antics. He was becoming more and more obsessed to the point of distraction from his day-to-day duties; which were few enough. Word got around within certain circles that he was willing to pay good dollars for items of circus memorabilia. As he left his apartment one morning, an ancient babushka, almost doubled over with age, stopped him in the street and opened a canvas bag for him to peer into, it contained a pink feather and diamanté headdress, which Rupert exchanged without argument for the quantity of dollars demanded by the old woman—who was amazed at his stupidity for not bartering. On another occasion Rupert answered the phone to a consular security officer, who said that he was restraining an over-excited, troublesome beggar down at the main gates. The man was insisting on speaking to Rupert, and despite warnings would not take no for an answer. This didn't surprise Rupert. If there was one thing that he had learnt during his commission, it was that Russians don't have a word for 'no'. Experience had taught him that 'da' meant 'yes', and 'niet'—although having a dictionary definition of 'no', also meant 'yes', only more emphatically. He put down the phone and walked casually down to the gates. There was indeed a beggar there, waving an old hessian sack and shouting in a strong accent, 'Chardleee Chapleeen! Chardleee Chapleeen!'.

Rupert thanked the two guards who were keeping the poor man at bay, and waved them away. He put a calming hand on the man's shoulder and led the tattered wretch to one side.

'Chardleee Chapleeen! Chardleee Chapleeen!' The man kept repeating, pushing the sack upwards to Rupert's face. Rupert tried to take the sack from the man's hands to see what it contained. Big as it was, it certainly wasn't big enough to contain Charlie Chaplin. But the man wouldn't let go. He clung on to it as if life depended on it. 'Chardleee Chapleeen! Chardleee Chapleeen!' He repeated again, even more insistently, as he reached into the bag to withdraw a very oversized, very battered, very dusty black leather shoe. 'Chardleee Chapleeen! Chardleee Chapleeen!' the man said again, and walked around in a tight circle giving a fairly accurate impression of that most famous of walks. It had been many years since Rupert had seen a Charlie Chaplin film, but he had to admit that the shoe did look uncannily familiar. And even if they hadn't belonged to the great clown himself, they were perfect. Rupert held up two fingers: 'Two? You have two?'

The man nodded enthusiastically: 'Da! Da! Da! Da! Dva!' He delved into the bag again and pulled out the other. Although not strictly circus. They had, if they were genuine, belonged to inarguably the world's best clown. Rupert hoped they were genuine, because he paid for them as if they were. He took the bag furtively, preciously, and headed back into the Embassy, leaving the dishevelled old man clutching more dollars than he had ever seen in one place in his life.

Rupert headed for the WC. He installed himself in an empty cubicle, locked the brass door catch and sat down on the wooden seat. He slipped out of his own polished, brown leather shoes, but kept his feet resting on their tops to prevent his socks from touching the floor. He withdrew the old, large, dusty shoes from the sack, put them on the floor and slid his feet into them. They were a little tight and not particularly comfortable, but he had managed to get them on, so as far as he was concerned they fitted. Rupert stood up and turned his feet outwards to get the feel of them, but the cubicle was cramped, he realised he would have to wait for the evening to really appreciate the full joy of owning such an historic pair of shoes (he'd already convinced himself they were genuine). He compiled a mental list of which of his regular women he might most enjoy in such attire, tapping one large-shod foot as he did so.

And so Rupert Smithereen's apartment became a shrine to the circus, his bedroom an altar to the ring. Sucked as deeply into his addiction as he was, he couldn't bear even to go back to London for his two weeks annual leave. Besides, there was no point: avoiding a certain property developer would mean remaining reclusive—hardly a holiday. His obsession began seeping more noticeably into his daily life—not that he made much effort to keep it under canvas. He started wearing garish ties made especially for him by his costumier, the white spotted red number being his particular favourite. He was also lax about removing every trace of makeup. The dark rings around his eyes were not totally down to late nights. The little work that he was expected to do began to suffer. It was inevitable that he would eventually come to the attention of the powers that be: in his establishment the ties alone were enough to warrant that.

Mr Rupert Smithereen had managed to slide, rather than work, his way up through the rank and filing using his roguish charm like warm massage oil. He did in fact have a natural skill for a certain type of diplomacy. He could encourage even the most heated issue to be settled at best amiably, at worst with repressed animosity. It was to his credit as a minor diplomat that Rupert's natural skill was helped by his investigations into the extra-curricular activities of upper-middle-ranking party officials, coupled with his knowledge of the petty shenanigans of his own colleagues. He was also a great favourite with the wives, not just the ex-pats, but right across the diplomatic stage. The general whisperings admiringly described him as 'cute', boyishly so with his blue eyes, fair hair, and—for those who fluttered closely enough to experience them—his endearing pseudo-aristocratic eccentricities.

Rupert's delicate balance between occupation and preoccupation was finally tipped by a snippet of news that lifted what little focus on work had remained, and cooked his concentration completely: He discovered that the circus was returning to town.

Saturday was the opening night. Unlike the rest of Moscow, Rupert didn't work Saturdays. He slept fitfully on Friday, drifting in and out of tantalisingly unfulfilling erotic dreams like a bee searching for nectar in a garden full of exquisite silk flowers. He slipped into a deep sleep as the sun rose and slept solidly, accidentally, until midday. He bathed and dressed, but couldn't eat. His stomach felt like a pillow in a washing machine.

There was no decision made about going to the circus. Rupert just went as inevitably as he was going to draw his next breath. He wandered dreamily between the caravans and trailers, inches from cages of lions and tigers, past decorated horses and chained elephants. There were thousands of people milling around, either employed intently about a task, or heading towards one.

He walked through the throng as if he was invisible. It was like wandering through some exotic, ancient dirty Medina. Some people were dressed in costumes, or parts of costumes to help them rehearse their routines—adding to the unreality of this transitional world.

Rupert was in his vital element, holding that same sense of centre he felt when he visited this very circus for the first time. From a narrow alley formed by a line of gaily decorated caravans he emerged into a small circular clearing in which several acts were being polished. A high wire artiste was practising with meditative concentration on a slack rope suspended six feet off the ground. A knife thrower was aiming axes at a spinning circular board on which was chalked the outline of a body which looked unnervingly like something from a forensic scene. A young woman ran through a routine with a dozen poodles, which yelped and wagged as they pushed a ball around, jumped through hoops and leapt onto tiny podiums. Rupert's attention was drawn to a small group of clowns. One was dressed in costume—complete with makeup. Another wore ordinary casual clothes—loose trousers and a shirt rolled up to the elbows. Yet another wore just baggy clown's pants, an old red vest and big shoes. There were also two midgets, both in costume. They were all running through an elaborately choreographed act involving plates and buckets, empty for the rehearsal. Rupert was amazed at their dexterity and agility. They were practising at half-speed, which made it look like a surreal ballet. Speeded up later in the evening with the addition of water, shredded foil and custard-foam it would be hilarious, but now it was a theatre of grace in perfect time. Rupert was rooted. At the end of the routine the fully costumed clown walked over to Rupert, 'What did you think?' Rupert, already mentally disjointed, was taken even further aback. The voice was that of a woman, obviously Russian, but with excellent English.

'Fab! Really fabulous!' Was all he could say, although his arms and hands were writhing as if also trying to say more. 'I've never seen… I mean, that was so… fabulous!'.

'What's your name?'

'Rupert. Rupert Smithereen. I work here, I mean at the British Consulate here…in Moscow.'

'I thought you might.'

'You speak excellent English. But how did you know I was English?'

'Thank you. But look at yourself! I could ask you how you know I'm a clown!'

Rupert glanced down and realised he was wearing brown brogues, corduroy trousers, a yellow sweater and a Harris Tweed jacket. 'I see what you mean!' He laughed.

'And as for my English; I've been to England with the circus many times. I like it. It's colourful and the people are so… stiff. Would you like some tea?' Rupert nodded. 'My name's Irina by the way, in case you're interested.'

'Oh, I'm sorry, I'm just a little—dazed by everything at the moment. Forgive me.'

'You're forgiven Rupert. This time…'

The clown took Rupert by the arm and led him back down a narrow aisle between the caravans. They talked on the way, and Rupert found out that Irina had visited just about every country in Europe and beyond. She had been to London and to Edinburgh—which she loved. He also discovered that she was not just a clown, but also a trapeze artiste, rode horses, and performed a variety of other duties involving shifting a small town from one place to another every couple of weeks.

Irina led Rupert up small steps into a wooden caravan. Inside it was half-lit by a shaft of light that managed to leak through the tight space between the caravan next-door, then through the half-closed velvet curtains. As his eyes slowly adjusted, he could see that the small space was crammed from top to bottom. There was barely a square inch of clear wall, ceiling or floor space. Costumes and clothes dripped from the few items of furniture, hung from hooks around the walls, or were sitting in small piles on the floor. A table was covered with makeup, trinkets, a half-full china tea cup, decorated boxes, large feathers, a couple of red noses, a stack of letters in blue envelopes and an oil lamp. A large gilt-framed mirror screwed to the wall held in one corner a black and white photo of a small girl. The painted wooden walls were covered with pictures—prints and photographs, small portraits and a circus poster, most of which were half-hidden by the hanging clothes. At one end was a divan covered in a heavy, ornate rug, peeled back to reveal a thick eiderdown and several pillows.

'Is this your dressing room?' Rupert asked.

Irina laughed as she pulled of her red nose: 'Yes. It's also my bedroom, living room, kitchen and bathroom. It is my home Rupert.'

Rupert liked the way she said 'Rupert'.

'But it's so... so compact!'

'Small. The word is 'small' Rupert. But I love it. My mother gave it to me, she was a contortionist and an acrobat, she teach me everything she knew. I teach myself to be a clown. Please, sit down…'

'Taught', Rupert said.

'I'm sorry?'

'Your mother, she taught you everything you know, not teach, it's the past, erm…'

'Ah, I see…'

'I'm sorry, that was very rude of me to correct you, especially as your English is so excellent.'

'Not at all, Rupert, you must correct me; it is the only way to learn. Thank you.' Irina lifted a heap of clothes from a velvet-seated chair and threw them on the bed. 'Make yourself comfortable'. She unlaced her shoes, then unzipped her outfit down one side, which obviously benefited from its own padding to protect her falls, and added to the overall image of a fat and happy clown. She was still wearing the makeup, except for the red nose. Her normal nose looked out of place against the white, red and black grease paint. 'A cute nose, if it is a little on the large size', Rupert thought to himself.

In one swift well-practised movement Irina stepped out of the costume and let it fall to the floor. This left her wearing nothing but her underwear and a clown's wig—bald with red nylon hair sticking wildly out from each side. She peeled this off, then removed a tight hair net, picked up a brush from the caravan's single cluttered table, and began brushing to free the compact mass. As she did so it began to fall about her shoulders, in long, red, loose curls.

Rupert was sexually captivated, physically speechless and absolutely fascinated. Standing before him was his heaven, his dreams, his awakenings, his desire, his iconic fetish. A tall, slim, red-haired woman dressed in nothing but simple underwear—a pretty vest and pants, and wearing clown's makeup. Rupert wanted her so badly he ached. An involuntary trembling had taken hold of his legs. He leaned forward, pressing his elbow down onto his thighs to try and contain it. His breathing became erratic as his lungs fought for the oxygen his beating heart was absorbing. All the colours in the room merged into abstraction. Highlights of the gilt on mirrors and frames became too bright to look at, but he couldn't even blink. The smell of makeup, dust, wood, paint and above all Irina, filled his head like opium, drawing him backwards into a bed of red velvet. He sighed deeply—like a dog that's just settled down for the night—and slid into delicious oblivion.

'Rupert! Rupert! Aah! You are here again. Where have you been. Are you OK?' Rupert fought to make sense as consciousness drifted back to him, along with gradually recognition of Irina's voice. But he was so bloody uncomfortable. His face was pressed against the floor. Something hard was pressing into his skull. His legs were doubled up underneath his body and his feet were jammed against something. His arms were the only parts of his body that didn't seem to be trapped, they flopped out either side like the spread wings of a dead bird. He snorted as he took a deep breath, then pulled in his arms to push himself up. Irina took him by the shoulders, helping pull him up into a kneeling position.

'Uuuuuh!' Was the only sound that came out of his mouth. He tried again: 'Uuuuuh, Oooh! Aaaah!' He was vaguely aware that the sounds he was trying to make with his mouth were not the sounds that were actually coming out. He seemed to have lost consonants as well as consciousness. 'Uuuuuh! I, I, I'm OK I think… Oh God! I'm sorry about that… Ouch!'

'That looks like a bad lump on your head. I think your eye might go black', Irina looked concerned.'

'Bloody hurts to!' Rupert's wits were returning. He decided to go for sympathy. 'Maybe I should just lie down for a minute or two. I feel a little odd!'

'Of course, here let me help you!' Irina helped drag him to his feet. Rupert noticed that she was strong for her size. He liked that. She hastily moved a pile of clothes from the bed back onto the chair that Rupert had inadvertently dived from, and helped him on. He lay back. He could smell her body on the bedclothes. He took a deep breath.

'Ooooh! That's so, so good. I'm sure I'll be fine in a minute…' He put his hand to his head, a bump was rising on his left eyebrow. 'Bugger!' He said.

'You rest here for a while. If you like I can get our doctor to look at you. I'll go and get him. He's very good with injuries, he takes care of all our animals…' Irina had genuine concern in her voice.

'No, No! Thank you, but I'll be fine in a little while. It's only a small bump. Please don't worry yourself.' Rupert felt a wave of self-satisfaction.

'Are you sure? It's no trouble for me?'

'No honestly. I'm really grateful, but it's not necessary. You carry on. I'll be fine. Honest.'

'If you're sure?'

'Yes, absolutely!'

'OK then, but you rest for a while. I have to go and rehearse with the horses. Are you sure you're fine?'

Rupert was a little disappointed, he thought he'd have Irina's undivided attention for an hour or two: 'I'm fine! You go. I'll be as right as rain in short while.'

'As right as rain? I don't understand.'

'It's nothing, just an English saying.'

'Why not as right as the sun?' Irina slipped into a pair of slacks. Rupert stole a greedy glance at her body as she pulled a sweater down over her head.

'I don't know, I guess because we see more rain than sun in England.'

'The English are strange. I'll be back in a couple of hours. Take care of yourself Rupert.' She grabbed a pair of soft satin shoes from a shelf by the door, waved, and disappeared.

'A couple of hours! Bugger!' Rupert muttered. He lay on the bed for a while, soaking up every aspect of the room, trying to cram into his memory. This kept him occupied for almost half-an-hour, but he knew he would be bored witless if he continued to wait. He had imagined something unfolding like a scene from a film, where he lays back, wounded; the beautiful nurse leans over to attend his forehead; their eyes meet; their lips part; they kiss passionately; he drags her towards him… 'Oh well! I suppose in the films they always cut at that point anyway.'

He sighed as he swung his legs over the edge of the bed and sat up. His head hurt. He looked down and realised that he had simply keeled forward from the chair, landed face down on the floor, and become wedged in the lack of space. 'How undignified!' He thought.

Rupert decided not to wait. Patience was not a Smithereen virtue. He also decided that he was in love. He wasn't of course, it was pure, unadulterated lust. He was just more in lust than he had ever been before, mainly because it was unsatisfied. He managed to convince himself that it was love due to the fact that there was no money involved—not as far as he knew anyway. A healthy bank account, or the promise of one, was a very attractive thing in a woman. But he found Irina attractive regardless—therefore it must be love. He scrabbled around on the desk and found a pencil and a pad on which he wrote a short thank-you note, adding that he hoped to see her soon. Rupert looked around for somewhere to stick it, if he left it on the table there was a strong chance it would be covered up and not seen, so he placed it on her pillow. After checking his bump in the mirror, he took a last look around the caravan, and left.

Rupert rode back to his apartment in a battered taxi that bounced and veered around like a wooden roller coaster. Any suspension had long since been destroyed by Moscow's cobbles and bad driving. The trip was more white-knuckle ride than taxi ride. At one point the cursing driver stopped the car in the middle of traffic at a busy junction. Clutching a large glass bottle, he leapt out of the car, wrenched the bonnet open, fought with a scalding radiator cap, topped up the steaming coolant, screamed abuse at the honking traffic, slammed down the bonnet, got back in the car and slammed the door shut—simultaneously discarding the bottle into the passenger foot well where it crashed into a large pile of similar glass bottles, some empty, some full—and continued the journey. The crashing bottles added an even harder edge to the trip as the car rattled, bounced and crashed over every cobblestone and tram-track. By the time Rupert got home his head was aching. He looked in the mirror. A blue and purple patch was beginning to spread down around his eye. He went to the kitchen and opened the fridge. There was no steak so he took some ice, wrapped it in a tea towel and went to lie down on the bed, where he gingerly applied the cold pack to the purple patch. He fell asleep. If he had dreams, he didn't remember a thing about them.

Rupert was convinced it was only a matter of time before Irina's conquest. He visited the circus every night and watched the show. And of course he couldn't take his eyes off her. She was the highlight of his evening, of his day, currently—of his life. He tried to see her after the first evening of the show, but it was impossible. She was running around, contributing her part to the thousand-and-one tasks demanded by the circus machine. He pursued her during the day, but again she was always busy. He managed to talk to her as she walked between rehearsals or when she stopped to take a drink, and he tried to be as calm as possible, but in reality he was becoming more and more frustrated in every way.

The week wore on and Rupert was getting nowhere.

He sent flowers. She thanked him, genuinely delighted, and kissed him on the cheek as she towelled the sweat from her body after an acrobatic session. Her smell drove Rupert wild. He bought her chocolates, which she opened immediately, to the delight of everyone in the vicinity who swooped in like pecking pigeons and demolished the box in seconds. They all thanked him for his generosity. He even bought her a puppy, thinking it would soften her. She took it into her arms and cuddled it tightly. Then, with a hint of sadness in her eyes, she slowly handed it back to Rupert, saying that it wouldn't be fair to keep it as there was no way she could take care of anything in the circus that didn't work: her days were just too busy, she didn't have a spare second. 'You keep it, Rupert, he likes you! Look!' The puppy was licking Rupert's bruised eye.

The circus had been in town for a week. Rupert was getting precisely nowhere. He walked despondently back towards home, looking for a taxi. He handed the puppy to a legless man selling a tiny pile of perfect red apples from a sack on the pavement. The man's head was as bald, shiny and red as the apples he was selling. He took it without a word and stroked it, talking to it gently as if to a small child. The puppy whimpered as it watched Rupert walk away. It then turned around, licked its new owner's cheek, and wagged its tail. A passer-by stopped, stooped to stroke the animal and bought a couple of rosy apples.

Rupert was kept busy at work all of the following day. No matter what excuse he tried to make to get away for the afternoon, he couldn't. There was an important visit from England that could prove to be diplomatically delicate and

Rupert was being dragged into it. Career-wise, it was one of those events that would do him a lot of good if he got it right, but his mind was not on the job, he needed to get away. When he eventually did it had gone seven in the evening. He borrowed an embassy car and driver and headed for the circus.

A big circus is like a small town. This particular one had more than seven thousand people working in it, as well as hundreds of animals. There were also hundreds of vehicles, including caravans, cars, trucks, buses and motorcycles. Unlike a small town, especially a small town in Russia, a circus is geared towards being totally efficient and completely mobile. Everything had gone by the time Rupert arrived at the park. All that remained were yellow islands of grass in a sea of mud. He stepped out of the car and looked around, feeling the emptiness. 'It was only a matter of time…' he said to himself, forlornly.

Rupert's decline was quick. He tried to satisfy his feelings by buying the services of a string of attractive professional ladies. He had them dress in red wigs, made them wear clown's make-up and plain but expensive underwear ordered by catalogue from Paris. He thought up routines for his 'actresses' whom he directed in earnest—driven by an unhealthy combination of deprivation and depravity. He began dressing himself up in various costumes and combinations. But nothing could fulfil him. Everything always seemed to start fine: the costumes turned him on, the women pampered him and performed as he requested—paying rapt attention to his smallest whim. His interest could be initially raised. But the harder he tried to bring the act to a satisfying finale, the less satisfying it became. 'Things were better before,' Rupert moaned, slumping back onto the bed with yet another flop.

Disheartened and distracted, Rupert's work slid still further downhill. His patience became shorter, which does not make for good diplomacy. He created several situations that had to be smoothed by colleagues. Enquiries were made about sending him home, but there seemed to be some powers in London quite happy to keep him in Moscow, at least for as long as they could count the capital benefits of tower blocks being thrown up by a certain IoM-based property company.

The KGB had been happily taking drips of information from Rupert for months and was keen to increase the flow. Rupert was at his usual rendezvous, sitting on a park bench, distractedly breaking small pieces of bread as if to feed them to a group of attentive pigeons, but feeding himself instead. His operator sat down. She was an attractive woman in an efficient kind of way, and Rupert usually flirted with her. Today it could have been anyone who sat down beside him. Rupert didn't remember much about the conversation, only that she wanted some information or other about someone or other. Either way, Rupert couldn't be bothered. The operator pulled out an envelope, from which she withdrew several black and white photographs of excellent quality. They showed Rupert, dressed in nothing but a clown's costume from the waist up, his Charlee Chapleen shoes and a pair of striped socks. A fleeting thought crossed his mind that the photos would have been better in colour—those socks were red, blue and yellow. One photo showed him in a sex act with a woman who was perched on the edge of a kitchen cabinet. She was also wearing clown's makeup, complete with a badly fitting wig and a custard pie on each breast. Rupert looked through the photos, then handed them back to the woman. 'Big Top', was all he said.

Just as Rupert's work for the Embassy suffered, so did his work for the KGB. He just couldn't be bothered. Which is probably why the pictures turned up on the news-desk of a popular Sunday newspaper in Fleet Street. The potential was there for the story to run for weeks, had he not been relegated by more prominent scandals. Rupert's pride was dented at this—it seemed that even his scandal had ended prematurely, with barely enough coverage to dine on.

In the clean-up that followed, and to the great relief of many of his colleagues in Moscow, Rupert was finally dismissed and recalled. As a parting present—mainly as an incentive to continue working for them, partly because it had been lying around gathering dust—Rupert's Russian friends presented him with the last Munter Drophead in their possession. In its glove box was a set of black and white prints and a reel of 8mm cine film. Rupert never did get to see himself in action, which was probably a good thing. He thought the car was the ugliest thing he had ever seen in his life. Apart from anything else, it was black. Rupert tried to imagine it in a more fashionable red, yellow or orange, but in his mind's eye it didn't look any better. In a final act of diplomacy he accepted it, simultaneously deciding he would sell it as soon as possible.

On arriving back in London Rupert decided to avoid

the office for a while—he knew he'd have to go in at some point to be reprimanded, probably formally dismissed and possibly charged. So the first stop was his house, which was very bleak indeed. It looked as though it was due for demolition. He tentatively knocked on the door, which was answered by a dazed and confused individual who peered at Rupert through bloodshot eyes, it took careful interrogation to discover that he was one of a commune of squatters—very much at home, having been there for almost a year. Next stop was the office of the agents who were supposed to be looking after his affairs. The 'To Let' sign said almost everything. What it didn't tell him he found out from his bank manager, who assured Rupert that not a single payment had been made into his account by the agents, and in fact his account was overdrawn because of bank charges, and interest on the bank charges.

Rupert, feeling ever more desperate, visited several estate agents in a vain attempt to put the property on the market, but was assured that it would be almost impossible to sell while filled with nonpaying guests. One did mention that he knew a property developer that might be interested, and that he could mention it to him when he next came over from the Isle of Man. Rupert declined the offer. The rattling, noisy, dusty, smelly, hot tube ride to Victoria summed up how he felt. He realised that in true Smithereen tradition, he was broke. He couldn't count on his charm as currency either—not now that he had been exposed to the nation via the Sunday papers, the cuttings of which he carried with some pride in his jacket pocket.

He lay back on the lumpy bed in his small hotel room

and stared at a brown stain on the ceiling. He was thinking about Moscow. He missed its red, greys and browns. He missed its smell, its people. He missed the circus and his missed chances. He realised that just about everything he owned was in the two suitcases he had with him. One contained clothes and personal effects. The other was packed with circus paraphernalia. The brown stain reminded of something…it was like an island in a sea. It reminded him of somewhere he hadn't visited since he was young. He lay for a while, staring up at the patch, projecting memories onto it.

He made a decision: there was no point in hanging around here waiting for who knows what. He knew that sometime soon, someone would come looking for him for something or other that he would want or need to avoid. He rose from the creaking bed, picked up his suitcases, opened the window and slid them down the awning beneath it. He casually walked out of the hotel, saying 'See you later' to the sour-faced receptionist. He walked along to the awning, reached up and lifted both suitcases down, then carried them to where the Munter was parked, and loaded up. He climbed into the driver's seat and sat silently for a few minutes staring into space.

After drawing a vague map in his head he started the engine and headed north, through the seemingly endless suburbs of London and onto the A1. He left his dreams of wealth and society in Park Lane as he slid around Marble Arch. He drove until he could finally feel the distance between him and London, then pulled into the car-park of a roadside café a few miles north of Huntingdon for a greasy lunch and a couple of hours sleep between lorries on the pot-holed gravel car park. He awoke, had a strong tea, then continued driving: up through the flatlands by Stamford and Grantham; up between Leeds and York; and across the dales and moors to Darlington and past Durham; onward through Alnwick and Berwick, Edinburgh and Perth. A night in grim B&B in Pitlochry, then up through the mountains to Inverness. It was only as he was driving between Inverness and Thurso that Rupert began to feel any kind of peace—as the ancient peat of the Plains of Caithness rolled westwards and the sky was as big and as grey as he had ever seen it. The wind rocked the Munter as he drove. He arrived at Scrabster too late to take that day's ferry, so checked into a cosy B&B. A plaque over the door announced it was run by Trevor and Venus, who proved to be a charming couple. The place was decorated with trinkets from holidays in Spain—plastic donkeys, castanets and the doll of a flamenco dancer that doubled as a holder for the spare toilet roll hidden beneath its black and red silk frock.

Rupert was semi-hypnotised from his journey. He couldn't focus on anything because he was so used to looking at a vanishing point and feeling the world rush by. His head was spinning. He was too tired to eat an evening meal, too tired to undress. He slid statically between the bobbly nylon sheets and was asleep by the time his head touched the polyester pillow.

Sleep is not always rest. Rupert's dream was one long, energy-packed tornado that seemed to have sucked up everything that had happened to him over the past few months. These were not happy images now being extracted from his non-conscious mind and dumped into his cradle of dreams. When he awoke he seemed to be more exhausted than before. He crawled out of bed and washed in cold water. He watched himself drying his face in the mirror. He held the towel over his mouth. He looked tired, drained. His eyes were red, his eyelids swollen. His skin was grey and his hair was greasy. He moved closer to the mirror and stared deeply into his own eyes, looking for something, some kind of sign that would tell him something about himself. He tried to imagine that he was someone else looking at him, trying to work out what he was like. But the eyes were too familiar. 'How can you be yourself, but not know yourself?' He thought.

Rupert didn't realise how hungry he was until he started eating breakfast: egg, bacon, black pudding, beans, a sausage which had been carefully carved lengthwise to give the illusion of there being two on the plate, tea, toast and marmalade. Rupert felt slightly better. After breakfast he paid the bill, walked to the ticket office on the quay and bought a ticket to Stromness. The ferry sailed at midday.

It was a comparatively smooth crossing; even so, someone managed to throw up on the deck above where Rupert was standing, depositing a small amount of regurgitated meat pie over one shoulder. He wiped it off with a handkerchief and watched a skua skim the surface of the rolling sea.

From Stromness he drove to Kirkwall. There he made enquiries then a phone call to arrange the next sea-leg to his destination. His transport was an ex-military landing craft that had suffered the minimum amount of conversion to enable it to be used to carry cars and vans, tractors and sheep between the various islands. Rupert drove to Tingwall to await its arrival.

The rusty ferry arrived several hours after Rupert, who had at first been alone enjoying the silence, but had since been joined by two other vehicles, along with a young man leading a tethered calf. One of the drivers was a woman who looked at least ten months' pregnant, and had been for an antenatal check up. They were all waiting for the craft to take them home on either Rowsay or Sanday. Rupert's destination was slightly different. The brown stain had reminded him that his family owned Smitsay, a small island out in one of the Orkney Sounds. He didn't remember much about it other than it had a farmhouse and an outbuilding—a barn, in which he had enjoyed playing as a child. He remembered the whiskered grey seals on the rocks, and the tiny beach that held innumerable imaginary adventures. Rupert knew that the house was uninhabited. It had been boarded up years ago. For as long as he could remember the little land that there was had been rented to someone from another island for sheep grazing.

There was no peace on the landing craft. Its ancient diesel engine thudded like a tired heart as it trudged through the water. The calf was wide-eyed with fear, but was being soothed by stroking and gentle words made gentler by the soft accent of the islands. 'We'll soon be there boy. Soon be there. Be easy now.' The words also began to have a soporific effect on Rupert.

Smitsay was the last port of call, a silhouette against a sea the same colour as the grey sky, but sparkling from a slit of low, but intense cherry-coloured sunlight that split the horizon. The landing craft landed and dropped its door onto the slippery green seaweed that coated the concrete ramp that served as a jetty. As Rupert prepared to drive the Munter from the craft, the pilot said:

'You sure you're going to be alright out here on your own lad?'

'As alright as I'll be anywhere.' Rupert answered, before adding, 'Don't worry, I was born on an island!'

'Aye? Which one was that then?'

'The Isle of Man' at which Rupert drove off the craft.

The pilot smiled to himself and shook his head slowly as he prepared to winch up the ramp for his departure. He paused as an afterthought caught him, then disappeared up into the wheelhouse and returned with a bottle of Navy rum. He walked down the metal ramp and handed it to Rupert, who was still sitting in the Munter. 'Here, take this. You might need it. I'll call by in a week in case you need anything.' Rupert took it with resigned thanks. A few minutes later the ramp of the landing craft was cranked noisily up, the engine roared and it slowly backed away from the island, black smoke gushing from its rusting funnel. Rupert sat in the car and watched it disappear into the distant shape of one of the low dark islands that broke the line of the horizon.

The sea was calm. Rupert twisted the cork out of the rum bottle and took a swig, twisted the cork back on, and got out of the Munter. It was so quiet here. His ears ached with the silence. He wasn't used to listening to so far away. The sea lapped against the narrow beach. Wind blew through the grass. There were a handful of sheep on the island: he could hear them ripping up the ground. A dog barked several miles away, echoing over the heads of a floating raft of Eider sitting in the middle of the Sound. Gulls floated silently in the near distance, adjusting their wings to the intimacy of the shifting breeze. The cherry-red sun slit threw out long, lazy, purple rays from under the grey clouds. Rupert dragged his cases out of the Munter and up the pebble and seashell path to the house. There was no lock on the door, but it was stiff on rusty hinges. He had to put his shoulder to it to shove it open, leaving flakes of faded blue paint on his thick, white woollen jumper. He pulled his suitcases inside and dumped them on the threadbare carpet, then walked back outside and opened the shutters on the living room window, which let some light in through the dusty, cracked glass. Back inside, Rupert's eyes began the slow adjustment to the lack of light. The windows weren't all that was dusty—everything was covered in a film of sand as fine as talcum powder which, driven by the wind, had sifted through every seam and crack of the house. The last time Rupert had been here was on holiday with an aunt and uncle when he was about eight. He vaguely remembered the house and in his memory it was clean and white. But now the walls of the living room were lined with wood from which the topcoat of paint had all but disappeared, revealing the pale-pink undercoat. There was an alcove bed in the same room, with a curtain across the front to keep out the winter cold and the summer's almost endless days. There was also an old stove, which burned peat brought over by a boat several times a year and stacked in a lean-to against the barn. The only furniture in the room was a low Orkney chair, its wicker back designed to embrace and conserve valuable body warmth; an old pine dining table with turned legs and a top that was probably scrubbed white once; several mismatched dining chairs, including one carved oak piece with rotting leather upholstery, and a rickety captain's chair with a pierced plywood seat. There was also a dresser, which must have been the pride of the room when someone was proud of the house. On it were several old plates, a metal jug, a china teapot, an oil lamp and a candleholder—all coated in a layer of fine sand.

For the first time in ages, Rupert felt contentment settling in. A knot untied in his gut, releasing a sense of freedom that flooded his head. There was nobody around for miles. No need to be diplomatic; no need for airs and graces; no need to be charming; no need to be polite; no need to pretend; no need to be afraid; no need to act; no need to answer. He decided the problem in his life wasn't himself, it was other people. This was obvious, because there was nobody else here, and he had never felt better. There was nothing for him in London apart from consequences and the need to find a job. He had heard on the grapevine that it was no secret that he was selling secrets. Rupert realised his minor misdemeanours probably wouldn't be overlooked, despite the fact that the secrets were probably inconsequential—and probably not even secret.

Rupert had run out on a lot of debts in his time, so he saw no reason why he shouldn't follow the same course for his debt to society. He had come here to escape, not to be enlightened. Inadvertently Rupert experienced an epiphany. He found himself in the silence. He realised everything all at once. He realised he was a total arse, or at least he had been. He realised that he had spent all his life chasing luxuries—an apartment in Mayfair, a Bentley Continental, holidays on the Riviera, Saville Row suits, Polo, Henley, Wimbledon, Ascot, beautiful women, the membership of a decent club, money—but every time he put so much as a foot on the first rung of the ladder, the rung snapped. He realised that all luxuries were now with him. The true luxuries of time, space, silence and privacy—and particularly his suitcase full of circus costumes. For the first time in his life, Rupert realised that he didn't need to pretend to be anything other than who he was, and for the first time in his life he knew what he was: conniving, dishonest, obsessed, selfish, uncaring and lascivious; and he really loved himself for it.

Rupert picked up the suitcase and tossed it onto the bed, causing the mattress to exhale a small dust cloud. He unclasped it and threw back the lid. In minutes he had selected a wig: a bald dome with long, straggly orange frizz hanging down the back and sides. He took out his prized Chardlee Chapleen shoes and placed them on the floor, they looked strangely comfortable sitting in the dust. He took out a large yellow jacket with a red tartan band running across it and massive blue buttons. He took out a stiff, coiled-spring shirt front and a giant green bow tie. Finally he pulled out a shocking pink tutu. Within minutes he had undressed and changed. From a pocket in the lid of the case he withdrew some theatrical makeup. He found a small distressed mirror on the wall and smeared away the dust so that he could see himself. A shaft of sunlight shining in through the window lit up one half of his face with a blood-red glow, the other side seemed to be in total darkness by contrast. He applied the makeup with the skill of a professional. Finally he placed the wig on his head, adjusted it for comfort, grabbed the bottle of rum, and walked outside into the beautiful silence. He couldn't remember ever feeling happier. He walked around, feeling the cool air around his naked balls beneath the tutu. A sheep stared at him, chewing.

'Baaaa!' Said the sheep.

'Fuck off!' Said Rupert.

The sheep shook its tail and carried on chewing.

Rupert walked down to the Munter. He laughed as he looked at it with his new vision. 'You are still the ugliest car I have ever seen in my life. I think we need to get you out of sight, you're spoiling the view!' Even so, he still couldn't help but carry some affection for the beast; after all, it carried him to Smitsay without a glitch. He sat in the driving seat; the leather was cold against his bare arse. He started the engine and carefully drove the car up the path to the barn. Leaving the engine running, he got out walked to the barn doors and tried to force them open; but they were locked from inside. He walked round to the side and found a small door of corrugated iron, which pulled open easily. He picked his way around bits of old machinery and salvaged wood, and opened the main doors by removing a stout wooden beam that had prevented the worst of the wind from tearing them open. It took a few minutes to clear enough area in which to park the Munter. He nudged it carefully in. The inside of the car was now familiar to him: its smell of leather and engine, the pattern of the wood on the dashboard. It also felt warm in contrast to the rapidly cooling air outside.

The last rays of the sun were clinging to the horizon. Rupert left the engine running to warm up the inside. He squeezed out of the driver's seat and inched along the side of the car to close the main doors. He shivered as he dropped the wooden beam back into place. He then inched his way back—stepping carefully over old bits of machinery, and climbed into the Munter again. He turned the heater up, and switched on the wireless, he found a light station that was playing some string quartet he almost recognised, Ravel, he thought. He twisted the cork out of the rum bottle and took a deep swig, then another. Then relaxed into his contentment and his exhaustion. He drifted off into a deep sleep of delicious dreams in which he was finally having gorgeous, extremely dirty sex with the delicious Irina—they were both in full costume: except that she wasn't in her caravan, she was in the wood-lined living room on Smitsay. Clouds of dust rose from the bed as they fucked. As fumes filled the barn, in his dreams Rupert Smithereen had the deepest, and the last orgasm of his life. Eventually the fuel in the Munter's tank was sucked dry, and the engine died.

13: The travels of scooter boy (ii)

Tadeuz had arranged to meet up with a cousin from Kiev. Their rendezvous was a particular place on the Polish border where his cousin knew the police and the local bandits. Of course the bribe was going to take some of his savings, but this was his gateway to freedom and what price freedom? He was pleased that he had a full 125cc of power to carry him along. His old 50cc scooter would have been too slow. He smiled as he thought about how he had used its old engine to power the pump that now provided water from the well to his mother's house. He was known around the village for being good with engines and machines. His brothers could take care of the vegetables, the pig and the rest of the family. Especially Lenny, who considered himself to be a bigshot criminal, but who was just a lazy petty thief. Tadeuz knew he had something to offer: good looks and a body kept fit and muscular from working around the farm. He strapped his helmet on, buttoned up his leather jacket, dusted off his faux-Nike trainers—a Black Sea import—took his position on the scooter, kicked it into life, and set off for Calais: via Poland, Czechoslovakia,

Germany and Belgium. There was also an unscheduled but very enjoyable detour into Hungary, courtesy of a kind girl called Katinka he met in Krakow.

He was on the scooter for around eight hours every day. What amazed him was the price of everything. He had saved up a small fortune, now exchanged into euros, but what was a small fortune in Ukraine seemed to be nothing in Europe. His money was disappearing at an alarming rate. He wasn't allowing himself any luxuries—except perhaps the odd beer, but even that stopped when a bar in France charged him three euros for a small measure, plus he felt that he should leave a tip, just to prove that he was a man of substance. That took care of another euro.

By the time he reached Calais he had less than a quarter of his savings left. He pulled up as close as he could get to the English Channel and stared out to sea. After several minutes he could make out the white gash of the cliffs of England. There it was, he could see it. Even from here it looked magical, tempting, white, clean. He watched the shuttling ferries with longing—the transport of his dreams. He stood on the end of the stone pier and focused on one of them until it disappeared into the horizon.

14: Point of departure

Nathaniel could normally focus very easily on what he was doing, but now, as he stood again on the ferry he didn't seem to be able to concentrate on the task in hand—which was to find a target vehicle that was a safer bet than the rusty van he'd picked last time. His thoughts kept wandering. He felt edgy, as if he was walking on stepping stones with sharks on one side and alligators on the other. He was usually a happy person—quiet, but happy. Now he was starting to realise that he wasn't happy. It was a feeling that he had tried to shake off, or at least put at the back of his mind, or deny, for some time, but it was there. He sighed heavily and made himself focus on the line of traffic.

'What's up?' Icarus asked.

'Oh nothing.'

'There is. I know you well enough to know when something's not right dude. You were a bit off last time we did this, remember? Are you nervous?'

'What about?'

'The job.'

'The job? No, not at all. Quite the opposite in fact. In

fact I wish I was a bit nervous.'

'So what's up man?' Icarus asked again, as he pulled a ham and cheese baguette out of a carrier bag he was holding.

'God! Don't you ever stop eating? I'm surprised you're not like him.' Nathaniel nodded in the direction to a fat-bellied guy in his mid-twenties standing against a railing. He was holding a pint of lager. His tee-shirt didn't quite cover his belly.

'Metabolism.' Icarus replied, as he took a massive bite.

'Metabolism! Rubbish! You know, I don't think I've ever seen you eat a proper meal!'

Icarus pointed to the baguette and obviously wanted to say something. He swallowed. 'It's got lettuce on it, and tomato.' He then started to pick it out and throw it to the gulls, as usual.

'No! I don't mean that! I mean I don't think I've ever seen you sit down and eat a proper meal—like a dinner. Only a greasy spoon. Your arteries must be like concrete.'

Icarus was just about to take another bite, 'What's up dude? I mean, there's got to be something up. Since when have you bothered about what goes into my guts? You know I eat crap. I've always eaten crap, probably always will. I like eating crap. It's never bothered you before?'

'I know but... Oh! I don't know. It's just... I don't know! I wish I did. Things just don't feel right.' Nathaniel face was screwed up with the exertion of trying to find the right words, but they just weren't there yet. 'I don't know!'

'What is it? Like knots in your stomach?'

Nathaniel thought for a second, mentally feeling his

insides: 'Sort of.'

'Mmhu... And are you having difficulty concentrating on things?'

That one required no thought, 'Yes,' was Nathaniel's instant reply.

'Have you lost your appetite?'

Nathaniel tried to remember what he'd eaten over the past few days, and realised that all he'd done is pick at his food. 'I guess so.' By now he was becoming curious about Icarus's questioning, 'Why do you ask?'

'Male menopause!' Icarus said, casually, as he sunk his teeth into his baguette again.

'Male menopause! There's no such thing!' Nathaniel said, indignantly. 'I should have known better,' he added, feeling as though Icarus had been having a joke at his expense.

Icarus, still chewing, with cheeks bulging, looked at Nathaniel, raised his eyebrows and shrugged as if to say: 'Male menopause is a fact, like it or not!'

'Absolute bollocks!' Nathaniel replied.

Icarus swallowed. 'I'm telling you, it exists. I read it in... what was the name of that magazine? Anyway, that's what you've got. It's because you're scared of dying, y'know, with being old and that...' Icarus bit into his baguette.

'All that rubbish you eat has obviously affected your brain. You do talk some rubbish! I am not scared of dying. I like being this age, it means I don't have to put up with all the shit that I put up with when I was your age! And I'm not old. I'm only bloody fifty-two for Pete's sake, probably only half-way through it all!'

Icarus's eyes bulged as he nearly choked as he swallowed

too much, too quickly. 'Listen to you!' He said, after recovering. 'Scared stiff! Male menopause! I tell you!'

'Double-bollocks! Anyway, I can't stand here talking to you as if we've got nothing to do!' Nathaniel felt even more uneasy. While Icarus may or may not have been right, he was sticking his head into a subject that Nathaniel didn't feel comfortable thinking about, never mind discussing. His attention turned back to the dwindling line of cars.

'That one!' He said, impatiently, nodding in the direction of a strange looking car now rolling down the ramp towards the ferry.

Icarus looked over the top of his large paper cup—the contents of which he was sucking up through a bent plastic straw. It hissed and bubbled as his mouth let go.

'What, the black one? What the hell is that! It's the ugliest thing I've ever seen in my entire life!' His voice had that deep tone that can only be gained by a large mass working its way down, slowly and painfully, towards the stomach.

'To be honest, I don't know what it is. But it's perfect! Some kind of classic thing—I'm not well up on cars, maybe an Alvis—I don't know.'

'It's bloody horrible! Do you think they'll let it into France? If it was my country I wouldn't! What's an 'Elvis' anyway?'

'Alvis! You idiot! But I don't think it is, it looks too American, and it's left-hand drive.' Nathaniel replied, feeling slightly better now his adrenaline was starting to flow.

*

Arthur parked up, pulled on the handbrake, took the

small bag containing his passport, money and camera, locked up the Munter and headed for the stairs. He liked this part of the trip. He could have gone via the Tunnel, but he always took the ferry, it made him feel as though he was on a journey: sailing across the sea to distant lands—even if it was only twenty-something miles, swimming distance for some, and you were never even out of sight of land. Arthur walked up the brightly lit stairs, squashed between the other passengers heading in the same direction. He was thinking about the time he hitched down to the south of France and into Italy, he was only a kid. He got a lift from Paris to St Tropez on the back of a Harley Davidson Electroglide. These memories were just fleeting thoughts: A lift had dropped him off in the northern suburbs of Paris and, without a map, he wasn't sure which direction to walk in, so he headed where most of the traffic seemed to be going. He walked for at least an hour before finding signs for 'Centre Ville'. But still wasn't sure exactly which direction to go, the centre of cities was never a good place to hitch from. He'd seen the bike parked up on a broad pavement, its owner was looking at a map.

'Excusez moi!' Arthur had shouted, 'Est-ce que vous savez…'

'What!?' The rider had shouted, looking puzzled.

'Are you English?' Arthur asked.

'Yeah! You don't know the way out of this fuckin' place do yer?'

'I was going to ask you the same! Where're you going?'

'St Tropez, to a Harley meet, but I'm fuckin' well lost. I've been riding around for hours, can't find the right fuckin' road! Where are you going?'

'I'm not too sure, I'm just hitching—south though.'

'Can you read a map?'

'Yes.'

'Can you speak French, because I've tried to ask the way, but nobody speaks English, at least they pretend they can't! Bastards!'

'I can get by, just about.'

'Do you want a lift?'

'Wouldn't mind.'

'Right then! Hop on, here's your helmet. It might be a bit small, I brought it in case I met some gorgeous French bird! Look what I end up with! Never mind.'

Now that was an adventure, thought Arthur. He thought about the walk from St Tropez to the Italian border. He'd only turned back once there because he realised that he had hardly any money left. His thoughts flashed forward to when he had his first job in London. He had flown down to Nice for a photo-shoot in Juan-le-Pin. Out in the morning, back the same evening. Same trip, different journey.

Arthur decided a half-pint of cold lager wouldn't go amiss—well it was the first day of his holiday. He also needed a pee. At the top of the stairs, he noticed someone holding a pint glass almost drained of beer. Although there was something older about him—possibly the empty pint glass, the person holding it looked as though he couldn't have been more than about sixteen years old. He had a smooth, bright red face, a shock of sandy-coloured hair, and a chin that would have arrived everywhere first if it hadn't been for the beer belly. He was also about six-feet-four-inches tall. Arthur looked up at him and asked him if he knew were the bar was.

'Aaar!' A nod accompanied by single word with the broadest West Country accent that Arthur had ever heard.

'Ee'll be up yarn stairs thar.' A massive, red hand pointed the way.

'Thanks very much.' Arthur replied, and went to walk in that direction, reasoning that there'd be a gents somewhere near to it.

'Horatio!' The man held out his hand.

Arthur stopped in his tracks, looked up at the man, puzzled.

'Horatio Thornbaarlock, Oi'm from a long line of Thornbaarlocks. My farther were a Thornbaarlock, 'is farther were a Thornbaarlock, and 'is farther afor 'im were a Thornbaarlock...'

'Pleased to meet you Horatio, I'm Arthur, Arthur Pod', but I've got to go... well you know, got to pee...'

'Aaar! Can't hold you from that. You'd be going t' France then?'

Arthur looked bemused. 'Er, yes?' Thinking: 'Well this is the Dover to Calais Ferry'.

'Aaar! Thort as much. Me too!'

'Well have a great time!' Arthur turned to take another step.

'Do you know whoi oi's going ter Fraance?' Horatio was smiling smugly as he asked this.

Arthur again felt the same kind of bemusement, replying

in a slightly patronising tone—brought out by his need to relieve himself. 'Erm? Let me see? Erm… No.'

'Oi'll tell 'ee whoi oi is going t' Fraance, oim goin' ter Fraance ter foind out whaat Meltingwherpe's loike.'

'Whereabouts in France is Meltingwherpe? I've never heard of it.' Arthur was vaguely curious.

Horatio laughed and slapped Arthur on the shoulder with such force his knees buckled: 'Taint in Fraance matey-boy! Meltingwherpe's where oi comes fram ain't it! 's-in Cornwaall.'

'Oh really?' Said Arthur, locking his knees back into position. 'That's fascinating, but…'

'Surproised you not knowing that! Big village loike Meltingwherpe! Almost 'undred-and-forty people lives there! Mostly Thornbaarlocks, mostly. Anyways Oi ain't never been nowheres else, an Oi gets ter thinkin' Oi wonder what it's loik, where Oi lives loik. An Oi figures the only way ter foind out, loike, was ter go somewheres else, so Oi decoides ter go ter Fraance loike. Oi coulda gone ter somewhere else in Engerland, or ev'n Scartland, but that tain't 'xactly faareign is it? Course Oi coulda gone ter Wales, but Oi can't make 'ead nor tail o' them. We 'ad one visit our village once—couldn't understaand a werd 'e said. Anyway's alus fancied France. There's nuthin' loike a noice onion! That's what Oi alus says!'

'Look Horatio, I don't want to be rude, but I'm going to piss myself if I stay here another minute! I'm gonna have to go.' Arthur said, partly out of genuine need, partly as an excuse.

'Aar! Oi takes yer point matey-boy. But you gets ter yon

bar aafter, an Oi'll buy thee one!'

Arthur grinned, nodded, and headed for the gents. He really fancied a cold lager, but thought it might be better to avoid the bar.

*

Icarus had bolted the diamonds to the underneath of the Munter, but not without some considerable trouble. The bolts and nuts were all weird sizes and shapes. As it turned out it took him longer than it should have, especially by the time he'd disabled the engine, which gave him a surprise, because when he opened the bonnet he discovered it was a diesel engine.

'Weird? On a sports car?' Icarus thought. He spent a few minutes deciding what to do, before settling on unbolting the cable to the starter motor, removing it, and throwing it in his bag. He then swapped a couple of wires that were connected to a small black box, just to make sure. He didn't know much about diesel engines, but he was sure he'd done everything he could think of to disable the car. He closed the bonnet, chucked all the tools into the bag—along with his overalls and rubber gloves—and headed for the stairs, where a deck hand almost caught him. He had to make some excuse about falling asleep in the car before the man felt easy enough to allow him back up to the deck. He was annoyed as he climbed the stairs but the thought of a beer consoled him.

Icarus arrived at the bar at the same time as the same large guy who had been on deck earlier. The man took out a ten-pound note to flag the attention of the barman, who was busy serving someone else.

Icarus adopted the calm, steely-eyed approach: 'Serve me first. Serve me first,' was the mantra he was trying to project from his own brain into the barman's brain.

The barman dropped some coins in the till, slammed the drawer shut and looked up, glancing quickly between the two men, 'Who's next?'

'Pint of lager please!'

'Point o' lager please matey!'

Two voices, almost as one.

The barman stuck two glasses deftly under the two taps and flicked a couple of levers. He topped both glasses and put them on the counter. Icarus fumbled in his pocket for some change he thought he had, meanwhile the barman took the waving tenner and clipped it into the till.

'Two pints of lager! There's your change,' said the barman, with an air of finality.

'But…' Before the Icarus could protest further, the barman had turned around,

'Who's next?'

'Wait!' Icarus shouted, now waving a tenner of his own in the air, 'we're not together! Here!'

'Don't worry Matey-boy! You can buy the next round! Horatio's the name…' Horatio held out his hand.

Icarus shrugged, it seemed like the easiest solution. He shook Horatio's hand. 'Sorry man, I had the dosh here… I'm Icarus.'

'Aaar! No problems! Horatio raised his glass and winked: 'Cheers matey-boy, 'ere's to a bon-voyage! Thaat's French, Oi've been learnin' it!'

'Cheers!' Icarus drank a long draught from his glass.

Horatio drained his: 'Bloody marvellous that! Oi think Oi'm ready for that other one now?' He looked at Icarus expectantly.

Icarus felt obliged to return the favour, even though his own glass was still more than half full. He flagged a barman and ordered a pint for Horatio.

He hadn't intended to order another for himself, but Horatio leaned over the bar, 'Oi, matey! Oon owtre beer poor mown ami owsi! Sil vous plate' He then turned to Icarus, Oi can't be drinkin' alone now can Oi, tain't sociable loik!

As the ship slipped gently away from England, Icarus had already sunk two pints, and was slipping down the inevitable slope of becoming one of the many friends that Horatio would gather during his travels.

'Matey-boy, what d'you think of this waatch then?' He showed Icarus a red-faced LED watch on a heavy chrome band; the watch was the size of small alarm clock.

'Great...' Icarus tried to be enthusiastic.

'Arij'nal this. Pulsar P1. It were brought from a Japanese businessman in noineteen seventy four for three 'undred dollars. Not boi me a'course, Oi only paid ten quid f'rit down the pub. Roit baargin if y'arsk me. Now Ic'rus, 'ow many watches d'you think Oi've got? Go on matey-boy, take a guess?'

Icarus didn't really care, but pretended to be thinking about it.

Horatio ordered another round, and without waiting for a reply, said: "Thirty-foive! An Oi'll praably 'ave more by the toim Oi gets back 'ome. An' you know whoi Oi've gat thirty-foive watches? Go-on matey-boy, guess!'

Icarus really couldn't think of an answer. 'You collect them?' He asked, feebly.

'Well, in a way Oi guess you ain't wrong, but Oi'll tell 'ee the real reason. It's caause they aall tells the toim different.'

'Ah! You mean as in the different time zones?'

'Whaat?' Horatio looked puzzled.

'Time zones. You know—London, Paris New York? Like now France is an hour ahead of London?'

'Well Oi can't say as to havin' a clue what you're taalkin' about. You seems a bit confused if yer don't moind me sayin'. But I'll tell yer why: They've all got the same toim on 'em loik, but they're aall different. You see some is 'arder, some is softer. Some is a round koind o' toim, others is more straight loik. Some's a bit wiggly. It's a bit loik diff'rent doimensions. Oi's sens'tive to 'em. This waatch 'ere, is me no-nonsense, straightfor'ard travellin' toim. Course Oi gat more in me baag loik, because the theng about toime is it's aalus a-changin'. The more Horatio drank, the less Icarus could understand, but despite the fact that he had around three drinks to each of Icarus's, this was the only noticeable effect. Icarus began to wonder how much time they had before the ferry arrived.

Nathaniel had been gazing out to sea, and down at the wake of the ship. He had been miles away, still trying to make sense of the way he was feeling. Maybe he was just depressed. Maybe it was the male menopause. He thought about going to see a doctor when he got back to England. He came back to himself and wondered if there were ever dolphins in the English Channel, and where Icarus was. After a quick scan around the horizon, he gave up on the dolphins and decided to look for Icarus in the bar. There could only be half-an-hour or so to go before they docked, and he still had to call Eve.

Arthur, meanwhile, had wandered around the ship, more out of boredom than anything else. He browsed the shop, but there was nothing of interest. The spirits were all too expensive, and most of the rest of the stuff on sale was crap of one sort or another. He'd poked his nose into the cafeteria and the restaurant, but nothing enticed him to investigate further. All of the seats dotted about the aisles and foyers were full, so he decided to head for the bar. He hoped that the jolly red giant might not recognise him.

A vain hope of course, as soon as Arthur entered the room he was spotted by Horatio, who had dragged him over to the bar and ordered almost before Arthur had drawn a second breath.

'Aaah, Aarthur! That wur a laang pee. Oi thort thee'd flushed thee self overboard!' Arthur could hardly make out a word that Horatio was saying. 'Here! Meet a friend o' moin: Ic'rus. Ic'rus this is Arthur if Oi remember roight.'

'Your not wrong, Arthur it is.' Arthur shook hands with Icarus.

'See! Oi never ferget's a name nor a face! 'ang on, Oi'll get us anuther drink in…'

Nathaniel entered the bar, saw the group and decided that he didn't want to get involved in what looked like a bit of a session. He decided to stand a little way off and try to grab Icarus's attention. He caught it in just a few minutes.

But despite the fact that he obviously knew he was there, Icarus made no attempt to come over, he just shrugged. Nathaniel pointed emphatically at his wristwatch. Icarus nodded and tried to break away from the barrage that was Horatio, who was on top form being his bombastic, good-natured, very, very friendly self. He noticed that Icarus's attention was being coaxed elsewhere, and followed his gaze to Nathaniel.

'Aaallo there matey boy! Come on over and join the paarty!' Horatio shouted across the heads of everyone between himself and Nathaniel.

Nathaniel tried to gesticulate towards Icarus, although he wasn't sure himself what he was trying to communicate. He realised the only way he was going to speak to Icarus was to enter the red lion's den. He wandered over. Irritated.

'Aall roight matey! Whaat youz 'avin' then?'

Nathaniel tried to protest and refuse, but like everybody else, he had no choice. He ordered an orange juice with ice. Horatio ordered the barman to stick a stiff shot of vodka into it, regardless of Nathaniel's protestations.

'Thaar y'are, yer looks as though yer needs it matey. Cheeers!'

For a moment there was silence within the group. It was broken by Nathaniel, who flashed a glare at Icarus: 'I didn't mean to interrupt. I just wondered how my friend Icarus here was. He...erm gets a bit seasick sometimes. He's on a special diet, not meant to drink alcohol with his medication'.

Icarus had settled in to the rhythm of drinking: 'Seasick? Well I er, started out a bit dodgy dude, but—the pills seem to be working fine. I'm good!'

'Is that good? Or good to go?' Nathaniel wanted reassurance. Icarus didn't have a clue what he was talking about, and looked at Nathaniel as if he was going mad. Nathaniel looked at Icarus and pointed down to the ground. Icarus began to understand.

'Oh, yeah dude! Good to go! Excellent! Smooth.'

'I hope is stays smooth.' There was the merest hint of a warning in Nathaniel's voice.

'It'll be fine. The weather report's good,' Arthur said helpfully. Which was about all he could say before Horatio grabbed the spotlight again, along with anyone within arm's reach. As the ferry approached France there was quite a party going on. Nathaniel had managed to slip away for long enough to call Eve with the necessary details. Icarus had already sent her the registration number by text. Eve would be waiting in her usual place when the ferry docked.

Finally, with some relief, the call came for all passengers to return to the car deck and the party began to dissipate.

'Well nice to have met you all! Thanks for the drinks, sorry I couldn't down them all, but you know—driving. Maybe I'll see you again sometime?' Arthur said, as he got ready to depart. 'Are you coming down?' He said to Nathaniel more to be polite than anything. It was the first time they'd exchanged words.

'No, we're on foot, only staying this evening—lads' night out. You know the kind of thing,' Nathaniel replied, 'back tomorrow, unfortunately.' He tried to sound regretful, but couldn't wait to get back onto home soil.

Arthur nodded. 'Well, you enjoy yourselves.'

'What about you?' Nathaniel asked, more out of courtesy than anything, he was too distracted to be really interested.

'A week I think. Just driving around. I've got some friends here who I might spend a few days with though. And a bit of shopping of course—a couple of cases of something or other.'

Nathaniel grinned, 'Well you enjoy yourself too'.

'I will, thanks.'

Arthur returned to the Munter, unlocked it and climbed in. He put the key into the ignition and waited for the line of cars in front of him to clear. The opening of the ferry's bow doors was the signal that most people took to start their engines. Arthur turned the ignition key. Nothing. He tried again. The same.

'Strange?' He said to himself.

He sat back in his seat and built a mental map of the engine. He had helped strip and rebuild it after eventually getting it back from the Scottish island he'd tracked it down to—and after forensics had finished with it. He also kept it carefully maintained; out of necessity because it was so unique: there were probably only one or two mechanics who had ever looked under the bonnet of a Munter, let alone actually taken a spanner to one.

Arthur decided the problem was probably electrical. He stepped out of the car as the row of cars to his left started to pull out. He lifted the bonnet and peered in, looking at the engine for anything that might give him a clue. Nothing obvious. At the first inspection all leads were in place. He went round; pushing various leads and terminals to make sure they were secure.

It was while doing this he realised the starter motor cable was missing. 'Strange? I wonder how that came off. What was even stranger was the fact that the nut was still on the retaining bolt, so there was no way it could have come off accidentally. He took a spanner from the toolbox in the boot, reached into the box of spares he needed to carry and found an old battery lead. It was longer than the starter lead, but the same thickness. Arthur got it to fit comfortably using a couple of washers out of his toolbox. After a final check to make sure it was secure he tried to start the engine again. Success! A few seconds later the Munter was purring perfectly.

'That was easy!' He said, revving the engine to confirm it was OK. But he was still puzzled as to how, or more importantly why, the cable had been taken. What Arthur had failed to notice was that not only was there a lead missing, but two wires had been swapped—Icarus thought they might help disable the car, in fact they just disabled the engine immobiliser and alarm.

While Arthur sorted out the Munter, the cars behind had been pulling out and driving around him. By the time he'd finished there was still one lane to clear. As soon as it was considered safe for him to join the line, a steward in a fluorescent green tabard waved him forward. The Munter bumped up onto the exit ramp, cruised down towards the passport control and Customs and drove through without stopping, out into the cool evening air. At the first sight of a French road sign Arthur felt relaxed. He now felt as if he was really taking a break. He thought about his route—it was only half-past-four, his timing was perfect. He wasn't as tired as he thought he would be, so he reckoned he'd be able to manage a good few hours drive to get him on his way.

Arthur needed to get some fuel for the car, and for himself—he was feeling a bit peckish. He thought about driving into Calais but decided that it would probably be easier to pull into a supermarket—he liked browsing around the gorgeous food on offer. He could pick up some cheese, dried sausage, of course some lovely fresh bread—and maybe some wine for later. With this in mind, Arthur aimed towards the Cité de l'Europe, just ten minutes down the road.

As Arthur parked the Munter, back at the port Eve was still waiting in the pickup. All the traffic seemed to have left the ferry. Any moment now she expected to be called to remove a stricken vehicle. Fifteen minutes later, no call. Twenty-five, and still no call. She got out of the pick-up and walked to where she could get a better view. Nothing was happening. Eve telephoned Nathaniel, who was already waiting at her garage in Calais.

'How's it going?'

'Nowt.'

'What do you mean, "nowt"?'

'Why as in nowt! Nothing! Rien, de nada! I'm sittin' here and there's nowt happenin'. I've had no calls, and it looks like everything's off the ferry.'

'But it can't be. I mean… are you sure? Maybe they're having problems?'

'Naah! They'll be loadin' soon. There can't be 'owt on there. I'll stay here ferra bit longer, maybe another ten or fifteen minutes, but then I'm coming back. I'll see you later.'

'What's up?' Icarus was slightly the worse for wear, but he could see the concern on Nathaniel's face.

'Nowt!'

'Oh that's all right then. For a minute there I thought...'

'No, I mean nowt as in nothing. Eve hasn't got anything. She's on her way back.'

'That's impossible! It must be there!' Icarus began to get a premature hangover.

'Are you sure you scuppered it?'

'Of course, I mean...'

'What, Icarus?'

'Well, it was a diesel engine, but I took off the cable to the starter motor, and chucked it overboard with the tools and stuff. There's no way it would have started without that. And I switched some wires, just to make sure.'

'Sounds fine, but where's the car? I mean, there's no other way he could have got it going is there?'

'No chance! That kind of cable's not something you'd have lying around.'

'Fuck!' Nathaniel started to rack his brain for a possible solution.

'Maybe...' Icarus started...

'What?'

'Well... maybe he decided not to get off. Maybe he's gone back on the same ferry. I mean, if you think about it, it's a pretty unusual car, so maybe the guy didn't want to risk being stuck in France. Maybe he, or she, decided to go back instead.'

Nathaniel thought about this. It was a distinct possibility. 'You've got to go back then, on that same ferry.'

'Me! Why me dude?'

'Why not?'

'Aw, come on dude! I've only just got here. I was looking forward to going out on the town tonight. Saturday night. Bit of clubbing, casual sex, you know…'

'Don't you think this is just a little more important! Don't you realise what's at stake here?'

Icarus stayed quiet. He was pissed off, but he saw the point. Nathaniel however, realised that he'd quite like to go back himself. There wasn't much he could do in Calais.

'Look, OK, you stay here and I'll go back, but I'm going to have to leave right now or I'll miss the damned ferry. See if you can find out anything. Find out what's going on! Why is everything so…' Nathaniel was getting goose bumps as the enormity of what might be happening began to crawl through his body.

Icarus wondered where he would start: 'Well dude, I mean I'll give it a go, but I don't see what I can do. I mean if the car's not on the ferry now, where the fuck is it? How am I supposed to find it? It could be miles away. The guy could be hammering down towards Nice, or Strasbourg, or even up to Belgium or Germany or anywhere.'

Both men stood thinking for a few minutes, eventually Icarus said: 'Look dude, I'm not one for logic, as you know, but look at this logically: Eve didn't see the car; the starter cable's at the bottom of the Channel—so the car's gotta be on the ferry?'

'OK, OK, I'll find out soon enough I suppose. But you stay here and look around anyway, just in case. Maybe he's spending the day in Calais, shopping or something; check out the hypermarket car parks—anything! I'll call you from the ferry. Give my love to Evey when she gets back, tell her I'll call soon.' And with that, Nathaniel left Eve's garage and left Icarus wondering what the hell he was going to do. Even though it wasn't his fault, he couldn't help feeling guilty.

15: The travels of scooter boy (iii)

Tadeuz had a heavy heart. He'd asked around but couldn't find anyone who could help him in the way he'd paid to be helped. Before he'd left Ukraine he'd paid up-front to get into England. He'd been told that all he had to do was make his own way to Calais and call a number. The number turned out to be a veterinary surgery, and they insisted that the only passports they gave were for pets. Tadeuz realised that he'd been ripped off. The visa, the ferry crossing, the hotel in London he'd been promised as a home, the job on a building site—it was all lies. His trip was wasted, as was his money. He curled up for the night beside his scooter, frustrated, his mind curled around different ways of revenge. But revenge meant going home and he didn't want to do that, he'd come this far, there had to be a way to cross the last few kilometres. The next morning he walked around the streets of Calais. Hearing a familiar language amongst all the unfamiliar languages, he stopped to say hello. One acquaintance led to another, and before long he had learned from Albanians, Chinese, Kurds, North Africans and a variety of other nationalities about all the ways there were of getting into England, all you needed was the right amount of money. He heard stories about those who had been successful, and those who hadn't. And about those who'd died or got injured trying.

After more than two weeks travelling between Calais, Boulogne, Ostend and Dunkirk, Tadeuz was back in Calais again, broke and despondent. His scooter was nearly out of fuel. He realised that he was stuck and that, for now at least, his dream was out of reach. Angry and frustrated, He knew he had to return home. And he promised he would take the revenge that had been fermenting in his frustration. However, that was later; first he took something else—purely on a whim.

There was something about this ugly sports car that he couldn't resist. It was purely the sight of it that inspired his reasoning, and his reasoning inspired his actions: If he was going home, he would go in some kind of style. It took him a few minutes to open the door, lift the bonnet and get the engine running. He was good with machines and this engine reminded him of a Russian tractor. It even ran on diesel, which Tadeuz thought was strange for a sports car. The Cyrillic script on the various labels and the engine confirmed its origin. It was a Russian car, but Tadeuz had never seen anything like it, not even in books. The chrome letters across the front of the polished black bonnet read 'Munter'. Tadeuz knew a lot about cars and trucks, but he'd had never heard of this one.

There wasn't much luggage inside, just a single bag containing a few clothes. He wondered if he could sell them for anything, but doubted it. He knew he could sell the iPod though, and there were some CDs lying around. He could probably raise enough to buy a length of plastic pipe and a fuel can. He felt guilty about leaving his beloved scooter as he jumped into the Munter and shifted it into gear. He stopped twice on the way out of Calais: once to sell the CDs to one of his new-found 'friends', he decided to keep the iPod, it might be useful later; his second stop was to buy the fuel can. He found a piece of tube sticking out of a rubbish skip at the side of the road. Then, driven by fear and adrenaline, he travelled for two days, siphoning diesel from parked trucks to keep him going back across Belgium, Germany and Poland.

Tadeuz drove to the Ukrainian border, where he was worried about losing the car because he had no money to bribe customs. He only got through because the officers were arguing fiercely with each other about who should take the iPod Tadeuz had given them. They waved him through as the horns of the traffic behind began to blow. Totally exhausted, he finally reached home.

His mother took one look at her skinny son and led him to a bed on which he collapsed and slept for thirty-six hours. His brother Lenny took one look at the car and decided to sell it. Within half-an-hour of Tadeuz falling asleep, Lenny had put on his best sunglasses and was on his way to Kiev at the wheel of the Munter.

16: One man's loss

Arthur was feeling very happy and relaxed as he left the hypermarket. His carrier bag contained exactly what he fancied: some fresh bread, a selection of cheeses and meats and some washed salad. He'd also picked up a few bottles of wine to give to Lytt and Nancy. He was looking forward to a tasty snack in the car, then a pleasant drive for a couple of hours through the French countryside to their place. He'd stay for one night then head off on his adventure. He'd been thinking about where, and decided the rugged hills of the southwest. There were some lovely roads around the mountains south of Clermont Ferrand; then the gentle countryside south of Toulouse; maybe then across to Collioure, or maybe the other way to Biarritz instead. He was enjoying exploring his options as he wove his way through the hypermarket car park back to the car.

He reached the spot where he thought the Munter was parked but there was just an empty space with an old grey scooter lying on its side nearby. He wasn't worried, he thought that maybe he had the wrong aisle, something that was easy to do in this place where everything looked the same. It was also late Saturday afternoon, so the car park was very busy. He wandered up and down several aisles, at first optimistically, but the longer he searched, the more sick and anxious he became. He just kept coming back to that same spot. He looked around, trying to get his bearings from the limited landmarks that were available—lamp-posts, the trolley bay, a pedestrian crossing. This had to be the place. He walked up and down a bit more. But nothing. Again he ended up back at the scooter. His instincts were screaming something he didn't want to hear. Inevitably ice-cold realisation washed over him, making his skin prickle. He froze as he realised the Munter was gone.

'Shit!' was the only word he could think of. His stomach churned, his throat tightened and tears began to blur his vision. He tried to swallow but his mouth was dry as he turned and ran back into the shopping centre. The sooner he could find someone in uniform, the better.

*

A gendarme, or any type of policeman was the last thing the two figures in the large silver van wanted to see. They pulled up in the spot previously occupied by the Munter. The cab doors opened simultaneously and two men jumped out, gold chains rattling as they moved. They were on their way to stock up with cigarettes and alcohol to sell at a pre-arranged meeting on a car park next to a busy A-road just outside Thurrock. One of the men saw Tadeuz's scooter lying on its side, obviously abandoned.

'Ere, Davey-boy! What do you fackin' reckon to this?'

'Erm, looks like a fackin' scooter.'

'I ain't fackin' stupid. I can see it's a fackin' scooter, but what kind of scooter?'

'Dunno. But then I ain't yer fackin' scooter expert am I? What's that? Some kind of fackin' East-Europe plate?'

'Could be. What's it fackin' doing lyin' there?'

'Dunno mate. Maybe it belonged to one of them fackin' asylum seekers. It looks as though it's been chucked. 'Ere, it's like one of them fackin, retro things what yer sees in the West End. Bit of a clean up and it might look fackin' cool.'

'Maybe. It's a weird lookin' facker though. Yer could be sure no other facker would 'ave one!'

'Would any facker want one!' They both laughed.

'No seriously though, it could be worth sammink, to a fackin' collector like,'

'You reckon?'

'Yeah! Fackin' dead right! On that fackin' Ebay! Get it on there, some facker'd buy it.'

'You fackin' reckon?'

'Yeah! I'm fackin' tellin' you! You can sell anything on there. It's like them fackin' Trabants—they go for a fackin' fortune.'

'What's a Trabant? Some kind of fackin' tropical fish?'

'Naaaah mate! It's like a Reliant Robin, but wiv four fackin' wheels—like a proper car.'

'Never heard of 'em.'

'That fackin' bloke out of U fackin' 2 drives one.'

'Fackin' naaah!'

'Fackin' right mate! Their dead trendy.'

'So what'ya fackin' saying, that we should take this

fackin' thing back to fackin' England?'

'Why fackin' not?'

'It'll take up valuable fackin' booze space fer one fing.'

'So fackin' what! We come over here every fackin' week anyway! Call yourself an entre-fackin'-prenewer?'

'OK. Let's stick it in the fackin' van...'

*

Arthur felt sick. He'd given his statement to the police, who seemed to be casually optimistic. What they needed was a photo of the Munter, which Arthur didn't have with him. He'd been meaning to put together a website for some time, detailing the history of the car—how it originated and how he'd restored it, but he hadn't got round to it. It would have been handy now, but he'd never banked on the car ever being stolen, especially from a supermarket car park in France. Arthur considered it to be unfair to have your car stolen at the beginning of a holiday. He was also angry, the Munter didn't belong to anyone else, it was his. He had researched it, rescued it, arranged and paid for it to be transported all the way down from a remote Scottish Island. He'd spent months helping restore it: stripping everything down, cleaning, repairing, replacing. Just finding the parts needed took a massive amount of dedication, and money. The end result was something that Arthur felt belonged to him. He owned it as much as anyone can ever own something not actually connected to their own body. Whoever had taken it didn't understand what it was, or what it meant, they would never appreciate the amount of love and care put into it. Arthur realised he was more angry than upset. Not furiously angry, but indignantly angry.

'Ownership should be absolute,' thought Arthur. 'At least until you lose faith or interest in it. People have got no right to take things. It's not as if it's an essential, like a loaf of bread or something that you can forgive someone for.' After considerable deliberation while waiting to be interviewed by the police, Arthur decided that it was probably OK to steal out of necessity, but there should be a ban on stealing the tools of a person's trade, or their best car.

It was a mystery why the alarm and immobiliser hadn't worked. The police seemed to think that it was a professional job—they were as helpful as they could be, given the circumstances. They took the registration number and a description and promised to make their officers alert and aware. Arthur was told there had been a string of thefts from the car park over recent weeks, mostly luxury sports cars and four by fours, and until now none had been recovered. The feeling was that they were being smuggled into Eastern Europe, probably loaded onto trucks. It was highly organised: the new EC members had opened new supply routes to countries that had otherwise been landlocked from European borders.

'Perr'aps ze most likely destinations are Russia, ze Ukraine, Latvia or Azerbaijan, alzough Armenia eezun't totally out of ze question. Of course eet could joost be—'ow you say: les joyriders,'

'Where the fuck is Azerbaijan? If you'll pardon my French…' Arthur was beyond despondency.

Two hours later, and Arthur walked forlornly out into the streets of Calais wondering what to do. The theft had knocked all the wind out of his sails. He knew the insurance company would provide him with a car and other expenses to get him on his way, but he didn't much feel like carrying on. He decided that the best thing to do was to head back home. He decided to stay in Calais for the evening. It was late anyway, and he was tempted by the thought of a fish restaurant and a glass of wine or two by way of consolation. He still clutched the bags of food and wine he'd bought earlier, but they didn't seem to hold the pleasure they had several hours ago. He would sort out a hire car when he got to Dover in the morning. First though, he had to call Lytt to tell him he wouldn't be arriving. Strangely, he didn't want to say it was because the Munter had been stolen. He didn't understand why he couldn't tell him. He just didn't want to talk about it. It was as if bringing out into the open would make it too painfully real, like changing the dressing on a fresh wound.

'Hi Lytt, it's Arthur.'

'Arthur! Where are you? What time are you arriving?'

'Aah, well... the thing is, I'm not.'

'Yeah! Right! What time do you get here?'

'Seriously! I'm not coming.'

'Arthur, I'm not falling for that, so stop messing around...'

'I'm not messing around Lytt, honest. I... well I think I've eaten something. I feel really lousy.'

'What you're serious? So where are you? In Manchester?'

'No, Calais. But I'm going back. I don't feel too good. It might be a bug and I don't want to spread it around.'

As soon as he said 'Calais', Arthur wished he hadn't lied. It made him sound pathetic that he was going back after actually getting to France.

'But Arthur we were looking forward to you, we haven't seen you for ages. We've even got a little party planned. Nancy will be really disappointed.

Arthur felt guilty, but just couldn't face a crowd of revellers: 'I'm really sorry. I'd love to be there. But I think it's best if I go back home and rest for a couple of days.'

'But you're a strange one Arthur! You've done most of the journey! Just come! We'll take care of you. You can rest here. We've got all kinds of things in the medicine cabinet to perk you up!'

'That's very kind, but all I need is a paracetamol, and besides…'

'Oh come on Arthur! You won't have to do any renovation work, I promise. You don't have to do any drugs either. You can just relax, laze around, take it easy. I mean it's your birthday, apart from anything else…'

'It's not my birthday until next week!' Arthur was getting a bit fed up of correcting people.

'Well there you go! You'll be better by then. Fit to party!'

Lytton was tenacious, and obviously not prepared to accept what Arthur could now see was a lame excuse. He realised that there was only one thing to do.

'Look, Lytton, the thing is, I'm feeling sick because… it's the Munter, it's been stolen.'

There was silence. 'Lytton?'

'I'm here… Tell me you're joking… Are you serious?'

Lytton sounded genuinely concerned.

'Come on Lytt, do you really think I'd joke about something like this?'

Nancy had obviously been listening, and after a quick word with Lytton, took the phone. 'Hi Arthur, it's Nance—that's terrible. How? When? Where from?'

'Don't know. A couple of hours ago. Calais. I only stopped to get some wine to bring, and a few nibbles. I should've kept on driving.'

'Yes you should have Arthur, you know we always have too much food and drink here anyway.'

'Well you know I don't like to arrive empty-handed. But I'm really, really pissed off about it, and I wouldn't be any kind of company there. Apart from anything else I'm furious about it.'

'I don't blame you.'

'I'd rather go home and see what I can sort out. At least I'll feel as though I'm doing something.'

'OK. I understand, I guess. But we'll miss you.'

'Thanks. I'm sorry. And I feel really guilty, honest.'

'Don't! Please don't. You do what you must. We'll let you off providing you promise to come soon. Promise?'

'I promise,' he said, with as much enthusiasm as he could muster in his deflated state.

'Take care of yourself.'

'Thanks Nance. Send my love to everyone.'

Arthur put the phone down, and as foolish as he felt, the tears began to roll.

17: Hacked off

Nathaniel had managed to catch the 'Spirit of Dunkirk' back to Dover. It was the same ship on which he'd made the outward journey. He made sure he was the first foot passenger to disembark and he hung around until all the traffic had cleared the ship. But there was no sign of the car. It was impossible to miss, which is why he'd picked it in the first place. He felt like an idiot, and was thinking that maybe Icarus had been right—they could have simply carried the diamonds over in a plastic carrier bag; nobody would have given them a second glance. He could kick himself. Of course everything had gone relatively smoothly up until now, but he should have taken the rusty white van incident as an omen.

'Stupid! Stupid! Stupid!' He said to himself, as he walked towards customs. He was still chastising himself as he walked casually through the green aisle.

'Excuse me sir...' the female customs officer beckoned him over. Nathaniel was initially shocked, but couldn't help noticing how attractive she was: attractive in a small, serious, uniformed kind of way. He was a little out of practise, but he could have sworn there was a hint of flirtatiousness, and not only from himself.

Perversely, it made him feel better that he'd been questioned and searched. He felt that his smuggling methods weren't too excessive. But he was a professional: he knew he'd made a mess of things and knew he had nobody else to blame but himself. He should have anticipated everything as he usually did. Planned things carefully down to the n-nth detail. He realised his mind had be all over the place recently: 'You can't afford to slip in this business. Not for a second,' he thought, as he climbed into his car for the drive back home. He hadn't noticed the folded note that had been slipped into his pocket by a certain small, serious, and very cute uniformed customs officer.

Nathaniel's mind was still churning as he drove. He was thinking about Sandra, and realised that he wasn't looking forward to going home. He began to think about their relationship. They were more like flatmates than partners. He began to wonder whether she was happy. All she seemed to do was shop, go to the gym and spend evenings with 'the girls'—a coven of companions who, when they got together, could sink chardonnay like it was going out of fashion. Nathaniel was lonely. What he wasn't getting out of the relationship was love. There was hardly any sex either. When it happened, it was cursory and they were each generally at least half a bottle of wine numbed. He tried to think when they'd last done it, but couldn't remember. He was sure she wasn't having an affair; then sadly realised that he almost wished she was. 'We've changed. But I wonder who's changed more?' He thought. He realised he was probably quieter these days, less physical. But maybe that was the nature of the relationship. He tried to remember a time when he had been number one in Sandra's eyes, but couldn't. He compiled a list in his head as he drove: First was shopping; second was nights with the girls; third was her nail business… Fourth? Being number four was bad enough: he gave up.

As he headed up the M20, Nathaniel realised he had to face up to what had been distracting him for weeks, if not months. Reality wasn't going to disappear, no matter how hard he wished it would—there was some kind of peace in denial, but not the quiet kind. Now, however, he understood that he had no choice. What was a whisper was now a scream. Sandra didn't care about him. He had become a habit, they had become a habit. But he also realised that he didn't love her. He told her many times that he did, but even that was a habit, like the flowers he occasionally bought her. He didn't love her and she didn't love him. They had simply slipped into a comfortable rut that was easier to stay in that get out of.

It was the contrast of taking up smuggling again that had shaped everything into perspective. He felt alive when he was working. It was a part of him that he shouldn't have to deny; that he couldn't deny. He'd given it up for Sandra years ago, and was happy to. She was exciting, their relationship was exciting. He remembered looking down at her blonde hair as she was giving him a blow-job in the kitchen not long after they met, and deciding then that he didn't need anything else in his life, she fulfilled it all. But somewhere along the line the relationship had faded. There was no specific time, no reason—no affairs or arguments, no major bust-ups, it had just drifted gently into a routine. More than that, it was boring: the killer.

As Nathaniel approached the M25 junction where he needed take the anti-clockwise route for the Dartford tunnel and the road home, he realised he had to make a decision: he could either turn left and back to Sandra, their designer flat, her forty pairs of designer jeans and innumerable sunglasses, or he could keep on going. If he didn't turn off now, he knew he would never go back. The decision turned out to be no decision at all. He drove straight past the junction and headed down the A20 into London. He felt lighter, like the pressure in his head had been released. He knew instantly that however it had happened, he was doing the right thing. His body started to shiver slightly in a mixture of nervousness and excitement. Possibilities began to flit wildly through his mind. Where would he go? What would he do? Where could he go? What could he do? He began to have flashes about what he was leaving behind. Pangs of regret. Cruelly, his mind was recalling images of the way he and Sandra were when they were first together. Especially the sex, which had been fabulous back then. But rationality fought back and Nathaniel realised that what he was leaving had already gone. The shivering started to subside.

He pulled into the next service station to call Icarus.

'Hi, how's it going?'

Icarus sounded pissed off: 'Terrible dude. Nothing. I've checked the hypermarkets, the main hotels, everywhere, but absolutely zilch! What about you? Please tell me you've called to tell me it was on the ferry?'

'I wish I could, but no, nothing. I waited around in Dover until the ferry was empty. Don't ask me where the bugger went. Just vanished into thin air.'

'So what are we gonna do?'

'To be honest, at the moment, I'm not sure. The best thing you can do is come back and we'll think about it. Oh, by the way, I got stopped at Customs on the way back, would you believe it!'

'Ha! You're joking?'

'No, seriously! Searched and everything.'

'Well there you go then. You don't sound too bothered about it though?'

'No. Well it wasn't as if I had anything to declare. Come to think of it, she was pretty cute. As in pretty and cute—but I'll tell you all about it later…' Nathaniel voice dropped as he tried to think of how to put into words what he'd been thinking about.

'What?' Icarus asked.

'What you do mean 'what'?' Nathaniel replied.

'Well you went all quiet man. What's up?'

'Nothing…'

'No, no, no! You're always doing this, dude! That nothing that means something! What is it? You're making me ponnie.'

'Making you what?'

'Ponnie. You know dude—uneasy, paranoid, uncomfortable, edgy, nervous…'

'OK! I get the picture.'

'So? Are you going to tell me what?'

'Well, I wondered if I can sling my hammock with you

for a few days?'

'No problems, why? Is something up?'

'No, not really.'

'Aaah!' There was a note of realisation in Icarus's voice.

'What do you mean "aaah!"?'

'I mean aaaah! You're leaving her!'

'I just need some space for a while, to sort things out.'

'Naah! I know you; you've left her haven't you? You'll never go back. It's cool, dude. Of course you can stay, as it's all in a good cause—leaving Mrs Makeover.'

'Don't call her that, her name's Sandra! And she's a sweet woman.'

'Yeah dude! Candyfloss is sweet too, but no good for you.'

Nathaniel felt guilty for feeling happy. He also felt guilty at the prospect of turning everything upside-down, then wondered if it really would. Sandra could keep the hotel, her salon—and there was always enough money.

'Let's face it, you only get one life', Nathaniel said aloud, as he drove around the South Circular towards London.

*

Monday morning and Nathaniel is sitting at a kitchen table covered with a plastic tablecloth. Icarus is grilling a mountain of bacon and dropping bread into the toaster, yanking down the lever irritably.

'Who the fuck carries a spare starter motor lead with them?' Icarus was miserable and going over the possibilities. Even though it wasn't his fault, he couldn't help but feel guilty.

'A car enthusiast, that's who. I should have thought

harder before picking that bloody car! It just seemed right at the time. In future no old sports cars of any make or nationality. In fact no classic cars at all!' Nathaniel was blaming himself. 'In fact no cars at all. And no white vans. Maybe we should rethink things. I mean, in theory it was a good plan, but in reality it's far too messy and… well, there's got to be a better way. I mean, it's not as if we're even suspected of lifting them in the first place.'

'That's what I've been saying all along. But come on dude! Don't beat yourself up about it. Anyway, I've been searched before and you got searched on the way back, so let's chill on it all a bit OK. Look dude, I'll admit that I thought it was all a bit OTT before, but in principle it's a sound plan, and it's worked so far, sort of, if you don't count the last two times.'

'Sound? It's hard to see what else could have gone wrong! Let's get real about this: The first time was OK; the second time we nearly lost out because we were dealing with a pair of idiots driving a shit-heap; now we've got millions of quids' worth of diamonds running around Europe somewhere, and we don't know where. It's a bloody farce!'

'Well you've been a bit distracted lately.' Icarus slapped the bacon onto the toast, decorated it with a squirt of brown sauce and dropped the plate in front of Nathaniel. 'There you go man, get your big gob around that!'

'Brown sauce? On bacon?'

'Of course! What else?'

'Red?'

'Don't be stupid! Red is for chips and hot dogs.' Icarus rolled his eyes at Nathaniel's ignorance about something so fundamental.

'If you say so, you're the expert.' Nathaniel bit into his sandwich, chewed slowly as his mind worked through the past few days. He swallowed, and sipped from his coffee. 'I guess I have been a bit distracted, but everything's going to change now. In fact I've got a feeling it's already started.'

'Have you called her yet?'

'No. Not yet. But I will—eventually, I just need a bit of time to get back to myself a bit.'

'Won't she worry that you've stayed out for a few days?'

'I doubt it. She probably won't even notice I'm not there if you want the truth.'

'Come on, she's bound to notice!'

'Not really. She'd be more upset if she lost a credit card.'

'Ouch!'

'You can laugh, but it's true!' Nathaniel took another large bite from his bacon sandwich. 'This is good!' he said, muffled, 'but it needs red sauce'.

'So what are we going to do? We haven't got much to go on?' Icarus asked after breakfast. 'I'm guessing we're still going to try and get the diamonds back?'

'Of course! We've got to. But like you say, we don't have much of a clue. We don't know where the car went; we don't know where it came from. I don't even know the make. I mean, I don't think I've ever seen anything like it before. We don't even know the registration number. How stupid is that!'

'MUN 05', the numbers rolled off Icarus's tongue a casually as saying his own name.

'What?' Nathaniel looked straight at Icarus.

'MUN 05, that's what was what was on each end of the car.

'Why didn't you say you remembered the number plate?' Nathaniel had perked up for the first time all day.

'You never asked me for it dude. It's not like it was that difficult to remember. Besides, what use is it?'

'What use is it? Why none at all...unless you've got a friend who's in the police force who owes you a favour, or you know someone who might be able to hack into the DVLA computer! No bloody use at all!'

'So you've got a friend who works for the feds?' Icarus, asked.

'If you mean the police, then no... well yes, but I'm a bit loathed to ask him anything to be honest. He'll be suspicious. He's not necessarily a good cop, but he's a bloody good policeman—if you know what I mean. If he sussed that there might something in it for him he'd be hanging around like a dog at a dinner table, so he's a last resort only. But I do know someone who might be able to hack into the DVLA computer...'

'Who?!' Icarus asked, his voice failing to disguise that he was pissed off, hacking into computers was strictly his own domain. Nathaniel looked at him with a: 'you idiot, you should know better' look. Icarus felt like an idiot and that he should have known better. 'Oh, me! Well, I, erm, suppose I could give it a go dude. Ain't gonna be easy but it's got to be worth a shot.' Icarus loved this kind of challenge.

'So, let's get to it! Where's the computer? Your bedroom?'

'Aah, well, if it's OK I'd like to sort it out on my own dude,' Icarus said, suddenly slightly panicked. He didn't allow anyone into his room. 'You know. It may take some time, besides, it's really boring to watch. I've got to get into it—it's like a different mindset thing, you know, plugging myself into a whole different weird, wired world. Anyway, I need to guard my secrets.' Icarus was actually thinking more about the state of his bedroom, which was a catastrophe of leisure, and the various porn sites still on screen from earlier that morning.

'Fair enough. I'll leave you to it. I need to go out and buy a few bits and pieces—I've got nothing except the clothes I'm standing in.'

*

'It's crazy! Bloody insane! I should write to someone!' Of course there was no way that Icarus could write to anybody about his current indignation, which was over the ease with which he had hacked into the DVLA computer and retrieved the address details for the current owner of something called a 'Munter Drophead' registration number: MUN 05, colour: Black; one previous owner. His indignation wasn't raised because this particular computer and its many security devices were easy to crack—they weren't easy; it was the fact that he had managed to crack it at all. Secretly he hoped to one-day find a computer or system he couldn't hack or crack, but so far he hadn't found one. He was indignant at cracking the DVLA computer, but he would be genuinely pissed off when he found that the information it contained was wrong.

18: A packet of custard creams

Of all the places the car could have been registered to, Peckham was probably not the first one that Icarus would have guessed at. He lived in Brixton, so it was only a bus ride away across south east London. It was early afternoon and a nice sunny day, so Icarus decided to go himself, rather than wait for Nathaniel who was still out shopping. There was a bus every few minutes, and the journey was no more than three miles but it took almost forty minutes: 'I could have walked it faster,' Icarus thought.

His suspicions were raised even further when he walked into the council estate. There was row of garages, one open and serving as a covered fly-tip, complete with a rotting mattress, upturned shopping trolley, piles of wet cardboard and black refuse bags, and flies. Other garages were closed and protected with anti-ram barriers, padlocks and metal security bars. All of them were covered in graffiti from the inanely obscene to the wildly artistic. There were also cars parked nearby, all almost new, expensive and sporty. Something Icarus hadn't banked on was the car belonging to someone from a south-east London posse. He felt decidedly nervous. It was one thing buying drugs from them, something else to try and get information out of them. The tenement block was typical of council estates in south east London: red brick and concrete around a large paved communal area containing optimistic patches of grass on which children played and bull terriers shat. Icarus looked around and decided that he definitely did not want to knock casually on someone's door and ask them if they had a weird-looking sports car, and if so could he please remove several million quid's worth of diamonds that had somehow become attached to it while it was on the Dover-to-Calais car ferry.

Icarus thought he'd simply find the house, or—as it seemed more likely—the flat, see what it looked like and maybe catch a glimpse of the owner. He had passing thoughts about a stakeout, but decided that this wasn't the kind of place he'd like to be staked out in. He was particularly nervous about a group of teenagers hanging around near a stairwell on the other side of the block. They were all wearing hoodies and gloves, so it was impossible to see any skin, just the occasional flash of the white of an eye. They looked like creatures of the night, waiting for darkness to fall. 'Maybe they're allergic to sunlight, or they could simply be zombies', Icarus muttered, nervously.

When he found the flat, it was the state of it that made him decide to knock. The windows were filthy: one broken pane had been taped up with brown packaging tape. The door was that special colour that only local authorities do well—impossible to tell whether it was blue, green or grey, also peeling and layered with grime. The flat was on the ground floor, with a small area enclosed with concrete bricks that served as some kind of garden. All it contained were lots of polystyrene fast-food containers dumped by the wind, an empty five-litre paint can, and an invalid scooter propped up on bricks with the wheels missing.

'Hmm!' Said Icarus, as he knocked on the door. The noise attracted the attention of the zombies, who looked over, faceless under their hoods. There was no answer. He knocked again, aware of the eyes upon him.

He was ready to give up and go, when he heard some shuffling from inside. It took more than three minutes for the shuffling to reach the door.

'Hello?' Said a frail voice from the other side.

'Hello?' Icarus replied.

'What d'yer want? We ain't got naffin''

'It's all right sir, I don't want nothin', just to ask you a couple of questions.'

'Well you can arsk 'em from there. I ain't openin' the door. Yer carn't be too careful these days.'

'No I agree. You keep yourself safe.'

'Fifty year I've lived 'ere. Fifty year! An' I ain't movin' nar!'

'It's alright Mr Pump. I only wanted to ask you if you have a car?'

'Caancil!'

'What?'

'Caancil! Me name's Caancil.'

'Sorry? Mr Cansil'

'Naa! Not Censil, Caaansil!'

'Council!'

'Yuhr! That's wot are said, di'n't are? Yer deaf yang-un?'

'Sorry, Mr Council. I just wondered if you had a car?'

'Used ter 'ave. 'ad a Ford Pop'lar, then a Morris Moina…'

'So you don't have one now?'

'Vox'aw!'

'You've got a Vauxhall?' Icarus asked, positive by now that this was not his man.

'Naaaa! Sowd it ter a blowk in Vox'aw—sixty foive!.'

'What? The bloke was sixty five?' Icarus just wanted to get out of this now.

'Naaa! Got sixty foive quid for it.'

'OK. Fine. Right then. Sorry to have bothered you.'

'Naa bovver mate—got ter go naa though, Caant'daan's on in arf-an-aar, an' I got ter get back ter me settee. Are down't serpawse yer 'ave any biskits on yer?'

'No sorry mate.'

'Jast fort are'd arsk.'

Icarus suddenly felt scared of growing old. He walked to a shop on the corner, it was completely boarded up and there was wire mesh over the boards. Faded fluorescent paper signs announced: 'Cheap Booze', 'Cut-price Cigs', 'Top-ups', 'DVD-Rental'. Inside the shop everything was on display behind shatterproof plastic panels. Icarus bought a packet of custard creams—figuring it would fit through a letterbox easily.

19: The queen of Mayfair

Arthur was miserable. He couldn't relax at home. He hadn't been able to sleep properly and he hadn't bothered with breakfast. He picked up a magazine to read, but couldn't concentrate for more than a couple of sentences. Even music provided no escape from the twisted, empty feeling he had inside. He'd already called the police in Manchester and given them all the details, but they admitted that there wasn't much they could do. He thought about phoning Ronnie to tell him the bad news, but didn't feel like speaking to anyone. In the end he decided to go into the studio. 'At least there's stuff I can do at work,' he thought. He'd been meaning to clear up for ages, and pottering about was just about all he thought he could manage. 'It will keep me occupied if nothing else.'

He arrived at work just before midday. The answering machine was flashing, but Arthur couldn't be bothered taking messages. 'I'm on holiday!' He shouted at it. He half-heartedly started to clear up—there were piles of paper that needed sorting, he also had to do his VAT and other admin stuff he'd put off because they were jobs he disliked.

He sat down at his computer, kicked it into life, and logged onto the internet. A quick glance through the titles of his emails showed nothing of interest. He started to browse around. Looking for pictures of the Munter—there were a few cursory mentions, plus a bad black and white picture on an American site of 'rare' automobiles. The site obviously hadn't been updated for at least five years. He read the day's news, and had an idle flick through eBay in case there was anything interesting being offered. At the back of his mind was a vague thought that the Munter might turn up on it. There was nothing. He looked in the weird stuff section, but even that was boring; although the auction of a single flip-flop and a string vest brought a momentary smile to his face, especially as there were two days to go and there had already been twenty-one bids. There was also a scooter, which looked very similar to the one that had been laying close to where the Munter had been stolen from. Arthur gave it a second glance but no more.

What Arthur needed was sympathy. If Sara had been around he could have called her. She wouldn't have been that sympathetic, but at least she would have pretended—and that would have been enough. She understood men. Absent-mindedly Arthur called Ronnie's mobile.

'Bonjour mate! How's France?'

'I'm not in France.'

'Where are you then?'

'In the office.'

'Doesn't sound like much of a holiday?'

'It wasn't.'

'What happened? I mean, why are you back?'

'Well, after I spoke to you on Friday, I went to this wedding reception party thing up in Derbyshire somewhere. Which was interesting. Then on Saturday I drove down to Calais. And on Saturday evening, someone nicked my car from a hypermarket car park.' Arthur felt choked again as he struggled to get the words out.

'Bastards! That's terrible! Someone's nicked M?' 'M' was what Ronnie called the Munter, mainly because his wife didn't like him calling it the Munter, because it sounded rude she said.

'Yes. Bastards.'

'Have you reported it?'

'Of course I've reported it, here and in France. Not much they can do though.'

'Bugger, sorry—it's difficult to know what to say. What about the insurance?'

'Oh there's nothing they can do yet, we have to wait to see whether it turns up or not. But that's not the point, I don't what the money. I want my car back.'

'Well I'm sorry mate. Really. I know how much the old thing means to you.'

'Cheers Ronnie. Look, I'm free all week, so if you fancy getting together one evening...'

'No problems mate. I'll have a word with Vix and give you a ring.'

'OK Cheers Ronnie.'

'Cheers Arthur. Call me if there's anything I can do.'

'Cheers.'

'Oh! Before you go Arthur!'

Arthur was just about to hang up: 'Sorry, what?'

'I just wondered where M had ended up?'

'I don't know. How would I know. It could be anywhere?' Arthur was puzzled at Ronnie's question.

'But I thought you installed the…' Ronnie finished his sentence, and Arthur finished it simultaneously.

'…the tracking chip! Of course! What a bloody idiot I am. I forgot all about that! Thanks Ronnie! Got to go. I'll call you back. I owe you one.' Arthur was shot with optimism as he put the phone down and furiously started to search through a file of papers that had been languishing on the floor.

He found his 'SaTrakIt' membership card, and called the company, after being warned that he was being recorded for training purposes, and after navigating his way around several complex menus via his telephone keypad, he eventually got through to a shrill-voiced girl with a Scottish accent and explained his situation.

'Aye, well you should really have let us know on Saturday, we could have done something about it then. Hang on! I'll just check whereabouts it is now. I won't be a minute… Ah yes! Well Mr Pod, it seems that we do have a signal, but unfortunately it's outside the realms of your subscription.'

'I'm sorry?'

'Well, the screen says you've only subscribed to Western Europe and the UK, so I'm afraid I can't tell you where the signal is coming from.'

'But that's ridiculous! You have the information there, but you can't give it to me?'

'I'm sorry sir, but I'm just following policy.'

Arthur realised there was no point in arguing. 'What

if I change my subscription? Can you tell me then?' There was silence on the other end of the line.

'I'm not sure about that sir, I'll have to ask my supervisor. One moment please.' More silence. 'Hello sir, thank you for holding, I've checked with my supervisor, and she said that's not possible. You can change your subscription by all means, but we can't give you any details about anything previously related to your current subscription. Stupid cow!'

'I'm sorry?'

'Well it's stupid isn't it?'

'What?' Arthur wasn't quite sure what he was hearing.

'Well, this is my first day live after a week's worth of training, and I think it's really stupid that I can see everything on screen, but I'm not allowed to tell you. What's the point of that!

'Well I agree of course...'

'And making you pay extra, well that's bloody stupid too. Especially as we still won't give you the information. Tae be honest, I've had enough. Listen, it was in Poland.'

'Poland?'

'Aye, that's what it says on my map—Poland. Then it crossed into, where's that? Ukraine is it? Aye, Ukraine, and it looks as though it's in a big town, erm...let's have a look...Kiev, Aye that's it, Kiev. Is that where the chicken comes from?'

Arthur was taken aback: 'I'm not sure... could be. You're sure about that? Kiev?'

'Well that's what the computer says, and it's supposed to be connected to some expensive satellites somewhere, beeping down a signal from somewhere, which is a bit frightening if you think about it.'

'I guess it is. But Kiev?'

'You OK mister?'

'Yes, just a bit shocked about my car, it was stolen from France. Anyway, look thanks for that. You won't get into trouble will you? Don't they usually record these conversations for training purposes?'

'Aye, I'll probably lose my job I guess, but I never wanted it in the first place, the Job Centre made me come here. But I did'nae want tae learn tae speak posh, I really want tae be a singer.'

'A singer?'

'Aye, I've been singing since I was three, would you like me to tae give y'a song? Who do'ye like? Whitney? Celine? Leona?'

'Well, I, I'm not sure…'

'Hang on, I'll have tae take ma headphones off. I cannae sing unless I'm standing.'

There was the sound of scuffling, then momentary silence, the song made the phone's earpiece crackle. It was one of those big power ballads that Arthur didn't much care for because they all sounded more-or-less the same, whether by Whitney, Celine, Leona or whoever. He could tell that this Scottish lass had some voice though—even managing the overworked diva trick of showing off an entire several-octave range in a single note.

'Get your hands off me!'

The singing had stopped and there were sounds of a different kind of scuffle, one involving several people.

'Let me go! I'll leave OK! But stop twisting ma arm!'

The voice was fading into a distance.

'You wait! I'll be famous one day! Shona McDuff—remember my name! Somebody call Simon Cowell!'

Silence.

Arthur put the phone down and clicked on the internet to study a map of eastern Europe.

Speaking to Ronnie had initially made Arthur feel a bit better. Now he was miserable again. Coupled with what the French police had said, it was almost certain that the Munter was destined to become a runabout for the east European mafia. He felt it might have been better if he didn't know where it was—just that it had simply disappeared. To know where it was and to be able to do nothing about it was frustrating, 'Ignorance really is bliss,' Arthur thought.

*

Arthur wasn't the only one frustrated. Icarus was sitting at his kitchen table, seething with enough steam to froth enough milk for a large cappuccino. He was talking to himself, although Nathaniel was standing nearby unpacking shopping bags.

'Fucking stupid people! How is it possible to be so wrong? What am I supposed to do if some fucking underpaid clerk can't input the details right. Shit in! Shit out! I've a good mind to write to someone about it.'

'Come on, we all make mistakes—what do you think of this shirt by the way?'

'Hm, it takes a real man to wear pink, nice.' He said calmly, before slipping into more vitriol: 'Mistakes, dude? This isn't just a mistake. I mean I didn't see the guy, but he sounded about a-hundred-and-eight! He could hardly walk to the front door, never mind drive to France. I doubt that he could steer a Zimmer frame, never mind a fucking sports car!'

'Maybe it's his son or something—who owns the car I mean?'

'His son would be about ninety! Trust me man, this guy is a relic. He lives on his own in a pokey little council flat. He probably wouldn't be alive without social services. And as for keeping a sports car there… I mean, don't get me wrong—there were the usual council estate drugs dealers' wheels—beemers with blacked out windows and four-wheel drive stuff. But this is not an area for classics—they'd even nicked the wheels off the old geezer's geri-scooter! And there were all these kids hanging around like the walking dead.'

'I see what you mean. What do you think of these jeans by the way? They were only fifteen quid.'

'Bargain. I mean come on! Nicking the wheels of an old guy's scooter! What's the world coming to?'

'Poor bloke.' Nathaniel was ripping price tags off the jeans.

'He doesn't need sympathy. They probably did him a favour. This guy's too old for any kind of wheels.'

'Well what about his name, surely that can't be wrong?'

'Totally bolloxed! He said his name was Mr Council, well he actually said 'Mr Caaancil'—you know in that way that ancient London people do.'

'So it's not 'Albert Pump', then?'

'Correct.'

'So who's Albert Pump, and where are our diamonds?'

Icarus shrugged, depressed.

Nathaniel put the clothes back in a large plastic carrier bag and sat down opposite Icarus.

'Well, what about the name of the car? What did you say the records said? 'Munter... Drophead. Munter Drophead, although I wouldn't put money on it being called that. I've never heard of it. It doesn't sound like a real word, maybe it's another mistake. Maybe it should be something like Mazda, or Messerschmitt or something-or-other. But Munter? What's that all about?'

'I don't have a clue. All you can do is check it out. Why don't you search around on the internet. There's bound to be something on there somewhere.'

'I'll give it a go. But I'm not optimistic.'

*

Arthur's head was hurting with the effort of thinking. The more he tried to think, the less seemed to come into his head. Even the red light on the answering machine was beginning to irritate him. He leaned over and pressed the button:

'Hello? Mr Pod? I've been given your name. I'm getting married—to Nigel and I wondered if you were free for the second week in September. That's not this year, by the way, it's in two years time. Could you call me so that I can tell you what we want and find out how much you charge. Nigel's in management accountancy, so we'd like something special. Video too. You can call me back as soon as you can, on...'

'Snapping the dead.' Arthur said, before the next

message:

'Erm, oh, a machine. Right, well, erm. I need a picture taking, and erm, I found your name in the, I think it was yellow pages, or was it the newspaper? I can't remember, anyway, erm, as you were, erm, well under, erm 'photographers', I erm, wondered if you could, I mean is that the kind of thing you, erm, do? I think it was the newspaper. Thanks.'

Arthur answered the answering machine indignantly: 'Yes! I'm a bloody photographer, of course it's what I do! But I can't take a bloody photo of you if you don't leave your bloody phone number!'

Third message: 'Mum! Mum! Are you there! Look I've decided that I'm staying here this week so you don't need to pick me up on Sunday evening because Ethan's like not going on his field trip now because there's been some problem with the visa remember I told you he was going to Mexico like for a week which would have been really exciting but now he's here for another two weeks so like I'm staying and I've got essays to write and like I thought you'd be pleased that you didn't have to like drive all the way up to Durham so anyway like I'll call you soon and love to dad and give Fritz a big cuddle from me love you bye.'

'God! Pause for breath girl! I bet you got a surprise when your mum turned up last night! ' Arthur said aloud. 'What is it today—nobody seems to have the time to even breathe any more?'

The answering machine beeped again, ready to deliver its last message. From the first word, Arthur was captivated.

All thoughts about the stolen Munter melted away. 'Hello? Oh! It's your machine, that's a shame. I was hoping to speak to Mr Arthur Pod of Pod's Photographic in person. Still, if you're not there, I can't can I? My name's Etta, I'd like you to do a portrait for me. Actually two portraits. Could you call me back when you have time? You can reach me on…'

Even though he had been preoccupied with the loss of the Munter, 'the voice' had remained on his mind. Now here it was again. And now it had a name: 'Etta'. He liked that. There was something jazzy about it. It was arty and colourful and—short.

'Etta, hmm. Etta, Et, Ets, Etty,' Arthur tried all combinations. 'Etta. Hm. I do like that!'

Wasting no time, he dialled the number.

There was no reply, instead her answering machine kicked in.

'Hi, you're through to Etta, if you leave a message I'll get right back to you. Bye.'

'Oh, erm, Hi. It's Arthur… Pod that is, of Pod's Photographic, and well, I can fit you in on Tuesday, as in tomorrow—which would be today if you don't get the message until today—as in today being Tuesday, I mean today's Monday and tomorrow's Tuesday. Oh bollocks! I'm making a bit of a mess of this. Anyway I can fit you in on Tuesday afternoon if that's OK with you. Can you call back and confirm, my number's 0161… oh—of course. You already have it don't you. Right then. Well, I'll erm, look forward to hearing from you. Oh, and sorry about saying bollocks.' Arthur put the phone down.

'Bollocky Bill the Sailor!' He stretched back in his chair and covered his eyes with his hands. 'She'll think I'm a total wanker!'

The phone message messed up Arthur even more. Now he had two things to worry about. He wasn't sure about which was affecting him the most. At least he'd managed to try and arrange the appointment for tomorrow afternoon—hopefully, which would give him the morning to clean up the studio. He thought about the voice again, trying to picture what Etta looked like. Then he started to have doubts: was it the same voice? Maybe not. Two people could have a very similar voice couldn't they? Maybe it was just coincidence? Then Arthur tried to reassure himself: No, it must be the same voice. He knew the second he heard it. It had the same, what was it? The same… thing, behind it. That's what made it special, not the voice, but what was behind it. Whatever that was.

That night Arthur slept restlessly. He fell in and out of so many dreams that he felt exhausted when he woke up just before five. This morning he didn't slip back into his pre-six-thirty snooze, but lay awake as thoughts flew through his head. It was like standing on the edge of a busy motorway as traffic roared past.

*

Icarus had been up half the night trawling the internet, which was not unusual, only this time he hadn't spent it on Facebook, Twitter, or surfing porn. He wandered in to the living room, where Nathaniel was still crashed on the sofa, channel-surfing through the morning TV.

'Morning.'

'Morning.'

'Fancy a coffee?'

'I've already made some, not long ago, so it should still be OK.'

'Do you want a refill?'

'No, I'm fine. How did you get on?'

'Sod all,' Icarus shouted in from the kitchen where he was now pouring coffee into a cracked mug, 'except for an old newspaper article about some diplomat being found in a similar car on some Scottish Island... Well, not all of him, his skeleton... dressed in a tutu and a clown's outfit... something about an honourable career in Moscow...' He was trying to sip the hot coffee as he spoke.

'What about the car?' Nathaniel asked as he started to get dressed.

'Nothing much, but the name's right. It's called a Munter Drophead, prototype made in Russia for export. Never made it to production though'

'And this guy's name, this dead diplomat bloke?' Nathaniel asked.

'Oh yes, Rupert, Rupert Smithereen.'

'When did they find him?'

'Oh, I think it was the late sixties.'

'Brilliant!' Nathaniel was genuinely delighted as he stood up and tucked his shirt into his trousers.

Icarus wandered back into the living room: 'Why?! I haven't got anything I can do anything with?'

'Maybe not, but you've got something I can do something with. What's the time?'

'Eight-twenty-six.'

'Good, almost half-past eight then.'

'Why?' Icarus was curious about why Nathaniel was all of sudden enthusiastic.

'I'm going into London to visit a queen…' he turned and took a step towards the door, 'a good friend who used to work in the foreign office. I'll see you later.'

Nathaniel grabbed a jacket he'd bought the day before, picked up his wallet and keys, and left. Icarus sat down on the sofa, sipped his coffee and took over the channel-surfing.

Although now retired, Christian Ruttersnape (pronounced 'Ternarnspay') knew lots about all kinds of people, especially in the Civil Service, where he'd spent all of his working life.

'Well, if one is going to spend one's time in an institution, one may as well get rewarded for it,' was his resigned view not long after entering it as a youth. It had proved to be much more of a pleasure then he could ever have anticipated. He soon discovered he was far from being the only gay in the village of Whitehall. In a shared closet with very flimsy doors, Christian Ruttersnape knew who had slept with whom, who had said what about whom, and who had benefited financially from whom. Of course he knew all about Rupert Smithereen: 'Reprehensible little creep. I always thought so. I interviewed him once for an internal promotion. Slimy little toad possessed by the demon of self-interest was my opinion. That's not bad in itself of course—it can be a positive boon if one wants to get on in politics. No, you see his problem was that he didn't know how to help others along the way, not even to help himself. He couldn't 'grease his pole' as it were...' Christian was sitting in his small, but comfortable apartment just off Jermyn Street, handily within walking distance of Soho. He was an old acquaintance of Nathaniel's—they had met at the opening of an exhibition of surrealist art—introduced to each other by one of Nathaniel's relatives, who had been an MP at the time. Natural instincts, keen social awareness and subtle communications made each realise that the other might be of use. Their relationship had grown over time: alongside the very private collection of twentieth century paintings and drawings that were displayed modestly throughout Christian Ruttersnape's apartment. Including many lesser-known works by the leading surrealists.

'I heard he was given a car or something, by the Russians?' Nathaniel asked.

'Oh that! Yes they found him in it somewhere off the north coast of Scotland. God knows what he'd been up to. Poisoned himself with the exhaust. Some think it was suicide, but it wasn't. He wouldn't have had the courage to kill himself. If you ask me, it was definitely an accident, but what I think doesn't really matter, the official verdict was 'Death by misadventure', which is an awfully dull way to go! 'Death by adventure' would be so much more romantic don't you think? Anyway, I know one shouldn't speak ill of the dead, but good riddance to bad rubbish, that's what I say. And I'm not the only one to think that way. He undoubtedly saved someone somewhere from himself.'

'That's a bit harsh isn't it?'

'Not at all, a decade earlier he could easily have

'disappeared'. But it was the sixties, there was far too much conscience around, too much preoccupation with what was right and what was wrong. And you couldn't rely on the press any longer to say what you told them. Bring back the days when you could simply tell people what was right and what was wrong. It was all that awful pop music and those drugs, it made people start thinking for themselves. Society simply went to pot. I blame the Americans!'

'Don't start on that again! I think I've heard it all before!' Nathaniel was laughing.

'But darling they were so, casual!'

'You're not the only person ever to be deserted by a GI.'

'So you keep telling me. But I'll never forget those shoulders,' Christian looked wistfully into the distance, snapping back to the present by saying: 'but despite what they say, their chocolate tasted like shit. It still does!'

'I hope you're not being disgustingly euphemistic!'

'Good gracious me no! I'd never be so vulgar dear! No, I really mean their actual chocolate. Have you ever tasted it? It's despicable stuff! I wouldn't feed it to a dog, and you know how I feel about dogs. Anyway enough of all this. A little more Lapsang? I want to talk to you about a little Giacometti drawing I've got my eye on.'

All in all it was a successful trip. Christian spoke to someone at the Foreign Office, who got someone else to dig through the old files. The result was a sales receipt, recovered, remarkably, that very same day from a box file in a secure, but semi-forgotten aircraft hangar in Essex. The young researcher found the hangar to be full of nothing more than thousands of old box-files, and crates of candles marked 'for national emergencies only': they lit dinner parties across London for months. A motorcycle courier delivered a copy of the receipt to Icarus's flat later the same day.

Icarus was impressed, 'Well I've got to hand it to you dude, you've certainly got some excellent contacts!'

Nathaniel tore open the envelope, read the note from Christian and smiled:

'Ha! At last we've got a name now, whether or not it's the name of the bloke who still owns the thing is down to luck.' Nathaniel flicked the note with his finger: 'It says here it was sold to someone called 'Arthur Pod'. The address is no good though, it says here it's been checked out and it's a big detached house in Putney in the middle of being converted into luxury apartments—a building site. But we've got to look on the bright side, we shouldn't have too much trouble finding him. It's not as if we're looking for a 'John Smith' is it?' Nathaniel was feeling a little happier.

'Arthur Pod? Leave it to me dude. Let the world wide web work wonders!' Icarus jumped up and disappeared into his bedroom.

Icarus emerged an hour or so later looking jubilant and waving a piece of paper:

'Well fuck me with the rough-end of a ragman's trumpet!'

'Has anybody ever told you you're a pervert?' Nathaniel said.

'No, but then I always pay them enough to enjoy it and say nothing!' Icarus sniggered. 'No it's this! Look!' He handed the sheet of paper to Nathaniel.

'Manchester!'.

'Manchester. South Manchester to be more precise, a trendy bit of South Manchester!'

'Are you sure it's him. Are you sure he still lives there?'

'Unless he died over the weekend!' Icarus and Nathaniel looked at each other in silence, before simultaneously saying 'Naaaaah!'

Nathaniel was delighted. 'At last, we're getting somewhere! But we need to think about how we do this. How long do you reckon to get our stuff off the car? Presuming it's there of course.'

'Don't freak me man! It's got to be there. It shouldn't take more than ten minutes, say twenty—just to be on the safe side, it was a bugger to work on that thing. Now that I know it was made in Russia, I can understand why.' Icarus replied.

'Right! Well that shouldn't be too difficult. I'm presuming he doesn't park the damned thing outside his house. Not in Manchester, not if he wants to keep his wheels!'

'You're in a good mood. First time I've seen you like this for a while.'

'I feel good. Now let's go see what Manchester has to offer,' Nathaniel started to pack a selection of new clothes into a new bag.

20: A kind of dreaming

Tuesday morning and Arthur was in the studio clearing up. He still felt sick whenever he thought about the Munter, exacerbated by his nerves at the prospect of that afternoon's visit. A message on the answering machine confirmed that Etta would arrive at two o'clock. By twelve he'd finished and the place looked spick and span. He began to prepare the studio space to take a portrait: arranging the lamps and fixing the camera to its tripod. That managed to kill another hour. He was left with one hour until she arrived and he was getting more nervous by the minute. His moths were very active.

'Stop being so stupid Arthur! You're acting like a teenager.' He lay down on the floor and did some deep breathing to calm himself down. His computer was tuned into an internet radio channel that was playing some chill-out music. Outside, the steady traffic turned into a gentle rhythm. It had been a traumatic few days and Arthur had missed his usual sleep. His meditation slid into a deep dog-nap...

...Semi-consciousness popped back. Thinking he'd

just nodded off for a second, Arthur lay still, enjoying the buzz of sleep that was still in his head. His whole body felt relaxed. He was entirely of that moment. He began to be aware of where he was. Sounds began to creep back into his head. The rhythmic hum turned back into traffic; the music from the computer peeled off as another layer. Arthur's eyes were closed and heavy. 'I must have had a pretty deep sleep,' he said to himself, still half-asleep.

He became aware of something else… a presence. There were other noises, breathing, the soft sound of another being. There was something else? Was that scent? No. Not scent. What was it? Almost not there. Drifting. Floating. Arthur stretched, and sat up, eyes still closed. Suddenly his sense of time returned and he realised where he was and why. He opened one of his eyes to let the light in gently, wondering what the time was.

'You must have been tired.' It was a woman's voice. That voice.

'It's erm…' Arthur was fighting to connect his brain with his mouth.

'Twenty-five-to-three. I thought I'd leave you to sleep for a while. You looked so sweet! Like a little boy, except you snore, by the way, like a rhino! But I nudged you and you stopped, so that's OK.'

'No, erm, I mean you're er..'

'What?'

'Etta?' Arthur was beginning to connect.

'I am. I can see you were expecting me!' Etta started to giggle.

Arthur turned to face her, but all he could see was a

silhouette against the light flooding in through the window. His eyes hadn't adjusted to daylight exposure. He squinted to try and see more as he hoisted himself up and into an office chair.

'What?' Was all that Arthur could say, he didn't know why.

'Nothing. I'm sorry, I shouldn't laugh.'

Arthur began to reconnect: 'No! No! You should! I don't mind. Laughing's good. And, I'm erm, sorry, I must have dozed off. It's been a strange weekend. I didn't plan on falling asleep, I just got down to relax for a bit and…' Arthur rubbed his eyes to get the last of the sleep out of his system, 'God. I don't know, I'm really…' Arthur stopped mid sentence. He could see Etta now, well he could see her eyes, dark brown, sparkling, magical gems that sucked all time from the room and Arthur with it. Everything in the world faded away, first to mist, then to infinity. There was no colour, no sound, no sense of touch, no odour, all that existed were those eyes and his own sense of self. Even though every nerve in his body was charged, he couldn't feel a thing. How long this state lasted for, Arthur had no idea, there wasn't a thought in his head. Gradually the world re-materialised, and it would never be the same again.

'No choice!' The words slid out of his mouth.

'I'm sorry?'

Arthur felt sheepish. He couldn't explain, although he was beginning to understand. 'Oh, er, probably still dreaming.'

'Are you OK Arthur?' There was concern in Etta's voice.

'What? Oh, yes! God yes! OK? Absolutely! Everything's,

erm, fine! Would you like a cup of tea? I need a cup of tea. Would you like a cup of tea? Tea! Yes! Or coffee maybe? If I've got any. Have I got any?' Arthur felt like an idiot, like he was talking through a mouthful of cream crackers.

'I'll tell you what Arthur, you sit there, and I'll make the tea.' Etta was already standing and walking towards a door, 'I guess this is where the kitchen is?'

'Oh yes, thanks. There's tea and cups and—stuff.'

'How would you like it?'

'I'm sorry?'

'Your tea! How do you have it?'

'There's some green tea in there, I'll have that, no sugar or milk, in fact I don't think I've got any milk, or sugar.'

'Don't worry, green's fine for me too.' Etta continued her conversation from the kitchen. 'So tell me Arthur?'

'Tell you what?' His head was spinning with a thousand disjointed thoughts.

'Tell me anything you want to tell me?'

'I don't know what I want to tell you?' Arthur felt perplexed. He knew what he'd like to tell her right this second: that she was the most amazing woman he'd ever seen; that he already felt like he'd known her forever; that he didn't want to spend a second away from her for the rest of his life; that he wanted to explore every single square centimetre of her body. In short, that he was in total, irresponsible and irrevocable love with her. But that was stupid, how could he be? He'd only just met her? It was infatuation. He'd get over it?

What he actually told her was: 'I've set everything up for your portrait.'

Etta laughed again. Arthur loved her laugh, it sounded like crystals in sunshine.

'What's so funny?' Arthur was a bit concerned that she seemed to be laughing at him a lot. He would have liked to have been a bit cool, less exposed, but realised that it was pointless.

'Nothing! Nothing. Just life, that's all. So did you enjoy yourself on Friday?

'Friday?'

'The party.'

'Oh god, yes! That! Was it only last Friday? It seems like ages ago. It's been a long couple of days.'

'Amazing place isn't it?'

'Was that meant to be a pun?'

'Excuse me?' Etta laughed again, 'Oh no! I wouldn't be so crass! I didn't scare you did I? The mysterious voice in the maze? At least you managed to find your way out, or should I say, in.'

'What happened to you? I looked for you in that dome thing, which was difficult, because I didn't know what you looked like.'

'Oh I had to go. I've got a sixteen-year-old daughter I had to get back to.' Etta walked back in, carrying two steaming cups of tea. 'She's responsible, but I don't like to leave her on her own. I worry.'

Arthur smiled, he'd never thought of her having children—a child. Etta caught something that flashed across his face.

'Do you like children?'

'Of course! Love 'em. I've got a couple of nieces and

nephews, and my best friend has three kids—monsters to be honest, but they seem to like me for some reason, they probably just don't know any better.'

'I hope you're not fishing for flattery?' Etta ribbed him.

'Flattery? You must be kidding. I'm very comfortable with everything you see. Well, I've at least learned to live with it.'

'It looks fine from where I'm standing.'

Arthur could feel himself getting hot around the ears. He needed to take the attention away from himself.

'Oh, I'm sorry, here, sit down. What's your daughter called?

Etta sat on the stool Arthur had set up for her portrait: 'Natti.'

'What's that? Natalie?'

'Officially yes. But really it's just Natti.'

'That's funny!'

'Why!' Etta had a vague tone of defensiveness in her voice.

'No! I don't mean funny in a bad way, I mean funny in a good way. It reminds me of 'Natty Dread', you know—Bob Marley? It's one of my favourite albums.'

'I'll forgive you then, because it's one of my favourites too.'

'You're joking!' Arthur was genuinely surprised. 'What does Natti think of it?'

'Oh she loves Bob Marley. She loves all music. She thinks it's 'cool' to be Natti, and thankfully there's no 'dread', she's a sweetie—not at all like teenagers are supposed to be.'

'It's a shame though: a couple of bad 'uns give them all

a reputation.'

'Yes, you rarely hear about the good ones.'

'I guess its a case of 'good news is no news."

There was a silence. They both sipped tea. Arthur wanted to stare at Etta, but confined himself to stolen glances. Etta just sipped, looked at Arthur, and smiled.

Arthur felt a bit awkward, he put his cup down and stood up: 'Well, I guess we ought to get this portrait sorted out then. What's it for, your passport?'

Etta frowned and her head pulled back slightly. 'Passport? It's not my portrait. I hate having my picture taken. It's my dogs.'

'Your dogs?'

'Yes, I need a couple of photos of them—it's a long story, but they're stars darling.' As she spoke, Etta crossed her legs and held an imaginary cigarette holder, looking for all the world like a beautiful actress. She then slumped again, and picked up her tea, 'well at least they were. You might have seen them: the 'Little Gem' pet food ads?'

Arthur thought for a second, and remembered a really annoying TV ad for dog food, and equally annoying posters. 'You don't mean those two bloody awful poodles?' Realising what he'd said he tried to back-pedal: 'I mean those awful ads with those two sweet little …'

'It's OK Arthur, you don't have to like them. To be honest they can be a complete pain, but they pay the bills, and have done for some time. The problem I have at the moment is that the contract's up for renewal soon and … well I have this feeling …'

'What kind of feeling?'

'Oh I don't know. Call it intuition. I think we might be dumped.'

'D'you think so? They must have invested a fortune in brand-building, those two are everywhere: posters, TV, magazines; I wouldn't worry.'

'I don't know. You can never tell. Anyway, I thought I'd better update their portfolio, just in case. Truth is, I need the money, and they've got experience. They're little gems as long as they're in front of a camera. The rest of the time they're a total pain the pair of them. Cute, in a way, but a pain all the same. Too yappy by far, and too picky about food. They'll only eat tinned sardines and rice, won't touch any kind of dog food, especially 'Little Gems'. To be honest if I was looking for a pet, I prefer bigger dogs, something like a Labrador.'

Arthur went quiet for a moment. Then said: 'Look I'll tell you what I'll do. I don't normally do pets. It's not because of the pets you understand. I like animals, it's because of the owners, who are generally a pain in the arse. No offence.'

'None taken.'

'But I'll do yours on two conditions.'

'Which are?'

'Well, if I charge you, then it becomes a job, which means that—officially, I take pictures of pets. And someone might find out. And before you know it there'll be a stream of people beating a path to my door wanting me to take pictures of Little Fluffy, or Honey, or Rex, or Felix or Wellington-Roaring-Windrush the third, and I tick over very nicely thank you without cleaning up Cambodia's cat pee or little Ramekin's dog crap. But if I don't charge you, then it's a favour from me to you, so I'll do it if I can do it for free, as a favour.'

'Phew!' Etta was looking a bit taken aback.

'I'm sorry. Like I said, I've had a strange weekend.'

'No, it's quite alright, I'm certainly not going to object to that, but what was the second condition?'

'What?'

'You said 'I'll do yours on two conditions.' That was only one?'

'Ah, sorry, that was it. I must be going a bit barmy.'

'OK Let me tell you what the second condition is.'

'Seems fair.'

'I'll let you do it for free, if you let me take you to dinner.'

'Hm ... I'll need to think about it ... Deal!' Arthur barely had time to think about anything, events were running things. 'Even though I hardly know you.'

'Not true. I think we know each other very well. We just don't know much about each other, yet, dinner should help solve that.'

'You could be a bunny-boiler or anything.'

'Don't be silly Arthur, I'm vegetarian.'

'Are you?'

'No. Not yet anyway.'

So it was arranged: dinner at eight in exchange for a set of prints and jpegs on a disk. Arthur reorganised the set and lights to accommodate two poodles instead of one human. The poodles were one black, one white, so Arthur had fun in monochrome. Etta was right about the animals. The yapped and yelped and snapped and fought continuously, right up until the moment they were put in front of the lights and the camera, then they became as malleable as modelling-clay animation figures, obeying every order. They didn't even mind props, such as the sunglasses that Etta perched on one of their snouts. Arthur enjoyed himself. It wasn't so much the photography as the conversation. As Arthur worked, completely occupied doing something that was by now second nature to him, he and Etta talked. It was a gentle conversation, during which they began to find out the facts of their lives.

Arthur told Etta all about his eventful weekend. She listened with total attention, genuinely concerned as gradually the tension that had been twisting up in Arthur over the weekend unwound. By the time he'd finished the photos, they'd shared stories about each others' lives and Arthur had told her all about the Munter: how he'd come to own it, and everything he knew about its disappearance—which wasn't much, he realised—on hearing himself talk about it.

He ran off some prints and burned a disk for a delighted Etta, who thanked him before leaving. They were both looking forward to the evening. With Etta gone, the studio was quiet. Much quieter than before.

Back home a little later, Arthur was sitting in an armchair with thoughts flooding through his racing head. He was trying to make sense of something that didn't demand logic. Maybe it was because of the weekend: he'd hardly slept on Friday night; Saturday he drove to France; Sunday he'd driven back again in the hire car; Monday was a blur;

Today was even more of a blur. He had feelings that he wasn't sure about. Except that it wasn't that he wasn't sure about them, because he knew he was. It just all seemed, well, strange. He was feeling something that he hadn't felt for years: the moths, light-headedness, no concentration. He was sitting simply waiting for evening to arrive. Time had slowed down. Minutes were distorted and stretched. Seconds ached by. He'd had a shower and was physically relaxed, but his head was a mess. He was trying to rationalise. Maybe it was anxiety? It was definitely anxiety. But it was anxiety about how he was feeling. He felt like he was holding back a reservoir with something inadequate, and that any moment it would snap and everything would come flooding out—that he'd drown and lose control. He took a deep breath and tried to calm himself down.

And why now? Everything was so easy now. Work was steady, the house was paid for. He was happy. He hadn't even thought about having a partner—a girlfriend, never mind falling in… 'What am I thinking!' How could he be in… whatever it was? He was approaching fifty, not eighteen. He wouldn't want that again for anything. He thought about that first love: the pain afterwards. Nearly two years of hurt—that churning hole in the stomach, tortuous awakenings every morning, constant nausea. At the time it seemed like the pain would never end, but one day it did, and he wasn't even conscious of when. He had gone about his normal life again without realising it. He thought about subsequent relationships, which he'd survived by never completely letting go. Nobody was going to hurt him like that again, because he was never going to feel that way again. Of course he'd been in love since, or at least he'd said he'd been in love, and he'd known some wonderful women. It had taken him years to realise that it wasn't fair, he wasn't fair, he hadn't been fair to them. Even now there were one or two whom Arthur felt sure would say they'd had a good relationship with him; but Arthur knew now that the problem always emerged in some way or other—he couldn't open up to them, couldn't give what a good relationship needed. He wondered how much frustration he'd caused, and how much hurt.

He had never given up though, he now realised. There must always have been hope that one day he'd meet someone and everything would be right. He was surprised at thinking this, because he hadn't considered it was something that was in him. He wondered what he had expected, how and when he'd expected it to happen. There were no rules, and no logic either, so it could happen any time, any place, any way…

…and it was here, now. Arthur was confronting something he never consciously thought he would have to face up to: Real Love. The first-sight thing, except this was more like love at first sound. What was frightening him was the fact he realised he had no choice. This time all decisions had been taken right away from his control. He wondered momentarily whether he could just deny it, but knew that was impossible. This was something that existed and couldn't be denied. It was like finding a new colour: once you know it's there, you can't ignore it, because it affects the way you see everything. The way you feel about everything. The way you experience the world.

Arthur felt sick. What if it all went wrong? What if he was wrong? Maybe it's delusion; maybe shock. Losing the Munter had left his emotions raw, he was surprised how much. He remembered watching a film on TV the other night, a romance, a bit schmaltzy but with a good story. By the end of the film he was really choked up; he almost shed a tear. He tried to think of the title, but he'd missed the beginning of the film. Then there was the news—some football team in an amazing comeback. He'd felt the tears in his eyes at the wild joy being shown by the fans—and he didn't even like football; well not that much anyway. Why all this emotion all of a sudden. Was it tiredness? Age? Then he recalled another film he'd seen about an old Italian guy watching a sad film: tears were streaming down his face unashamedly.

Arthur began to realise that this was what getting older was all about. You didn't have to make excuses about how you felt about things—about life, art politics, religion. You could stop worrying about what other people thought of you: about how you acted and looked; about how you felt. You could cut loose a bit, just be who you are. You could start learning to ditch your self-consciousness. And if the worse thing that happened was that you got hurt again, well it was about time. It was time to find courage. He'd handled it before, he could handle it again. Arthur got chicken-skin as the warmth of what he was feeling washed over him—then the tears came, and flowed. For loss, for pain, for joy, for love—these tears had been a long time coming.

21: Open faith

An age on and evening finally happened. Arthur and Etta were sitting at a table, looking for all the world like a couple in love. They had flirted, touched and talked like lovers, companions and friends. If Arthur had any reservations, they had been washed away in the flood. Arthur loved looking at Etta; she was the most beautiful person. He also loved listening to her, she was interesting, thoughtful, intelligent and funny.

'What I'd like to know Arthur, is why you're still single? I mean you seem to be perfectly normal. Why didn't someone snap you up years ago? Do you have some dark secret you're not telling me? Something to hide? Tell me if you do, I love a scandal!'

'Scandal? Not that I'm aware of. I wish I had, it would make me more interesting. As for not being snapped up, well, to be honest that's my fault, I didn't think it was fair on anyone else.' Arthur stopped and thought for a second or two. 'In a way I thought I was kind of settled already. Work's always steady. The house is convenient, I've got a few close friends, had the odd fling and things,'

'Not too odd I hope?'

Arthur laughed: 'No, well—there was this one time… but that's another story!'

'You must tell it to me sometime.' Etta asked, raising an eyebrow.

Arthur took a sip from his glass—mainly so that he could hide behind it: 'I might, one day, anyway, I've had a couple of long-term relationships—they can eat up time: three years here, six years there, I even tried marriage for five years…'

'What happened to that?'

'Oh I don't know really, well I guess I do. I mean I could say that she was unfaithful and all that, which she was, but I guess she wouldn't have been if everything had been fine. It's funny, because I've been thinking about it recently,'

Etta's head tilted into another listening position.

'I've been thinking about a lot of things recently—I think it's to do with being forty-nine, nearly fifty.'

'You don't look it!'

'Flatterer.'

'No really!'

'Thanks. So, I was thinking about it—the marriage I mean, and the conclusion I came to was that it just stopped.'

'Stopped?'

'Yes.'

'Interesting.' Etta was leaning on the edge of her palm, thinking about what Arthur was saying. 'I'd never thought about that before. You always presume there's a reason, such as an affair, or violence, drunkenness, something like that, but I'd never thought about it just stopping—but I guess it happens with people. Did you love her?' Etta could see that Arthur felt uncomfortable with this question: 'You don't have to answer if you don't want to.'

'No, I don't mind. I was just thinking about what you would consider the right answer to be, which is stupid.'

'There isn't a right answer as far as I'm concerned, only an honest one.'

'That's what I thought too. Did I love her? You know, I don't think I did, not really, I mean… I guess in a way I did, but it was more a case of taking care of her. I was thinking about this the other day; do you want to know why I really married her?'

'Of course I do. If you want to tell me.'

'Because I was flattered.'

'Flattered?'

'Yes. Crappy reason for getting married huh?.'

'Was she beautiful?' Etta could see that Arthur was uncomfortable again. 'Be honest.' She added.

'I'd like to be honest, but you might think it's bullshit?'

'Well at least it would be honest bullshit.'

'Well, I thought she was beautiful. I was bowled over. Physically she really was. In fact she worked as a photographic model, which was how I met her. But in the end, for all kinds of reasons, she was a just a victim looking for sanctuary, somewhere to escape from the world. I was that somewhere, her route to a comfortable home, safety, but in the end she was more like a daughter than a partner. I was blinded by flattery, by the fact that she was prepared to be with me. It's funny, because I was thinking earlier today, or yesterday—sometime recently anyway—that I haven't changed. I feel the same now as I did when I was thirty-five, even twenty-five. But I guess if you live with change you don't notice it. The funny thing is that right now I feel like a different person. I can't believe I did what I did for the reasons I did.'

'So why did you think I'd think that was bullshit?'

'Well, you asked me if she was beautiful, and now I'd have to say yes—in a physical way; but also no, because now I think I have the sense to understand beauty, because there's something about you that's the most beautiful thing I've ever sensed.'

Etta took Arthur's hand. 'Arthur I would never think that was bullshit. That's probably the most wonderful thing anyone's ever said to me.'

Arthur looked at Etta, and he could feel himself filling up again. He tried to take control of himself, his body moving slightly in his own discomfort. Etta missed nothing. She put her hand on his hand:

'It's alright Arthur, everything's alright.' She lifted his hand and kissed his knuckles.

Arthur didn't know what was happening to him. Maybe this was his mid-life crisis? Maybe the events of the past few days had all become just too much for him.

'I'm sorry Etta, I...'

'Arthur! Please don't apologise to me. I don't want you to apologise to me ever. Especially for the way you feel.'

'I think I'm only just realising how I feel. I think I've been sheltering in my own comfort for far too long. Do you want the truth? Of course you do.'

'Always.'

'You've completely unsettled me. If I hadn't met you I think I would have ticked along in the comfort zone for the rest of my life, without being aware of it. Which is really funny.' Arthur couldn't help but laugh at himself.

'Why?'

'Because only the other morning I was lying in bed, thinking—I did say I'd been thinking a lot lately—I kind of have this aim that when I'm on my death-bed, I want to think that I couldn't have done any more with the time I've been given.'

'Well it's a bit morbid, but I see your point. So what's funny about it?'

'Well, I wonder if I'd realise that I'd been avoiding the most important part of life.'

'Which is?'

'Love.'

'And were you?'.

'I think I was.'

'You have to have faith, Arthur.'

'I guess I've always been too scared.'

'What of?'

'Pain. It's easier to play safe.'

'Easier, and some people choose that, it's like choosing to be Religious with a capital 'R'. But if you know the difference it will never be fulfilling.'

'How?' Arthur's emotions were settling a little, he was feeling much happier and relaxed.

'Well religion should be spiritual guidance. But somewhere along the line it became 'Religion', and hijacked faith for the sake of politics and power. It's like you can only have faith if you have faith in God, or Jesus, or Allah, or whoever. But that takes away all the responsibility from life. What's wrong with just having faith?'

'You're not Religious then?'

'No, not at all.'

'Me neither. So what responsibility, you mean like conscience?'

'Exactly! Religion, the one with a capital 'R', is an easy option. The church is like a bank where you can deposit your conscience, and as long as you keep paying in a small amount every week, you can feel like you're doing your bit for the world.'

'So you can sit back and rest easy.' Arthur said, 'like I've been doing.'

'I'm not criticising you. In fact I'm not criticising anyone. It's just the way of the world. I mean, people always talk about freedom, but in a way that's what people want to do, just talk about freedom. Freedom means responsibility, having to make choices about things.'

'So you think that most people don't really want that responsibility?'

'Honestly?'

'As you said! The only right answer is the honest one!'

Etta flashed a smile. 'I don't think they do. I think most people want the easy option: they want other people to make decisions.'

'Which explains why people like Hitler were so successful?'

'Extreme, but yes. And it's still going on. It's like Africa now—we say that our governments should be doing something about it—debt and Aids and poverty, because we've voted away our responsibility. We're happy to think it's their responsibility as our elected representatives to have a conscience about it. So we just get on with our daily lives. We're the same about the global warming.'

'Isn't that a bid hard, I mean what about charities and stuff like Live Aid?'

'They're wonderful. Don't get me wrong, but when we give money, why are we doing it?'

'I know what you're suggesting, but it sounds a bit cynical.'

'I know, Arthur. I know. But that's the way the world makes me feel sometimes. It's like there are two worlds—one big wonderful, creative, deep, faithful, sensual soup of a place; the other a hard, faithless, cynical, superficial, uncaring money grabbing, overheating, destructive war-loving failure.'

'All that in one breath!'

'I'm sorry. It just makes me so…'

'Angry?'

'Actually, no Arthur, I don't think it's anger, I think it's a kind of despair.'

'I like the idea of a sensual soup, by the way. I understand what you're saying, and I'd love to agree with you. But if people don't want responsibility, why should they have it forced on them?'

'Well, that's where it gets difficult Arthur, because if freedom is the ability to make choices, then you have to be allowed to make the choice to limit your responsibilities. You can't make people be responsible.

'So what do we do?'

'I guess we make it a criterion that anyone who takes responsibility on our behalf—those who we hand our conscience over to—are chosen because they fully understand that.'

'And don't you think that happens now?'

'What with the politicians and religious leaders? No way. I mean there might be a few, but on the whole I'd say they're in it for status and power.'

'Hell of a conversation for a first date!'

'Oh Arthur, I'm sorry. And look, the food's gone cold!'

'Don't worry, curry's good cold—especially for breakfast. Anyway, I wasn't complaining. It kind of makes a change from 'what's your favourite kind of music, stroke film, stroke colour, stroke soap. If you start off on that foot, you know just what kind of relationship you're in for.'

'What kind?'

'Short.'

Etta laughed, 'I know, try being a thirty-four-year-old single mother. You'd be amazed how conceited some men can be. Of course there have been some sweeties, but some just think you're desperate, scared of being on the shelf and they're your last chance. And then we have dinner and I start rabbiting on about something, like now, and they think I'm weird and that's it, off they go! Of course what they really wanted me to do was to sit there and ask 'What's your favourite kind of music, stroke film, stroke colour, stroke sexual position. You see, so many people are scared of being themselves, because of other people.'

'Bugger!'

'What?' Etta's fork stopped midway between plate and lips.

'You've ruined my chat-up line.'

'Funny guy! Anyway I know you're not the same.'

'Why? I mean you don't know much about me, at least you didn't.'

'No. But I do have faith in you. Hasn't it occurred to you that I might feel exactly the same way about you as you feel about me?'

'Why? I mean I could be a complete bastard, or a complete dork.'

'Don't be silly Arthur, you don't have a bastard bone in your body.'

'OK, I know, but I might have been one, I mean—you didn't know that.'

'Arthur! You're not a bastard, there's no 'might' in it. I mean if you take that logic then anything might be anything. But the fact is they're not. 'Things is wot they is!"

'Who said that?'

'Me of course, who did you think it was? You have to have faith Arthur. This life, this society, its politics, its religions—they all kill real faith. Faith means taking responsibility.'

'In what way?' Arthur picked up a naan bread, but rigor mortis had already claimed it. He picked with his fork at some sticky rice.

'In yourself. Take love for example. You have to have faith in love, give yourself to it—even though you might get hurt so much that life doesn't seem worth living.'

'I've been there, and I wouldn't wish that on anybody.'

'Me too, and in a way, neither would I. But we need to take that risk. That's what life's all about—using all our senses, risking them, taking responsibility for ourselves and the world we live in.'

'I suppose we should all try and be more of what we are?'

'Exactly Arthur! On a fundamental level. The problem is finding out who we really are.'

'I guess that's down to environment—creating the conditions that let you be who you are.'

'That's got a lot to do with it, but religion is the antithesis of that.'

'I guess politics is too,' said Arthur as he struggled to swallow a chilli.

'Religion is politics.' Etta was waving her fork as she spoke; any food it contained had long since fallen off.

'I can see you feel strongly about this Etta!' Arthur glanced at Etta's fork.

'I'm sorry! It's my turn to apologise.' Etta put the fork down on the side of her plate.

'And it's my turn to say you shouldn't apologise. I love listening to you. I guess I feel similarly to you. It's all really interesting, only I don't think I've given it all enough thought yet. It's that comfort zone again, I think it got me. But I want to talk to you lots.'

'Me too, with you. But we've got time.' Etta gripped the napkin on her lap tightly with both hands and leaned forward, 'Oh Arthur, I really want you to have faith. I mean I know you have it. That's why I'm here. When I saw you at the wedding I could feel it in you. I knew you were special.'

'You were at the wedding?' Arthur was surprised, he didn't remember seeing her.

Etta leaned back, 'Yes, but you were far too busy working to notice me. You made me laugh, the way you handled the children, and Uncle Cedric.'

'I'm…'

'Arthur! Don't say you're sorry! Why should you be! You were doing your job. Anyway I wasn't going to go to the reception because I couldn't find a sitter for Natti. But when Aunty Meek said you'd be there, I pulled in a favour. Only trouble is you were late.'

'Last minute decision. So you hid in the maze.'

'I wasn't hiding. OK in a way I was hiding, but I had to get back home. I thought it would be more mysterious that way. I got your business card off Cedric, so I knew I could get in touch.'

'But how did aunty Meek know I was going? Even I didn't know I was going until about ten minutes before I set off!'

'Oh she just knows things, she lives by her faith and people have faith in her.'

'Sounds like some kind of magic?'

'Not where she comes from, it's to do with life. It's like I was saying earlier, there are two worlds. Aunty Meek lives in the other one, except it's all part of the same one. To her, and lots of other, what many would call, 'primitive' people, faith and the world are naturally inseparable. They don't separate what we call spirituality, from the physical. Maybe it should be magic, and maybe we should believe in it.

'I like the idea of that.' Arthur was musing.

'What?'

'Faith and life being inseparable. It has a truth about it.'

'But can you live by it d'you think?'

'Honestly? I'd like to think so, but sometimes it's difficult to know how ingrained things are in you, I mean in me.'

'Do you want to kiss me?'

Arthur answered in a quiet voice: 'I've wanted to kiss you since the first time I heard your voice.'

'So why haven't you done it yet?'

'Well, partly because you were hiding behind a hedge.'

'Ha! But why didn't you kiss me today, in your studio, I wanted you to?'

'I don't know. I guess I was the one hiding behind a hedge. I was waiting for the right time? But of course the right time is when you want to do it.'

Etta smiled.

'I can see that it's going to take some courage to have faith in myself. But I can see that it's worth trying. I think I can cope.' Arthur thought he could resign himself quite happily to this fate.

Etta stood up, walked over to Arthur, took his hands and gently pulled him to his feet. She put her hands on his face and kissed him. Arthur was willing.

'That was because I wanted to,' Etta said.

Arthur put his arms around her, pulled her close and they kissed again. Somewhere deep inside, something dissolved.

'Mmm. That's better than an entire conversation.' Etta said.

'You're so right, I should have done that ages ago.'

'I don't think I could eat any more? You?'

'No, I think we talked the food to death anyway, besides, everybody's looking at us, even though they're pretending not to', Arthur replied. 'What would you like to do then?'

'Well, what I'd like to do, and what I can do are not the same thing.'

'That seems to be the theme of the evening.'

'What I need to do is to get home to a certain sixteen-year-old girl. Which is a shame, because I'd like to come back with you for a coffee. If you were asking of course.'

'Well. I wouldn't probably have asked in case you thought I was euphemistically asking to sleep with you, and I wouldn't have wanted to spoil things, because I really like you.'

'So you're saying that if you liked me less I might get to spend the night with you? Or are you simply saying you're lousy in bed?'

'Argh! You've got me there! First of all, I'm not going to say I'm lousy in bed—I'm a man, so how could I? As for the coffee, I'll have you know I make a really lousy cup—and I've probably got no milk or sugar—or coffee come to that.'

'Oh well! That makes me feel better. I think I'll go home and make some Camomile tea. I can't sleep after coffee anyway.'

'Aaaah, Camomile tea—the new cocoa! Let's pay-up and hunt down a taxi for you. I can get a bus from just outside here.'

'But Arthur it's raining?'

'Not that much. Anyway I like the rain, it will cool me down.'

'Not too much I hope?'

'No, not if I can see you again? If you want to that is?'

'There you go again! Of course I want to! How about tomorrow, Natti's on a sleepover?'

'Great! I'll cook if you like. Is there anything you don't eat?'

'That would be telling,' Etta said coyly, what about you?'

Arthur grinned and raised an eyebrow.

22: Mersey Lizards

In principle, it was simple. All that was required was a good old-fashioned stakeout. 'A bit like a take-out but with steak?' Icarus mused.

'I hope that wasn't meant to be funny!' Nathaniel groaned. With the postcode and a street map from the internet they thought they'd tracked down Arthur's road. All they needed now was to find out which house it was. The 'development' consisted of one road leading to three small cul-de-sacs, which contained around twenty executive and cottage-style homes. Behind these an earth bank planted with shrubs led up to the banks of the River Mersey. With only one way in or out, in theory it was easy: just sit at the entrance to the main road and wait until the Munter drove past.

They took turns, one watching and one relaxing in hourly shifts. Nathaniel took first watch: he listened to Radio 4 while Icarus trawled the internet using a laptop and a doctored mobile phone. Icarus's watch consisted of keeping one eye out of the window, while he simultaneously rolled and smoked tiny Californian-style pure-skunk reefers.

Nathaniel, who was now having very vivid dreams as he slept soundly on the reclining passenger seat, wouldn't let Icarus smoke fat spliffs in the car on account of the tobacco and the damaging effects of secondary smoke.

Two people came and went—one looked like an insurance salesman, the other was an old lady pushing a wicker shopping trolley. Two bicycles came and went—one carrying the postman. A dog came, sniffed, peed and went. A variety of cats went. The inevitable Manchester rain came, went, then came again. Between 8.00 and 8.30am several cars went. Between 5.30 and 7pm the same cars came. Arthur came and went, on his bicycle—along the riverbank, which was the quickest way to his studio. A whole day came and went with no sign of the Munter, before Nathaniel decided: 'This isn't working. Are you sure he lives here?'

'Well, only from the information I've got...'

'A postcode isn't much information Icarus. We don't even know what the guy looks like. And we've got to do something. The diamonds are floating around somewhere. At least I hope they are. We could be here for days, even weeks, without finding anything out. What if he only uses the car at the weekend? Apart from that, look at the state of it in here already,' Nathaniel was looking at the inside of the car, 'we've been here for less than a day and it's like sitting in a rubbish skip. I need some proper food—preferably something without salt or sugar.'

'Dunno what you're talking about man. I'm quite enjoying it. Anyway there's no such thing as proper food without salt or sugar. Have you tried these meat and potato pies? Delish!' Icarus popped the last of it into his mouth; screwed up the silver tray it came in, and threw it over his shoulder into the foot well of the back seats. 'Why can't you buy 'em in London?'

'Do you mind! You can clear this lot out later; it's mostly your stuff anyway. I don't know where you put it all!'

Icarus shrugged and grinned; there was gravy on his chin.

Nathaniel was restless. 'We need to find out what the guy looks like. Then we might be able to find out where he lives, which garage is his.'

'We could just knock on all the doors and ask,' said Icarus as he pulled down the vanity mirror and wiped the gravy away with a paper napkin.

'Oh, and what if someone says: 'Yes. I'm Arthur Pod?' Do you say: 'Ahh! Mr. Pod, we believe you have some of our diamonds stuck underneath your car. Would you mind terribly if we retrieved them?'

'No, but technology might help.' Icarus was in a stoned-kind-of-thinky-kind-of-mood.

'How? Because I really need something to happen now.'

'Weeeeell, dude, I've been thinking that we could do a survey. I could make a false ID card. Then I can buy a small hidden camera for a few quid, which I could hide in a baseball cap and attach it to my own camcorder so that nobody will see it. We can make up a short questionnaire and get whatever information we need.'

'You're stoned!'

'Yes, they do have some very nice stuff up here, but that's

not the point. Have you got a better idea?'

Nathaniel racked his head for something that sounded better than a bad idea, but his store of good ideas was currently in a mess. 'So what kind of questions?'

'Let's go back to the hotel and sort it out.' Icarus wound down the window, carefully picked a tiny scrap of burnt paper from between a pair of tweezers, and flicked it into the street. He started to wind the window back up.

'Leave it down for a bit,' Nathaniel said, 'I need some fresh air.'

'Fresh air? We're in Manchester dude?'

'I wish you'd stop saying 'dude'!'

'OK dude.'

*

For the first time in as long as he could remember, Arthur didn't wake up at four, or at six-thirty. He slept soundly until almost nine o'clock. When he woke he decided to take a bath rather than a shower, he needed to think about stuff.

Arthur soaked, thinking about Etta. It was all so paradoxical. He flicked some water towards the taps with his left hand. On one hand nothing had ever been stranger; on the other nothing had ever been so natural. It was such a cliché to say it, but he really felt like he'd known Etta for years. In fact he felt like he'd always known her. She felt completely right. He was trying to remember their conversation from the previous evening. What she said about... was it honesty or truth? He wondered if you could really be totally honest with someone. There always seemed to be things that you had to hold back, because that was the thing to do. A kind of social and sexual etiquette. But in a way that was only necessary as a defence, but a defence against what? Arthur thought about himself when he was younger: he'd happily have a one-night-stand, and had no conscience about it afterwards. He wondered about how many women he'd hurt by being clumsy. He felt a sadness inside as he remembered some of the lovely women he'd had flings with. Some who he knew had expected more. He had no emotional responsibilities then. 'In a way, I'm one of the reasons that kind of etiquette exists,' Arthur thought. He also realised that there had been situations when he had expected more, but had been disappointed. 'Maybe it's just part of growing up,' he thought. One of the reasons that he'd stopped having casual relationships was that he realised every relationship, no matter how casual, has some emotional responsibility attached to it.

It was so different being honest. And what was happening was so out-of-the-blue. Arthur shifted in the water to immerse his knees. Etta seemed to fill him up, yet he didn't feel insecure about her. It was like she was just there—always had been and always would be. He didn't feel nervous with her; didn't feel that he should make conversation—try and be funny or intelligent. It was just easy with her. He just knew that he didn't want anyone else in his life.

One thing that did perturb him was that he realised he'd felt this way from the moment he first heard her voice. 'How could that be? I mean I didn't know what she looked like, what she was like—nothing about her.' He had never dismissed the strange things of the world, ghosts, the afterlife, parallel dimensions and such, because he understood that there was much more to life than we could possibly know about. He'd had one or two strange experiences himself—a couple of very weird coincidences, and one scary out-of-body experience that was nothing to do with drugs. This was kind of in the same vein. Etta had talked about faith. Arthur felt that perhaps he was a fraud in this department. Because having faith often meant having blind belief in something you can't prove. But he didn't need faith in Etta, because how he felt about her just was, it didn't need proof. He considered the paradox that not needing to have faith gave him total faith. It was an undeniable state. Having faith meant making an absolute choice. Except it didn't, because Arthur knew that he didn't have a choice, didn't need to make a decision. Whatever happened now was completely out of his hands. He wasn't scared of getting hurt. He wasn't afraid of the future. He relaxed his knees and slid down so that his ears were underwater. He could hear his heartbeat pumping the blood around his body. He knew everything would be just fine.

*

It was still officially Arthur's holiday. Initially pissed off about the France trip and the Munter, he was now enjoying just pottering about. Besides which, fate may have removed him from the Munter, but it had also delivered him into Etta's arms. He knew he didn't have too much to be upset about.

After a couple of hours in the studio he went shopping. He loved cooking, particularly when he had a good reason to do it, and he had an excellent reason this evening. His head was buzzing with ideas: Thai curry, paella, fish, but no: 'What do I really like to cook and what do I really like to eat?' He didn't want to be faffing around all afternoon: 'Chicken in red wine! Perfect! Good old reliable Coq-au-Vin! A bit seventies, but it will put something French back into the week.'

By the time Etta rang the doorbell Arthur was very relaxed. The house was warm with the delicious smell of roasting chicken, garlic, wine and herbs. The goat's cheese salad starter was ready to serve. A bottle of wine was already open and a glass had made its way into the chef.

He opened the door, as he did so two excited, yapping, fuzzy creatures—one black, one white—dashed through his legs, straight into the house, and started sniffing every surface.

'I'm sorry Arthur, I hope you don't mind, I didn't want to leave them in case they chewed the house to pieces.'

Arthur laughed nervously. 'No! No! No problem.' He watched them scampering too and fro, sniffing the walls, the floor and dig between the cushions on the sofa. This wasn't on his plan for a romantic dinner. 'They can chew anything they fancy here.'

'Don't worry they'll settle down in a minute. I've put some food and their bowls in a bag.' Etta held up a carrier bag to show Arthur. 'I'll just settle them in a corner and they'll be fine.' In her other hand was a bunch of flowers. 'These are for you.'

'Thanks! They're gorgeous.' Arthur was delighted.

Etta sorted the dogs out, and true to her word, they

settled as good as gold. She looked around.

'Well, I don't think I'd imagined your house would be like this. I kind of pictured you in a bachelor flat of some kind—you know, smeared chrome, tatty shag pile, and a zebra-print bed-throw!'

'Thanks a bunch!' Arthur could tell Etta was ribbing him, 'I only get the zebra-skin out on special occasions!'

Etta was casually investigating the room: 'I'm surprised, it's really homely! Interesting. I mean—I love all these bits and pieces.'

Arthur had returned to the kitchen, tending to the food and putting the flowers into a vase. The food was almost ready. He walked into the living room holding the vase. 'Not many people would think of buying a bloke flowers, but I love 'em. These are great! Thanks very much.' Arthur was smiling as he put the vase on a windowsill. 'Fantastic—look at the colours of those lilies, like fire!'

'Glad you like them. I love flowers too. They're all out of my garden you know.'

'You're joking! You haven't got green fingers, you've got golden hands.'

'...well my garden and my greenhouse. I love gardening.'

'I don't bother much. Someone comes to cut the grass every couple of weeks. I tidy up a bit in-between, and that's it. I lived in a flat before—you would have passed it on the way in—just up the road. I was there for years, so I'm still not used to the gardening bit.'

'Ah so you did have a bachelor pad!'

'Sadly, I have to put my hands up to that one. And it

had spotlights, a waterbed and an aquarium!'

'A right old shag-pad I'll bet!'

'I wish! A shagged pad more like. I was going to redo it all, but I realised it was too small anyway, and they were building these houses, and—well I like it round here, so I thought I may as well move. The garage is useful too, I had one with the flat but it was in a separate block.' Arthur suddenly remembered the Munter was gone: 'Well it was useful before some bastard nicked my car! It's only got my bike in it now. Anyway, it's a relief to have extra space. I mean this has three bedrooms and it looks full; you can imagine what it was like with all this cramed into a one-bedroomed flat. And I chucked out as much stuff as I saved.'

'Any news on your car?'

'No, not yet. I thought I'd make a few calls tomorrow. Find out what's going on. But to be honest, I don't hold out much hope.'

'Have you got a picture of it?'

'Yes.' Arthur stood and walked into the hall, where he took a framed photo from the wall. He came back in and handed it to Etta. She looked at it, eyebrows raised.

'Well. I don't know what to say. It's ...unusual isn't it? What's that big chrome nose thing on the front?'

'That's the big chrome nose thing.'

'Cheeky! It looks a bit like a plane in some places. It's...'

'Ugly?'

'Well I wouldn't go so far as that, it's certainly different though.'

'Don't worry, I know it's ugly. But there's a strange kind of beauty in it. It's the way it's all so disjointed yet smooth. I know it's difficult to explain but it's got so much character—it's more than an object.'

'Well, I can sort of see what you mean?'

'It's better in real life. In fact it's even uglier.'

Etta handed the picture back to Arthur, who looked at it wistfully, before placing it on a bookshelf within arm's reach.

'To be honest cars are all more or less the same to me. Whether it's a Skoda or a Porsche, I don't really appreciate the difference,' Etta said, in a matter of fact way, 'As long as it gets from A to B'.

'Aren't women supposed to be impressed by a man with a sports car? And don't get me wrong I don't expect anyone to be impressed with the Munter, it's purely a personal pleasure.'

'I don't know? Are they supposed to be impressed? All I know is that I'm not interested.'

'Fair enough. We can't all be interested in everything.'

'I went out on this date once—I'm sorry, it doesn't bother you: me talking about this does it? It was ages ago.'

'No! Not at all. I'd be surprised if you hadn't had any, a gorgeous woman like you!'

'Flattery will get you everywhere!'

Arthur grinned. 'Keep talking, I'll get you a drink. Red wine OK?'

'Lovely, thanks. Anyway, he kept steering the conversation around to his car, like he really wanted me to ask him what he drove.'

'Did you?'

'Of course not! He was so boring. Anyway, we got to the end of the evening and he asked me if he could give me a lift home in his Bentley Continental. He actually said that! Can you believe it' Etta put on a mock-man voice: 'Would you like a lift home in my Bentley Continental? It was all I could do to keep a straight face. Anyway, I turned to him and I said 'Goodness gracious! You have a Bentley Continental! How wonderful! Isn't that an extremely expensive car?'

'You didn't say it like that surely!' Arthur returned with the wine.

'Of course!'

'What, like a cooing Marilyn Monroe? I'm surprised you didn't add: 'Mr. President'. He must have cottoned on that you were taking the mickey?'

'No. He was an idiot. He actually said to me…' and again Etta put on the same deep voice: '…Oh I don't know my dear, I suppose about £175,000'—like that amount of money was nothing to him.'

'So what did you do?'

'Nothing of course. Went to the toilet. Paid the bill. Got a bus home. I left him sitting there.' Etta giggled: 'He could be still there for all I know. God, he was so full of it, a hundred and seventy grand on a car! What an idiot! What a waste!' Etta had been laughing, but suddenly stopped. 'Oh Arthur! I'm sorry. I mean this… your car? It…'

Arthur glanced at her face. It looked so beautiful, lit soft by the candlelight. 'What?' Etta asked, seeing Arthur looking at her in a distracted way. 'You're not upset about what I said are you?'

Arthur switched back. 'God no! I'd never spend that much money on a car! I wouldn't! Apart from anything else I couldn't—I haven't got that much money. The Munter cost me next to nothing, I bought it from the Civil Service. It was a total wreck when I found it. Well it wasn't a wreck, but it was in a really bad way. It cost me more to ship it down from Scotland than I paid for it. I did most of the work on it myself, with a bit of help from here and there. Well, to be honest with a lot of help, it was a job-and-a-half.'

Etta smiled, but Arthur could see that there was another thought on her mind.

'What?'

'Oh sorry! I was listening. I was just thinking about dating. I hate it.'

'Thanks!'

'No! You know what I mean! I hate all that going out and first meetings, and expectation and disappointment. So many men are, oh I don't know… sad I guess.'

'Thanks! I'll take that as a compliment!' Arthur said. 'But it's not just men. It's people. But it's not their, our, fault. Or rather it is. We have a hell of a capacity for damaging each other. If you know what I mean.'

'Yes, you're right. But you're different—I can tell you're basically a happy person. With a lot of men it's like they're looking for therapy, or a mother—desperate for someone who's going to give them happiness. Like it's someone else's responsibility, my responsibility, to make them happy. It's so disappointing. They have so much expectation just kind of hanging there. Not all of them, of course. Some just want sex. In some ways I'd rather deal with them, it's easier.'

'That's a bit damning isn't it. I'm sure you can't generalise about all of us? Besides women can be as bad. I learnt to avoid anyone who sends you anything to do with cats.'

'Why cats?'

'Psychos.'

'Talk about generalising!'

'It's true! Cat postcards, cat pictures on emails, photos of themselves with their cats, cat mugs, cat diaries and calendars, conversations about cats. I've never met anyone who owns cats who's not ever so slightly bonkers. The more cats they have, the more bonkers they are. That's my theory anyway.'

Etta was laughing: 'What about dog owners then?'

'Different breed altogether!' Arthur said glibly, waving them off to one side.

'You're funny Arthur! But you know I don't mean you, it's just my own experience. I tried the whole dating scene for a while: Internet dating, speed dating, executive dating, ads in newspapers. It makes me sound desperate but it's not that I was looking for just anybody. I don't need anybody. But I always believed I'd meet somebody, my somebody, and knew that the world wasn't going to come to me—I had to go to the world. I also knew that I'd know who that person was. I mean I didn't have a preconceived idea about him, or her come to that: you have to be open-minded about these things. But I knew there was somebody for me out there somewhere. Do you understand that? Or does it sound a little bit strange?'

'I think you're asking the wrong person. I'm still a bit shell-shocked by everything. It's kind of the opposite to you, a bit like what we talked about the other night. I wasn't looking for anybody. I was safely in the comfort zone. When 'Bang!' Any thoughts I had before are right out the window! I'm still trying to make sense of it all. The only conclusion I can reach is that there is no sense to it. I don't have any choice. It's just something that exists. It's like living in a black and white world and suddenly discovering colour!'

'Are you happy about it though?'

'Happy! Honestly I've never been happier.'

'That's good then, isn't it?'

'Yes! Of course. And you?'

'The same. I don't feel like the odd one out any more.'

'In what way?'

'Well, my gaggle of girl-friends and I go walking together and cook meals and get drunk sometimes, laugh a lot, talk a lot—including about men of course, and sex and relationships, and places we've been, people we've known. We try and put the world to rights—like you do when you're drunk. They've all been married, like me, and are divorced like me, we're a gang of sisters really. But they're happy being single, or at least they say they're happy being single—although to be honest they've all got relationships of one kind or another, mainly casual or on-offs, you know the kind of thing. Anyway sometimes I feel like the odd one out because I like men, I like being with a man, I like being taken care of by a man, and taking care of a man. It's a fundamental part of life for me. The strange thing is I've been on my own longer than I've been in relationships, and I hate that word 'relationship'—it reduces everything to the level of a soap opera.'

'But what about Natti's father, if you don't mind me asking.'

'No, I don't mind. I got married. I was young, eighteen. Believe it or not a dashing young Englishman swept me off my feet. I was living in southern France at the time. My parents lived in a small town north of Paris. My father was dying and needed constant care from my mother, so she sent me down to the south to stay with her sister. I was seventeen. That's where I met Hector. He bred racehorses. He was older than me. He seemed to have so much experience of life. He had his own plane, a big estate in England, a villa on the Riviera.'

'A Bentley Continental?'

Etta laughed, 'Cheeky! No, far too big and slow for him. He liked speed. He raced cars—one of his many hobbies, he played tennis, went skiing, rode horses, climbed mountains. He made me feel so special. I was very beautiful...' Etta slipped into momentary reverie.

'And then?'

'Oh, I'm sorry, but that's all boring! Let's talk about something else.'

'No, carry on, it's interesting.'

'Well... we had a wonderful wedding, and for a couple of years everything was fine. Then I became pregnant and had Natti, and from there he lost interest. I realised afterwards that I was just like one of his hobbies. He didn't love me. He admired me. He thought I was beautiful. He wanted me to have his child. To him I was an exquisite table decoration when we threw dinner parties, something beautiful to wear when we went to Ascot or a charity ball. I was something to make his friends envious, like his Lagonda or one of his precious racehorses. After I had Natti he became more impatient with me. I think because I wasn't completely focussed on him. I think he loved Natti—as much as he was capable of that kind of love, but I think he was jealous. He thought she was stealing part of my love for him. As if love has a finite quantity. It's easy to see everything now of course, but at the time I was so confused and upset, I couldn't understand what I'd done wrong. I felt almost guilty for having Natti, like she was my fault, but I loved her so much,'

'So what happened then?'

'Oh Arthur, I'm sorry. I'm sure you can't want to listen to all this, it sounds so... so Mills & Boone!'

'No! I'm genuinely interested! Besides I've never read a Mills & Boone. So more please...'

'Well you can probably fill in the rest yourself. We had stopped having sex almost as soon as Natti became a bump. Well at least I thought we had. As it turned out it was only me that had stopped. He'd been having affairs all over the place. I should have guessed. I suppose I really knew but just didn't want to admit it to myself. I was happy with my beautiful Natti, I lived in a lovely big house, someone came in to clean every day, we even had a cook and I love cooking! Also my father had died not long after Hector and I were married, so I guess he sort of fulfilled that role'.

Etta went quiet, before adding quietly, 'but of course he nothing could ever replace Poppy'

'Poppy?'

'My father, everyone called him Poppy.'

'Ah!'

'Anyway I had a lot to lose, and I suppose I told myself I was doing it all for Natti, but I think that was an excuse. I was comfortable—house, clothes, car, money, but really I was so lonely. All I really had was my beautiful daughter, she was everything, she still is. But I remembered how it was when I was a child, how my father and mother were with each other; there was a feeling of ...family. We didn't have that feeling Hector and I, we weren't a family. He wasn't interested in being a father and a husband. I think we were just something he felt that he ought to have. Eventually I realised that all I was doing was wasting my life. There was no love. I wasn't happy. So I left him. I took Natti and we moved to London. We divorced Of course he was angry at first—ego mainly. First of all he begged me not to go, and swore undying love, then when that didn't work, he threatened all kinds of things: he was going to take Natti back, not give me any money. He said I'd never survive without him, but I think he was secretly relieved, it meant he could be even more of a playboy. He bought a house for us in Battersea, and of course he wrangled his finances so that he only had to provide the minimum amount of money for Natti—but that was fine, I didn't care, I was happy, I was also in a better position that many people. Anyway I found a job—working in a shop selling eastern clothes and jewellery, and that's about it.'

'So how did you end up living in Derbyshire?'

'Oh that happened later. Natti had a real thing about music. She started playing guitar when she was at primary school in Battersea and was naturally so good at it. The school suggested that I get her into a specialised music school, which she wanted to do even at the age of seven. Well we had an audition in Manchester—I'd never been up here before. Never been north of Watford. I couldn't believe how beautiful it was. I mean there were all the clichés about it being 'grim up north' but not 'green up north'. I just fell in love with it. Luckily Nat got into school here, otherwise I don't know what we'd have done, stayed in London I guess.'

'Well I'm glad you didn't. Here's to Natti!' Arthur raised his glass; they drank. 'So then what happened?'

'Do you really want to know, or are you just being polite?'

'Of course not! I'm fascinated. I love hearing about your life.'

'Well if you're sure…'

Arthur nodded. 'Carry on. I want the next episode! It's that or me talking about myself.'

'Well—if you put it like that! So her father was furious of course—about the move. He wanted her to go through the public school thing—then of course the Oxbridge mill. But she's my child and she had her own mind. Anyway, I sold the house in Battersea and we bought a house—not that far from here, in Heaton Moor.'

'I know that area, it used to be a bit of a bedsit-land.'

'Yes, you're right. I bought this massive house for next

to nothing, I mean I couldn't have bought anything like it in London for the price. It was bedsits before, but had been empty for a year or so—and in a bit of a state. Perfect to do up.'

'Sounds like you bought at the right time.'

'I suppose we did, I never expected to get anything like what we did for it.'

'Well it's a trendy suburb now.'

'I know, that was a good reason to move. But at the time it was great for Nats because we could get a train straight into the centre—I took her for the first five years or so, until she was about twelve, then she insisted on going with her friends; she used to meet them at the station. God I used to worry about her! I made her phone me when she'd got on the train; when she got off the train; when she arrived at school. Do you want to know a secret?'

'Do you have to ask me?'

'For the first couple of months I used to get the same train in as her, but sit in a different compartment. Then I used to go into Manchester in the afternoon and get the same train back. She never knew. Is that a bit crazy?'

'Not at all! You must love her very much.'

'She's everything to me. My life! I'd love you to meet her. But…'

'What?'

' I'm really nervous about it. I mean, I really want her to like you. And you to like her.'

'Don't worry. If she's anything like you how could I not like her. So she's sixteen now, still at music school?'

'Yes, still playing guitar, and doing really well. Up to her ears in exams at the moment though. Revision, revision and more revision.'

'What about boyfriends?'

'She gets a lot of interest. But at the moment she's having a good time with the girls. Boys. That's what frightens me the most. It's the one thing I can't protect her from.'

'We all have to learn the only way we can.'

'That's what worries me.'

'What about her father?'

'Oh she sees him during the summer holidays. And sometimes at Christmas. She flies out to Nice. She loves him, and she misses him too, but he's never really been a part of her life, so it's all normal for her. She's well-balanced about it.'

'Do you see him?'

'No. Not deliberately anyway—there's just never the need. Which is probably a good thing. We talk on the phone if anything needs sorting out. But he just leaves me to it. I don't think he's changed.'

So how did you end up in Derbyshire?'

Well. I met the girls via Martha. Martha's daughter Rhia is at the same school as Nats, we met at the station, got talking and it turns out the girls walked. Martha invited me out for a walk in the Peaks with them. I tell you Arthur, these girls really walked! I was exhausted the first few times. But I soon got into it. We tramped those hills and talked. Walked and talked.' In her head, Etta was walking with the girls. Her face glowed.

'Sounds as though you enjoy it.'

'It was a breath of fresh air. Not just the actual air: the

company as well. They were so funny and irreverent. We walked in sunshine, we walked in rain, we walked in snow. We got wet, we got hot, we got tired, we got stoned, we got lost, but we always got to the pub!'

'An essential part of a good walk I always say.'

'Absolutely! Anyway I just fell in love with the Peaks. We were walking one day, looking for a pub in a small village, and I saw this cottage for sale. It was mine; I knew it. So I came back and talked to Nats about it. She could easily get the train from there: all she cared about was having the ability to meet her friends; also it would mean a few more sleepovers, which she was happy about; so that was that. I put the house on the market sold it within a week, made an unhealthy profit and moved into the hills.'

'Sounds like fate.'

'Absolutely. But enough of all that, I've been talking forever, let's eat. It smells delicious and I'm starving.'

'You wait right here. I'll get it.'

The meal was delicious in every imaginable way. Etta and Arthur talked, listened, explored, debated, flirted, laughed, drank, ate and enjoyed. The only glitch came from the doorbell. As it rang the dogs jumped up yapping and growling menacingly, making Arthur jump out of his skin:

'Drat! Who's that at this time of the evening?!' Arthur was irritated at the intrusion. 'I'm not answering it! It will be someone selling something.' But, despite Etta's efforts to shush them, the dogs carried on barking, running too and fro between her and the front door. Their yapping escalated when the doorbell rang for a second time. 'I'll be back in a sec.' Arthur said, as he rose.

'It's OK I've been dying for a wee for ages, but I've only just realised!' Etta replied.

'Follow me, there's a handy toilet under the stairs. You might have to climb over the vacuum cleaner though.'

Etta stood and followed Arthur. The dogs followed closely behind Etta. As Arthur opened the front door the dogs growled menacingly, but Etta knelt and grabbed hold of their collars. Etta smiled up at the skinny young man in the funny yellow baseball cap. He grinned back, nervously.

'Nice dogs!' He lied.

'Thank you.' Etta replied. The dogs were pulling at their collars, needle-sharp teeth bared.

'You can put them in the garage if you like,' Arthur said, 'It's empty and heated.'

'Thanks. I will if they don't settle down, but they should be OK.' Etta dragged the dogs back into the living room.

'Sorry about that,' Arthur said to the young man at the door, who he thought must be on some kind of drugs rehabilitation scheme, judging by the look of him. 'What can I do for you?'

Icarus re-gathered his composure: 'Oh hi! I'm collecting names on behalf of a local organisation trying to protect the river bank.' Icarus waved his arm in the direction of the Mersey '—that riverbank right behind your house. Did you know there are seven rare species of plants, and a couple of rare butterflies living there? It's also the only habitat for one of Britain's rarest lizards, and there's dragonflies and all sorts of stuff!' Icarus asked, holding out a clipboard and a pen. He was trying to be as geeky as possible, without realising he didn't need to act it. He thought the black-rimmed spectacles were an especially nice touch. 'We're trying to get it made into an area of special scientific interest.'

The clipboard contained a sheet of paper, with various signatures and addresses scrawled on it, as well as an identity tag with his picture on.

'But it's the River Mersey!' Arthur was truly amazed,

'That's exactly why we're trying to raise people's awareness. Most people just don't realise what a natural treasure it is,' Icarus was convincing 'here, just sign there…'

'I haven't got any change,' Arthur apologized.

'That's OK we're just collecting signatures, a petition to stop the authorities from destroying a unique microcosmic habitat by extending the golf course.'

'What organisation did you say you were from?'

'The Society for the Protection of the Environment of the River Mersey.'

'Sounds like a noble cause. Anything to stop the spread of golf.' Arthur signed and handed the clipboard back.

'Sorry to have disturbed you. Thanks for your support.'

'No problems.'

Arthur walked back into the room. He couldn't help but think there was something vaguely familiar about the young man he'd just spoken to, but he had other things on his mind

'I heard something about the river—did I hear him mention lizards?' Etta was kneeling stroking the dogs, who were laying on their backs with their legs open, balls shining like small brown marbles.'

'Yes. I've lived here for years, cycle up the river almost every day, and I never knew that! Just shows you what can go on under your nose without you knowing.'

Arthur decided to serve dessert on the sofa. He and Etta took advantage of an evening with no further interruptions.

23: Moths and sunshine

As he walked back down the garden path. Icarus didn't know whether he was more pissed off than pleased, or more pleased than pissed off. He'd just checked the signature. It was a bit of a scrawl, but unmistakably 'Arthur Pod'. It was clearly Arthur Pod who he'd just heard say 'The garage is empty'. He decided to call Nathaniel.

'Well I've got some good news and some bad news.'

'Ah! Icarus. I'm glad it's you, I was just about to call you…'

'I've found him!'

'Who? Oh our man—Arthur. Right! Yes! Good…' Nathaniel didn't sound too excited about it.

'What's up dude, I mean man?'

'Nothing. Why?' Nathaniel was defensive. He had something to tell Icarus, but he wanted to pick his own space.

'You're doing it again! I thought you'd be excited.'

'It's Sandra.'

'What? Has something happened?'

'She's finally realised I've left.'

'Well it's only taken her, what is it? Three days? You can't be surprised she's found out?'

'Actually, she didn't. I called her and told her.'

'Why?'

'Oh I don't know. Anyway, I'm going to go and see her. I need to sort things out one-way or the other. It's niggling me. It's too much of a distraction.'

'Respect. I'll come back to the hotel; we'll have a look at the video, and sort out what we're going to do. But there's something I need to tell...'

Nathaniel interrupted: 'Actually, when I say I'm going to see her. I man I'm actually going to see her, now, as in I'm already on the train to London.'

'Fuck me! That was a bit sudden. I've only been gone for a couple of hours. You could have warned me.'

'Sorry mate. It was all a bit rushed. Look I'll be back in a couple of days, maybe sooner. But I've got to get this thing sorted. It's hanging over me. You sort things out there. I trust you.'

'Fair enough.' But it wasn't fair enough: Icarus was pissed off.

'I'm sorry. I've left you an envelope at reception. It's got some money in it. Enough to keep you going until I get back. The hotel has my credit card details, so that's all taken care of. Stay as long as you need to. I'll call you.'

'OK. Look, I understand. You get things sorted with Sandra and I'll see what I can do here. If I have any problems I'll call.'

'Fine.'

'I'll see you dude, I mean, man.' Icarus remembered

he hadn't finished…but it was too late, he tried to call Nathaniel back—there was no answer.

At the hotel. Icarus checked the video he'd taken using his 'baseball-cap-cam'. He had a good facial of Arthur and a bonus shot of Arthur's girlfriend and the two yapping little monsters. Icarus hated dogs, especially small yappy-type dogs. He hadn't met a small dog yet that didn't look as though it wanted to chew off his head. He captured the images into his computer and printed them out. After flicking through everything that was available on the TV, and discovering that the porn channel wasn't bookable for another hour, he decided to get some food and a couple of beers.

The hotel was a typical businessman's suburban stopover. Icarus's room was the same as any one of the other 60 in the building. It had a Jacuzzi corner bath, too many layers of paint on the woodwork, a box of tissues by the bed and a complimentary industrial-strength condom in the plastic imitation wicker basket of toiletries. The pool and gym downstairs held no interest for him. There was a large, softly lit bar next to the armchair-littered reception area, which was adjacent to a soul-less restaurant. A nightclub occupied a separate building tacked onto the side of the main hotel. On the front of the nightclub a neon sign glowed with the ominous invitation to 'meet - eat - sleep.' The hotel's large car park contained the incentives of evangelised commerce: the odd BMW, Jag and Mercedes, but mainly lots of Vauxhalls and Fords—the badges of which communicated a symbolic hierarchy as subtle as a single 'i' or a few square centimetres of pseudo-walnut trim for those aspiring to be at the top of their tree.

The hotel was not Icarus's scene. There were far too many suits in the bar. He wandered down the road in search of a pub where he could work out a plan of action, and a kebab house where he could get some proper food afterwards. He discovered a small pub with sticky carpets down a side street not far from the hotel. He ordered a pint of bitter and a bag of Hoi Sin flavoured pork scratchings, found a table and sat down to think.

It was alright for Nathaniel to say 'you sort something out', but what? If the Munter wasn't in Arthur's garage, where was it? He could follow Arthur and find out if it was somewhere else. But why keep it somewhere else if you've got an empty garage in your own house? Maybe it was in a workshop somewhere? Maybe he'd taken it to be checked over after the incident on the ferry? That wouldn't be unusual. All this stake-out stuff was getting a bit stupid. Icarus peeled a beer-mat to pieces, he had the feeling of being stuck in some kind of limbo. He just wanted to go home and relax in front of his computer, play a few games, enjoy a bit of social networking, watch some stupid videos and chill out. Instead he was in some scuzzy pub in Manchester trying to find an ugly car with a small fortune in diamonds bolted underneath. All he wanted to do was to find the thing, get the box with the diamonds and go home. He thought about just giving up, after all he didn't care about the money. He only helped Nathaniel because it was a buzz. It was like doing an extreme sport but with a lot less effort, which suited Icarus just fine, however there was no adrenaline involved in just sitting around, waiting.

Icarus was facing up to the prospect of having to follow Arthur until he found the car. 'It could take days!' Just the thought of it was frustrating. He decided to give it one day. He'd follow Arthur, and if there was no joy, at least it would give him time to think up an alternative plan.

Nathaniel and Icarus made a good team for good reasons. Nathaniel had the benefit of experience. He was a careful planner. He had excellent contacts. He didn't take unnecessary risks. He always kept things as simple as possible. And—importantly—he was well aware of his own weaknesses, technology being one of them.

Icarus, on the other hand, was brilliant at anything to do with computers, electronics, machines, codes and numbers. He was naturally gifted, a genius in fact, in the true sense of the word. Undisciplined genius can be a very volatile thing—dangerous even. Working with Nathaniel created the balance needed to get the best out of Icarus's talents, and get the best out of a situation. On his own, Icarus had the tendency to be over-complicated, single-minded and sometimes obsessive. The main reason that Icarus had never got himself into serious trouble was because he regularly dulled his brain with drugs and drink. His brain was like a monster that needed regular feeding. If it was fed it was a pussycat, if it started to go hungry it turned into a wild cat that needed to consume. His brain's need to consume was linked directly to Icarus's need to consume: he ate constantly to replace his perpetually-burning mental energy. If Nathaniel hadn't been so distracted by his own emotional affairs, he would never have left Icarus to 'sort things out'.

The following day wasn't as easy as Icarus hoped. From early morning he sat in the car within sight of Arthur's house. He felt claustrophobic. He saw Arthur's partner leave in her car with the two dogs. Then waited for hours until Arthur finally emerged. He watched Arthur open the garage door—sure enough it was empty, and watched as he came out pushing a bicycle. After locking the garage he rode down a path at the side of the house and up another path onto the riverbank. Icarus scrambled around for a map amongst all the rubbish now piling up in the car. A quick check showed that the river ran behind a suburb, affectionately called locally a 'village', about a mile away, before disappearing off through some industrial estate and past a sewage works. Icarus worked out that the village was probably his best bet. Although to get to it meant at least twice the distance by road than along the river.

After a frustrating drive through suburban traffic, frustrating minutes at traffic lights, then the problem of having to find somewhere to park in what turned out to be a thriving shopping street along a main road adorned with far too many double yellow lines, Icarus arrived. 'Some village!' He said to himself, as he locked the car and walked out along the busy road; taking in all the trendy shops, café bars, estate agents and offices he passed.

Finding 'Pod's Photography' was a damp revelation. It was obviously Arthur Pod's place, but it was shut. Icarus wandered around the back, he didn't know what to expect, and didn't find much except for the company van parked behind a steel fence. He hung around for almost an hour, but the proprietor didn't show.

The reason why there was a no show, was that Arthur had cycled—not to go to work, but to visit the police station to see if they had any more information for him. He was full of the joys of new love and the afterglow of the best sex he'd had in as long as he could remember. He felt genuinely happy as he cycled along the bank next to the brown waters of the Mersey. He was enjoying the sheer experience of existing. He often talked or sang to himself as he cycled, today he had lots to talk and sing about:

'Well, maybe this is it! It certainly feels like it! I like the way this feels! Whoever said life begins at forty obviously hadn't reached fifty. The sun was shining from an azure-blue sky dotted with white clouds like cotton wool stuck to a child's painting.

Arthur looked from the sky, to the trees and shrubs along the river: some of which were in full blossom, some of which were just starting. A blackbird hopped out of his path and up into a branch, from where it glared wide-eyed down its yellow beak at Arthur. 'You don't have to be rich to be my girl…' he sang, before thinking out loud: 'but maybe it's all a flash in the wotsit,' then that thought flashed and the puff of doubt dissipated, 'Naah! It's the real thing. Moths, sunshine and the future and love and I give in to it all, because…I have no choice! You are the sunshine of my life, ooooooh…'

The police had nothing, which was nothing more than Arthur expected, but it was a wonderful day anyway, so he decided to buy a few bits and pieces of food and cycle back gently along the river.

By late afternoon, Icarus was itching with boredom.

Nothing was happening. What was needed was a plan. If Arthur wasn't going to go to the car of his own accord, something would have to be done to make him go to it.

Icarus was walking through a park, smoking a spliff and racking his extensive, if slightly tangential, brain for an idea. As it happened, the flash of inspiration came from his feet rather then his head: Distracted, and slightly stoned, he stepped in some dog shit.

'Fuck! Fucking dogs! Why don't people clear up their effing crap after them! Little bastards.' Icarus hopped over to a wooden bench, sat down, removed his trainer and started to scrape out the shit from between the tread with a twig. It was while he was looking around to see if there was any water anywhere—a pond or a drinking fountain, that he noticed the poster across the road on the other side of the park. Grinning across at Icarus were two gigantic images of small poodles, one black, the other white. The slogan read 'Little Gem, perfect for Them.' Icarus was furious. He stood up, simultaneously trying to put his shoe on, and stumbled towards the poster, mumbling as he went: 'Fucking dogs! What do they do for anyone! How did the sly little bastards get human beings to take care of them, eh! Sneaking into our homes, eating our food! It's not like you can milk them, or get wool from them. Fuck me you can't even eat them! Well not without some fucking do-gooders kicking up a fucking stink!' Unchilled, Icarus reached the fence at the edge of the park. The poster was straight ahead. He picked up a stone and threw it as hard as he could. It hit on of the animals square on the tip of its black nose. He was just about to search for another stone to inflict the same punishment on the other dog, when he froze. Deep in his brain, sparks flew as connections were being made. He looked hard from the black poodle on the left, to the white poodle on the right, and back again. 'Naaa! They can't be! That's impossible! I mean what are the chances of that!' Not daring to hope, he took out his mobile phone, stretched over the fence as far as he could to get a good photo, and snapped. He couldn't get back to the hotel fast enough.

*

Etta had left Arthur's early to get home and change, then get back into the centre of Manchester for a meeting with Jenny at the agency. She wished she'd taken a change of clothes in the car to Arthur's, to save time.

Jenny had tried to insist on taking Etta for lunch, but it was the last thing Etta needed. She had a good idea what was coming and didn't see why she should help by consenting to a comfortable social environment. It took some considerable tact and determination to refuse: Jenny could be very insistent. Etta had just about got her act together as she entered Jenny's office.

'I'd rather have discussed this over lunch darling. But, it's your choice…'

'Discussed what, exactly?'

'Well… Oh! I didn't really want to do this!' Said Jenny, lying easily through her bright red lips.

'Do what?'

'I'm with you darling, you know that! I fought for your side, truly!' Etta knew Jenny well enough to know that she would take whatever side would gain her the most points.

'Fought for what? Come on Jenny, you've let half the cat out of the bag...'

'OK, well, the thing is...we're animating.'

'Animating what?' Etta knew damned well what, but she wanted to make Jenny squirm as much as possible.

'Well, the poochies of course, what else? Apparently CGI is simply THE thing these days, so realistic, even the fur.'

'CGI?' Etta asked.

'Computer generated graphics darling. Simply everybody's using it!'

'I know what it is, but isn't that horrendously expensive?'

'No darling, it used to be, but I did some research and...'

'You did some research?'

'Oops, sorry darling! Well, yes I might have suggested that...'

'It was your suggestion?!'

'Well Tim and I went to see this film with his daughter, and it was so cute darling—the little monsters and everything, it just got me thinking...' In Etta's experience thinking and Jenny didn't occur in the same place at the same time.

'Well thank you! Talk about being stabbed in the back! But surely there will be some royalties or something? I mean you're basing them on my dogs.'

'No royalties darling, sorry. It wouldn't make financial sense if there were. I've spoken to our legal department and, well, it's all in your contract, or not in your contract, or whatever, darling.'

'So that's it?' Etta was trying to keep as calm as she could.

'Sorry darling, but we had to do something, I mean they're only doggies, they aren't going to be around forever. Besides we've got to protect the brand!'

'Protect the brand!'

'Of course darling! Thanks to your little darlings we're now number one you know!'

'Exactly the point! My little darlings! So what do you get out of this? A promotion, a raise?'

'Well I have heard rumours…' Jenny was discharging pride like static; she grinned revealing lipstick on her teeth.

'Well I'd be careful if I were you. You're only human and you're not going to be around forever. They can replace the simplest things with CGI these days. Goodbye darling!' Etta stood and turned to leave, adding: 'Et tu Brutė!'

'I'm sorry?' Jenny was puzzled, but she found herself questioning a door that had just shut.

Jenny got on the internal phone to a young account executive: 'What was the name of that aftershave that everyone wore in the mid-seventies?' The young exec shrugged, he wouldn't know, he wasn't born until 1984; however he made a mental note to ask his dad. When he'd Wiki'd the answer he passed it to Jenny, who was puzzled as to why this young man had suddenly come into her office a couple of days later and blurted out the name of one of the three musketeers. She suspected him of having Tourette's, and made a note on her e-diary to get rid of him at the first opportunity.

24: Dogged planning

'I should have told her where to go!' Etta was giggling. She'd called in to see Arthur on her way home, 'Instead of being so polite.'

'She sounds as though she deserved it. At least you don't sound too upset considering you've just heard your sole source of income's ending.'

'To be honest, I'm actually pleased. I mean, I'd already been thinking about doing something else, and I hadn't realised how fed up I was with the whole advertising thing. We've been doing it for, what, more than five years now.'

'So have you thought about what you're going to do?' Arthur was more curious than concerned: Etta was intelligent and he was sure whatever she turned her hand to would work.

'Well, I've been thinking—but I haven't come up with anything yet. But whatever it is I'd like it to be something with a little more credibility attached to it. I mean really, advertising dog food: Where's the merit in that?'

Arthur really didn't know, 'Maybe you could do something creative, such as painting, or writing, or pottery or something.'

'Well I would, except that I've got Natti to think about. I couldn't write though, tried it once. I thought I'd write a straightforward romance, but I ended up getting diverted into all kinds of pseudo-philosophical and psychological stuff, even I couldn't make sense of it after a couple of chapters. So I gave up. No. Not writing. Maybe a shop, or property developing, I don't know.'

'Property developing? Would that mean selling your cottage?'

Etta nodded.

'But I thought you loved it?'

'I do, but it's worth a small fortune now. I could buy a house closer to the centre and another one to do up and sell, or rent out. Don't get me wrong, I'd hate to sell it, but needs must.'

'From what you've said, it sounds lovely. I think it would be a shame.'

'Of course! You've not seen it yet have you? What are you doing this evening? Why don't you come over to my house for dinner? You won't be able to stay though—it's probably not a good idea.'

'Because of Natti you mean?'

'Yes. I'd feel a bit odd announcing 'Arthur, Natalie; Natti, this is Arthur, and by-the-way he's staying the night.'

'Mmm, I see what you mean, but don't worry, I'd love to meet her anyway.'

'You might. She'll be studying and practising at Beatrice's house; she's due to come home but sometimes stays over if it gets too late.'

'There's only one problem.'

'What's that?' Etta looked concerned.

'Three nights, three dates.'

Etta laughed with relief. 'So! Who cares?'

'Not me.'

'Although officially, that will make you my boyfriend.'

'I can live with that, as long as you don't expect me to come quietly.'

Etta smiled mischievously.

*

Icarus was in high spirits. It seemed that his luck was changing. Even the sun had come out. In the hotel he compared the two images: the one from the poster and the one he'd produced from the video footage he'd taken with his 'baseball-hat-cam' of the dogs being restrained as they tried to jump up to rip out his throat—at least that's how he remembered it. While he couldn't totally confirm they were the same two dogs, they certainly looked identical enough to make him ninety-nine per cent certain. It was the small pink spot on the nose of the white one that was the clincher.

Things were getting complicated enough now for Icarus to put a plan together. He like complicated things, which is why he inevitably made problems more complicated in the first place: it was only then he could work out a way to solve them. Simple problems were a puzzle to Icarus. Partly because he couldn't see the point in them, but mainly because he was always suspicious that they were more complicated than they seemed to be. He didn't trust simple problems one little bit. Of course none of this was conscious. He thought all his own plans were elegantly simple; just like the one he was now hatching.

First he had to make sure where the dogs were kept. Maybe the woman lived with Arthur? He had to find out somehow. He remembered that there were two cars in the drive when he'd called the previous evening. One must be hers. He decided to check out the registration numbers.

As he drove to Arthur's house, Icarus decided that he'd never make a cop, not that he had even thought of being one, but stakeouts were the most boring waste of time ever invented. He paused for a second to wonder whether boring wastes of time had ever actually ever been invented. He tried the basic sustenance of the American detective movie—coffee and doughnuts, but they offered little if any comfort. The sugar and caffeine just made him more restless. Out of boredom, Icarus set himself the task of finding the perfect stakeout food: Pizza was OK, hamburgers not too bad, but donner kebabs were the best—fiddly, messy and time consuming. He bought himself a kebab, now laying wrapped in foil on the passenger seat as he pulled up within sight of Arthur's house, where he was delighted to see the same two cars in the drive he'd seen a few days before. He casually drove down the road and made a mental note of the registration number of each of them. He stopped out of sight of the house to write the numbers down, then opened his laptop, picked up a local Wi-Fi hotspot and hacked into the information he needed.

The results showed the car registered to Ms Etta Corbett. The address was in Derbyshire. She was 34. He decided to try and find out something about the dogs, but before he could start searching, he saw Etta's car start to move out of Arthur's drive. Impulsively he decided to follow. He inadvertently squashed the kebab as he dropped the laptop onto the passenger seat, started the engine, and slid the car into gear.

An hour or so later, Icarus was pleased to discover that, for once, data and the physical world matched. He watched as Etta parked her car, took a set of keys from her pocket and disappeared through a gate between high hedges. He wound down the window. He was almost pleased to hear the familiar yapping of the two poodles, which faded as the door closed. 'Fantastic!' The seeds of his plan began to germinate. He did a three-point-turn and headed back into town.

Back in his hotel room, Icarus sat smug about the elegance of his plan, which was simply to kidnap the dogs and ransom them for the car. He wondered whether dognapping was a crime in England. Of course he didn't really want the car, only the diamonds, but he needed to get to the car, preferably without being seen, in order to get the diamonds. He thought about wearing a mask, and ran through the options including the pope, a clown, or maybe a white bunny with big pink ears. But dismissed that idea as all too trippy. Help was what he really needed, he decided. He couldn't do it on his own. Nathaniel was obviously up to his emotional ears in Mrs. Makeover, and Icarus knew that he probably wouldn't approve of his plan. 'But you've got to take risks if you want to make a profit man,' Icarus reasoned, thinking that would be the kind of thing Nathaniel might say.

Deciding he needed help was one thing, but where from? He didn't know anyone in Manchester. He was sitting on the lid of the toilet, using the hotel room's bathroom extractor to take away the smoke from the small spliff he'd almost finished, when he realised that he might know a man who did. He had Bob the Dog's number in his mobile. He dumped the roach in the toilet and flushed before dialling:

'Bob? It's Icarus'

Icarus?' Bob sounded as though he was jogging.

'You know—Nathaniel Boot's friend?'

'Oh! Hello mate! (Pant! Pant!) What can I (Pant! Pant!) do for you? (Pant! Pant! Pant!)'

Icarus felt good, as if he was a proper criminal organising a job. 'Well Bob, I've got this thing going down in Manchester, but I need a couple of helpers.'

'Sorry mate! (Pant! Pant!) I never go up north. (Pant! Pant!). Makes me nervous (Pant! Pant! Pant!)'

'That's OK but I was wondering if you might know of anyone up here?'

'Hang on mate… (Pant! Pant!) (Pant! Pant!) (Pant! Pant! Pant!) (Uuuuuurgh!)'

Icarus thought Bob must have strained a muscle. If he had, it was a quick recovery.

'Are you OK? What are you doing, jogging?'

'Ha! Ha! (blow out and pause for breath) Ha! No! Jogging? Me! That's a good 'un. I don't walk unless I 'ave to, never mind jog! No mate! I was having a bit of Posh 'n' Becks with the good lady missus here! And very nice it was too. But I'm all yours now. Now what was it you needed?'

Icarus nearly threw up into the phone. 'I, well, you see I've got this problem I need to sort out in Manchester. I wondered if you knew anyone?'

'What kind of problem?'

'Well, it's difficult to explain. But I need one or two people who will do what they're paid to do, without asking questions.'

'Hmmm…' Bob was thinking, 'Well there is these two… …Naaa!'

'What?' Icarus dived in quickly.

'No they'd be no good. Ain't normal.'

'Ain't normal' sounded good to Icarus, he needed ain't normal, 'Who?'

'Nah, seriously Icarus, they're a bit mum and dad, the pair of 'em.'

'Well maybe I could meet them, suss them out.' For Icarus, it was a case of any breath of wind in the Doldrums.

'Well, they're secure enough. Wouldn't grass yer up nor nuffin', but, well I s'pose it's your loaf. But watch 'em. 'ere I'll give you their number.' There was a brief pause as Bob disappeared. He returned and gave a number to Icarus, who entered it into his mobile.

'What are their names?' Icarus asked.

'Oh yes! What a darft barstard I am! They're called Des and Les, they're twins. Des and Les Mattress. Most people calls 'em the Mattress twins.

*

Les and Des Mattress would do anything for money. They would do many things for the sheer twisted pleasure of it. But they would do literally anything for money.

They'd always been like that. At school Les ate a whole chinchilla for a quid. It wasn't as cruel as it sounds, because Des had already separated it from existence for another quid. Onlookers, in between throwing up, would have thought that Les drew the short straw, except that the pair had a fist fight to decide who did what. Les won, and got to decide who would swallow it.

The fact that they would casually accomplish just about any dare made them initially popular with whatever social group they were in, briefly. Eventually their inevitable drift towards extremes repulsed even the hardest spectator. Besides which many couldn't cope with the responsibility for what the twins were capable of doing.

Of course extreme actions create extreme risk. Broken bones, scars and burns in delicate places were some tokens of their exploits. But the twins always collected the money, whether they succeeded or whether they failed. They worked on the basis that if they tried, they should be paid. Nobody could knock them for trying.

Inevitably they had grown up to make the most of their talents. The were regularly called upon by all kinds of people including criminals and lawyers, disgruntled businessmen and dishonoured wives, all of whom required something doing for money. Generally things that they either couldn't do themselves, or didn't have the stomach or courage to do: burglary, kidnap, beatings, theft, arson, strange sex, and so on.

What added a twist to the twins' talents was their angelic appearance. They were more-or-less identical, given the odd visible scar: A whisker over six feet tall, with blonde hair that fell foppishly over their beautiful, blue-eyed, boyish faces. They were both fit and lithe. Women stopped talking when the twins walked into a room, and if they went back to their conversations, their eyes would still dart hungrily across.

In a way, this added to their shock element. Watching a still-warm chinchilla being dismembered and eaten by something resembling an ogre is one thing, it was quite something else to watch it be calmly enjoyed by a small blonde boy with a face that looked as though it could summon a choir of angels. Des and Les were also charming, polite and well mannered—the result of a good, but very strict upbringing. It was all wasted of course; in fact it was purely superficial because neither twin had the slightest shred of a conscience nor a glimmer of guilt in their being. They were true innocents who didn't need to see the point in anything. This made them lousy friends and even lousier boyfriends. They would have sex with anyone who was vaguely interested without even considering the word 'faithful', and lots of women were vaguely interested. They're angelic looks attracted no less attention from men. The women and the men tended to get hurt in different ways. As for friends, the twins didn't need any: they had each other. To call the Mattress twins 'evil', as some did, was to not understand them, because to be 'evil' implies knowing the difference between good and bad. As far as the Mattress twins were concerned, if you got paid for it, it was good.

As far as Icarus was concerned the pair seemed perfectly fine. He organised to meet the twins in the same pub he had been in the previous evening. The twins were polite, quiet, seemed to be fairly thoughtful, and listened intently. If Icarus had the two boys' brains wired to a monitor, the only activity he would have seen would have been peaks in the parts that handled the questions 'What?' and 'How much?' Icarus felt very comfortable with them. And happily employed their services, thinking 'Natty-boy would be proud of me!'

Icarus's simple plan was that the twins would kidnap the dogs, hide them somewhere, and keep them safe until needed. Icarus would arrange a ransom note, and organise a meeting point—somewhere remote and dark. The deal would be that Etta gets driven to the drop by Arthur, in his car. There would be a token amount of ransom money of course: the twins had to be paid after all. A couple of grand should do it—nothing too heavy. The twins would make the swap, which would happen some distance away from the Munter. Then Icarus could nip underneath with a spanner and remove the box, recovering the diamonds. Simple. Of course the twins didn't know anything about Icarus's part in the plot. As far as they knew, it was just being done for the money. Not that they cared anything about the whys and wherefores, just the whats and how-muches.

Icarus gave the twins the address where the dogs were. They seemed very confident, which made Icarus feel much more relaxed. Breaking, entering and dognapping weren't his thing. Give him a safe, a website, a bank account, a code, and he'd crack it. But the thought of trying to handle two yappy little bastard dogs made him shiver. That was without the worry of having to find somewhere to keep them and feed them for a couple of days. 'Thank god for Bob the Dog!' Icarus thought, as he looked for a kebab shop on his way back to the hotel.

25: Smitten and bitten

Looking at Etta's grey stone cottage as he walked towards it, Arthur couldn't help imagining it as a box. Not a box as in the thousands of modern homes that seem to pop up overnight—so bland that they have to be sold with a lifestyle as well as an en-suite. The box Arthur had in mind was more a glorious container of life, warmth, love and colour that was enclosed so that nothing could be seen from the outside except the plain grey of the raw material. Stone and slate the colour of old-fashioned speckled-grey cardboard—the type that peeps from the well-worn corners of the covers of old books, or made boxes that toys always came in at Christmas when Arthur was a kid. That kind of box had a quality all of its own, it could contain great adventures, romances, mysteries, thrillers, it could hold an entire imagination.

As he walked up the path through the garden the scent of plants shifted with each step: light and sweet, heavy and slow, green and sharp, deep. Arthur wished he knew the names of more plants. Yellow light flooded a warm invitation through the half-paned door. Arthur rang the bell and saw Etta through the glass. As soon as he saw her he wondered what he'd done to deserve her.

The home was bigger than Arthur imagined it would be when outside. There were low beams, a massive fireplace, flagged floors, and an enormous stove that radiated heat faithfully from the kitchen. Everywhere there was evidence of art: pictures and words made with love and shared by Etta and Natti; strangely shaped or beautifully coloured wood, stone and metal foraged from adventures. Arthur could see that the walls held work from every step of Natti's life, probably from the first time she'd held a crayon. There were poems, notes, photographs, postcards and scraps of all kinds. The living room was half-lined with books. The bookshelves had overflowed into piles on the floor and crept up the side of the stairs. There were also newspapers and magazines kept for cuttings that hadn't yet been cut. There were framed prints of work by artists such as Titian, Cezanne and Sutherland, mingling comfortably with posters for concerts, films and exhibitions. But it was clear that Natti's work, or play, took pride of place.

'You're quiet Arthur, is everything OK?'

'I'm gob smacked.'

'Is that good?'

'Wonderful! Everything's so ...'

'What?' Asked Etta, after waiting for Arthur to get the word out.

'I don't know! Really I don't know how to describe it! Homely? Interesting? Colourful? Artistic? Everything all mixed together.'

'Well, thanks. That's good then.'

'It's … honestly, I'm … I don't know what else to say.'

'It's children really. This is what they do. Their heads spill out all over the place.' Etta was smiling.

Arthur thought she looked so at home here, then felt stupid when he realised that of course she would. He was glad he didn't say it out loud. 'It's not just all this,' Arthur panned the room with his arms, 'it's the feeling in here. It feels like family, like home. It's really wonderful.'

'So you like it then?' Etta was teasing Arthur's enthusing.

'I love it. I love it because it says everything about how I see you. It's like…' Arthur paused for thought, 'It's like how I feel about you.'

'In what way?'

'It's difficult, but… it's like your personality, what you are, how I feel you are as a person. It's like the sense I have of you when you're not around. The bit of you I carry around with me, the bit that's always there—even if I'm not thinking about you,'

Etta looked at Arthur and laughed, not because of his clumsy explanation, but out of delight because he was trying to get his feeling out. Feelings like that needed a whole lifetime and then some. She walked over to him and put her arms around his waist, he wrapped his around her. 'I think I understand you, and I think that might be another one of the nicest thing anyone's ever said to me.' She reached up, and they kissed.

'Where is Natti? I'm looking forward to meeting her?'

'Oh, not here I'm afraid, she's revising and practising at her friends again, they've got a concert in a few weeks. She's staying over, but she's going to ring me later. The concert's a part of her exams, they start next week so she's nervous. But she really doesn't need to be, she'll sail through them.'

'Well I don't know her, but I imagine she would. I can tell she's very creative, she obviously gets it from you.'

'Oh we love doing things together. At least we did. She changed recently, more into her friends, music and, inevitably—boys. She still has her moments though: Christmas and birthday cards. She's made our Christmas cards since she was three. I get them printed and send them out to all our friends and family.'

'You're obviously very proud of her. It's a shame she won't be here.'

'Oh you'll meet here soon. She's curious to meet you too.'

'Curious?'

Etta laughed, 'Her word, not mine. She's at that age—it must be something she's reading.'

Arthur smiled.

'Now Arthur, I've got an apology to make.'

Arthur looked concerned.

'Oh it's nothing serious! Don't worry!'

Arthur felt relief.

'It's just that I didn't get back until late and I haven't cooked anything. I'm really sorry—especially after your lovely meal the other night.'

'Don't worry. A slice of dry bread and a glass of water will do fine.'

'Well, I can rustle that up for you if it's what you really want. But I was thinking we could go down to the pub.

They do proper country food. I hope you're not on a diet though, because it's a bit lardy—steak puddings, venison sausage, roast pheasant, fish in cream sauce—that sort of thing?'

'No, you're OK I'll stick with the slice of bread and the glass of water, as long as it's white sliced bread.'

Etta looked pained, 'Oh, I'm sorry, no. I've only got wholemeal, fresh today from the bakery in the village.'

'Oh well!' Arthur shrugged, 'I guess it's the pub then.'

Etta pulled on a thick jumper: 'It can get chilly up here in the evening, especially at this time of year.' She then knelt down to stroke the dogs, which were curled up together on the rug in front of the fireplace.

'You two be good. I won't be long.' She then stood up and switched on the TV, flicking it to a cartoon channel. 'They love cartoons, and anything to do with motorcycles, they'll sit and watch either for hours, I don't know why. Dogs are strange creatures.' And with that, Etta and Arthur went to the pub. Etta was unaware that this was the last time she would ever see the animals in such a sedate state.

Des and Les were ready to do anything necessary to take the dogs: given that they were being paid for doing it. They sat in their rusty BMW convertible parked a short distance from Etta's house. They were waiting. Not waiting patiently, because patience is a virtue and the Mattress twins weren't virtuous. They were waiting purely because it was part of what they were being paid to do. They'd discussed the plan with Icarus. Les favoured a knock on the door, a forced entry, lots of tying up and bundling. Des's suggestion would have had even those with the strongest stomach searching for a bucket. Icarus tried to put them as straight as he could, explaining each step of the task in detail. Somewhere on a faraway hillside in Icarus's head a solitary warning bell pealed slowly—reverberating distantly due to the effects of the rather strong skunk he'd spliffed up earlier.

The twins would have waited for as long as they needed to: days or weeks, it didn't matter. They had little sense of time. They saw Arthur arrive. They waited. They saw Etta and Arthur leave and walk up the road. That was good enough. They got out of the car and walked over to the house. The shrubs and bushes provided excellent cover. After a quick scout around they crept to the back of the house. Getting in was easy. Des found a small open window, reached through and opened a larger one. He climbed in and opened the back door. From the living room came the sound of children's TV and what sounded like cartoon mayhem. Les walked as quietly as he could to the living room door, which was ajar. Des peered over Les's shoulder. The TV was clearly in view, as was the back of the sofa, other than that, no sign of the dogs or anyone else. Les pushed the door further open and the pair walked quietly into the room. On screen a mouse was misshaping a cat's head with a mallet. Des sniggered, Les giggled and gestured to Des to 'Ssshhussshhh!'.

There was a gentle growl from the other side of the sofa. Des and Les stepped forward, paying more attention to the cartoon than they should have. They were almost touching the back of the sofa when two tiny fur-and-fanged figures came hurtling over the top, yapping and snarling with a viciousness which far outweighed their size. Les reacted instantly by putting out his hand to protect his face from the snarling needlepoint-filled mouth that was hurtling towards it. He felt the teeth sink into his hand. It would be some time before he noticed the missing fingertip. Des lost his balance while trying to avoid the other animal, which had connected with all its lupine instincts and, somewhat ambitiously, was ready to rip out his throat. Des grabbed at the sofa-back to steady himself, but there was not enough counterweight in it to hold him: he and the sofa fell backwards. One corner of the sofa landed square in Des's balls. It was small consolation that it also threw the poodle off-balance; it missed his throat and instead clamped its teeth onto his earlobe. In the several seconds it took for the pain in his balls to subside enough to allow any kind of defensive action, the lobe had been bitten off and swallowed.

Anger and bitterness were not in the twins' limited range of emotions, which was very fortunate for the poodles. After a scramble around the living room, which resulted in smashed lamps, upturned tables and significant amounts of blood being trailed around, the dogs were finally caught and bundled still snarling into the twin's respective rucksacks. On the TV the cartoon jingle played along merrily. Understandably, Les wanted the end of his finger back, he was sure that the dog now squirming and growling in his bag had eaten it. There was only one way he could think of getting it, but because he was being paid to do a job, he thought he'd better check with Icarus first. A quick phone call attracted the stressed reply: 'Alive! Definitely alive!' Les reconciled himself by deciding that he had never planned to play a musical instrument. They were halfway down the path when Des remembered to go back and leave the note.

The room looked like a murder scene. There were blood smears all over the place, hardly a stick of furniture had not been misplaced, upset or broken. A framed photo of the two smiling dogs lay smashed upon the floor. The phone rang and the answering machine clicked into life: 'Hi! Etty, it's Jenny from the agency, please could you give me a call darling—when you've got the time. Speak to you soon darling!'

Etta and Arthur had enjoyed a fine meal. The pair walked back huddled together, sharing each other's warmth. It was a clear night bright with stars and the air was crisp enough to mist the breath. Etta pulled her key from a pocket of her jeans and opened the door. What she saw was too difficult to absorb instantly, several seconds passed as her eyes delivered the message to her brain, which rapidly compared what was where and what should be where. It finally clicked:

'Oh dear!'

Arthur looked from the room to Etta and back again, several times—waiting for a reaction that would tell him which way she would fall. Whichever way, he would be there to catch her.

Etta's hands started to tremble as she thought about what might have happened if Natti had been there. Even though she knew exactly where Natti was, she panicked and needed to phone her. Her hands were shaking so much that Arthur had to dial. Natti was of course fine. Arthur could feel Etta's relief. With Natti safe, Etta was free to explore what had happened. It was the silence that made her realise there was no sign of the dogs. She called them…but nothing. She went into the kitchen and found the door open.

'Don't touch anything!' Arthur shouted, thinking of fingerprints. Etta ran into the garden shouting the dogs' names. There was not even a whimper. Arthur ran after her, concerned that the intruders might still be nearby. Suspecting that the dogs may have been frightened, she searched under the beds and in any space big enough for them to hide in. Nothing. She called the police.

It was while she was on the phone that she noticed the note propped up on the TV, she waved to Arthur and pointed to it. While Etta tried calmly to explain to the police what had happened, Arthur looked for something with which to pick up the note. He was still thinking of fingerprints. He found a pair of pink rubber gloves in the kitchen, and after snapping them on; he carefully picked up the note. He mimed opening it to Etta, who was trying to remain calm with the police, even though her patience was being tried. She nodded, pointed down the mouthpiece of the phone and looked to heaven. Arthur ripped open the envelope and took out the contents just as Etta ended her call. Standing beside Arthur, she giggled—a release of nervousness. Arthur looked at her questioningly.

'The gloves,' Etta said.

Arthur unfolded the note, which was put together from cut-out newspaper letters. 'How cliché!' Etta said, mockingly, but trying to hide her anger.

Arthur read the note out loud: 'We've got your dogs. We are the Black Claw Group Against Animals in Advertising. If you go to the police you will never see them again. We want something. We will contact you. Write a mobile number on the back of the door of the second cubicle in the Swine and Trasher in the village. No funny stuff!'

The word 'claw' had actually been spelt 'clow' but someone had crossed out the 'o' with a felt-tip pen and written the letter 'a' above it. The same pen had also crossed out the word 'something', and written in 'some money'.

'Idiots!' Etta said, her anger slipping out.

'I wonder why they wrote: "we want something" first, what thing?' Arthur asked.

'Probably just money. But whatever they want, I do know what they've got. And I'll tell you Arthur; they'll soon find out that they've bitten off more than they can chew!'

Etta made tea for the pair of them as they waited for the police. Cup in hand, she walked slowly around the room, checking to see if anything else was missing. All she wanted to do was tidy up—put everything back where it should be. Make her home her own again. She especially wanted to tidy and clean before Natti saw it. Arthur had insisted that Etta tell the police about the dogs and the note. But Etta was adamant that she wouldn't—at least not until she'd had time to think things over, 'And right now, my head's a mess,' she said

The police were almost as much help as they could be. Later described by Arthur as the 'Laurel and Hardy' of the local nick, the pair looked around, seemingly more curious about the house than the crime. Ollie, the officer who took the statement, seemed to exist purely as a life support system for his belly. Etta wondered what his shirt buttons were sewn on with; whatever it was, it was tough stuff. He balanced a clipboard on his belly, and using a tiny ballpoint pen borrowed from a betting shop, filled in the crime sheet with handwriting the size of an ant's footsteps. He asked a question: then there was an agonising wait while he wrote down the answer:

'Name?'

'Etta Corbett.'

Ollie repeated the name, 'Etta Corbett', inhaled deeply and dived into his sheet of paper. He wrote at least two lines just for Etta's name. Throughout the interview, every time he reached a full stop he looked up, and—with the demeanour of an academic who had been concentrating on translating some ancient text and just discovered a gem of wisdom—gave of his long experience on the force. For example:

'You must have disturbed them, that's why there's nothing missing.'

The other officer, Stan, was busy taking pictures of most of the house with a digital camera, striking the melodramatic poses of a fashion photographer as he did so. 'Very arty. Very House & Garden,' he enthused, peering into the back of the camera at a nicely framed shot of upset objects on a windowsill. 'Nice curtains! Where are they from?'

Etta's glare was unseen by Stan, who had already been distracted.

‘Blood! That’s good!’ He said, zooming in for a close up. After clicking the shutter he said, loud enough for everyone to hear: ‘It’s good if we find blood or shit—sorry Miss, I mean ‘faeces’—because we can get it tested.’

Ollie nodded and said sombrely ‘That’s right, DNA’, as he laboured the pen.

The double act finished almost two hours later, a lot of which involved Etta and Arthur listening to mainly gruesome tales about being a police officer. Finally, the pen was popped into an inside pocket and the officers stood to leave.

Etta was looking forward to getting the place cleaned up. Arthur was looking forward to bed. Stan and Ollie seemed to have no sense of time.

‘Don’t worry ma’am, I’m sure your dogs are just frightened, they’ll probably be back when they get hungry!’

‘They’re always hungry,’ thought Etta, but didn’t say anything in case it triggered another anecdote.

‘Very nervous animals, poodles—my brother’s wife’s got one,’ said Stan, while tucking his camera back into its bag, ‘He can’t go near her without it growling at him. They’ve not had sex since she bought it, two years ago.’

‘Oops! Silly me! I almost forgot to ask you to sign the statement.’ Ollie said, taking his pen out of his pocket. He handed her the clipboard containing two sheets of ant steps. She read through it. Even though she didn’t remember using phrases such as ‘proceeded towards the village’, ‘it came to my attention that…’ and ‘forced entry via an aperture in a glazed panel above the water inlet valves and waste-water outlet area', the general gist was correct. She signed.

'Thank you ma'am I'll arrange for CID to call first thing.'

'First thing! What, you mean I've got to live in this mess all night?' Etta looked pleadingly at Ollie.

'Er, well CID is a specialist division. They only work from nine until five, unless it's a murder of course!' He looked at Stan: 'It's a fine mess, but I don't see any dead bodies here!' They both smirked, said their goodbyes, and left.

The house was quiet. Etta looked around and sighed.

'Well there's not much we can do, we may as well go to bed.'

'You don't have to stay here if you're not comfortable with it. We can go to my place. I can help you clean up tomorrow, after the CID has been.'

'Oh I don't mind Arthur, really. They've not touched upstairs, besides, I'm not letting a bunch of idiots keep me out of my own home.'

Etta didn't sleep well. She lay in Arthur's arms for most of the night, thinking about the future: about what she was going to do, and why anyone would want to kidnap a pair of poodles. It was early morning now, and Arthur was no longer sleeping.

'I don't understand. I mean it's insane,' she said, quietly.

'Well, look on the bright side, if they've been taken by an animal rights group, at least they'll be treated well.'

'Mm,' agreed Etta. 'I don't know though. But whatever happens I really need to do something else, find another way of making a living. Don't get me wrong Arthur, I like them, they're real characters—but their not really lovable, not really pets. They can be quite vicious: I doubt very much that it's their blood downstairs. At least I hope it's not—I don't want them to suffer, I love dogs, but I'd rather have something bigger and softer…' She snuggled up to Arthur.

'A Labrador, if I remember right.'

'Mmm. Poodles just yap and growl at everything and everyone. I can't complain of course, they've paid the bills, but… I don't know. I mean I know my hand has been forced by the agency, but I wasn't happy—you know, promoting dog food and being part of an international brand. Anyway, now I'm just repeating myself. Let's get some breakfast.'

'I think that might be difficult before the CID get here.'

As it was, they didn't turn up until almost midday. 'They' was in fact a 'him', a quiet, middle-aged man with grey hair and grey beard, both a little too long. He pulled up at the front of the house in an unassuming blue van. He was already dressed in a white coat, and carried a blue plastic toolbox. After a polite introduction he snapped on a pair of surgical gloves and began dusting for prints and collecting samples of dried blood, as well as minute objects picked up with the end of a scalpel. Everything was placed in small plastic tubes or bags and carefully labelled. He didn't really say much. He accepted a coffee after Etta checked that it was OK to make one. When he'd gone it was still sitting untouched where Etta had put it for him.

'Got dogs?' he asked.

'Yes. Two. Poodles.'

'Thought so. Smell 'em. No matter how much you clean, you can't get rid of the smell. Good though, poodles. Don't lose much hair. Makes my job easier. Hate dogs though me. And bees...' He spoke without lifting his head from examining a section of carpet that had been underneath the upturned sofa. He was engrossed in inspecting something.

'Have you found any prints?' Etta asked, looking around at the powder smeared all over her doors, furniture and windows.

'Not really, all smeared. Got one perfect one though.'

'Good, that should be useful?' Etta was trying to prompt some reply.

'Not really. It's still on the finger. Useful prints are those not on the finger—then we can find the finger, the hand and hopefully the person—all nice and intact like. Course he could have a criminal record, in which case a finger is very useful indeed. But criminals are normally very careful not to leave bits of anatomy lying around, p'ticularly their own—and especially bits with fingerprints on—in my experience anyway.' He dropped the fingertip casually into a plastic bag. Arthur grimaced.

'What about the blood? Is it human do you think?' Etta needed some consolation. The grey-head lifted and, from under a raised eyebrow a turquoise-coloured eye stared at the fingertip in the bag, then looked at Etta.

'Human then,' she concluded.

The man nodded slowly: 'Ninety-nine per cent certain! Mostly from one human fingertip, severed by canine.'

Arthur helped Etta clean the house. He donned the rubber gloves: 'This is becoming a habit!' and washed down all the surfaces. The fingerprint powder was particularly stubborn. Etta put everything back in its place. Her main concern was that Natti didn't suspect anything—she didn't want her to feel uneasy. By the time they'd finished it was almost three o'clock. Neither had eaten since the previous evening. Arthur felt his stomach protest.

'We should eat.'

'I'm not hungry.

'That's the adrenaline and the stress. You should eat.'

Etta was leaning against the frame of the kitchen door, looking out into the living room, and thinking.

'I guess you're right. But let's go to the Swine and Thrasher, then we can kill two birds with one stone.'

Arthur was concerned, 'But you're not really going to do what they want are you?'

'What choice do I have?'

'You don't have to give them your own mobile number for a start.'

Etta looked at Arthur, waiting for him to continue. He hadn't thought that far ahead, but needed to come up with something.

'Use mine. I've got an old pay-as-you-go phone at home.' You can give me mine back when this is all over.

Etta smiled, Arthur may be nearly fifty, but he still had something to learn about women: 'Have you really got another phone at home?'

'Yes, well … no, well yes …'

'Well? Is it yes or no?'

'Yes I've got one at home, but no because it doesn't work. I dropped it.'

'Thanks anyway Arthur. I mean, I'm grateful and everything, but I really don't mind if they have my number.'

'It's not that I'm worried about; it's leaving it written on the back of a toilet door that worries me. You could get all kinds of weirdos and pervs calling.'

'That could be interesting. But I guess you're right. But if I use your phone, then you'll get all the pervy calls, that's not exactly fair is it? Maybe you just want them all for yourself!'

Arthur grinned. 'Drat! Discovered!.'

'I'll tell you what, I'll give you my mobile number and you can make a pervy call. Then I'll know who it is.'

'Now you're just being silly. Besides, I already have your number.'

Etta smiled as if to say 'Well, what are you waiting for?'

Arthur smiled. Then jolted with an idea: 'I know what we can do. Natti must have some water-based felt-tips?'

Etta nodded.

'We can use one of those, then, after your first call, we'll nip back and wipe it off.'

The Swine and Thrasher had once been a lovely old place that existed mainly because of its excellent food. Etta had enjoyed spending the odd evening there, usually on her own—it used to be good for a quiet drink, and sometimes a bit of banter. But it had recently been taken over by some chain or other, who had ripped out all of its genuine 18th century interior, and replaced it with a genuine reproduction of an 18th century interior, which included all kinds of old farm implements, stuffed animals and images printed on canvas to make them look like oil paintings. Dried hops were draped from fibreglass wooden beams. The place still served food, though of course the kitchen and dining area had been revamped to make better use of a freezer, microwave and deep-fat fryer in order to serve more customers with delicious authentic country-style food. As in the styles of the countries of Thailand, Mexico, Italy, Greece, and India.

As soon as they entered the pub, Arthur caught the smell of stale cooking oil hanging in the air; he knew he'd be wearing the same smell on his clothes when they left. Etta smiled at the smartly dressed young man who was serving behind the bar and ordered a beer for each of them. They sat down. The note didn't say whether to leave the number in a cubicle in the gents or in the ladies. Arthur went to the gents and there was only one cubicle. Etta went to the ladies. Angrily, she wrote her mobile number on the back of the second door.

She was still angry when she returned. They decided not to eat: left two barely-touched pints of fizzy, tasteless beer, and went to another pub.

26: 42nz g8

Considering that one had lost an earlobe and the other had lost the end of a finger, Icarus was surprised just how calm the Mattress twins were. He paid them each a £200 bonus for their troubles. The twins pocketed it without thanks.

The bonus was given more as an offering to the gods—to ensure that roaming tigers didn't eat the baby. Icarus was nervous. What had seemed like a brilliant idea at conception had the potential to become a difficult offspring. It had already kept him awake last night. The reason for his nervousness was that all his jobs to date had involved objects or computers in which options were calculable. He had always dealt with things he understood. This was something different: there were elements over which he did not have complete control. Icarus wasn't a gambler, he didn't get a thrill out of chancing the unknown, but from discovering what he needed to to eliminate chance. Knowledge gave him control. When he hacked into a website, or cracked a code, it was the taking control that gave him the buzz. Even downloading money into accounts he'd set up in Switzerland and Panama wasn't the objective.

He could have taken millions; instead he only ever took a token amount as his reward for his own success. He saw it as providing a service, because losing a five-figure sum was a small price for a bank or multinational to pay, or more accurately to lose, if it helped them stitch up a loophole in the security of their systems. Icarus knew that even if they could catch him, the institutions wouldn't prosecute him because he was protected by their share prices: a crack in Internet security was privately embarrassing but publicly damaging.

This was a different kettle of fish, and they were beginning to smell a bit off. A lot depended on people, and Icarus was aware of how you couldn't always depend on people. The plan was straightforward enough, and Icarus had gone over it again and again, and now again: Des and Les would pose as the animal rights activists. Arthur and his girlfriend would turn up somewhere remote in the Munter; while the money-for-poodles exchange was being made, he would retrieve the diamonds. It was definitely simple enough. How wrong could it go?

Because he wasn't too familiar with the area, Icarus asked Des and Les if they knew a suitable spot for the swap: somewhere dark, accessible and private. The twins knew lots of places that were dark, accessible and private, but trying to think of one that was big enough to park a car in was difficult. They began a verbal tour around most of the places they could remember visiting—mostly on day trips and school trips. Blackpool Pleasure Beach was too bright and too public, the Lake District and Snowdonia too far. That was more or less all the twins could suggest.

They mentioned a place they'd visited once on a school trip—some run-down industrial museum, and it was the fact that it was in the Peak District that caught Icarus's attention. Icarus looked the place up on the Internet. It seemed ideal—and interesting. It looked as though it had been developed considerably since the twins' school trip. It was now called the 'Fortune's Gate' complex, a slick heritage site with an underground river that could be explored by boat, and, above ground, a rope making machine that had been refurbished and actually worked on Tuesdays, Thursdays and Saturdays throughout the summer. In its productive years it had made rope for some of the most famous ships, including the Queen Mary. The place was easy to find, quiet at night and it had three car parks. Another advantage was the location of the rope-making museum itself—in a cave set into a hillside, a good walk away from the parking area. Now that the scene had been set, Icarus's nerves relaxed a little—everything seemed to be working out fine, on one level anyway.

Outside of Icarus's control was the fact that a small problem was brewing with the twins. They were developing their own brand of fondness for the two animals in their care. It was hard to say why—given the twins' lack of commitment to any kind of emotion. It could possibly have been because the poodles looked so cute, yet growled ferociously and tried to bite and nip at any opportunity; or maybe it was because they ate anything and everything that was put in front of them, something that would have surprised Etta. Whatever the reason, as the prospect of a place and time to hand over the dogs drew closer, the twins' mood began to change. Not that they'd show emotions involving any kind of tears or sadness—these were the Mattress twins after all—they just became increasingly imbalanced. Les fed his favourite pooch—imaginatively christened 'Mr. White', with a live mouse he had found in the old Victorian house they lived in. The house had been left to them by a pair of aunts whom the twins never knew existed until the reading of the will. The mouse was happily consumed in one bite and two swallows. Des was throwing cockroaches at his own favourite: 'Mr Black', who was catching them in mid air and crunching them gleefully. Des giggled with some kind of twisted glee.

The twins had written down several numbers from the toilet door in the pub. It took Icarus some time to sort out the correct one. He saved at least one of the other numbers for a rainy day, then remembering he was in Manchester, he decided to keep it for a sunny day instead. He composed a text message and sent it from his computer, making sure there was no way he could be traced. This involved hacking into a computer in Florida, via another in the Philippines, and bouncing the message around the world before it eventually arrived at its destination. Etta's mobile buzzed. She hastily picked up the phone, tapped a couple of keys and read the message while Arthur looked on.

'It is from them, but it's difficult to understand'

'Let's have a look,' Arthur said. Etta showed him the message:

'meet @ 10 dont b L8. b n boyfrndz kr bring 3000 qid. 2nyt 42nz g8 complx. rope makng mchyn ntrns.

Arthur was baffled. Texting wasn't his medium: 'God!

What language is that? I mean I understand the odd word, such a 'meet' and 'bring', but apart from that…'

'Ssshhh! I'm trying to work it out. When you've got a sixteen-year-old daughter you soon learn to break this code!' Etta was studying the message, scrolling up and down. 'I think I've got it! 'L' '8' is 'late. I think it says "meet at ten, don't be late – B N boyfriend's, BN that must mean 'be in', 'k, r' means 'car', what's '42nz g8?' – Hang on, 'G8' is 'gate''

'What about 'forty-second'?'

'That's not forty-second. It's four-two-nz: 'Fortunes'— the 'Fortune's Gate' Complex?'

'I know it! I went there on a school trip when I was a kid. It wasn't called that back then though. It was interesting, but a bit of a dump. I remember reading something in the paper ages ago about it being developed. Not been there since.' Arthur was pleased to have at least cracked a bit of the code.

'What about the rope making machine?'

'Yes, that's there, or at least it was thirty-odd years ago when I went. God! Was it that long? Time flies!'

Etta jokingly consoled Arthur by patting him on the shoulder. 'Right old-timer, so we've got to be at the Fortune's Gate Complex, at ten-o'clock tonight, at the rope making machine entrance, with 3,000 quid and we have to be in your car!' Easy.

'Less of the old-timer! I'm not even middle aged yet. Not for a while anyway. What time is it now?'

Etta looked at the time on her mobile, 'Nearly six. Almost your bedtime!'

'Funny-girl! On a more serious note, where are we going to get £3,000 from at this time of night?'

'We?'

'Yes, we.'

'I don't really know. I've got a string of cards—for emergencies only of course—so I can get some from cash points, but nowhere near £3,000. Maybe £1,800 at the most.'

Arthur's brow furrowed as he thought: 'Hm, well I've got a bit of cash in my float-tin at work—probably about £400. I've got another £200 in cash on me, and I should be able to get about £200 from a cash point, so what's that?'

Etta did a mental calculation: 'Hm? Eighteen, two, six, four… £2,600. Do you think that will be enough?'

'It's close.'

'It will have to do!' Etta decided, before adding resolutely: 'They should have given us more notice.'

The next few hours were nerve-wracking—seemingly more for Arthur than for Etta. To comply with the blackmailer's request, they took Arthur's car—the hire car he'd been using since the Munter disappeared—and stopped at a cash point via Arthur's studio to get his float money. On the way out to Fortune's Gate, Arthur tried to convince Etta that she should stay out of harm's way. He offered to make the drop alone.

'No way Arthur, I don't want any heroics from you. I'd rather have you safe. I'm coming with you!'

'No! That's not a good idea!' Arthur said firmly.

'Arthur, have you got any martial arts training?'

'No, I did judo for a while when I was nine years old …'

'That'll be useful!'

'Not really, I don't remember a thing, apart from how to fall.'

'Well, you're prepared then! It's a good job one of us is armed.'

Arthur was shocked; he couldn't imagine Etta carrying a weapon—a knife or a gun hidden in a handbag, or a baseball bat under the car seat, 'Armed?'

'In a manner of speaking, I've done kickboxing for the past six years. Only to keep fit though. So I guess we both go, and no arguing!'

'I'm not arguing. I'll go and that's that. You've got Natti to think about.'

'Arthur. Nothing is going to happen. They're obviously idiots!'

'Yes they are, which is why anything can happen. Maybe we should go to the police?'

'Now you're just being ridiculous!'

'Why?' Arthur was slightly miffed.

'You mean "proceed in a brisk and determined manner to the location occupied by police officers Laurel and Hardy to impart verbal information vital to the progress of their ongoing investigation?"'

Arthur had to admit that she did have a point.

As they drove to the rendezvous, Arthur recalled the day when the coach rattled to a halt on the car park on the trip to the rope making machine. The door hissed open and thirty children, himself included, gushed out into the grey, damp mist. It was the first and last time he'd ever been on a field trip. They climbed a hill to look at some geological strata. Arthur tried to remember the different types of rock they'd been shown, all he could come up with was 'sedimentary'—which was self-explanatory, and 'igneous' but couldn't remember what that meant. After the climb, the group descended, and had been due to descend even further into the mine—they'd all been excited about the prospect of an underground boat trip. Arthur remembered having a mad crush on a girl in his class—a tiny, pretty redhead called Ruth. He'd never had the courage to ask her on a date, but fancied her for the whole time he was at secondary school. The mine was shut as it was out of season, so they'd had to make do with a walk up to the rope-making machine. He was probably the only person impressed by the enormous beast that lived in the cave. It was brown with rust and black with grease and filled the dripping cave with the smell of iron and tar. The wheels and cogs in the giant cast-iron frame still turned in those days, spewing rope out of the cave and down the hill, where it was coiled and loaded onto lorries to be taken to shipyards in Belfast, Barrow, Liverpool and Glasgow.

Brown heritage signs now pointed the way to the 'Fortune's Gate Complex'. Arthur tried to remember how it all used to be, to compare how it was now: the asphalt car parks with not a pothole to be felt, the signs pointing to the different attractions: the restaurant, visitors' centre and inevitably, a gift shop.

They drove into a parking bay even though they were in the only car in the car park. It was dark. Arthur switched off the engine and looked at Etta, he could tell she was as nervous as he was. His mouth was dry. Etta opened her bag and pulled out a small bottle of water:

'Want a sip?'

Arthur took the bottle and the water worked wonders. Etta leaned over and took the plastic carrier bag containing the money from the back seat.

'Well we can't sit here,' she said. They looked at each other decisively and got out of the car.

They followed the route directed by a signpost pointing the way to the 'Rope Making Workshop'. Arthur was still trying to superimpose everything he was seeing with what he remembered, but there wasn't much of a match. The general direction up a path was about the only connection he could make.

The path led to steps, which led in turn up to an area of wooden decking built in front of the entrance to the cave. Arthur was amazed at the difference. Where he remembered the cave as being open to the elements, it was now glowing through a metal and glass frontage.

'Wow! It was nothing like this when I was a boy!' He was looking through the glass at the machine inside. It had been restored to its original glory. The cave was dry, the floor concreted and the entire space lit with subtle blue and red lights—highlighting different parts of the machine and the cave. Dotted around were display panels and cases containing all the materials and equipment associated with the rope-maker's trade.

'Amazing! Now this is worth a school trip!'

'It's certainly impressive, but what do we do now?'

Arthur looked around—there was no sign of anyone. 'I guess we just wait.'

It was a pleasant spot to wait. The pair leaned against the wooden railing that surrounded the deck and stared into the clear sky. Masses of stars shone as there was hardly any light pollution except a distant, dim-orange glow from Manchester to the north-west. The flashing lights of an aircraft tracked its flight across the dark space. A fox screamed in the distance.

'Have you got the dosh?' The voice made Arthur and Etta jump back into the reason why they were where they were. They looked around; there was nobody to be seen.

'I'm sorry?' Etta asked.

'The dosh? Have you got it?' The voice hissed a loud whisper.

'Most of it. Have you got my dogs?'

'Most of it?' The voice hissed again. 'How much of it?'

'Two-thousand-six-hundred,' Etta said.

'Two-thousand-six-hundred!' Two voices hissed in unison. There was a pause, before one of the voices said: 'There was s'pposed to be three-thousand!'

'Well it's not my fault. You didn't give me any time. You're lucky I could get this much together!' Etta was indignant.

'What about the slots?' Des hissed.

'What slots?' Etta didn't remember anything being said about slots.

'Slots! Cash machines!' Des hissed again.

'I used cash points until they're dry! Where do think I got this from, a piggy bank!'

'Well we don't know if that's enough...' said Les, looking at Des, who shrugged. 'Stay there, we need to think about it,' which was not something that came easily to the twins.

Icarus, meanwhile was walking along the shrubbery at the edges of each car park, looking for the Munter. But no matter where he looked, there was only one car in the otherwise empty car parks: an anonymous, newish hatchback.

'Shit!' he thought, wondering what to do. He started to walk back up the track, towards where he knew Les and Des were.

Les and Des, meanwhile, had come halfway down the track and were whispering an argument, 'Three-thousand we said. Shit, she doesn't even care about 'em enough to bring the right money!'

'Right!' Les replied, 'So what are we gonna do, take what they've got and give up Mr Black and Mr White, or what?'

'Dunno? It seems a shame, poor little things. I mean what's three grand anyway?'

'Les, it's cash money! Alcohol. Clubs. Drugs.'

'Yeah, but apart from that, what is it?'

'Women!'

'Yeah, good point, but apart from them what is it?'

'I suppose yer've got a point.'

There was a pause.

'Des, I don't wanna give mine back.'

'Me neever. Maybe we could take the money and the dogs?'

'I dunno.'

The twins had been paid to do a job. That job was to collect £3,000 in exchange for two poodles. But there wasn't £3,000 to collect, which gave the twins enough reason to consider an alternative plan, given the circumstances.

'Fuck the money!' Des said.

'Yeah fuck it! Let's go.' The twins each hoisted a rucksack containing a contented animal over their respective shoulders and headed down the track. They met Icarus coming up.

'Where are you two going, have you got the money?' There was anxiety in Icarus' voice.

'Naaaa! Fuck the money! She's not bovvered, so we're not bovvered. We're goin'. We're keeping 'em. She never brought enough money! If it was my dogs I'd've got the money—robbed it or summat.'

'But you can't just keep them!' Icarus said.

'Why not?' Les asked.

'Yeah, why not?' Des added.

Icarus was thinking hard. 'Look just ask him where the other car is?'

'What uvver car?' The twins had no idea what Icarus was talking about, he was beginning to make less and less sense.

'Just ask them please, then you can keep the dogs!' Since the whole point had been to get the diamonds, Icarus decided he didn't care what happened to the dogs—for the moment anyway.

'Honest?' Des asked,

'Seriously?' Les asked.

Out of desperation, Icarus said 'Yes!' which he would later realise was a very stupid thing to say.

'OK then, it's a deal! What about the cash?' Les asked.

'Fuck the money!' Icarus was getting frustrated.

'Exactly!' Des and Les grinned: 'Fuck it!'

The twins went back up the track. At the top Les hissed: 'Where's the other car?'

Etta jumped again. It had been strangely quiet for a good five minutes. She and Arthur had been wondering what to do. 'What other car?' Etta asked.

Des and Les looked at each other. ' 'ang on a minute!' Les hissed.

'Stay there!' Des hissed to Etta. The two walked back down the track to where Icarus was waiting.

'She say's what uvver car?'

'The Munter!' Icarus was not chilled. Des and Les looked at each other, frowning with a lack of understanding, then looked back at Icarus.

'The what?'

'The fucking Munter!'

Des and Les climbed the track.

'The Mun……' Les had forgotten. He turned to Des:

'The fucking Munter!' Des hissed.

'It was stolen. In France!' Arthur shouted back. 'Now please can we do what we came here to do!' There was silence, apart from a rustling of bushes below.

Icarus didn't seem to be happy with the news: 'Shit! Shit! Shit! Shit! Shit!' he hissed, as he did an Indian rain dance halfway up the track, much to the twins' amusement.

'I think he's stressed out.' Des whispered to Les, 'Come on, let's fuck off.'

'Where the fuck are you two going?' Icarus was still dancing.

'We're fuckin' off.'

'You can't just fuck off!'

'Why not?' The twins waited expectantly for Icarus's reason.

'... because you just can't!'

That was no reason at all, so Les nudged Des and pointed down the track. The pair set off.

'Well fuck off then!' Icarus sprayed.

'You need to chill out. Take a holiday!' Les whispered, helpfully, back up to Icarus.

'Rhyl's cool!' Des added.

'Cold more like! Blackpool's better,' Les replied.

'Naaah! Crap in spring. He needs to chill, in Rhyl.'

'Yeah, but Blackpool rocks!'

'S'pose.'

Icarus was left standing alone; he shivered in the chill of the evening air.

Ten minutes had passed and there had been no activity. It was clear that nothing was happening. Etta peered as best as she could into the blackness in front of her and called, 'Hello?' There was no reply. Arthur peered down over the railing, trying to see if he could see where the voices had come from. In the distance a car started and drove off. A few minutes later, another car did the same.

It was silent. There was no one around.

'It was obviously not enough money,' Arthur speculated.

Etta was furious: 'I'm so annoyed, bloody morons! And what was all that animal rights stuff about! They were just bloody common crooks! What about my dogs?!' Etta was furious.

27: Busy waiting

'This is an important new development! Said Ollie, who's real name was actually DS Norman Bates. Stan had also been called in to the office. He'd introduced himself at Etta's house as DC Bailey. It had been too much for Etta not to ask if his first name was David.

'No, it's Bob, but it's amazing how many people ask me that!' He'd looked genuinely baffled.

'Yes, an important new development!' What do you think Bob? DS Bates held up the ransom note that Etta had given to him.

'Important? Could be! Could be!' He replied, taking a photo of it.

Etta and Arthur had just recounted the story to the two officers.

'You see, you fell into a classic trap there.'

'Which is?' Etta asked.

'You should have let the professionals deal with it. Isn't that right Bob?'

'Aye Mr Bates, the professionals!' Bob looked puzzled as he answered, then added: 'Yes, the professionals. Erm, who would that be then Mr Bates?'

'Us Bob! Us!'

'Oh yes of course! The professionals!'

'Never, I repeat never, pay the ransom. You're just giving them what they want. Isn't that right Bob?'

'Aye Mr Bates.'

'You see that's why they left. If they can get some money out of you, they can get more out of you. They'll be back—you mark my words. All we have to do is wait. What do you say Bob?'

'Aye, Mr Bates. Waiting—that's exactly what we have to do.'

Exasperation was creeping up on Etta: 'So you're going to do nothing then?'

'No! No! No! Mrs. Corbett. We won't be doing nothing. We'll be waiting. Isn't that right Bob?'

'Aye Mr Bates, busy—waiting.'

'If these, scum—and excuse me but I'm sure you'll agree that's not too strong a word to use for them—contact you again, you get in touch with us straight away.' Ollie smiled at Etta, then Arthur.

'What a total and utter waste of time!' Etta was furious as they walked out of the police station. 'Useless! That's what they are, useless! There must be something we can do? We can't just sit around 'waiting'.'

Arthur was quiet.

'Arthur?'

'Oh! Sorry, I was just thinking.'

'What about?'

'Well, there's something that I don't understand. You

remember the text message?'

'Yes, what about it?'

'Well it said something about going in your boyfriend's car with the money ...'

'Yes?'

'And when we were at Fortune's Gate, they were asking about my car too—even by name—the Munter.'

'Yes, I remember.'

'So why? Why not your car or any car? I mean why specifically say go in my car. What difference could it possibly have made what we drove there in?'

'I see what you mean. That is strange?'

'A bit, yes. Only thing is, I can't think of a reason.'

Arthur was frustrated. Nothing seemed to be happening with the Munter. Nothing seemed to be happening about the dogs—Etta had promised to call him if she heard anything. He was at a loose end. The last he'd heard of the Munter it was in Kiev. There was something about Kiev that Arthur realised he should know, apart from the fact that it was the location of the 2005 Eurovision Song Contest, the home of the Dynamo Kiev football team, and it had a chicken dish named after it. But there was something else. He decided he needed a bath: he needed space to think.

The bath was relaxing, but there were no eureka moments. Afterwards Arthur sat and browsed through his Munter scrapbooks. He thought again about that website he'd been meaning to put together. He'd always kept anything to do with the car: cuttings from old magazines; photos of the car in the barn he'd rescued it from; there were newspaper cuttings about Rupert Smithereen, the disgraced diplomat whose body had been found—and thankfully removed from the car—before Arthur had bought and collected it; there was a picture of the design team standing around the first prototype. It was this that finally gave Arthur his eureka moment.

The head of the design team had sent the picture to him. Arthur had contacted Sergei Zadinsky many years ago, and he'd been a great help in providing information and technical data. Sergei had been the head of the original design team in Khrushchev's day. Sergei had even sent a box of spares salvaged from the original project. Sergei and Arthur had remained in touch, on and off, ever since—at first corresponding by mail, but for the past few years by email. Arthur had sent him prints of the finished Munter project, much to Sergei's delight. For many years Sergei had lived in Russia, but after Ukrainian independence he'd moved to Kiev.

Arthur's initial flash of joy was extinguished by the realisation that there was probably little that Sergei could do. Apart from anything else, he was now in his seventies. But the seed of an idea was germinating in Arthur's head. Sergei had said many times that Arthur should visit him in Kiev. It was something that he'd thought about, but never done, as is often the way with such things.

A quick search on the internet revealed that, thanks to the Orange Revolution, he didn't need a visa. Then he emailed Sergei that he was thinking of a visit to Kiev, but decided not to write anything about the theft of the Munter. He tried to rationalise a reason for this, but in the end had to admit that it was mainly down to his own embarrassment. Then he called Etta to tell her his plan.

'Why?'

'Because there's nothing happening here. At least if I go there, I can do something?'

'What?'

'Report it to the police. Ask around. Pay someone to look for it. I don't know. But something is better than nothing.'

'When?'

'Well, that's one of the reasons I called: Tuesday.'

'What, next Tuesday?'

Arthur confirmed.

How?'

'Well, there's a direct flight from Gatwick, which means going down to London on the train. So I'll stay in a hotel on Monday night.'

'Do you think that's the best thing to do?'

'I don't know, possibly not, but I've got to do something.'

'I suppose so. Well I suppose you know what you're doing.'

'I wondered if you'd like to come with me?'

'Oh Arthur, that would be wonderful, but I can't—Natti—'

'She could come too.' It was a desperate stab by Arthur.

'I'm sure she'd love it, but she's in the middle of revising and practising for her exams, so it wouldn't be a good idea. But it's sweet of you to ask.'

'Just a thought.'

'And I really appreciate it. I'd love to go away with you somewhere, but you'll enjoy yourself I'm sure. I'll miss you though.'

'I'll miss you too. But what will you do? What if you hear anything?'

'Arthur I'll be fine! If I do hear anything I'll call in Laurel and Hardy.'

'You promise?'

'I promise! Don't worry about me.'

'Well, I will worry, but if you're sure. Anyway nothing's fixed yet. I haven't heard from Sergei.'

'Will you call me and let me know?'

'Of course I will. As if I wouldn't!'

'I love you.'

'I love you too.' Arthur had put the phone down before being hit by the full impact of what Etta had said. She loved him!

Sergei replied on Sunday morning. He was delighted that Arthur was planning to visit at last. And not only would he be happy to meet up, but Arthur should stay with them in their apartment which was just off Kreschiatik—right in the centre of town. If Arthur sent details of the flight arrival, Sergei would meet him at the airport personally. This was better than Arthur had hoped for. After reading Sergei's mail, Arthur stayed on-line and booked his train ticket to London and his flight to Kiev.

28: Arrested development

Nathaniel returned to Manchester after a traumatic few days with Sandra. He was carrying a well-stuffed rucksack when Icarus picked him up from the train station.

'How did it go then?' Icarus said—by way of polite conversation, and also to try and suss out his overall mood.

'Hmm! Don't ask.'

'Not good then?'

'It was never going to be good, but it could have been worse.'

'Chicks, eh? So bloody difficult.'

'It's not women that are difficult, it's relationships. I mean I got home, and she started telling me she loves me and has missed me and cares for me. I start to think maybe I was wrong about it all—maybe I should give it a second chance, but as soon as she thought I was fine again—she was off! Out at lunch and shopping with the rest of her crew. And what do I get? "There's plenty of stuff in the freezer if you're hungry." I've had enough! That's her idea of caring—buying frozen meals from M&S. I think she was only concerned about losing the hotel and her salon. I told her she could have it all, and the flat. I just want to get out of it.'

'So what are you going to do?'

'To be honest, nothing. Get on with what I enjoy doing.'

'Thieving?'

'It's not thieving! It's smuggling. Thieving is just a miniscule part of it. Anyway, it's not like I'm going to be short of money. Especially after this little job. How's it going by the way?'

Icarus spent the rest of the journey out of town explaining to Nathaniel what had happened. Nathaniel became more and more aghast as he the story unfolded.

'Bob had no right to mention the bloody Mattress twins! He should have realised! They're psychos. Double trouble! You should have told me what you were going to do—and who you were planning to do it with!'

'I didn't want to disturb you, and I did sort of try, but you were sorting out your private life and…'

At first Nathaniel was livid. But he realised that it was partly his own fault for not being around: 'I'm sorry. It's not your fault. You did the best you could under the circumstances.' Nathaniel was slipping into planning mode, unaware that Icarus was saving the worst till last.

'So you say the twins want to keep the dogs?'

Icarus nodded.

'Why? They haven't got a caring bone in their body.'

'I don't know! They just said "Fuck the money" and disappeared,'

'Have you called them?'

'Tried to, but there was no reply. I left a message but, nothing yet.'

'Bugger! Well we need to get the dogs back, or we're not going to get the car.'

'I don't think that's an issue any more,' Icarus said, tentatively.

'Sorry?'

'The dogs, I don't think they're an issue any more— getting them back and that,'

'Why? I'm not sure I'm with you?'

'Well I think I know why we haven't seen the Munter.'

'Why? Come on, what do you know?'

'It's been nicked.'

Nathaniel was silent.

Icarus was nervous, 'So? Aren't you going to say anything?'

'What do you want me to say?'

'I don't know. Call me a fucking idiot or something! Please, just to make me feel better.'

'What's the point? That's not going to get the stuff back. Besides, it's not your fault. Where is the car? Any idea?'

'Ah! That's another thing…'

'What's another thing?'

'It's in Kiev.'

It took a few seconds for Nathaniel to absorb what Icarus had said: 'Kiev?'

'Kiev,' Icarus confirmed.

'Fuck!'

'That's exactly what I thought.'

Nathaniel was laying in bed that evening, wondering, 'Why me?' Some jobs had the odd glitch. This one had turned into a nightmare. 'I should stick to art. You know where you are when you nick a good painting', he thought. He fell asleep eventually, but woke frequently between frustrating dreams—including one in which Sandra was standing with two uniformed men in an airport arrivals area. She was pointing at him. He was trying to conceal a large, framed painting which kept slipping down from under his jacket. The two men had poodles in black dog coats on which 'Revenue' was printed in white. The dogs yapped and strained on their leashes as they tried to get at him. His dream zoomed in to the leering faces of the two men—the Mattress twins.

By four in the morning he'd had enough of trying to sleep, and lay awake in the grey light, thinking about work, love and life. By morning he'd decided that desperate situations demanded desperate measures. As he rinsed out his mouth after cleaning his teeth, he resolved that it was time to take control and sort this thing out—once and for all.

Fifteen minutes later, and he was at breakfast with Icarus, who had already taken advantage of the hotel buffet to pile his plate with sausages, bacon, eggs, beans and fried potatoes.

'I can hear your arteries cracking from here,' Nathaniel said. Icarus just grinned, displaying bits of bacon between his teeth.

'Can you eat and listen? Or should I wait?'

Icarus nodded and mumbled something through his meaty mouthful.

'Well. I think I've got a plan.'

Icarus swallowed hard and looked at Nathaniel: 'Is it cunning?'

Determined to be serious, Nathaniel ignored Icarus's weak attempt at humour: 'Do you know where a lot of the paintings we acquire end up?'

Icarus swallowed a mouthful of tea to help dislodge the ball of food now stuck in his gut: 'Honestly? I always thought they went to some rich bastard's underground private studio in America or Switzerland or somewhere.'

'Very 007. No, that might have been the case fifteen or twenty years ago, but the real money is in Eastern Europe now. And believe me we're talking real money. As long as it's dollars of course.'

'Isn't there some kind of irony in that?' Icarus mused.

'I guess there is,' Nathaniel smiled. 'Anyway, over the years I've built up some very good contacts, including one or two people who owe me favours.'

'Uh-hu, so?'

'So I'm going to arrange a meeting with a friend of mine, and we'll see what he says.'

'So what's the problem?' Icarus could sense there was some hesitation in Nathaniel.

'No real problem, it's just, well these people are heavy-duty. They won't tolerate any messing around, or any risk.'

'Aah…' Icarus said, trying to sound as if he knew what Nathaniel meant.

'It's a risk on our part. But for what's at stake I think it's worth it.'

'So?'

'So we can't fuck up again.'

Icarus nodded the fact that he now understood it was himself who couldn't fuck up again.

'And there's one more thing.'

'What?' Icarus hated it when there was one more thing; it was usually the worse thing.

'The dogs.'

'What about them?'

'You've got to get them back.'

Icarus frowned a 'Why?'

'For two reasons: a) we might need them for leverage later on; and b) if we leave them with the Mattress twins, there's no telling what will happen to the poor little things.'

'Who? The twins?'

'No the dogs, you dummy!'

'It's not gonna be easy man. It's weird I know, but they did seem kind of attached to them. Des even said that he felt like a part of him was in one of them, but I suppose he could have meant his earlobe.'

Icarus tried but despite repeated calls, there was no answer from Des and Les. He continued trying for days. Eventually he tucked three grand in his back pocket and went round to the deteriorating Victorian monolith they lived in. It was in one of the last seedy suburbs that remain after Manchester's cosmopolitan uprising. But, despite the area, even the price of this rotting monstrosity was rocketing by the month. The area was rough though, he was propositioned several times for sex on the way there and offered a variety of substances. He turned a corner and—twenty metres or so from the house—stopped to take in the sight of the decaying pile. A shiver ran up his spine.

'Hi there, Marlene's the name! I'm on the game! Fancy a blowjob luv? No rubber!' The voice, decorated with a broad Glaswegian accent, came from across the street.

Icarus was so preoccupied that he wasn't even vaguely interested: 'Not right now, but thanks for the offer,' he replied, politely, without taking his eyes off the house.

From across the road, the woman watched him push the broken gate aside and walk up the path to the front door.

'Weird them two. I'd be careful in there if I were you!'

'Thanks for the advice. You haven't seen them have you?' Icarus turned around to look at Marlene, who did nothing to hide her man's body beneath a tight-fitting black dress, slit almost all the way up one thigh.

'Me? Och No! I've no' seen 'em for days.'

'Cheers.' Icarus walked up the steps to the front door. He banged the lion's head knocker, which caused flakes of the faded green paint to flutter to the step. Somewhere high above, a roof tile slid, then stopped. The knocking echoed through the house. The echo was followed by silence. He banged again, and again nothing. There was a small round doorbell which Icarus pressed for ages. He could hear its feeble ringing, but it seemed nobody else could. He walked around the perimeter of the house, peering into as many windows as he could. But the entire place looked as if nobody was at home and as if it was no one's home. The window glass was brown—etched with decades of pollution, the window frames were rotten. Against a side-wall slumped a filthy mattress, held in place by a rusting motorcycle half-covered with a tarpaulin. The back garden was large, but overgrown. There seemed to be a path around its perimeter, but from the edge to the centre was filled with impenetrable vegetation: a contorted mass of wrist-thick brambles that strangled a variety of ancient, uncared-for fruit trees now in full and magnificent blossom.

Strangely there were more types of insects and birds flying around than Icarus had ever seen in one place, 'Looks like nobody's touched that for years, it's a miniature nature reserve!' He said, as he turned and walked back around the house.

Indeed no one had touched it for years. It had belonged to Flight Lieutenant Wilfred Mattress, who disappeared. It was his sisters who inherited the house, and who had inadvertently left the house to the twins. No one had touched the garden since 14 February 1943.

'Not in then?' Asked the broad Scottish lass, as Icarus walked back down the garden path.

'Naaah! But if you see them, tell them Icarus called.' Stupidly, Icarus then pulled the three grand out of his back pocket, peeled off a twenty and handed it over.

Icarus was still reflecting on his stupidity forty minutes later in the reception of the police station. He was sitting opposite Marlene.

As he was being arrested, Icarus had implored to the officer handcuffing him that the money was not being handed over for favours received, or even those about to be received, but the officer was having none of it: 'This is

Operation Bangkok, we're cleaning up this area of filth like you two. It's time that respectable married families—with clean children, two jobs and a strimmer—reclaimed this neighbourhood! Zero Tolerance, my lad, that's what we operate here. We'll soon have supermarkets making home deliveries around here, instead of scum like you!' He said, before inviting them to ride to the police station in the back of the police minibus.

'Och, don't worry about it!' Marlene tried to comfort a fidgety Icarus. 'I've been arrested seventeen times in the past two years.'

'Seventeen times? Bloody hell! You've been busy!' Icarus said.

'Aye, the last time was the worst: I was walking down past the University there, near the centre, where those traffic lights are?'

'Oh yes, I think know where you mean, near the business school?'

'Aye! That's it. Well there was this car stopped at the lights, the windows were open. There were these two men in it—gorgeous they were—and I'll swear one o' them was giving me the eye...'

As she spoke, Icarus tried to imagine what anyone saw in Marlene: a thickset man with enormous hands and a straight, blonde, ill-fitting wig. Immaculate make-up though, except for the too-long, heavily blackened false eyelashes. His voice was a cross between a deep manly, heavy Glaswegian growl, and Marilyn Monroe pillow-talking.

'Anyway, I shouted across 'Fancy a blowjob luv! And

bugger me if they weren't both police officers!'

'Maybe it's time you changed your sales pitch.' Icarus said, by way of advice.

'Ha! Maybe. Anyway, I should've recognised one o 'em, because he caught me for speeding when I was a truck driver.'

'You used to drive trucks?' Icarus asked.

'Aye! For years! Internaaationally!' The way he said this made it sound as if he'd been a star of stage and screen, 'And always in a frock. 'The Jock in a Frock' they called me. Aye! Once I was in the cab I was a different woman. I was famous for it, especially in Eastern Europe you ken: Romania and Hungary and that. And Turkey! Oh God! Please don't get me ontae Turkey! Anyway, they arrested me, again. I was inside for three months.'

'What? For speeding?'

'Och no laddie! For offerin' tae give 'em a blow job.'

'That must have been terrible.'

'Terrible! Och nae laddie! It was fabulous. I was the princess o' the block!' Marlene lent across to Icarus and whispered: 'I even gave wee favours tae some o' the warders,' then leant back and said aloud: 'It was one o' the busiest times I've ever had.' Marlene took out a compact, stared casually into its mirror, and tweaked an eyebrow.

It took some time for Icarus to think of an acceptable reason for being in an area renowned for drug pushers and prostitution with almost three grand stuck in his back pocket. He was searched for drugs, and had to give his fingerprints and a urine sample. He was thankful that he hadn't taken anything heavy for a day or two. Despite protesting heavily, he couldn't convince the police that he hadn't been kerb crawling. He was begrudgingly pleased that he was let off with only a caution. Marlene was arrested, strip-searched thoroughly, then released. They swapped verbal notes about their respective fates as they left the station together in contrasting moods. Icarus was pissed off. Marlene seemed almost jubilant: 'They always do the same thing, it's a wee bit o' entertainment for 'em. They always have a female in as well as the men, I think they think it's PC or something; and d'you know—I think the women are almost worse than the men! I don't know what goes on in their heeds—Come tae think of it—I never have with women! What they don't realise is that they're only degrading themselves. I keep ma dignity luv! So bollocks tae 'em!' Marlene's voice dropped an octave on the expletive. She smiled at a smartly dressed but overweight man who walked past her towards the station. 'See him, I've had him.' She whispered to Icarus: 'Detective. Gave him a BJ in the gun store. Did'na do me nae good though, I still got sent doon!' She then slipped a piece of paper to Icarus with a number written in the neatest handwriting he had ever seen: 'Just in case dear, ye never ken.' Icarus thought to himself that he damned well did ken. But anyway he put the number into his pocket: he didn't want to hurt Marlene's feelings by throwing it away right there and then.

Icarus was completely pissed off by the time he got back to the hotel. Nathaniel was in the bar.

'How did it go? Did you find the twins?' But it was easy to tell from Icarus's mood that he hadn't. A mood that wasn't helped by Nathaniel trying to suppress his laughter as Icarus told him what had happened.

'Well, thanks Icarus! I needed cheering up a bit.'

'Well I'm glad you think it's funny, man!'

'Oh come on! You got away with it, what are you worried about?'

'I didn't get away with it! I've been cautioned for kerb crawling! I'm pissed off. And there was no sign of the twins. What are we going to do?'

'Forget about them for now. I mean, we don't actually need the dogs. We'll need to get them back, but we can do it later. They're bound to turn up.'

'I guess,' Icarus's pride was slightly bruised.

'In the meantime, we've got to work out where this Munter thing is. I've been making enquiries, and apparently there's a scam going on at the moment—luxury cars being nicked and exported to Eastern Europe—Beemers, Mercs, Porsches, four-by-fours—that kind of thing. Anyway it's well organised, so there's some hope.'

'Hope? What do you mean?'

'Well chances are the Munter's been taken by an organised ring.'

'You mean the Russian mafia?'

'It's not like that, they're just businessmen, like us. And Kiev is in Ukraine, not Russia.' Nathaniel replied.

'OK, Russian businessmen, Ukrainian businessmen—it's all the same thing: Shoot first and fuck the questions! Where's the hope in that?'

'Well, the good thing about organised crime is the fact that it's organised. For example, Ukraine isn't like

England. I mean the police, customs and the bandits work together.'

'Bandits?' Icarus was curious.

'Yes, bandits, police, customs—they all work for the same firm. You can take anything over the border for a price.'

'So it's easy then?' Icarus asked.

'Well, I wouldn't say it was easy. But at least it's not impossible.'

'Not impossible, doesn't sound that easy to me…'

Nathaniel smiled: 'Anyway, I've been in touch with those business associates I mentioned, and arranged a meeting. We need see what kind of playing field we're in.'

'One with the Russians in it?' Icarus was now morbidly curious.

'We'll find that out. Why don't you hang around and meet them. Don't worry, they're charming. Just…'

'Just what!' Icarus asked.

'Just —well, be careful.'

'I dunno man, this isn't what I expected when we started this thing—Russian mafia and that.'

'Stop calling them that. They're just businessmen. They're fine—you wait until you meet them. Anyway, I'm not even sure they're Russian.'

'So when do I get to meet them?'

'Tomorrow morning.'

29: Vodka and bones

'Ahh! Nathaniel! Good to see you again.' Bogdan spoke excellent English.

'And you Bogdan. It's been some time.' The two men kissed each other's cheeks. Nathaniel introduced Icarus, who shook hands with each of the three men. Bogdan introduced Stefan, and another man whose name slipped right through the comprehension of both Nathaniel and Icarus. Afterwards he became known as 'Mr. Silent' due to the fact that he never said a word. Nathaniel thought he'd sussed the guy's role from the outset, due to a noticeable bulge under his jacket. All three men were casually dressed, but Icarus noticed that it was casual and very expensive.

Throughout the conversation the three Russians, if that's what they were, paid careful attention to everyone in the room. Anybody who came or went received a casual, but qualified visual shakedown. Icarus couldn't help but follow their line of sight. Stefan leaned over and, in Russian, asked Bogdan for something. This was relayed to Nathaniel in English.

'He wants to know if they serve chilled vodka here?'

'Well, you might be able to get a vodka with ice, but not chilled.' Nathaniel replied.

'No matter. We always take precautions!' Said Bogdan, who seemed to speak for all of them. He looked at Mr. Silent, and then nodded towards the table. Mr. Silent reached into his jacket and pulled out three glasses, then a gold hip flask—all of which were slammed noisily onto the table. Bogdan then beckoned to a waitress for two more glasses. Bogdan swept back his long hair; a heavy gold bracelet glinted on his wrist. He unscrewed the flask and poured five hefty measures.

'The best way to start a meeting, in fact the best way to start anything!' Bogdan said, raising his glass and beckoning the others to do so, 'Nasdarovia!'

The vodka was ice cold, much to Icarus's amazement. It slid down much easier than he imagined it would.

'Hm? Good stuff that!' He smacked his lips as he put his glass down. Wondering how he could ask, diplomatically, where he could get a bottle for himself.

'And always best cold!' Bogdan said, picking up the flask: 'A miracle of modern technology! A small device, which uses radioactive material no bigger than a grain of sand, powers a fuel cell to keep it at just the right temperature! Expensive of course—but who can put a price on perfection.'

Nathaniel looked at Bogdan to see if he was, as he hoped, joking. There was no sign of it.

The meeting began. Nathaniel had already agreed that he would do the explaining. Icarus was happy to let him. Nathaniel had spent half the previous night running through the story in his own head, now it was time to tell it…

'… so you see we hid the diamonds in the car to get them across the Channel,' said Nathaniel, coming to the end of his tale.

On hearing Nathaniel mention the diamonds, Icarus shifted nervously, an action not missed by the three 'businessmen.' Nathaniel, however, continued calmly: '… diamonds in a necklace that I, well let's say I 'acquired' them for my wife. Of course she never realised the value of this necklace, or where it had come from. But, as the relationship is now over, and as I'd given her the hotel, I thought it only fair to take them.'

Bogdan shrugged, he could see the logic in that.

Nathaniel continued: 'You see it was the necklace from the Hymer collection…' At hearing this, it was obvious to Icarus that Bogdan had suddenly become much more interested. It was also obvious to Stefan and Mr. Silent, who suddenly started paying less attention to other hotel guests, and became totally attentive to Bogdan's reactions. Bogdan pushed his vodka glass aside and leaned forward. Four other figures around the table also leaned forward and the tone of the conversation became more conspiratorial.

'The Hymer collection? Interesting. And tell me, how did this necklace from the Hymer collection happen to be in the possession of Mrs Boot?' Bogdan asked smoothly.

'It was a gift—from me.'

'So where did you get it from?'

'Let's just say it 'appeared'.'

'Appeared not long after it disappeared I'd imagine!'

Bogdan was laughing. 'Did you steal it?'

'Bogdan, you know I don't steal. I'm not a common thief, I'm a…'

'A smuggler, I know, you've told me before. You're a businessman, I'm a businessman—we're all businessmen. But tell me, what happened to the rest of the collection?'

'You mean the brooch, the bracelet and the ring? How would I know Bogdan?' There was a playful tone in Nathaniel's voice.

'I mean the 'Heart of Africa' and the 'Pink Tiger', or perhaps they are names not familiar with you?'

'Well it was a long time ago…'

'What value is time?' Bogdan said, laughing, 'You are a cunning man Nathaniel, I will have to watch you!'

'Reliable, Bogdan, reliable, that's why you used me remember?' Nathaniel's tone had shifted slightly.

'Used? Yes I suppose so, we are all used. But it was your cunning that saved you. Perhaps I knew it would.'

'Perhaps.'

'I'll tell you what I'll do, I'll see if anyone has seen your Munter. We'll see what we can do for you. But if it is in the wrong hands, you must understand that there is not much that I can do. The imbalance of power is what keeps us all moving.'

Icarus leaned back and looked at Bogdan questioningly. Bogdan noticed: 'It's like walking, my friend. Think about it: when you walk you lift up one leg, then move your body forward until it's out of balance, but you save yourself from falling by putting your other leg forward to take your weight, and so on. So you need to be in a constant state of imbalance to keep moving. Of course if you want to run, everything has to be more extreme. To establish equilibrium, you put both feet down and stop moving. And so it goes. So you see it's imbalance and the lack of equilibrium that keeps everything moving so smoothly. What we do is help maintain, and enhance, that state of imbalance, and in doing so we help the course of progress.' Bogdan then turned to Nathaniel, 'I'll see what I can do, and I in return, maybe you will forgive any past indiscretions on my part?'

Nathaniel gave a single nod. 'There's nothing to forgive. Any help you can provide would be very gratefully accepted!' He knew that if there was a diamond necklace, Bogdan would gratefully accept it without question, in fact without saying anything.

Bogdan had stood and slapped Nathaniel heartily on the back: 'I'll never understand you British! Too complicated. You should be more like the Americans!'

'I think we're trying…' Nathaniel said, as he stood and took a gasp of air to replace what had been slapped out of his lungs.

'Now Nathaniel, show me this city of yours. I'm in the mood to invest…football I think.'

*

In one of the last remaining seedy suburbs in Manchester, behind the boarded-up windows of a still functioning pub (the boards being a legacy of a shooting eighteen months earlier), a tiny figure dressed in the colourful, worn, multilayered clothes of a festival urchin, was tearfully sipping from a pint which was almost as big as she was.

She replaced her glass carefully on the table, and slowly wiped the sodden dreadlock that had accidentally fallen into it: 'Dog's gone missing. I've looked everywhere,' she sniffed, 'I've been up and down the street all last night and all today: calling him: 'Dog!' 'Dog!' everywhere, but he's not come home, (Sniff!) I've searched garages and stuff and all the usual places where cats get stuck—but nothing. I love my little Dog. I miss him so much. Sniff! He come to Glastonbury with me last year. I carried him all the way in my rucksack. They don't allow cats, but I smuggled him in. Sniff! You know how much Dog means to me.'

'Mate! Yeah! God mate! I'm really, like, sorry. Mate you should've texted me! I would've come to help, that's what mates is for mate.'

'I would've texted you. Sniff! But I was busy looking.'

'S'funny though; coz I was wiv Freddo yesterday,'

'White-Rasta Freddo, or Freddo from the Hell's Kitchen squat?'

'Squat Freddo! Well he said he was going 'ome to see 'is mum this weekend on account of e's dead upset…'

'Why's that then? (Sniff!)'

'Mate, it seems that 'is cat, Jemimah I fink she's called, 'as gone missin' too. Mind you 'e'll be alright. 'is mum lives in Cheshire, they've got a pool and stuff: 'e said 'e's gonna chill for-a-bit.'

'Poor Freddo. Poor Dog. (Sniff!)'

In another part of the same seedy area very early the following morning, the door of a ground floor flat is open. In its frame, stewing in a stinking haze of cat-pee, stands a short, plump female figure with lank, greasy hair. She is wearing a dirty red skirt over trousers tucked into leg warmers over exhausted leather walking boots, none of which had been removed for months. She is anxiously stretching the sides of a drab-green woollen cardigan with dirty, worrying fingers. The hairs on her chin twitch as she shouts out into the grey morning air: 'Fluffy! Fluuuffy! Fluuuuuuffyyyyy!

Meanwhile, in a dark corner of a certain dank cellar there was a growing pile of small bones.

30: Kiev

Kiev's Borispol airport seemed to Arthur to be just like any other city airport: A short walk from the gate to the luggage reclaim area; an average wait by the carousel; a queue to get his passport stamped, and a little more paperwork for Customs; then another queue to allow a uniformed official to poke through his luggage—which Arthur had managed to keep down to his usual single bag, plus an extra bag containing gifts for Sergei and his wife Nadia.

He left Customs and walked towards the exit—two heavy wooden doors with glass panels in their centre. He grabbed the large brass handle to push one of the doors open, but didn't get the chance—it was yanked open, several hands grabbed his arm and he was dragged through; his bag almost flying off his shoulder. He wasn't prepared for the arrivals hall: he was besieged by cab drivers, shouting and grabbing at him and his bag while elbowing and screaming protests at each other as if driven to a frenzy by the smell of dollars. Arthur clutched his bags tightly and repeated 'Niet! Niet! Niet!' Through gritted teeth as he tried to push through. Suddenly, something strong grabbed the shoulder of Arthur's jacket, and he was pulled forcefully sideways straight through the pack. He was too surprised to react. By the time he regained his balance and his composure he found himself facing a powerful figure shouting aggressively at the protesting drivers, one hand still clutching the shoulder of Arthur's jacket, the other waving threateningly. Within seconds the big man had turned back and was hugging and kissing Arthur as if he was a teddy bear. There were tears in his eyes.

'Arthur! Arthur! My dear friend! I am so pleased to meet you at last! But come—let us get out of this zoo. There is plenty of time to talk in the taxi.'

Before Arthur could reply, Sergei Zadinsky had taken Arthur's rucksack from his shoulder, thrown it over his own and was briskly marching Arthur towards the door.

'This way, it's waiting outside.' Sergei dismissed the pack of cab touts with a contemptuous wave, 'We don't bother with these cheating parasites, they'll try to charge you twenty dollars for a two-dollar ride into town!'

Nobody stood in Sergei's way. He was well over six-feet tall with grey hair, and a tan that comes from working outside, rather than relaxing outside. He moved with strength and determination. His face was lined with intelligence and worry. Sergei was the first person Arthur had ever met who really did have 'piercing blue eyes'. He was dressed in that naturally shabby way that only intellectuals seem to inadvertently achieve with chic: a baggy pair of jeans, scuffed brown shoes, open collared pale green shirt and an old grey cardigan, one worn elbow of which had been carefully darned. The pair burst outside into the Kiev sunshine. Arthur was surprised how warm it was. There was a Mediterranean feeling in the air. Sergei strode towards a row of cars parked haphazardly along the road.

'I would have picked you up in my car, but I hate the Kiev traffic. It is full of crazy people.' They settled into the back seat. The taxi was a comfortable modern saloon, a make that Arthur didn't recognise.

'No problem Sergei, it's just great to be here, and to meet you finally. I'm really grateful for this—you know, you letting me stay and everything.'

'It is my pleasure! I looked forward to meeting you for many years. I wanted to see with my own eyes what kind of man actually likes this terrible car we designed all those years ago!' Sergei laughed and slapped Arthur's knee. Sergei pointed out of the window: 'Welcome to Kiev!'

They drove down a broad, tree-lined avenue that led from Borispol airport and onto a motorway towards the city. The driver was cracking a pace, but traffic was still overtaking them on both sides. Arthur had never seen such a variety of transport on a single road: there were black-windowed four-by-fours, Mercs, expensive Audis and Volkswagens; battered trucks and buses that looked as though they were held together by blind faith; a horse and cart and several cyclists were travelling the wrong way down what Arthur could only presume was the hard-shoulder; cows and goats grazed on any patch of grass, including the central reservation. As they drove, Sergei talked about the changing city.

'All this is new,' he waved towards a suburb of high-rise

buildings, 'Everywhere they build. And the price!' Sergei sucked through his teeth, 'So expensive, you would not believe how much for an apartment, maybe two-hundred-fifty thousand!'

'Hrivnas?' Arthur asked, mentally trying to compare the price in sterling. Sergei laughed,

'Hrivnas! No, dollars! Quarter of a million dollars. And where does the money come from? How can so many people afford a-quarter-of-a-million dollars for an apartment—when the average salary is maybe one hundred dollars a month? You'll see the centre soon Arthur, apartments everywhere. As soon as they go up, in fact before they go up, they sell. I do not understand it.'

Arthur was stunned, he had no idea that Kiev was so big. The high-rise suburbs they drove through were each the size of small towns, and Sergei was right, there was building happening everywhere.

As they drove closer to the centre the traffic became increasingly insane. Arthur had a theory that you could tell the nature of a country by the way its people drive. He tried to work out the rules in Kiev, and concluded there was just one: 'Get there'. Traffic lanes, where they were defined, were ignored; as were traffic lights. At one busy junction there was a static queue to turn right—impatient drivers simply drove up onto the footpath and along the inside of the waiting traffic, only to end up in another queue along the footpath, horns blaring, trying to get back on to the road.

'See! See Arthur! Crazy people! No respect for anything! And they say we are better after communism! Look at them, BMWs, Mercedes, Toyotas—no patience! They think money entitles them to anything they can take. They think it buys them respect! Pshah! Rich fools!'

Arthur noticed a police car parked at a junction ahead. He was talking into the driver's window of a modern-looking saloon car. Sergei noticed Arthur's interest.

'Ah yes. All over Ukraine you will see them. They stop you and fine you for anything they can think of. See that man standing behind him?'

Arthur looked to where Sergei was indicating. Standing some distance away from the uniformed policeman was a thin man with cropped hair. He was wearing a leather jacket over a thick roll-necked jumper. Overdressed for such a warm day.

'Criminal. He takes a cut from the police.'

'Mafia?' Arthur asked.

'Mafia, businessman. Businessman, mafia—what is the difference? Criminals!'

The taxi drove along a wide expressway beside a river, the width of which surprised Arthur, but before could say anything, Sergei said:

'The Dnieper, we swim there in the summer and cut holes in the ice in winter to fish.'

'It's big,' was all that Arthur could think of saying.

Arthur was mesmerised by the traffic, his was also hungry to take in as much of the city as he could en-route. Sergei pointed out any famous landmarks they passed. They drove past beautiful churches, monuments and buildings, and all the time the traffic became increasingly chaotic. The taxi weaved and squeezed in and out of anywhere there was almost space for it to fit into. Horns blarted. Cars lurched carelessly into the main flow from side-roads. And the mêlée wasn't supported by skill: the taxi passed accidents that seemed to happen every few hundred yards. At one point the traffic swerved around a police car that was only half parked on the central reservation, laying on the ground nearby was a black plastic body bag.

'I could never drive here.' Arthur said. The driver glanced at the Englishman in his rear view mirror.

'You do not need to. There are buses, the metro, taxis. I rarely drive here also—only to get out of the place at the weekend,' Sergei said.

'Where do you go?'

'We have a place in the countryside. It is only a small house but it has good land, we grow many vegetables and fruit—you must come with us, it's a good time of year to be there. In fact any time of year is a good time of year to be there, away from this crazy stuff!' Sergei waved his hand towards the city around them.

'Great! I'll look forward to that.'

'We will soon be home Arthur. We stay near the centre, next to Kreschiatik, which is the most famous road in Kiev. You heard about our Orange Revolution?'

'Of course! It was on the TV every day. It was amazing what happened!'

Sergei smiled proudly, 'I had the best view in the city—it happened right next to our apartment.'

'You must have been very happy.'

'I cried like a baby to see what faith can do.'

'I'm hearing that word a lot recently.'

'They say faith can move mountains, and I still believe it can. Sad to say I think I lost mine for a while. But now, I am happy to say it is back again. Although it's sad that the faith of so many people was betrayed again.'

'Why?'

'Because the new dogs learnt the old tricks. But I have faith that one day we will have a government who deserves the faith of the people. Off course Kiev will always be the good and bad, crazy place it has always been!' Sergei slapped Arthur on the thigh again, and then said something to the driver in Russian. The driver turned into a side street and pulled up. The two men got out and Sergei paid the driver. 'Here we are. That is the music school and this is my apartment block,' Sergei pointed to a large stone building, then to another one opposite. 'You can hear the students practising their music, sometimes from five-o'clock in the morning. If they are good it is wonderful!'

Arthur wondered whether his room was at the front or the back of the building.

'Wait a moment,' Sergei ducked and dived across the wide, busy road to a stall selling flowers, and picked up a large, exotic bunch wrapped in purple crepe paper and an enormous pink ribbon; then weaved his way back through the traffic.

'That was a dangerous thing to do for a bunch of flowers,' Arthur said, genuinely concerned.

'The things we do for love,' Sergei replied.

Having seen the traffic Arthur thought Sergei was slightly mad. Something must have flicked across Arthur's face, because Sergei said: 'Don't worry! I love my life almost as much as I love my wife! And if anything happened to me, she would kill me!' Then laughed as he beckoned Arthur to follow him.

The apartment block must have been a very grand place eighty years ago. The vestibule was tattered, bruised and peeling, as was the concierge—a tough-looking woman with an etched scowl of suspicion. Her dark eyes tracked Arthur as he walked by. Sergei barked a couple of words to her as they passed. Whatever he said seemed to work, she moved rapidly into a small office at the back, picked up a phone and talked into it angrily while staring disapprovingly as the two men walked up the ancient, threadbare carpet of the broad main stairs. At the top they doubled back onto a landing lined with paintings of harsh landscapes, nicotine stained or sun-bleached to a degree that made them almost Impressionist. From here Sergei led Arthur down a long corridor, the only light for which came, totally inadequately, from a small stained glass window at the far end. Arthur wasn't sure whether it was some kind of optical illusion, but it appeared to be more than seventy-five metres away. As they neared the end, Arthur saw there was another corridor running perpendicular. Before they turned into it, Arthur stopped and looked back, then ahead: the second corridor ran at least the same distance they had just covered.

A few steps further and Sergei stopped in front of a large, solid wooden double-door. 'Home,' he said as he knocked. After a few seconds came the sound of locks being opened. Cautiously, one of the doors opened a little, then recognising her husband, Nadia pulled the door open wide.

Nadia kissed Sergei, relieved to see him safely home. He gave her the flowers and she blushed. Arthur was introduced and Nadia kissed him on both cheeks then fussed him into the apartment. She shared the same lean, healthy glow as Sergei, a glow that came partly from the fact that the pair absolutely doted on each other. Nadia's hair was long and pure white. She also was tall, and carried her beauty into her seventieth decade. Sergei and Nadia looked at each other in a way that Arthur had never seen in a couple before, as if they tried to make every second stretch into an eternity. She turned her attention to Arthur, and—while she was asking him whether he'd had a good trip and what he thought of Kiev—she picked a speck of dust from Sergei's cardigan. He leant forward and kissed her cheek tenderly; she kissed his, squeezing his arm as she did so.

After they'd talked about the trip, and after making sure that his guest was at ease, Sergei showed Arthur to his room, which was spacious and sparsely furnished: white walls and a dark parquet floor; a small camel-hair rug beside the large bed; a single wooden chair; a small table with a lamp on top. There was a large print of one of Van Gogh's sunflower paintings on the wall above the bed, and a few books on the windowsill—some with English titles. The only conspicuous luxury was the fact that the room had its own bathroom. Arthur was pleased that the room was at the back of the building, reasoning that it would be quieter than being opposite the music school at the front. The road in front was always busy too. The prospect of music students starting to practise at five in the morning was not something he thought he'd appreciate.

Sergei looked out of the window, his focus was beyond a line of trees, which were blowing in the breeze: 'I am sorry there is not much of a view. From the front you can see the fountains on the square'.

'Oh it's not a problem. It's perfect. What else do I need? It's a lovely place.' Arthur replied, noticing a smile flash across Sergei's face.

'There are towels in the bathroom. You just relax for a while. Soon we will eat. Are you hungry? Can I get you something now? You must be tired?'

'I'm fine honestly Sergei. Don't worry about me. I couldn't relax anyway, I'm too excited about being here.'

'Good, good. Then I will leave you alone for a while. Just come through when you are ready.' Sergei soft-saluted Arthur on his way out, and closed the door gently behind him.

Arthur dropped his rucksack on the floor and placed his carrier bag on the chair, he sat on the bed and flopped back; feet still on the floor. All he could hear was the faint white noise of traffic punctuated by horns and sirens. He stared at the ceiling. The room smelt of polish and soap, which melted comfortably into the underlying smell of age. Shadows from the trees outside flickered across the ceiling and seemed to animate the sunflowers above the bed.

Arthur relaxed a little, and began to think about his predicament. It was one thing to come to Kiev, another to actually find the Munter here. Just driving from the airport was enough for Arthur to realise that he was looking for a grain of sugar in a sand dune. Kiev was big and chaotic on a massive scale. Every suburb was like a separate city. There also seemed to be so many people here. He'd tried to find some information from the Internet before he left. One site he'd looked at said the population of Kiev was around four million, but Sergei had said there could be as many as twice that, nobody really knew for sure. Arthur wondered where and how he was going to start looking.

He stood up, took his bag from the chair, put it on the bed and began unpacking the gifts he'd brought for his hosts. There was a bottle of good single malt for Sergei; a box of Belgian chocolates, and a large hand-painted silk scarf that Etta had suggested as a gift for Nadia, plus a couple of bottles of decent red wine and some French champagne 'for the table'. After laying them out on the bed, Arthur showered and dressed in fresh clothes, ready for dinner. Before leaving the room he slid his feet into the pair of new slippers that had been placed by the door. Arthur knew it was the custom not to wear shoes in the home.

The door leading to the large sitting room was open and the air was rich with the smell of cooking. At one end of the room was a large, round table prepared for a splendid and generous meal. There were plates, dishes and bowls of all sizes filled with salads, meats, fish and sauces. A bottle of chilled vodka stood ready, coated in condensation that had already started to trickle down and form a pool. Arthur thought there was enough food for thirty, never mind three.

'You shouldn't have gone to so much trouble,' Arthur

said to Sergei, who was standing looking out of the window. He turned and moved from his distant thoughts back to the room:

'What? Ah, Arthur. I'm sorry, I was watching people down on the square. I like to look at people. Are you rested?'

'I'm fine thanks. The shower worked wonders.' Arthur nodded towards the table: ' It looks wonderful—you really shouldn't have gone to so much trouble.'

'Oh shush! It is no trouble! No trouble at all.'

Nadia walked into the room carrying another bowl: 'Trouble? Trouble is what you will have if you don't sit down here!' She said to Sergei.

There was a knock at the door 'Perfect timing!' Sergei excused himself and disappeared, returning with a large ice bucket containing several bottles of Russian champagne—the ice the result of a barked order to the concierge.

'Sit down! Sit down!' Nadia urged Arthur.

There was all kinds of food on the table. A whole fried carp cut into small portions, slices of pork and ham, small bowls of pickled fish and vegetables, a basket of dark and light bread and various types of salad. There were also several other places set. 'There's so much food! I'm glad to see you're expecting somebody else,' Arthur said.

'Oh, just a few friends. This is a celebration! Because at last our friend Arthur has come to Kiev. Let us drink!' Sergei poured vodka into shot-glasses and handed one to Nadia and one to Arthur, 'Although we should punish you for leaving it so long!' He added.

Arthur looked at the glass he was now holding, it was

brim-full of vodka, 'I think you're going to.'

The meal one of the best Arthur had ever eaten. The food was delicious, but it was the pace of the meal that he particularly enjoyed. No silently sitting through set courses here—instead everybody just ate what, when and as they wished. Nadia kept offering food to Arthur, Sergei and their two later arrivals and good friends: Uri and Valentina, neither of whom spoke English. Arthur soon learned that there was no saying 'Niet!' Especially to the vodka, which was always taken by the shot—but always with some tasty morsel of food, and almost always accompanied by a toast to something or someone, according to how the conversation progressed: to Arthur; to Uri & Valentina; to Nadia and all our women; to Nadia's wonderful food; to Nadia and Sergei; to love; to Ukraine; to health and happiness; to finding the Munter; to long life; to wisdom; to truth; to freedom; to Nadia for being such a wonderful wife for so many years; to Arthur for being such a true and good friend; to faith; to the love of friends; to family. Arthur had no idea how many toasts there were, and he was beyond caring.

There were also quiet moments, when everyone drifted on the warm-as-toast afterglow of a good meal: enjoying a memory, the taste of the food; or the simple feeling of being happy at a good table with good company. One such moment saw Sergei sitting back in his chair, he started to hum—at first quietly to himself. Nadia put down her fork, smiled as she wiped her lip with her napkin, and pushed her own chair a little away from the table. Uri and Valentina smiled at each other. Sergei's humming stopped for a second. Then he started to sing the tune he'd been humming. At first he sat upright in his chair as he sang, then he stood to let the voice pour from a deeper place. It was a long, beautiful song, which Nadia explained later was about love: about lovers losing each other but not losing their love for each other. Sergei sang it beautifully in a deep, rich, mellow, well-practised voice. The end of the song was just the beginning, because the music carried on throughout the evening—much to Arthur's pleasure. Sergei and Nadia sang unaccompanied and with each other—as if it was the most natural thing in the world to do, which of course it was. Valentina sang a song of many verses and Arthur wished he understood Russian, because from the reaction of the others around the table it seemed to tell a tale that was funny in some places and risqué in others. There was applause of delight when she finished. Nadia picked up a guitar and strummed gently as she sang a beautiful song that sounded religious; a fact that made Nadia laugh when Arthur asked her: 'No! No! It's about an old man betraying his wife! A young woman has tempted him. But he can't, well—you know, he can't make love!' It was obvious from the way she looked at Sergei and he looked at her, that this was not a problem they shared. As the evening passed, Arthur was amazed at how drunk he didn't feel. At one point he tried to work out how much vodka and champagne he'd consumed, but gave up.

'I think it is your turn Arthur!' Sergei said.

'Yes Arthur! You must sing for us now!' Nadia clapped her hands in anticipation.

Arthur tried in vain to say no—saying that he had no

voice and that he couldn't remember any songs—but as he had already discovered, there was no way of saying 'Niet'.

'Well, if you insist. But I normally only sing to myself, out of consideration for everyone else.' Arthur picked up the guitar and strummed, to check if it was in tune and to edge off his nervousness.

Arthur enjoyed playing, but it was a personal pleasure. Over the years he'd collected a small repertoire—not necessarily his favourite songs, but those that were easy to play and sing. Talking Heads' 'Psycho Killer' was a great one for a drunken evening, but Arthur wasn't sure how it would go down right here, right now. He mentally ran through those he thought he could do: 'Drugs Don't Work,' 'The Man Who Sold the World', 'Hotel California', 'Waterloo Sunset', 'Come As You Are', 'No Woman No Cry', 'Losing My Religion'...amongst others.

'Do you know 'Hey Jude'?' Nadia asked.

'Well I used to play it, but ...' Arthur actually knew a few Beatles' songs. Nothing could have been better for Nadia and Sergei, for whom the Beatles were something special—a taste of something squeezed through a transistor radio all those years ago. Colour in grey times.

Although nervous, the first song was received with delightful applause. The rest of the evening was a medley of pop tunes, including lots of Beatles' numbers—not just sung by Arthur, but by each and all of them. Including Uri and Valentina who didn't speak English, but could sing in English just about anything by the Beatles.

It was, as far as Arthur could remember, a wonderful evening. He could even enjoy recalling it the following morning as he seemed have a fairly clear head: miraculous, he thought, considering he had no idea how much he'd had to drink. 'That is because you ate food with it. Always eat when you drink,' Sergei told him later.

Arthur got up around ten. Nadia was already up, had cleared up and left for the countryside to tend her garden. It was only during a conversation, which started after he asked Sergei where Nadia was, he found out that all the food on the table the previous evening had been grown by the couple.

'We are going to meet her there tomorrow, so you can see for yourself,' Sergei explained as he made coffee for Arthur, 'But today I am going to show you Kiev, and you can tell me all about your problem.'

In the music school across the road, a lone trumpeter began practising scales. Arthur wondered how much it would cost to phone Etta from his mobile. He was missing her more than he imagined he would. It wasn't just that he felt that he was missing her; he also felt that there was something of himself missing without her.

31: The Wild East

Whoever Nathaniel was talking to on the phone and whatever it was about, it looked serious, but Icarus didn't give it much thought. He was just glad to be home again. Not just glad to be back in his own flat, but glad to be back in London. The endless traffic, its too many people, its littered streets, polluted air and noise—this was all home to Icarus, and he'd missed it. Nathaniel ended his call. He looked serious.

'What's up man, you look like you've seen your own arse?'

'If that was all it was I wouldn't mind.'

'Was it Mrs. Makeover?'

'No, she's the least of our problems.'

'Our problems?'

'Well that was Bogdan, and the good news is I think I know where that bloody car is.'

'But that's not just good, it's fucking fantastic!'

'Not quite.'

'Come on then, give us the bad news.'

'It's near a place called Tiraspol.'

'Where's that then? Somewhere near Kiev?'

'It depends on what scale you're talking about. It's a lot nearer to Kiev than London. But that's not the problem.'

'Well come on then! Don't keep me hanging on like a twat!'

'It's in Transdniester, and why do you have to swear all the time?'

'Trans-de-who?'

'Transdniester. It's a strip of land between Ukraine and Moldova.'

Icarus managed to create an expression of blankness, combined with one looking for more answers.

'The easiest way I can explain it is—imagine the Wild West, with bars, gunfighters, cat-houses, bank robberies, outlaws and whatever else you can think of.'

'OK, I can do that.' Icarus was building up an excellent picture in his mind's eye.

'Right, well transfer that to eastern Europe, and bring it up to date, with drugs, arms, money laundering, corruption and whatever else you can thing of—and you'll have some idea of the general picture.'

'Sound great! When do we go?'

'It's not that easy. Officially it doesn't exist.'

'What do you mean it doesn't exist?'

'I said officially it doesn't exist. But it exists real enough. It's just not a proper country, not a real place.'

'How do you know about it?'

'It's the smuggling hub of Europe. That's how.'

'So it's kind of like a 'Wild East' instead of a Wild West, but without the sheriff.'

Nathaniel laughed.

'What?' Icarus asked, laughing nervously.

'That's really funny. Because they do have a 'sheriff'—the football stadium!'

'What?'

'The football stadium in Tiraspol is called the 'Sheriff' stadium. It's fairly new; there are all sorts of rumours around about how it got built.'

'Sounds like a wild place. When do we go?'

'We don't. I do.'

'Ohh maaaan! Come on! You can't leave me here! Not when you're going to somewhere that sounds like the Las Vegas of Eastern Europe!'

'It's more Dodge City than Las Vegas. No, I have to go alone. I'm meeting one of Bogdan's men in Odessa.'

'Well I'm not happy. I was stuck in fucking Manchester for days while you sorted out your love life. Then I get lumbered with the psycho-twins, thanks to your mate Mr. bloody-Shaggy-Dog! Now you're going off on your own to Trans-fucking-jester or whatever it's called—to what sounds like some kind of giant party—and you're leaving me behind!'

'Finished?'

'For now, and pissed off.' Icarus was sulky.

'Anyway it's 'Transdniester', after the river.'

This was of no comfort to Icarus: 'I couldn't give a flying fuck whether it's Trans-fucking-vestite! I'm not happy.'

'Look Icarus, it's a dangerous place. It's not the East End of London we're talking about here. Anyway, like I said, I might need you here.'

Icarus knew that he wasn't going to change Nathaniel's mind.

'So when are you going?'

'I'm flying out this afternoon.'

32: Voyages of discovery

Arthur liked Kiev despite the seemingly endless suburban sprawl. The city was like a nugget of gold in an enormous grey rock. The centre was much more elegant and interesting that he'd imagined—even though he realised he didn't know what he'd imagined. Sergei was a perfect and proud guide as he walked with Arthur along wide boulevards and down narrow streets, into magnificent churches and through tree-lined parks. As they walked they talked incessantly: Arthur asked Sergei all about the Munter, about Russia under Khrushchev, Brezhnev and Gorbachev; and about how he came to be in Kiev and what life was like here.

Sergei in turn listened with close concentration as Arthur explained about the missing Munter; about Etta and the dogs—Sergei was amazed that it was possible to make a living out of two poodles; about the ransom note, and the fact that the Munter had been tracked to Kiev. After telling Sergei everything, Arthur realised that he didn't actually have that much to go on. Sergei only confirmed this.

'Well Arthur, I don't know,' he was shaking his head

slowly, 'You don't seem to have much we can do something with. All we know is that the Munter was in Kiev at some point, and as you can see, Kiev is a big city. It is also a big corrupt city'. The lines in Sergei's brow deepened with his thinking, 'But I am optimistic, and I always like to make the problem work for me. I think that's what we should do here. Also, the Munter is…' Arthur noticed a smile no more than twitch across Sergei's face: '…unique.'

'So do you think there's a chance?'

'Ha! One thing you learn from living in Ukraine, or Russia, is that there is always a chance, and even where there isn't one, you take it anyway! I think I know somebody who might be able to help. You might find her to be something of an unusual woman though.'

'Unusual? In what way? Crazy?'

'Oh, she is not crazy. She is just—how can I put it? As you would say: 'from the old school'. She used to have lots of power and influence, she is a businesswoman, or should I say she was. However her businesses are suffering at the moment, because her business is old business, and the new government is investigating many old businesses. So for now she is bear with no claws—but her bark can still shake the bones of the dead!' Sergei was laughing again. 'I'm sorry. I have made her sound a lot worse than she is. But if anyone can help, she can. She has no money at the moment, and her influence is not so strong as it was, but she still has many, many contacts.'

'So how do we get in touch with her?'

'Oh that is the easy part, she's spending lots of time in her countryside house at the moment. We drive past her place tomorrow on the way to ours, so we can call in to see her—we will take her a basket of fruit and, with your permission, that bottle of French champagne you brought with you. I cannot promise you anything, but there is a small chance.'

Even the smallest chance was better than Arthur had come to expect since being in Kiev. Since he'd arrived he'd wondered what had possessed him to make the trip when he had nothing to go on. He was enjoying being a tourist, so it would be a good holiday whatever happened, and now he began to hope that perhaps it might not be a complete waste of time as far as the Munter was concerned. Either way, he'd have lots to tell when he returned home.

*

Nathaniel should have felt elated at being in Tiraspol: this was after all the smuggling capital of Europe—and he was, despite recent setbacks, arguably the best smuggler in England. One thing that he couldn't argue about was the fact that this entire job had been a balls-up. His head was now much clearer than it had been for months, especially as he felt he'd finally sorted things out with Sandra. Although 'sorting things out' had meant giving her everything they owned except for a few personal things. This didn't bother Nathaniel: he'd never been that materialistic. Besides there were a lot of Boot family things that Sandra didn't know about, such as the art collection, his own stash of booty, his bolt-hole in Spain, a couple of bank accounts here and there, and a few properties he rented out around the UK—including apartments in Edinburgh and Brighton and the house in Penzance. Oh—and that small terraced house in Grimsby. He didn't feel guilty about leaving Sandra in ignorance of these assets; aside from the fact that many had been in the family for generations, her ignorance was also for her own good. What she didn't know she couldn't talk about.

It worried him that this job had turned into such a mess. It wasn't like a Boot to be in such a situation. He wondered if he was losing it—professionally speaking, but reassured himself that it was only because he'd been so distracted by his own problems. He had to admit that it might seem slightly strange to an outsider—sticking millions of £s worth diamonds under a strange car. And of all the bad luck, a car that had been nicked and ended up in this, this … he couldn't think of a way of describing the place. His head must have been all over the place recently. It was his own fault of course, he should have thought of everything, should have thought in more detail about every possible risk. If he had, he wouldn't be in this Wild-Eastern frontier town. He felt ashamed that he had performed like an amateur, and the situation needed to be resolved to maintain the good name and reputation of the Boot dynasty.

After his self-chastisement, Nathaniel's thoughts turned to how he'd get the diamonds from Tiraspol to Belgium. It wasn't so much the customs that worried him as having to deal with Bogdan. If he caught a hint of what was really going on, he would devalue the entire job—by taking a very large commission, possibly including several body parts. Stefan had been given the job of being Nathaniel's guide and almost certainly he would have been instructed to keep his eyes and ears open and report back to Bogdan. Nathaniel knew he would have to be very careful.

He'd flown into Odessa where he'd met Stefan, who'd driven him across to Transdniester and into Tiraspol. Going back the same way with the diamonds would be risky. Ending up in a Ukrainian prison wasn't one of Nathaniel's ambitions. But even that was more favourable than ending up in the Transdniester equivalent. At least Ukraine was a real country. Nathaniel realised that he was counting his chickens before the stable door had been opened—or whatever the expression was. There was no point in worrying about the number of eggs until he'd found the horse. Annoyingly, it took twenty minutes of stitched time before Nathaniel stopped translating his thoughts into mix 'n' match proverbs.

After a restless night in a six-roomed, cheap hotel, Stefan drove Nathaniel out of Tiraspol and into the countryside. Goats and solitary cows grazed on any available patch of grass; ancient babushkas sat by small piles of fruit and vegetables, trying to earn a pittance from passing trade; cottages huddled in hamlets like gossips around a conversation, each home separated by fences of any available material—old planks, sheets of ply and rust-laced corrugated iron.

Stefan pulled off the road onto a dirt track, passing through a hamlet of about eight or nine houses. The road continued, running alongside green fields containing growth too new to recognise, and past more wild spring flowers that Nathaniel had ever seen in one place. The car jolted along the rutted track, but Stefan made no compensation in speed for the lack of concrete or tarmac. As Nathaniel bounced around feeling sick he envied Stefan his steadying grip on the steering-wheel,.

The car slowed then stopped at the edge of a forest. Stefan got out and slammed the door shut and beckoned to Nathaniel to follow him.

'Car shit. Road shit. Now we walk!'

Nathaniel felt nervous. Anything could happen here and probably did, and there was nothing anyone could do about it. The two carried on walking along the track into the forest, which was all thin silver trunks. Nathaniel wished he knew more about nature. He could recognise an oak, sycamore or weeping willow, but wasn't sure about these trees: were they birch or beech? Birch, he thought. They left the track and cut through the woods, Nathaniel was aware of something brushing against his skin. Something brushed his face and stuck. Spiders' webs! He focussed and could see that almost all the trees had webs stretched between them. In the centre of some sat ominous looking yellow and black spiders.

'Are these poisonous?' Nathaniel asked Stefan.

'I do not know, I never eat one.' He replied. He didn't look as though he was joking. 'See?' Stefan was pointing to a large area of roughly ploughed up ground.

'I see?' Nathaniel replied

'Pigs. Wild pigs. Very dangerous.' Stefan said, matter-of-factly. 'We see, we run.' He pulled a pistol out of his pocket and cocked it. Nathaniel hoped it was for the pigs.

They rejoined the track. 'That little trek between the trees must have been a short-cut,' Nathaniel thought.

Ahead, he could make out the dark shape of a group of buildings.

'Is that where we're going?'

Stefan just looked at him, in a way that said: 'Of course, where do you think we're going, you idiot!'

Stefan walked past what Nathaniel took to be the main house, and towards a large shed. All the buildings were made of wooden planks. All were a similar size. He pushed open the door and Nathaniel followed him inside. At first, because of the contrast between the light outside and the dark interior, all he could see inside was a pattern of silhouettes and shafts of light. But gradually his eyes adjusted. Light jabbed through the cracks between the boards like conjurers' swords. The air smelt of rotting wood and damp hay. Birds flew in and out of holes in the roof. Nathaniel heard a muffled cry from somewhere close by, and instinctively tracked the noise. It took him a few seconds to focus into the darkness, but laying on a pile of straw against one side he saw two figures, bound, gagged and tied to a two-wheeled cart.

'Skinny one, Tadeuz; other one, Lenny. Brothers. Tadeuz steal your car. Other one bring here to sell. We question them little, but when Bogdan hear you come here, he said to keeping them alive for longer—for you want ask questions.

Nathaniel was upset and angry. But he knew he'd have to keep himself in check.

'All I wanted was some information.' He said to Stefan.

'We got you information?' Stefan was puzzled at

Nathaniel's attitude. 'What is problem?'

'Nothing. How are they?'

Stefan looked as though he hadn't understood the question. Which wasn't strictly true. He'd understood the question, but didn't understand why Nathaniel had asked it. After all, who cared how they were?

'Don't know. Maybe you ask them,' Stefan said, before giving a single equine snort—which for him passed as laughter.

'Can we untie them?'

Stefan shook his head: 'Not good idea.'

'Well can we at least take off the gags so that I can hear what they have to say?'

Stefan shrugged to say: 'OK.'

'Do they speak English?' Nathaniel asked.

Stefan shrugged again to say: 'Don't know.'

Nathaniel knelt down and looked at Tadeuz. His face was bruised on one side, but he glared at Nathaniel defiantly. He then looked across to Lenny, who was unmarked, but obviously terrified and looked as though he'd been crying.

'If I you, I do Lenny first, is easier, talks like babushka; this one, not speak.' Stefan advised. Nathaniel removed the gag from Tadeuz, then from Lenny.

'Do you speak English? He asked Lenny. Lenny flinched and started talking rapid Russian in a nerve-stretched voice. Nathaniel looked at Stefan questioningly.

'See—talks like babushka.'

'What's he saying?'

'Nothing important. He ask you not kill him.'

Nathaniel was already uncomfortable with the fact that

these two—hardly more than boys—had been tied up and questioned on his account. The bruise on Tadeuz looked fierce, 'So what are you going to do with them?' He asked Stefan.

'When you finish with them? Kill them.' Stefan replied, in a matter-of-fact way that led Nathaniel to believe him.

Nathaniel noticed that the comment made Tadeuz flinch slightly, 'You speak English?'

Tadeuz looked at Stefan, then at Nathaniel. He nodded.

'So tell me about the car. The one you stole.'

Tadeuz looked at Nathaniel, frowned as though he didn't understand, then looked at Stefan.

Stefan replied: 'Oh we know all about car, she is in other building. We already know that information.'

Nathaniel felt a jolt of optimism: 'So where is it? In other building where?' At the back of his mind he was anticipating yet another uncomfortable trip.

'Here.' Stefan answered.

'Here?'

'Here.'

'As in here, here; or as in here somewhere else?'

'Here, in other building next to tractor shed.'

'Can I see it?'

'Of course! Is only outside. I stay.' Stefan pointed to the two young men.

Nathaniel stood and walked towards the door, then paused and turned to Stefan: 'Don't kill them.'

'I do nothing. I wait you to finish.'

Nathaniel walked across to the other building. It was

about the size of a double garage with two sets of doors on the front. He wrenched open one of the doors. Inside was the Munter. At the sight of it, his optimism crashed in flames.

It was obviously the same type of car, but it was not recognisable as the same car. All that remained was trussed up with rope and suspended from the building's heavy wooden roof beams. It looked like some gigantic alien cocoon. All that was left was a metal shell. The wheels, hubs and suspension had gone; the interior had been stripped of seats, carpets, dials, switches and wires; all the glass had gone. Nathaniel walked around to the front and looked into the engine compartment to confirm what he already knew: the engine, gearbox—and consequently the diamonds—had gone.

Nathaniel went back outside. He looked up at the leaves swimming steadily through a breeze so gentle he couldn't feel it on his skin. The sky was covered in a sheet of high, light grey cloud. Up there it could have been any European country on a cool day in late spring. But he was in a country that officially didn't exist, with—in one buiding—two boys tied up and being watched over by a man of indeterminate eastern European nationality and a casual approach to life; and the empty shell of his reputation hanging in another building.

He turned around, walked over to the stump of a tree and sat down. He propped his foot on a log, his elbow on his knee, and his chin on his hand. He had never smoked, but he realised that this was one of those times when if he did, it might help.

'What was it? Why was nothing going right recently? And at what point do you give up several million quid?' He thought.

It was a casual thought that did it: it simply crossed his mind that you don't have to have a mid-life crisis to have a crisis in mid-life. He started laughing. He realised what an idiot he'd been. Several times over the past few months he'd felt as if he'd lost it. What he now realised was that he'd found it. The reason that everything was a 'fuck up' as Icarus would say, was because he was going against his own natural law. He'd been changing for years, but only just realised it. He had been ignoring all the signs and simply ploughed on regardless: trying to be as good as he'd always been at the things he was always good at. But never once had he asked himself was it what he wanted.

He'd got as far as asking that of his relationship, but it was easy to deflect your feelings onto another area. His relationship was an easy vehicle to hook up his problems to, because he should have got out of it years ago. But it was only part of the problem. What he hadn't done was question himself. He had always been so much the same. He used to say that he felt the same at forty-five as he felt at thirty—or twenty come to that. But now he realised he felt differently. In a way he'd been doing things purely for the sake of doing them. He'd smuggled because that's what the Boot family did. He was a brilliant smuggler, but that didn't necessarily mean it was what he had to do. But what did he want to do?

Nathaniel stood up. He felt good. What did he want to do? He wasn't sure, and now wasn't the time to make a decision. What he didn't want to do was to be in this situation. He walked back into the barn.

Stefan was sitting on an old wooden stool, smoking a cigarette. He looked up as Nathaniel came in.

'You find it?'

'Part of it. Not much of it left to find though. The wheels are gone, the engine's missing, the seats have disappeared...'

'Why you want car anyway. Is ugly most thing I ever see?'

'It's a long story.' A story that Nathaniel wasn't about to repeat.

'So, you want I kill them now, or you have question?'

At this Lenny started whimpering. Tadeuz shut him up with a contemptuous stare.

'Kill them?'

'OK! No problem...'

Nathaniel panicked when he realised his question had been taken as a statement. 'No! Wait! I don't want anybody killed! I hate violence! Let them go!'

'Let them go? Not possible.' Stefan shook his head slowly. Lenny started whimpering again.

'Why not?'

'Because I responsible for them. Is my job taking care of them. What you think would happen if I let them go and they decide for revenge? Maybe they go to police—even if no good in this no-god country. Why I leave this rubbish when I can clean it now, and feed to wild pigs in forest? I would have to be fool. Besides, I do job not properly, I have Bogdan problem. So, I take care of them. Simple.' Stefan sounded resolute.

Nathaniel thought.

'What if I took care of them for you?'

'What? You kill them? Well it would save me job probably—'

'No, I mean what if you told Bogdan that I would take responsibility for them. And that if anything went wrong in the future he could hold me accountable?'

'Lots of big words, me not so good English. Perhaps I speak to Bogdan?'

'Speak to him. In fact I'll speak to him if you like?'

'No, I do. Then I am sure.'

Stefan pulled out his mobile and called Bogdan. There was a long debate, which ended by the phone being handed to Nathaniel, who explained what he wanted to do:

'You sure you want to do that?' Bogdan asked.

'I'm sure. I'll take care of them, I give you my word.'

'Ha! And your word is your bond?' Bogdan was laughing.

'Funny! I forgot you get all our old TV programmes, you're welcome to them.'

'OK, Nathaniel—it's your decision but I don't want any comebacks. By the way, what happened to the necklace?'

'The necklace?'

'Now don't be coy with me—the Hymer collection, remember?'

'Aaah! That necklace! Well I think it got misplaced somewhere, but I'm sure it will turn up soon.'

'Misplaced? Hmmm. Well if is should happen to turn up, don't forget my commission. There's also the little matter of your travel arrangements, and your travel insurance of course. I would imagine you would like to settle your bill as soon as possible?'

'Of course—do you take American Express?'

'As many as I can get my hands on! Ha! You're funny Nathaniel, sometimes.'

'Thanks, I'll sort something out with you as soon as I get back to England.'

'Ha! It's a good job I trust you Nathaniel, probably one of the few people on this planet who does.'

'Thanks, I'll take that as a compliment.'

With that Nathaniel handed the phone back to Stefan who, after a further conversation with Bogdan, sighed, and put the phone back into his pocket.

'Well, I guess if Bogdan says is OK, then is OK. But it would be pleasure to kill babushka,' Stefan pointed at Lenny, who was crying with relief, 'but shame to kill skinny-boy, he has big talent with machines. But we go now. If I not needed, I go back to family.'

'Just one thing Stefan, could you ask Tadeuz what he did with the engine and gearbox, I'm just curious.'

'You ask, I think he know English very good.'

Nathaniel turned and looked at Tadeuz.

'Well?'

There was silence.

'Speak to him! He save your miserable life!' Stefan barked in Russian.

After a pause, Tadeuz said: 'It's in the tractor.'

'The tractor?' Nathaniel was curious.

'In Ukraine, our family has a small farm. The tractor

is dying for many years. Engine is no good. Brother fix it many, many times.' The explanation came from Lenny.

'Shut the fuck up Lenny!' Tadeuz did speak excellent English, except that it was more American.

'Look. My family works just about every day on that farm, just to make enough food to keep us going. We sell a little at the market. My mother's sick, but she still works every day. Even my grandmother works, picking potatoes, digging, and she's eighty-six, OK? So I took the engine from your lousy car, took it back to our farm and fixed up the tractor with it. Now it's fine. So I don't give a damn what you do to me. You're not having that block back!'

Nathaniel could tell by the tone of Tadeuz's voice that he was serious.

'So what? You put the whole lot, engine, gearbox, everything into a tractor?'

'Of course.'

'How did you get it back to Ukraine. I mean why? I mean wasn't the car in Kiev anyway?'

'Only for a couple of days, this idiot brother of mine tried to sell it while I was asleep. I was very tired when I got back. He drives it to Kiev and starts asking around to see if he can sell it. I was crazy when I woke up and found out what he has done. I phone him and told him to get it back home. He has no luck selling it in Kiev anyway. He thinks he's some kind of big-shot businessman, but he's just a dick-brain,' at this point Tadeuz glared at Lenny, 'so he has this crazy idea on the way back, and takes the highway to Transdniester, instead of coming straight back to our home near Odessa. They'll buy anything here, if they can't steal it first.' Tadeuz called Lenny something in Russian, and a fierce argument broke out between the two brothers.

'Listen them! Is how we find them, fight like cat and bitch!' Stefan said.

'What you mean those bruises? You?'

'Me?' Stefan said: 'Niet! Niet! I professional, I like clean ...' he mimed a slit throat, '... but I not do boxing—too much time, also bad for hands. No, they box each other!' Stefan snorted like a horse again, by way of a laugh. 'Well Nathaniel, we go. What you do with them?'

'Let's untie them.'

'OK, but they kill each other, not my fault.' Stefan shrugged in a matter of fact way.

As Nathaniel and Stefan untied the brothers, a thought crystallised in Nathaniel.

'How did you two get that engine back into Ukraine?'

'In a trailer behind our automobile.'

'You have a car here?'

'Of course, how do you think we got here? By bus?' Tadeuz's contempt for Nathaniel's stupid questions was growing.

'So how do you get across the border?'

'We pay of course. Ten dollars, no questions.'

Nathaniel turned to Stefan: 'Look, Stefan, I've made a decision. I'm staying here. I'll take care of these two; you get back to your family.

'What? You crazy. You want stay this place?'

'Not exactly, but I can take care of myself from here. Here take this,' Nathaniel reached into his pocket and pulled out a wallet, from which he took a bundle of dollars, which he handed to Stefan, 'Treat your family to something'.

'Treat my family? Mister, I have wife and nine daughters, I treat myself to something!'

Nathaniel laughed, 'Fine, you do that. And thanks for everything. Thank Bogdan for me.'

'Goodbye Nathaniel. I not so sure about this, but you take careful.'

The two men hugged each other, out of etiquette rather than affection. Stefan turned to leave. As he neared the door, Nathaniel called after him: 'Be careful of those wild pigs!'

Stefan turned and grinned, patted the pistol in his pocket, then left.

*

As they drove towards the border, Nathaniel and Tadeuz talked, and the more they talked, the more Nathaniel realised what an extraordinary person Tadeuz was. Nathaniel learnt that the brothers' father had left them many years ago—he'd gone to Spain to work and never returned. He'd sent money back for a while, but that soon dried up, and the family had struggled along ever since. Tadeuz also realised that Nathaniel was not the total idiot he'd first taken him for. He told him the story of how he'd ridden to France on his scooter with the intention of going to England to find work so that he could send money home to his family. He told Nathaniel how he'd seen the Munter outside the supermarket, and decided to take it on impulse.

'I'm not a thief; I just thought the guy that owned it

would be rich, and wouldn't miss it too much, or at least could afford another. And anyway, I didn't wanna go back empty handed.' Tadeuz said. 'It was only when I was on the way back I started to think that I might be able to get the engine into the tractor. It's strange, but the engine's not so different from the old one I took out. That's why I didn't sell it for the money: the bits were more useful, and I wouldn't have gotten a good price for it anyway. To be honest, I've never seen anything so ugly as that car, but it was kind of interesting.'

Nathaniel was astonished at Tadeuz's tale. He couldn't imagine the kind of determination needed to ride a scooter from Kiev to Calais. He was also amazed at the devotion the young man had for his family.

'There's one thing I don't understand though,' Nathaniel said.

'What?'

'If you'd already taken the engine back to your farm, why did you bother to go back to the car?'

'The seats.'

'The seats?'

'Yeah, the seats were really comfortable. I thought they would be perfect for our house. I could convert them easily: they were leather, with electric ... the position and stuff. They would have been real cool—perfect for my mother.'

'So what happened?'

'It was his fault!' Tadeuz prodded Lenny in the shoulder. Lenny swore in Russian.

'How come?' Nathaniel asked.

'Well after driving into Transdniester, he'd put the word

around to sell it, but got scared with the people he was dealing with. He ran back home like a chicken. He came back with no car, and money. He was too scared to drive the car any more in case he got hijacked, so he hid it in that place in the forest. It was my mother's grandparents' place; they died years ago, before independence. We had a fight and I made him come back with me to get it so I could drive it back. But when we go there, the wheels had gone. Probably thanks to big mouth here. So we took out the engine and transmission and brought them back. While I was fixing up the tractor, I was thinking about the seats. I decided to come back and get them. We drove back, but you saw what happened, everything had been stripped out. We were lucky we'd already taken the engine and stuff. I was crazy with idiot there. We started fighting again when those mafia guys caught us. They tied us up and...'

'What?'

'Well they just kept asking me about some necklace. I told them I didn't know nothin' about no necklace. They threatened me with all kindsa things. They said they'd stake me out in the forest for the wild pigs. But I couldn't tell 'em what I don't know. Anyway squealing pig here freaked out and starts talking about the car and apologising for it. I decided the best thing to do was to say nothin'.'

Nathaniel wasn't surprised they'd been asked about the necklace, he knew Bogdan well enough to know he'd try and get the necklace for himself if he could. Nathaniel had played on this by using the necklace as an incentive to get Bogdan to find the car. He also knew he'd have to sort out something with Bogdan when he got back, as he'd promised. It might mean losing the necklace, which was real enough, and which he did have stashed away in a safe place for a rainy day, but avoiding a storm was just as valid.

Sliding through Customs into Ukraine was a breeze. Nathaniel gave Lenny the ten dollars for the bribe, plus an extra ten to make sure he didn't get a stamp in his passport. Too many stamps could mean too many questions. By the time they arrived at the family farm it was dark and Nathaniel was exhausted. Tadeuz had phoned ahead to tell his family about his guest. If Nathaniel expected to rest, which he did, then he had no inkling of Ukrainian hospitality. There was a spread waiting for them: a table that included a bottle of vodka and wine made from home-grown grapes. The day had been long; the night would be long—but the morning would be longer.

Nathaniel awoke tucked under a colourful blanket on a small single bed with the squeakiest springs he'd ever encountered. Every time he moved a muscle the springs complained. There were two other beds in the room: both were empty. Nathaniel's mouth felt like somebody had lined it with dirty suede—he desperately needed a drink. He heaved himself up onto his elbows, which drew an ill-tempered tirade from the bed. Whatever he'd had to drink last night had shrunk his skull but not its contents and the mismatch was painful. He tried to swallow, but the necessary mechanism had dried up. Nathaniel's first steps on This Earth were probably less tentative than the ones he now took as he got out of bed, pulled on his trousers and shoes (the socks were a step too far, so he tucked them into his pocket) and headed for the door. Taking the shortest route between the bed and the door proved impossible, he had to negotiate an obstacle in-between—his own lack of balance.

Everyone was out working in the fields, except for babushka, who was wise in the ways of wine. Nathaniel nodded a 'good-morning', babushka's response was to leave the kitchen and go outside. Nathaniel had barely had enough time to think about how or why he might have offended her, before she returned with a chilled beer which she handed to Nathaniel. It seemed churlish to refuse. A few seconds later he was sure that this was the best beer he had ever put to his lips, the cold jolted a string of still-dormant nerves back into life; the fizz stripped the suede from his mouth; the fluid soaked into his brain, slating dehydration and calming the big-footed beast that had been noisily stomping around in there. Nathaniel sucked like a baby on the bottle until it was drained.

'Aaaaahhhh! Spasiba! Spaseeba babushka!' Which, along with 'Nasdarovia', was just about all the Russian he knew. She grinned, showing off her four remaining teeth and gave him the thumbs up. She then pointed outside, and said something in Russian, which Nathaniel didn't understand, but—as he had already benefited from her experience—he followed her like a lamb.

Outside it was a bright, sunny morning. A little too bright for Nathaniel, but he spotted a bench and table under the shade of an apple tree, which he headed for: it looked like the perfect place to recover. He slumped down and absorbed his surroundings which were, by all appearances, idyllic. The farmhouse was a single-storey cottage painted white on the outside and inside. The table was on one side of an orchard in full blossom; on the other side was a line of grape vines. To the left of the orchard was a flower garden, which Nathaniel would love to have investigated if his limbs hadn't felt like lead. Next to the house were several wooden out-houses, including storage sheds and what looked like an outside toilet. Chickens pecked, clucked and chick-stepped around in the stamped-hard earth outside the kitchen door. Under a tree slept the dog that had obviously seen everything, twitching as he ran across his fields of dreams. The sky was almost turquoise and clear. But by far the greatest luxury was the silence. Once Nathaniel had noticed it he couldn't tune his ears away from it. There was no hiss and drum of traffic, no planes, no alarms, no radio or TV. A donkey brayed somewhere in the distance. Flies and bees buzzed impatiently and lazily in turn. There was also birdsong, not just the occasional whistle or tweet, but real three-dimensional, musical birdsong. Butterflies in blue, orange, red, white and purple dipped into flowers. A preying mantis poised deathly patient on the twig of a shrub. Everything felt too real to be real, especially as Nathaniel still had much of last night's alcohol in his blood, topped up with this morning's beer. The more he looked, the more he saw: more insects, more flowers, more birds. A breeze of sadness passed through him as he realised that this was what it must have been like in England before farms and supermarkets started sterilising nature. He also realised that it would never come back to this. It was too late, England would never be so rich again: 'We're chasing the wrong kind of wealth,' Nathaniel thought. He also wondered how much it would cost to buy a farm here. He realised that it wouldn't be too many years before it was soaked into Europe, and the insidious march of the supermarkets would begin to slowly sterilise and homogenise yet another country.

Lost in his thoughts, he didn't noticed Tadeuz walking over from a gap in a hedge, naked to the waist and wiping his brow. He had a basket overflowing with vegetables slung under one arm.

'Good morning Nathaniel! How are you this morning?' He was grinning as if he already knew.

'A lot better than I might have been if it wasn't for your grandmother and a cold beer!' Nathaniel shouted back.

Tadeuz walked over and dropped the basket on the table.

'For lunch,' he said, looking down at the green leaves and new potatoes.

'They look fantastic.'

Tadeuz was obviously proud, but stifled his smile.

'So do you want to see the tractor?'

Nathaniel had all but forgotten why he was there.

'Oh! Of course. Very much!'

'Follow me.'

Nathaniel stood, expecting his head to start pounding again; he was relieved when it didn't. He followed Tadeuz back through the gap in the hedge. In front of him was a wide expanse of field divided into different crops: potatoes, corn, tomatoes, cabbages, lettuce and row upon row of green leaves Nathaniel couldn't recognise—he'd never been much of a gardener. The entire family was busy about their work, backs bent into the ground, pulling up weeds or thinning new growth. As each caught sight of Nathaniel they stood, waved and shouted their greetings, Nathaniel waved back. To one side a couple of goats munched on a pile of weeds.

The tractor sat to one side of the field. An old, solid flatbed was attached to the back.

'Here she is. She's old, but she saves a lot of work for my family.'

The tractor was decades old, but had that look that said it was determined to go on forever. Everything had been brush-painted grey: the wheels, bodywork, seat, levers, radiator—even the tyres had faded to a dull grey.

'Do you mind if I see the engine?' Nathaniel asked,

'How can I say no? It's your engine.' Tadeuz's response perplexed Nathaniel, until he realised that of course Tadeuz presumed the Munter was his. It hadn't occurred to Nathaniel that Tadeuz wouldn't have known to whom the Munter had belonged. Nathaniel also reasoned that this was why Tadeuz was being so hospitable. Why else would he have brought someone to his own house, someone who he suspected of turning the mafia onto him? Nathaniel also suspected that Tadeuz was probably afraid of him, thinking that he also was a 'businessman'. It wasn't a situation that he felt completely comfortable with, he didn't have that sort of ego.

Tadeuz opened one side of the bonnet and lifted it clear. Nathaniel peered inside. He was by no means an expert on mechanical things, but he knew a little, and if he hadn't been told that the Munter engine was in the tractor, he would never have guessed it wasn't the original. Icarus had told him where he'd bolted the diamonds.

'Do you mind if I look underneath?' Nathaniel asked,

'Like I said, it's your engine, of course I don't mind.'

He knelt down and looked up to where the gearbox joined the engine. The box should have been at eight o'clock. There was nothing. Nathaniel decided that enough was enough. He stood up and sighed heavily.

'I can take the block and transmission out, and we can take it back to Transdniester and put it back in the car. I might be able to fix it up again, but not with the original parts.' Tadeuz said, apologetically.

'Well, I can see you've done a brilliant job. I'm amazed it fits so well.'

'It's no problem, the block is the same as an American car—a Cadillac I think.'

'I don't understand? Why should that make it easy?' Nathaniel asked.

'Aah, well some old Russian tractors, like this, were built with Buick engines.'

'What as in American Buicks?'

'Of course! They were supplied by Buick.'

'Well! It's a small world! But tell me Tadeuz, were there any parts that you didn't fit?'

'Like what? The prop-shaft?'

'No, that wasn't what I had in mind. I'm thinking of a small metal box that might have been attached to the gearbox.'

Tadeuz thought for a few seconds, then his face lit up.

'Ah yeah! There was I remember. I didn't know what

that was. It didn't seem to do anything, so I threw it away. Everything works fine without it.'

Nathaniel's felt elation and slump in the space of ten seconds. He was very close to realising exactly how far he was prepared to go for several £million, and this was probably just about far enough.

'But then we gave it to the goat.'

This didn't register with Nathaniel. He was thinking what the expression 'Giving it the goat might mean, was it something like 'Giving up the ghost?', or 'Getting on someone's goat?'

'I'm sorry?'

'The goat! See!' Icarus pointed to the two goats furiously eating a pile of weeds. 'The brown and white one gets into the flowers and eats everything, my mother found the box, tied a spoon to it and tied it round the goat's neck, so we can hear when it comes near the house. That was the idea anyway, but it didn't work very well. I promised her I'd cut the bottom off and make it into a bell. I was supposed to do it two days ago, when we got back with the seats from the car, except...'

'So, the box is still in one piece?'

'Sure, take a look, but tuck your shirt in first, she'll eat anything.'

Nathaniel and Tadeuz walked over to the goat. Around its neck hung the box, intact. It had been painted with brightly coloured flowers.

'Very pretty.'

'Yulia painted it.'

'Talented girl.'

'She practises on her nails.'

Nathaniel realised that he was at a crossroads. It was tempting to leave the box where it was, enjoy lunch with this wonderfully hospitable family, and then get back to Odessa for his flight home. There was something poetic about leaving the diamonds here. It would remind him that this is where true wealth was. However Tadeuz had said he was going to open the box, if he did, he would definitely find the diamonds. Aside from everything, Nathaniel didn't think he was ready to value altruism quite as high as that.

'I'll start taking the engine out now should I?'

'No Tadeuz. There's no point. It will do much better left where it is.'

'Are you sure?'

'Of course I'm sure. But there are a couple of things I'd like you to do for me.'

Tadeuz paused in his relief and looked at Nathaniel with suspicion.

'First of all I'd like a lift to Odessa, this afternoon if you like, but if you don't mind putting up with me for another night, tomorrow would be fine.'

'I will speak to my mother, but I'm sure she would be pleased for you to stay until tomorrow.'

'Then, I'd like a small memento of the car.'

'Memento?'

'A souvenir. Something to remind me of it.'

'No problem, but what?'

'The goat's box.'

Tadeuz looked puzzled. In order not to make him

suspicious, Nathaniel added:

'I like the way it's painted, it's traditional, and it will remind me of where the car ended its days.' He looked at the goat, which was now munching on a sock that looked vaguely familiar.

'Ah yeah! I understand. Of course. Here I'll take it off now. I can make something better anyway.' Tadeuz started to untie the string around the goat's neck.

'And there's one other thing.'

Tadeuz was busy with the goat.

'You said you were trying to get to England?'

Tadeuz stood; the box was hanging from the string now in his hand.

'Yeah?'

'Well do you still want to go?'

'Of course. I want to earn money for my family—you see how hard my mother works!' They both looked over to where she was busy pulling weeds from between cabbages, she caught sight of the two men watching her; straightened her back, waved, wiped her forehead, and went back to her weeds.

'Then how would you like to work for me?'

Tadeuz looked at Nathaniel suspiciously. 'What do I have to do?'

'It will be hard work.'

'You can see I'm not afraid of hard work!'

'Well, I'm thinking of buying a farm. I need someone who knows what they're doing. It will be organic.'

'Organic?'

'No chemicals.'

'Why would you want to use chemicals on food?'

'It's a long story. It will be the same as you do here, but bigger. Also we'll have more animals—pigs for example.'

'How much bigger? It is hard work for me here and there are a few of us.'

Nathaniel laughed, 'Don't worry! You won't be working alone. You can choose people to help you, I'll help of course.'

'So I would be like, desyantnik?—The boss?'

Nathaniel laughed again, 'If you like. I'll pay you, and you can have a share of the profits. So if you do well, you'll earn more. How does that sound?'

'It sounds good, but is it true?' Tadeuz sounded unsure.

'What's up, you don't sound too enthusiastic?'

'It's just… well…' he sighed and said: 'I wanted to be a pop star or an actor maybe.'

Nathaniel smiled. 'I understand. But look at it this way, you'll be earning money, you can go to classes in your free time, learn to sing and act, and who knows?'

'You don't mind?'

'Of course not, as long as you work when you're supposed to.'

'But what if I become famous?'

'Then you have to find me a replacement, somebody as good as I think you're going to be.'

'Here in Ukraine there are plenty of good farmers. Maybe not as good as me, but good. But what about a visa?'

'I'll organise a visa.'

'It will cost you lots of dollars. I cannot pay now, but you can take from my salary maybe?'

'No! No dollars. I mean a real visa, to work in England—I'll take care of it. You've got skills I need, besides, I have contacts.'

Tadeuz grinned broadly, then he frowned.

'Maybe you're just playing a trick on me because I stole your car? Maybe you'll go back to England and leave me waiting every day. That would be cruel, but maybe you think it is what I deserve?'

'Tadeuz, I couldn't be so cruel. I promise. It might take some time. I haven't bought a farm yet—it might take a few months, but I promise you can come and work for me. Just have faith.'

'Mr. Nathaniel, if you promise, I wait!' Tadeuz beamed from ear to ear. It was more than he could have ever hoped for—to be going to England, never mind being legal and becoming a boss. Even becoming a pop star didn't seem quite as good now. He turned to Nathaniel: 'I want to tell my mother?'

'Then tell your mother.'

'You sure?'

'As sure as I can be after a night on your home-made vodka.'

'No tricks?'

'I promise, no tricks.'

Tadeuz shouted as he ran over to her. Sensing alarm, the other members of the family ran over to their mother as well, Tadeuz could hardly explain what was happening through his tears. Nathaniel looked on, wondering what on earth had possessed him to reach such a decision. He'd heard his own voice coming out of his own mouth as if it was coming out of a radio, like it was someone else talking. He certainly hadn't given it any conscious thought beforehand. After a single rush of fear had subsided, he realised he didn't feel a single pang of regret. He felt a greater sense of satisfaction than he could ever remember.

That evening, around the table under the apple tree, a wonderful celebration took place with Nathaniel as the guest of honour. The chicken, every vegetable and fruit placed on the table had been grown and raised on the farm, and were either fresh that day, or had been stored expertly since the autumn. There was more flavour in the food than Nathaniel could remember ever having enjoyed. He raised a glass quietly to his lips, and toasted the taste of things to come.

33: Muddy water

The French Champagne was delightfully received. However it disappeared instantly into the house and didn't reappear. Instead, Rita Klochkova returned with a bottle of chilled sweet Russian champagne and several glasses. Rita was not at all what Arthur was expecting; he got the impression from Sergei that she was some kind of tough businesswoman type. If this was the case, it was well camouflaged. Outwardly she was very hospitable and seemingly considerate. She made a fuss of Sergei and Arthur, offering them a bowl of fish soup she'd just made. Arthur felt obliged to accept. After it had been served he wished he hadn't been so obliging, it looked like a dirty pond with a lump of long-dead greyish fish laying on the bottom. Thankfully it didn't taste of much, but it was still an effort to eat. After taking the empty bowls away, Rita returned with a plate of strawberries, which she sprinkled with sugar and placed in the middle of the table.

'I grew them myself, here in my garden. I only picked them this morning.'

Arthur tasted one; they were sweet and delicious. He

complimented her on her gardening skills.

'Thank you Arthur! I grow lots of fruit here, but all my neighbours say my strawberries are the best.'

'You certainly have green hands, Rita Klochkova, to grow such wonderful strawberries so early in the year. You'll have to share your secret with me,' Sergei said in a charming voice.

'Sergei Zadinsky! You know I cannot tell you my secrets. If I tell you one, who knows how many others might come flooding out. But tell me, what is it that brings you here?'

'Ah, straight to the point as always. Well you see, we have a little problem you might be able to help us with.'

'Sergei, it's always a pleasure to help a good friend.'

'Thank you Rita, however this is of more concern to Arthur, my friend here from England.'

'Then of course it is also my pleasure to help if I can.'

'Well, his car was stolen, which in itself is not unusual, not in Ukraine, and not in England, however the car is unusual. It is almost unique, and the last information Arthur received about it was that it was in Kiev. I explained to my friend Arthur that you were a woman of influence, and that if it was here, you would perhaps know someone who might be able to cast a little light on this event.'

'Ah Sergei, you credit me with more than I deserve. Perhaps once I could claim to have influence, but we live in changing times. However, I think that what is happening here must be more than coincidence.'

'Coincidence?' Sergei asked.

'Well I had visitors two days ago who were asking me very similar questions to those you now ask. If I am correct,

I managed to provide him with exactly the information he needed. I also believe that they were looking for exactly what you now search for. I believe the car that you search for is called a Munter, is it not?'

'But Rita that is astonishing! Who else could want to know such a thing?'

'A business associate of mine—a Russian. He has a very successful import and export business. He also has many restaurants and hotels across Europe, including in England.'

'But why is he interested in the Munter?' Arthur asked.

'That, I'm afraid I do not know. But it must have great value to be of such interest to him.'

Arthur looked at Sergei, who gave only a quick glance to Arthur before turning back to his questions:

'So was your associate able to find the Munter?'

'Well Sergei, it seems that perhaps I have to bring you good news and bad news.'

'How is that?'

'Well I heard that the car was found, in Transdniester.'

'Where's Transdniester?' Arthur asked, seeing how Sergei had been so taken aback.

'Nowhere.' Sergei replied.

'What do you mean, nowhere?'

'He means that it is not a recognised state. It is a narrow, enterprising strip of land between the Dniester River and Ukraine,' Rita answered.

'Enterprising is one-way of describing it,' Sergei said, 'it's an arms-smuggling centre, a cut of land that has been trying to shake itself free of Moldova for some time. I am afraid, Arthur, that we must give up on your search. In muddy waters it is hard to catch a fish.'

'Hard, Sergei, but not impossible. The little fishes were caught,' there was a tone of gentle self-satisfaction in Rita's voice.

'Fishes?'

'Two little fishes to be exact.'

'And what happened to these two little fishes?'

'Ah well Sergei, I said there was good news and bad news.'

'So what's the bad news? Did they escape?'

'No, not exactly, let us say that they were too small, so they were thrown back into the muddy water.'

'And the car?'

'I do not know anything, but I hear that it is not much of a car.'

'Rita, you hurt my feelings! How could you say that? I was its head engineer.'

'Would I hurt my good friend? I mean there is not much of the car left, it was nibbled away to its bones.'

'By the Transdniester vultures you mean.'

'Vultures, piranhas, wolves, wasps—they are all the same.'

Arthur had been listening to this conversation, which had been held in English out of politeness; even so, he was still not sure that he'd understood everything. At least he hoped he hadn't understood what he thought he'd heard. Sergei turned to him:

'Arthur, what can I say. I'm sorry?'

'Don't be sorry Sergei. Why should you be sorry?'

'Because it seems that your trip has been in vain. You have travelled all this way for disappointment.'

'But maybe it's not so bad? I mean there must be something left?'

'Arthur I will be honest with you for the sake of being kind. If it is in Transdniester, it has been stripped down to bare metal, and that would have probably been used for something. I know what happens: the engine will already be in someone's old truck; the wheels on someone's rusting heap of a car; the seats will have pride of place in a crumbling apartment; in fact everything will have been stripped off and either used or sold. Perhaps 'enterprising' is not so inaccurate after all.'

If Arthur was anything, he was optimistic: 'Bare metal? Well there you go then! It's a start?'

'Forget it Arthur. You know I would be the first to help you if there was any hope at all. But trust me. There is no hope. Even if we found it, even if there was enough left to be worth rebuilding, even if we could somehow get it out of Transdniester in the state it's in; even if we could get it to Kiev—or over to England; what would we do? There are not enough parts left in the world to rebuild it to its original state, and I should know. No Arthur, it would be impossible. This is a sad, sad day for you Arthur, but it's a sad day for me also.'

Arthur could see that Sergei was devastated. The Munter was his project; each one was like family to him. Now he had lost one of his family. Arthur thought he should be upset himself, but he was much more upset for Sergei.

'Oh well, look on the bright side. At least it's been

recycled.'

The rest of the visit to Rita was sombre. But they parted with warm goodbyes and future invitations.

*

Sergei's sadness turned to anger in the car. He cursed country, politics and people.

'There is no grace any more Arthur! No grace!'

'It's worse in England; at least here it still exists. Rita seemed OK.' Arthur replied.

'A snake Arthur, she is honest, but you cannot trust her.'

'How do you mean?'

'Did you like her strawberries?'

'The were delicious.'

'She bought them from the market.'

'No! How do you know?'

'Because you can't grow strawberries at this time of year outdoors in Kiev. But that's not the only reason. I will tell you a story about her: One day I went to visit, with Nadia. We had a meal—as you have tasted she is terrible cook, but of course nobody criticises. It was early in the evening. Just as we, stand, er, stood, to leave, somebody in a house a few hundred metres away sends up some fireworks. Rita Klochkova instantly claps her hands and says 'I arranged that especially for you!' Of course we had to thank her many times and tell her how wonderful she is.'

'So? It was a lovely thing to do, very thoughtful,' Arthur wondered what the point was. As he drove, Sergei looked sideways at Arthur.

'Well, we drove away—to the edge of her village, and we saw a house with a bonfire in the garden—it was a birthday celebration with lots of children. That is what the fireworks were for.'

'But she wouldn't have known that?'

Sergei raised his fingers from the steering wheel and raised his eyebrows as he looked at Arthur to silently express: 'Exactly!' Then continued: 'And neither would anyone else. You see how devious she is? And that's just one example. She can react with her instincts to anything and make her advantage—even steal a child's party. She is one-hundred per cent politician.'

'That's amazing! But you have to admire her for that. I mean, to have the front to lie so blatantly.'

'Front?'

'I'm sorry, erm, the nerve; the cheek.'

'Ah, yes, I understand. But with Rita Klochkova it is more dangerous—she lies without guilt, and for her own gain.'

34: The curious engineer

It was only forty minutes' drive from Rita Klochkova's house to Sergei's place in the country. For most of it Arthur was in a contemplative mood. He had invested a large part of his life in tracing, restoring and maintaining the Munter, without questioning why. Now it had gone, and he was amazed how little he felt about its loss. He missed Etta much more. The Munter didn't seem real any more. It was like it hadn't ever existed. He couldn't explain why, but he suspected it was something to do with Etta. Arthur felt a validity to everything when he was with her. He hated being without her, nothing seemed real; it was like being in a permanent state of waiting—to get back to Etta and back to reality.

Nadia was already at the farm. She had taken an early-morning bus, partly to do some work around the place, partly to prepare for Arthur's visit. She welcomed the two men: Arthur with kisses on the cheeks, Sergei with kisses and hugs.

'I missed you boys. There's some cold beers in the fridge, I'll get them for you.'

'Relax Nadia I can get them, you look tired, you've been working all day.'

'It's no problem. I want to get them. You sit down and rest.'

'No you rest Nadiuchka, and I will fetch the beer,' but it was too late, Nadia was already on her way to the kitchen.

'What a wonderful place you have here!' Arthur said, looking around.

'Thank you. I'll show you around in a little while. I think you'll like what you see.'

'I'm sure I will.'

'Sit down! Sit down!' Arthur sat on a wooden bench and leaned forward onto the scrubbed white wood of the table.

'So, have you had time to think about what Rita Klochkova said about the Munter?' Sergei asked.

Nadia returned and placed two beers on the table, she was also carrying one for herself.

'Nadiuchka! Please sit down! I want you to rest for a few minutes.'

'But I have to prepare the vegetables for dinner...'

'Sit down Nadia, please!' Sergei implored.

'...for a few minutes then.'

'I'll help you with the food,' Arthur offered, 'I like cooking.'

'No! No! You're our guest, I can manage, it's only a few vegetables,' Nadia said.

'I'd like to help. Really.'

'Well, only if you are sure.'

'I was just asking Arthur how he felt about his car.'

'Ah, so tell me, what did Rita Klochkova say?'

Sergei told Nadia all about the conversation they'd had, and the sad conclusion about the state of the Munter.

'But that's terrible Arthur! You must be heartbroken, to lose it in such a bad way after all these years.'

'You know Nadia, Sergei just asked me how I felt about it. And I'd already been thinking all about it while we were driving here. And, honestly, I'm fine about it. I apologise Sergei, because it must sound like a terrible thing to say about the car you put so much into, but something's happened recently. Happened to me, I mean. And, well it sounds strange even to me to say this—because that car has been something of an obsession since I was a kid, a child, but . . . I don't know exactly what it is…' Arthur paused and watched condensation run down the side of his beer bottle. Nadia and Sergei let him explore his space. After a few minutes, without lifting his eyes from the droplets, Arthur said: 'Or maybe I do.' He reached out with his hand, and wiped the condensation from the neck of the bottle, creating small rivulets that ran down and soaked into the white wooden table. He raised his eyes and looked at Nadia and Sergei. 'It's partly from watching you two together, and partly because I've met someone. I've loved being with you both, even though it's only been for such a short time. Seeing you both together is so wonderful. You still seem so in love, even after however long you've been married.'

'We have been married for more than fifty years, and I still love my wife more with every day that passes.' Sergei stroked the back of Nadia's hand.

'But what's so amazing, is that you seem to value each other more than anything else. And you obviously value people more than things. I think I lost faith in relationships—a bad experience when I was younger.,' Arthur paused momentarily, 'someone asked me recently if I had faith, and it started me thinking: In England it seems that things have become more important than people. Bigger houses, better cars, more satellite channels, bigger shops, clothes, holidays, more money—or at least access to it: people borrow so much money you wouldn't believe it. We have a new religion in England it's called shopping…'

Sergei smiled.

'I'm not joking. I wish I was. The more I think about it, the less funny it is. Our cathedrals are gigantic shopping centres. It seems that people matter less and less—the value of them I mean. Children are given computer games and televisions to keep them occupied instead of being with their parents. They're given fast food to stop them from making a fuss—which instead makes them overweight and hyperactive: Not a good state to be in, they end up being rude and obnoxious. Parents are generally either divorced or both working, and always too exhausted to enjoy being a parent. If you're single you go out every night and drink yourself stupid; in fact you don't have to be single for that!'

'Just like in Ukraine.' Sergei added.

'Not from what I've seen. Here you take some time to sit around and share food and conversation. You entertain each other with folk songs and pop songs. You're proud of your culture. You drink lots of course—and I'm not saying it's not a problem, but it's certainly not just to get drunk. It's part of being social, part of expressing your culture. In England we don't have the same type of conversation, and there's no national culture to enjoy. Young people drink to get drunk as quickly as possible, for as long as they can afford to. Any culture we do have, we make jokes about.'

Sergei and Nadia looked puzzled.

'Oh, we call it 'folk' and it's not fashionable. Not 'cool', That's why it's just about disappeared. The only culture we have seems to come from those who we devotedly call our 'cousins' in America, and that culture seems to be based on violence, guns, drugs, dangerous faith and a total lack of respect. And here's an irony: the young kids—teenagers, have this thing they call 'Respect', except it's not 'Respect' it's fear. It's like…the more people that are afraid of you, the more respect you have. It's crazy! I'll tell you something I learnt recently: I went to a wedding—between an Irish family and an Inuit family.'

'From Greenland?' Sergei asked.

'I'm not sure exactly, I seem to remember something about Baffin Island, but I could be confused, it was a long night with lots of home-made whiskey. Anyway, this guy, a great guy, Jack, the groom, was telling me things about their own changing culture: one of the things he said was that traditionally the elders in their communities were only seen as successful if they had power without fear. If anyone was seen as being afraid of them, then they didn't attract the respect necessary for their position.'

'I suppose it takes a wise person to use power without fear,' Sergei said, before adding: 'the kind of person we need in Ukraine.'

'They're the kind of people we need heading all our countries. But we won't get them, because power itself is what drives people to become leaders. Greed if you like.'

Sergei and Nadia both nodded in agreement.

Nadia shrugged and said: 'That's why communism failed. In principle it was fine, but there will always be people who want more than they need; who want more than other people just for the sake of it—people who want to feel better than other people because of what they have. And they will do anything to get more. With such people, and there are always such people, it was always doomed to failure.'

'You know what makes me sad?' Arthur asked. He didn't wait for a reply: 'Everybody thinks England's so wonderful. People come from all over the world to try and make a new future for themselves; especially now Europe's expanded, with Polish, Czechs and so on. But what if they're leaving behind the things with most value? Who said what Europe, and England specifically, has to offer is better? So good that everyone should automatically want it? Superficially England's more glossy, arguably cleaner, and probably more colourful than some of these countries, but beyond that what is there? Debt? Ignorance? Dissatisfaction? The most idiotic television you can possibly imagine? Lack of difference? It's like everybody's scared to be different and desperate to be stupid. It makes me scared to admit it, but I think stupidity has become a quality. You may think this is too incredible to be true, but lots of young kids in our schools think that it's not 'cool' to learn anything unless you learn it on 'the streets'. On top of this, we criticise the French and worship America: which says a lot about our own culture and logic. We damn religions and cultures we don't understand as being dangerous, and moan about all the East Europeans coming in and 'taking our jobs' just like our parents moaned about the Asians and West Indians back in the fifties. Why? Because we're stupid. We have cameras on every street corner, in every building—more than any other country, and we accept it. We allow our liberty to be peeled away like the skin of an onion, not because of terrorism, but because we're too stupid, or too lazy, to learn the reality of what's happening, or at least to face up to it. And do you know the worst thing of all?'

Sergei and Nadia looked at each other, and looked at Arthur. The pause made Arthur realise that he had perhaps been going on for too long. 'Oh god! Please forgive me, I must sound terrible. I don't know what started me off on this...'

'No, please! Carry on! It's interesting. You sound as though you're just getting to the best part—about the worst part!' Sergei said. Nadia smiled.

'The worst part is that it's not a conspiracy; if it was, you could almost forgive people for being victims, and attach some credit to the Government for being intelligent.'

'What do you mean Arthur, that it's not a conspiracy?' Nadia asked.

'Because we're doing it to ourselves. Everything. We're all victims of our own incompetence, our own stupidity, and our own perceived comfort. We either don't want to use the intelligence we have, or don't want to see what's happening to our lives, our culture, our families, our environment and our bank accounts. We can maintain a certain standard of existing, and that's comfortable enough to allow us to keep being ignorant. In our 'western' culture, it doesn't profit anyone to think, because if you think then you have to start asking questions. And questions need answers, but nobody wants the answers, or hardly anyone; the ignorant majority just wants to be comfortable; just want things to stay how they are. That's why they watch more stupid TV; drink themselves stupid or take stupid drugs; encourage their children to be stupid; accept stupid laws from a stupid Government, and sit back and get involved from their armchairs in stupid wars. That's why they're stupid about how bad England really is. Stupidity is sad, and dangerous, once you have created the need for it, it begins to feed its own necessity. In the end there is not enough intelligent energy to do anything about it.'

Sergei laughed and said: 'But it makes me think that perhaps your society is a bit like communism after all!'

'In what way?' asked Arthur. Nadia too looked at Sergei questioningly.

'Well the majority of us had houses, heating, electricity, jobs and so on. Many people still think it was better than what they have now. But if you make people too comfortable, then they find the space to complain about things. If you keep people hungry, then they also will complain. They eventually complain in large enough numbers so that someone somewhere does something about it. Sometimes this is good; sometimes not so good. So what they used to do was to make food scarce, but not impossible to get.

You could get carrots if you queued for a few hours; you could get meat if you queued for a few hours; you could get oranges if you queued for a few hours. At the end of a hard day's queuing, you had enough food for that day's meal. Everybody had been kept occupied. Of course you could complain while you were in the queue, but that's all you could do—you were too busy queuing to do anything about it; and you could complain after you'd eaten your meal, but there was no time to actually do anything about it, besides, you were exhausted from queuing all day.' Sergei laughed out loud. Nadia laughed and nudged his shoulder affectionately. 'Maybe I'm just being cynical.' He said.

'Well if that's true, then you're right, it is similar, except that what keeps us occupied is not queuing, but work. Having to work every hour to pay for our bigger houses, bigger cars, bigger demands of our kids and bigger debts. Believe me, if you want to control a population, get them all into debt and give them all a TV, it works wonders. As for complaining,' Arthur laughed, ' …the English are famous for complaining and not doing anything about it, even if they do have the time!'

'Aah! That explains why you haven't had a revolution for such a long time,' Sergei, nodded, knowingly. The three of them laughed, and took the opportunity to sip from their beers. 'Ha! You think there's a lot to think about now, wait until you're seventy! Then you really don't have time for regrets!' Sergei lifted his bottle a few centimetres off the table, then put it back down again.

'But surely England cannot be as bad as you say?' Nadia asked.

'Maybe not, maybe I'm just angry with myself and my own stupidity. I'll probably go home and slip back into the comfortable existence of it all.' Arthur laughed and leaned back in his chair. 'But I doubt it. I guess it's taken me this long to find the art in everything.'

'But I thought you went to art school?' Sergei asked, frowning.

'No! No! I went to a crap college that kept me away from the real world. I didn't learn anything. I wasn't really expected to. The tutors, with probably one exception, were as bad as the students! What was I saying about stupidity feeding its own needs? Anyway, you don't get art from a college. You get it from life. It's the same with writing.'

'So, you're going to go home and write a book then? Arthur the author! It has a ring to it!' Sergei was laughing, Arthur followed.

'Ha! I don't think so! I couldn't write to save my life! But I might start using my camera for something with more value than taking soulless pictures for advertising agencies, or weddings. I mean look at me Sergei! I'm a photographer and I didn't even bring a camera with me! I'm disgusted with myself. I've been here for a couple of days, but I could have captured another life. I can't even take a picture of the two of you!'

'Then there are some benefits to it!' Sergei laughed, 'because of me of course, but some time you must take a portrait of my wife, she gets more beautiful with every year.' Nadia nudged him again in mock embarrassment, too familiar with his frequent displays of love to be truly embarrassed.

'So what about your Munter?'

'That's the point. As much as it's, or should I say, it was, a beautiful object—in my eyes anyway, and as much as its fate is a terrible shame, it's not worth getting too upset about. Even though a part of me has gone with it; it's people that really matter. In a way I'm ashamed at how upset I was when I first came out of that supermarket and saw it had gone. Still, they say you're never too old to learn…'

'That's true, I'm still learning every day, that's the wonder of life,' Sergei said.

'And I'll bet you're still learning about each other?' Arthur added.

Nadia and Sergei looked into each other's eyes, without diverting his gaze, Sergei said: 'If I lived a million years, I wouldn't know everything that goes on in my Nadiuchka's mind, but I would love a million years to find out.' Nadia blushed and brushed a stray hair from her husband's cheek.

'You see! Look at you both. Look at what I could have been enjoying, instead of devoting my attention—and probably even diverting some love, I'm ashamed to say—into an object; a beautifully strange, idiosyncratic, illogical and wonderful object; I know you helped create it Sergei, so I apologise, but it was still an object, a thing. Maybe it's because it was easy. Maybe it was just a diversion. Maybe because it was never going to hurt me, not emotionally anyway.'

'So Arthur you've just flown thousands of kilometres to try and find a car you now say that you don't care about; and when you get here you realise that what you really love is right back where you came from!' Sergei laughed; Nadia nudged him in the arm.

'Well, it was worth the trip just to spend this time with you. Anyway maybe I'm just going crazy.'

'That's not crazy Arthur, it's love. Being able to love is part of the miracle of living, and staying in love makes us wise,' Nadia said.

'How do you mean?'

Nadia continued: 'Love is fresh when we are young, wild and physical and free—the world is full of beautiful flowers; but the flowers do not live forever, they blossom and they die. And I think some people travel through life searching for flowers that will live forever. But when we find someone, our own someone; we enjoy spring together. And when spring and summer have passed and the flowers have disappeared, we find something deeper. I think then we begin to understand love. But it takes work: We have to work with each other; to care for each other; to want to be with each other. I hear some of my friends, and they complain about their men. They say: "men are so difficult", and I am sure that men say the same about women…'

'You can't live with them, you can't live without them,' Arthur said, partly to himself, then added by way of explanation: 'It's a saying from somewhere.'

Nadia smiled, 'But it's not men or women who are especially difficult. It's relationships.'

Sergei nodded: 'How complex and wonderful is one single person? We all have feelings that we sometimes don't even understand ourselves. Just like you, now. We have desires, hopes, dreams, history, memories, families, ancestors, influences, prejudices, skills, expectations. And of course these can change as we move through life. Yet we expect to be always understood by other people, especially the one we are closest to, who themselves carry the same complexity?'

Nadia nodded, 'As I said, it's relationships that are complex.'

There was a few moments silence between the three. In the background, the evening song of a bird echoed across the countryside. Night insects began to wake up and call into the warm, still air.

Sergei turned to Arthur: 'I will tell you something Arthur; you say that it's crazy to feel like you do. Well think about this: This Universe came from a single explosion, which formed the stars and planets. And one particular planet was in the right place to allow certain conditions to exist to create chemicals for life, and that life developed. And from a single cell came primitive organisms that reproduced to form other more complex animals and plants, and those animals became more diverse and more sophisticated eventually to make us: men and women. And those men and women suffered from diseases, they were eaten by wild animals, they died in wars, they were persecuted for their beliefs, they were victims of politics, power and genocide. And yet you and I can sit here today and share a bottle of beer and talk of love.'

Arthur started to say something, but Sergei continued: 'A conversation and a bottle of beer. It doesn't seem like much of a miracle does it. But think about this: if at any point anything had happened to any of our ancestors—stretching right back through to the very beginnings of time itself, then we would not be here. Maybe our little island in space would have settled a few hundred thousand kilometres away from the sun. Maybe a stupid little life form with no more than a few cells would have been dissolved by something only slightly more complex. An ape could have been killed by a tiger—or another ape. A primitive man might have frozen in a mountain, or drowned in a sea. Maybe a great, great, great, great, great, great grandmother would have died giving birth to her stillborn first child. Someone may have been stabbed in the dark by a jealous rival; or strangled for a loaf of bread. What if your grandfather had been killed in a war or my father hadn't survived for as long as he did. People search for miracles Arthur, but this bottle of beer, and this conversation is a miracle. And when you wake up in the morning it's a miracle. Because every one of our ancestors survived: yours, mine, Nadia's. They survived from the dawn of time—they survived war, they survived disease, they survived evolution, they survived religion and politics. If they hadn't, we wouldn't be here enjoying this conversation, this beer, this garden, this house, this country and this time. And it makes me angry Arthur; so angry; that people are so selfish and so dissatisfied with life.' Sergei was banging his bottle on the table; Nadia pressed his arm to calm him. He took hold of her arm, and wrapped his fingers around hers. He caressed her fingers as he talked: 'Every breath we take is a miracle, and even more than this, we don't just exist, we love. How is that possible?' Sergei turned his gaze from Nadia's fingers to Arthur. 'That, Arthur, is the miracle of all miracles. Philosophers search for the meaning of life

Arthur! Have you ever heard of anything so stupid? It's here, all around us! The meaning of life, is life. And love? There are those cold scientists who say 'Love? It's genetic motivation, that's all.' Idiots! So you think you are crazy? No Arthur, you are not crazy. I am an engineer, a curious engineer. I became an engineer because I wanted to know everything, and the most difficult thing to learn was that I would never know everything. Not just because there is too much to know, but because there are things I will never understand. Even in everyday life there are ordinary things that I will never understand: why does some music make tears in my eyes? Why do we paint, or write poetry? Why did I survive to be here when others didn't? These things I do not know. Maybe it is luck, maybe it is fate, maybe it is pure engineering, but why do I love? That is a mystery that turns every fact into a mystery. You see Arthur, do we need to love to survive? We need sex, we need to avoid conflict, we need food, drink and shelter. There are advantages to survival in being intelligent, in learning. But love? The existence of love, like the existence of art, music or poetry, makes no sense at all. In fact love probably causes more problems than it solves. I love my wife more than I love my own life. What is the sense in that for our evolution? But this question is of no importance to me. What is important is the fact of my love, the fact that it exists, the fact that I feel so much love for my wife and for my children. For me, it exists as part of the structure of everything. Oh! But listen to me! You must forgive me Arthur. Old men become sentimental! You think you are crazy? Wait until you get old! The thoughts that go through your head then are crazy! The good thing is that being old is a good excuse to think of them! I like being old, it's a paradoxical mixture of freedom of mind and restrictions of the body.' Sergei laughed and raised his beer. 'Let us drink to the miracle of beer and conversation.'

'And putting the world to rights!' Arthur added, as three bottles clinked together.

'That, I am afraid, is something we can never do.'

35: The whole point of pecking

Nathaniel was restless. He still didn't know what to do with the diamonds. On one hand he was tempted to leave them. On the other, they were worth a fortune. He was sure he could just walk through Customs with his little painted metal box. It looked like a piece of folk art. However he knew it would go through the x-ray machine, and the stones inside would show. He could say they were exactly that: stones. He could attach it to a small stick and say it was some kind of musical instrument, a rattle of some kind; maybe an ethnic device for rounding up sheep or cows or something. But Customs could be very thorough if they were suspicious. If they decided to keep it for analysis who knows what might happen, and if it did happen—whatever it was—Nathaniel didn't want it to happen to him.

The other problem was that he didn't want the stones back in England. Even if he managed to get them there, he'd be back at square one. It seemed stupid that he was on the continent he wanted to get the diamonds on, yet he couldn't get them to the city he wanted to get them to. While discussing travel plans with Tadeuz, Nathaniel had discovered that it was possible to take a bus from Kiev to London, changing at Antwerp, which would have been perfect. However, in casual conversation, Nathaniel had discovered that before Poland joined the EC, crossing the border between the two countries was easy—the customary ten dollars and no questions. Now it was much more difficult going than returning. You could bring almost anything into the country using the ten-dollar method, but taking things out had tightened up considerably. Nathaniel decided it wasn't worth the risk of letting Tadeuz take them by bus, because anything could happen. Besides which it wasn't fair on Tadeuz to make him sit on a bus for two days, and take the risk of being caught. Tadeuz could fly.

It was the tractor firing into life that triggered the idea and switched on the old instincts. He was hit by the realisation that he hadn't lost the will to carry on being a smuggler; he'd simply lost the point of it. There's no point in doing something that has no purpose. He knew his idea to start an organic farm was exactly what he needed to do, something worthwhile, something that would satisfy his sense of value, something that had a point—had purpose. The idea of it excited him. And because he was excited about that, he became excited again at the prospect of smuggling. It hit him that he had become too aware of the value of the things he was smuggling, which had taken the value away from his reason for doing it. He had to get the diamonds to Brussels, but not because they were worth three million. If he was smuggling pebbles he would feel the same way. The actual value of the diamonds meant nothing. The real value to Nathaniel was in smuggling them. 'Value is in what you do.' He said to a chicken pecking the ground nearby. The chicken looked up briefly, cocked its head at Nathaniel, and then carried on scratching around in the dirt.

Before they left for the airport in Odessa, Nathaniel explained that he thought the small painted metal box was a token of luck, and should remain a part of the tractor—'a kind of fertility token for good crops and a long working life'. This was not at all unusual to Tadeuz, who understood completely, and happily bolted the box back into place. Nathaniel then explained that he felt the tractor itself was something special, with its engine and its lucky token, and the fact that Tadeuz had kept it running so well. He said to Tadeuz that he thought the tractor should go with him to the new farm in England.

Tadeuz looked pained: 'I agree Mr Boot, it would be good to have the tractor in England, but—it is needed here. My family need it.'

'Tadeuz, please just call me Nathaniel, or Nathan. I understand what you're saying, but I have a proposal. It's an old tractor, and old things need lots of attention, what would happen if it broke down and you weren't here to fix it?'

Tadeuz looked worried, but said: 'There are people who could come and fix it, the neighbours are good guys, we help each other out here.'

'Fine, but listen to what I propose: I'll buy your family a new tractor. It will be more modern, smaller, and more comfortable—so even your mother can drive it easily. I'll also buy some tools to go with it. I don't know anything about farming so you can tell me what you need. I guess something like a small plough would be useful—things like that. Don't go mad though! I'm not stupid.'

'Really? You would do that for us? But why?'

'Oh I have my reasons. But is that an arrangement your family will be happy with?'

'They'll be on the moon with it!'

Nathaniel laughed: 'Over! It's over the moon—where did you learn English anyway, you speak it really well?'

'I learnt a bit at school, but the rest I picked up from American films. We've got some old films on video, I've watched them many, many times. When my father left us he left the videos and an old Russian-English dictionary, that's how I learn. You think my English is good enough for England?'

'You'll have no problems, I'm sure. Believe it or not, there are English people who don't understand what other English people are saying, even though they only live a few hundred miles apart.'

Tadeuz drew up a shopping list for Nathaniel. They went to an agricultural suppliers to price things up. Nathaniel was amazed at how expensive everything was. He could smell a rip-off from the 'take-it-or-leave-it' attitude of the seller. He decided to leave it, at least until he'd had the chance to price it up in England. He had a plan which meant that it would be no problem sending the equipment over.

And so, with his luggage, plus a small mountain of food packed for the journey by the boys' mother, Nathaniel was driven to Odessa for his flight home. He said his goodbyes to Tadeuz and Lenny, reiterating his promises to Tadeuz to sort out his visa and bring him to England.

As the plane took off. For the first time in years Nathaniel was excited.

36: The ghost of the machine

Arthur had enjoyed his stay with Sergei and Nadia, but it was time to go. He was sad to leave such graceful company, happy because he would soon see Etta. He was packing his rucksack as Sergei knocked and walked into the room.

'Ah good, you've almost finished! Bring your bag, and come with me. There's something I want to show you.' Sergei was grinning broadly, Arthur recognised this glint of mischief as something he'd felt in Sergei previously. He zipped up his bag and slung it over his shoulder, then followed Sergei out into the yard and around to one of several wooden buildings at the side of the house. Nadia's car was parked in front of one of them. Sergei opened the boot and Arthur dropped his bag in. After slamming the boot lid, Sergei silently gestured to Arthur to follow him. He unlocked a large padlock on a wooden door, and swung one door open. He then swung the other door open.

Arthur couldn't believe what he was seeing. 'How on earth? What? I mean…'

Sergei laughed as Arthur fought to process some of the thoughts now flying through his head. Stretched out in front of him was the bonnet of a gleaming, perfect Munter. Arthur was too stunned to speak.

Sergei, still laughing, heartily slapped Arthur's back.

'But how?' Arthur began composing his thoughts, he thought he knew the whereabouts of every Munter ever made, and this wasn't one of them.

'Oh there were a few pieces left over after the project, nobody else wanted them so,' Sergei held out his arms, palms up, to say: 'There you are.'

'But that's amazing. It looks totally original!'

'It is original. I keep it as a reminder. I buried the pieces all over the place, until I had the time and space to put it all together.'

'Well, I'm stunned. You don't mind if I…'

'No! Go ahead, here's the key. You can start the motor, but we can't drive it. I keep it hidden away. There's only a few people who know it's here.'

Arthur took the keys, unlocked the car and sat in the driver's seat; he leaned over and unlocked the passenger side for Sergei, who also climbed in.

'It's fantastic! Everything's here. And look at that! Is that right?' Arthur was pointing to the odometer.

'Four-thousand-nine-hundred-and-ninety-five kilometres. Yes that is correct. That is all it has done from the day I built it, and most of that on one trip!'

'But it's amazing. I can't believe it's here. It's… amazing!'

'It's amazing then?' Sergei repeated, making fun of Arthur.

Arthur started the engine. It purred into life and ticked

over contentedly.

'Wonderful! Wonderful!'

'I maintain it. I run the engine for a while ever week—the tail-pipe is connected to a tube that runs out of the roof, so the air stays clean.'

'Why don't you drive it?'

'Like I said, I hate driving in Kiev, everybody is crazy. Also it would attract too much attention, and in this city that is not a good thing.'

Arthur turned off the engine: 'Well, it's great. I'm so happy that you've got one. It makes losing mine seem less of a loss somehow. If that makes sense?'

'I think I understand. But we must get going if you are not going to miss your flight. Nadia's driving.

'Are you sure? I mean I can always get a cab?'

'No! No! It's no problem; we are going back to our apartment after we have dropped you off. But you can help me load up the car with vegetables.'

'My pleasure.' Arthur watched wistfully as Sergei closed the doors on the Munter.

37: Home again, home again

'You want to do what?!' Icarus was wondering whether or not he was hallucinating.

Nathaniel told him again.

'That's what I thought you said dude! A fucking organic farmer? What the fuck is happening? I mean Nathaniel, you're not a farmer. None of your family are farmers, what the fuck do you want to be a farmer for? Apart from anything else it's fucking hard work! You have to get up at two-o'clock in the morning to milk chickens and stuff! You're outside in the freezing rain and snow, and up to your ears in cow shit! I thought you were having a mid-life crisis before, but you're talking about a whole-life crisis.

'Look Icarus. I'm not going to go into it right now. I have my reasons, but I'm definitely going to do it. I want to do it. I don't care about the freezing rain and milking the chickens and getting up early and cow shit! I want to do it. As it happens I've already got my first piece of equipment. A tractor in fact.'

'A tractor! What the fuck are you going to do with a tractor?'

'Well for a start, I'm going to arrange for it to be picked up from Ukraine.'

'Ukraine! Why have you bought a tractor from Ukraine! You can buy tractors in England. Perfectly good tractors. A proper left-hand-drive tractor with a roof and iPod dock and brakes and air conditioning and stuff!'

'I know, I've already bought one of those too. Small, but very powerful, lots of bits to go with it. Cute thing. And, by the way, they don't have right or left-hand drive, just one seat in the middle.'

'So! Mr. Nathaniel Two-Tractors is an expert all of a sudden! I give up! Maybe all this is a weird dream and I'll wake up in a minute. Maybe it's a bad trip, except that I haven't taken anything. But I still don't understand! Especially why you bought a tractor in Ukraine?'

'Ah, well, you see it's a very special tractor.'

'It must be! How're you going to get it back? Whereabouts is it?'

'Near Odessa.'

'Great! You can drive it down the Potempkin Steps!'

'The what?'

'The Potempkin Steps. You must have heard of the fucking Potempkin steps?'

'No. Is that where they grow all the wheat?'

'Not Steppes! 'Steps', as in stairs, as in the Battleship Potempkin!'

'Oh! Right! The film. One of the greatest ever made they say. Never seen it. Mind you, I've never seen 'Citizen Kane' either. Personally, I like something with a bit of swashbuckling, moonlit coves and lots of treasure.'

Nathaniel had closed one eye as he imagined himself unloading rum into a cave on a dark night.

Icarus became less agitated and smiled, films were just about his favourite subject: 'I should have guessed. Like that 'Pirates of the Caribbean'.'

'Not seen that either. In fact I haven't been to the pictures for years.'

'The pictures! You're showing your age. People don't go to the pictures any more, they go to the multiplex!'

'Whether they do, or whether they don't. I'd rather go to the pictures, it's more romantic. Anyway, enough, we need to find a haulage company that will bring my tractor back. You don't know any do you?'

'No, but I'll check on the Internet for you. What's so special about this fuckin' tractor anyway?'

'Oh? Did I forget to mention that? It's worth at least three or four mill. A bargain considering what it cost me.'

It took Icarus a second to absorb the significance of this. 'You found them?'

'Uh hu!'

'Well fuck me! And I thought you were going on some wild goose ride.'

'Chase.'

'Whatever. So where were they? Did you find the car?'

'It's a long story, which I'll tell you all about, after I've cleaned up a bit. Meanwhile I need you to find out how much it's going to cost me to ship one tractor to a small farm near Odessa and bring another one back.'

'OK, you have a shower and I'll check it out.'

'And there's a bottle of vodka in the bag over there for

you.'

'Cheers man.'

'And while you're on the Internet, see if you can find a farm in Cornwall, preferably by the sea—if it has caves too, that would be perfect.'

*

An hour of surfing and phone calls trying to find a haulage company proved a waste of time. There were only one or two companies who would even consider it, and even then they wanted to charge a fortune.

'Plenty of companies will do Hungary or Poland, but Ukraine—that's difficult,' Icarus explained to Nathaniel

'Hmm. What we could do with is a man and a van.' Nathaniel thought through a mental list of contacts. He was concentrating hard and didn't notice Icarus holding a small scrap of paper.

'I think I might have an idea.' Icarus said, but he didn't sound too sure.

'What kind of idea?' Nathaniel was worried, he was still repairing the damage of Icarus's last idea.

'I think I might have someone.'

'That's good! Who?'

'Well it's not exactly a man and a van; it's more like a Jock in a truck. In fact more like a Jock in a frock in a truck.'

'A woman driver, that's even better! Less suspicio…'

'Not exactly,' Icarus interrupted 'when I say a Jock in a frock, I'm not talking about a lassie, more a lassie-laddie. But let me phone first and find out.' Icarus keyed the number into his mobile. Nathaniel looked puzzled.

Icarus had decided the best place to meet Marlene was

in an old, greasy Italian cafe off Oxford Street. Marlene was coming down from Manchester by train. Icarus and Nathaniel took the tube from Icarus's flat. They walked into the café and looked around at the clientele. Marlene was nowhere to be seen. Icarus wasn't too worried; they were almost five minutes' early. He ordered himself an all-day full English and a mug of tea to pass the time. As he turned from the counter, his attention was caught a heavy-set man waving at him from a table at the back of the café. The man was wearing a black, knitted woollen hat, and a green army jacket with pockets for every occasion. His black tee shirt bore the legendary 'Triumph' motorcycle logo. The man looked like a very large, very fit and very dangerous doorman.

'Icarus! Icarus! Is that yer-self?'

Nathaniel stopped to collect the drinks while Icarus walked over to man, who was now standing by his table.

'Marlene?'

'Oh! Call me Donald.'

'I'm sorry mate, I didn't recognise you. I was looking for…'

'I'm only Marlene when I'm working overtime. Well it's good tae see y'again. Although I must admit, it was a surprise tae get yer call. At first, when you said you had a job fer me, I thought it was another kind o' job!' Donald started laughing heartily as he thumped Icarus a bit too warmly on the shoulder, catching him off-balance and knocking him sideways down onto a seat. Other diners glanced nervously over newspapers and mugs.

Nathaniel arrived at the table carrying a couple of cups

and Icarus made the introductions. Nathaniel instantly warmed to Donald; intuition was important for a smuggler. After checking there were no casual eavesdroppers, the three set about discussing plans.

An hour or so later and everything seemed to be working out fine. Donald knew were he could hire a truck, and get the necessary paperwork to transport the new tractor to Ukraine and bring the old one back. He was more than willing to take on the job: 'Tae tell you the truth, I've been thinking it's time ter hang up ma frock. I've had a fine auld time of it, but I'm no gettin' any younger. It's no' even fun gettin' arrested nae more. I've been thinkin' of switchin' tae another means o' income. I didna' want tae go back on the road. But I wouldn't mind one last trip. 'The Swan Song o' the Jock-in-the-Frock! If yer ken ma drift.' Donald then leaned forward and, in a subdued voice asked Nathaniel: 'I'm thinkin' o' somethin' a wee bit special tae wear fer the occasion, 'the Jock's last Frock' if ye will, I don't suppose I could tap ye fe'a few bob?'

'No problems. Of course I'll sort something out. You'll be needing some expenses to, er, 'smooth the way' anyway.'

'Aye! Only the usual—a few bottles o' Johnny, some ciggies and a fistful o' dollars gets ye just about anywhere! Some things don't change! One thing I wouldna mind doin' though, if it's no problem tae yerselves, is visiting a few o' me auld stompin' grounds on the way? Just for the odd night! No' fer a holiday nor anythin'!'

'Where did you have in mind?' Icarus asked.

'Well, if it's right what Icarus says, an' I'm gannin' tae Odessa, I'd like tae drop by Hungary, Romania, and, erm,

Transdniester.'

Icarus and Nathaniel looked at each other. Icarus grinned.

'I don't want to stick my nose in, but why that way?' Nathaniel asked, 'especially Transdniester, I've been there and it's not exactly a place I'd like to go back to'.

'Well, apart from the fact that it's just about the most direct route. Ah used tae drive fer a wee charity—tae a couple o' orphanages in Romania. In Hungary there's this family I know—a wee lassie I took a shine tae when I was a laddie in Glasgae—she left me wi' a broken heart when her family moved back tae Hungary—but I've been visiting them almost as long as I've been drivin'. An' as for Transdniester—if you've been there then you'll know the less said the better!' Donald started laughing out loud again.

'I don't suppose you need some company along the way?' Icarus asked.

Nathaniel looked at Icarus questioningly; he simply grinned back and shrugged, then turned back to Donald in anticipation of an answer.

Before Nathaniel had a chance to intervene, Donald replied: 'Aye! Nae problem laddie! Nae problem! We'll have a wee adventure! Lot's o' dull roads, but the stops'll more than make up for them!'

Nathaniel wanted to protest, but realised that there was nothing to protest about. After a few seconds thought he decided that it might even be the best thing. There was nothing to do here now, and besides, he wanted to spend a few days in the southwest, looking at some properties.

There was also one other errand he felt he had to do.

'OK. OK. What can I say? Just be careful! And try not to lose anything. It's just as important that the tractor gets to Tadeuz's home as it is that the other one gets back here, via that very important stop in Brussels!' It seemed that everything was in place.

Donald raised his coffee cup: 'Here's t'ae a successful trip. An' the swansong o' the Jock in the Frock!'

Nathaniel and Icarus raised their cups and toasted in lukewarm tea and coffee 'So what are you going to do when you've hung up your driving gloves, or should I say your driving frock?' Nathaniel asked.

'Well, me dad worked in the shipyards, but the rest o' ma family were all fishermen, an' I used tae go out with one o' my uncles a lot when I was a nipper. In fact fer most o' me young life. So maybe I'll have bash at that. I've always loved the sea, and boats ye ken. Nothing big though, a wee, nippy thing'll see me fine.'

'So you can sail then?'

'Och Aye! It's in ma blood! A 'natural' my uncle used to say. I guess I only went to the drivin' to be master o' me own vessel. What wi' fishin' an' the yards being just about stuffed!'

Nathaniel grinned: 'Well, in that case let's drink not just to a successful trip, but to many more little adventures!' He could sense the beginning of a long working relationship.

As the cups clinked together, Icarus's full English arrived, the fried bread done to a perfect crisp.

*

Arthur stood in his living room, his bag over his shoulder

still. He looked around—it was boring. He'd only bought the house because he liked the area, but had run out of space at his old flat. He began to wonder if in fact he even liked the area, or was it nothing more than convenient for his studio, coupled with habit—because he'd lived here for years. He dropped his bag on the sofa, sat down beside it, picked up the phone—which was blinking the fact that he'd got several messages—and dialled Etta. Her answering machine clicked into life. He left a brief message to say that he was back, and would really, really like to see her. He walked into the kitchen, paying more attention than usual to its new bleached-oak units and cold granite surfaces. He walked back into the living room, searching the walls for something that would satisfy his senses: a decent photograph, an interesting object, but everything seemed soulless. He couldn't believe he was standing in his own house. He walked over to the CD player, and searched through his shelves for something suitable, picked out a couple of hopefuls, and tried them out one-by-one, but they were annoying. Eventually he settled on a disk he'd never played: a selection of overtures by Wagner. He'd never taken to Wagner, or Elgar. He tried the first track – the overture to 'Tristan und Isolde'; it was rich, soothing and quiet. He turned the volume up slightly, sat back into an armchair, and fell fast asleep within minutes.

Exhaustion had grabbed him. Now, from some distant place a cacophony was calling him. There were violent things happening somewhere and they were summoning him to awake. But this soothing place he was in was so peaceful, he wants to stay and enjoy it. But how can he with that racket going on above him! Up there! At the other end of that very bright tunnel! It is so peaceful and dark down here, and now he's moving upwards, and it's getting noisier and noisier. Why does he have to go there? Why can't he just stay down in the dark? But he's pulled and pulled and pulled closer and closer to what most surely be hell...

Had Arthur bothered to read the list of rest of the CD's contents, he would have seen that the last track was 'The Ride of the Valkyries', which was now playing at a deafening volume. He jumped out of the chair and dived over to the CD player, flicking a button to turn it off. There was still a steady knocking in his head, which a few more seconds of being dragged towards consciousness made him realise was actually the door, which he heaved himself towards while trying to shake off the sleep that was dragging behind him like a shadow with the mass of an old overcoat. He opened the door to Etta.

'I never had you down as Wagnerian?' She said, jauntily, as Arthur showed her in.

'Never was! Not now! Never will be!' He replied, scratching his head with both hands to try and massage some life back in to his brain.

'That's not what the neighbours will think!'

Arthur yawned: 'don't care what the neighbours think, especially neighbours who play the sound track from 'Cats' on a Sunday morning. Great to see you though. I tried to phone from Ukraine, but like an idiot I forgot to take the charger for my mobile with me. I called you as soon as I got back though'.

'I know, I got your message, I just dropped Natti off at the station.'

'More studying?'

'More studying. I've tried to persuade her to take some time off, but she's worried about her exams poor thing. Also she's due to visit her father next week, so she's trying to cram as much in as possible.'

'Does that mean I'll have you all to myself for a while then?'

'Possibly; why, would you like that?'

'Yes! I missed you.'

'I missed you too.'

'No, I missed you, really missed you. Lots.'

'You sound as though you didn't expect to? I don't know whether I should take that as a compliment or not!'

Arthur took Etta in his arms: 'I'll be honest, I did miss you more than I could have hoped for.'

'Arthur, that's almost romantic! Be careful.'

'Now you're just making fun of me.'

'Maybe,' Etta smiled, they kissed. 'You look tired,' she said, 'take me to bed.'

38: Portraits of an artist

Later that evening, Arthur and Etta lay in each other's arms. Arthur was feeling much more relaxed. 'Don't take this the wrong way, but when I got back today, I looked around the house and realised it's boring. I thought about my work and it's boring. I thought about my life and, apart from you of course, it's boring. I am boring. You'll get bored with me, I know you will.'

'Arthur you're not boring, and stop fishing for compliments! Even if you think you're boring, you're not, you probably just don't realise it yet!'

'Thanks, but it sounds as though you're just trying to bamboozle me!'

'Bamboozle! Arthur where on earth did you dig that word up from?' Etta was laughing.

'What's wrong with it?' Arthur sounded a little hurt.

'Nothing, it sounds like some kids' cartoon character—'Bamboozle and Draggle's Adventures in a Rubbish-Plane.'

'Now you're just being silly! And I can see what you're trying to do: you want me to ask you what a Rubbish-

Plane is! Well I'm not falling for that one.'

'What do you mean? A Rubbish-Plane is one that's made from the contents of a skip!'

'Oh, I thought you were going to say it was one that couldn't fly.'

'No, I hadn't thought of that.

*

At breakfast late the following morning, Etta asked Arthur about his birthday, she knew it was soon, but realized that they hadn't discussed specifics. She asked him when it was.

'What date is it now? I've lost track a bit.' Arthur asked. Etta told him the date.

'It's two weeks' away. Bugger! One of the reasons I went to France was to buy fifty bottles of champagne to celebrate with!'

'So you'd planned on having a party then?'

'Not exactly. I thought I'd just invite different people around during that week, whenever they were free, and have lots of pleasant evenings.'

'Pleasant? Sounds a little bit boring to me, certainly no way to celebrate your fiftieth?'

'See! I told you I was boring! Hmm… I may not have known you long, but I recognise that tone, have you got a plan?'

'A plan? No! No! I was just wondering what you're going to do, that's all.' There was a pause. They both sipped tea. Arthur was thinking. Etta had already thought.

'You know what you were saying last night,' and remembering they'd talked about everything, Etta added:

'about being boring?'

Arthur frowned and nodded.

'Well, I disagree.'

'What do mean?'

'Well, what you said got me thinking; and I've been looking around the house this morning: there's quite a few of your pictures here aren't there? Those on the walls in the living room, that big one in the bathroom, and that set down the stairs? And if I'm not mistaken, I saw you taking a couple of pictures in the church that didn't look as though they had much to do with the wedding? That funny old organist for example: the one that looked like a parrot.'

'Ah, you noticed her too! What a great character, like something out of Dickens or Mervyn Peake.'

'Exactly! Well, I think you're being a bit hard on yourself.'

'How do you mean?'

'Well I think you can't keep a good artist down!'

Arthur still looked puzzled.

'You really don't see it do you? How many more pictures have you got lying around that are nothing to do with work?'

'Dunno, quite a few I suppose. There's loads of them at the studio. I used to snap off to use up the film. I guess I still do it even with the digital stuff.'

'So you're telling me there's loads more like these?' Etta gestured towards the walls.

'Oh yes! I didn't pick these for any special reason. I just wanted something to put on the walls. I must have hundreds of them in the studio, mostly rubbish though.'

'Right, that's it then. You're taking me to your studio today, and we're going to go through your drawers.'

'Oooh er, missus!'

'Don't be so juvenile! You know what I mean. I want to see this 'rubbish' you've not thrown away. How long have you been doing it for?'

'I don't know exactly, I've always done it.'

'So you've got more than thirty years' worth of prints lying around somewhere? All rubbish, without one good one amongst them?'

'I guess if you look at it like that, there might be the odd one or two. To be honest I never look through them. There never seemed to be much point.'

'No point! Arthur! How can you say that! You may have thought the man is not an artist; but trust me, the art is in the man, some of these pictures are wonderful.'

'Only some? Are you sure you haven't got a plan?'

39: Better to give than to get

Nathaniel Boot needed to clear his conscience. He had no qualms about 'borrowing' paintings from galleries; diamonds from vaults; or national treasures from, well—nations. The way he looked at it was their beauty was their permanence. Who ever owned something with the permanent quality of a true work of art, or a beautiful diamond, couldn't own them forever; eventually they would always find their way back to where they belonged. As far as Nathaniel saw it, he simply borrowed things, then loaned them out for a small fee. Well actually sometimes for a substantial fee. The Rembrandt, for example: that was one of his first jobs after he'd finished his 'apprenticeship'. It was sold to a rich collector—who just happened to be a justice of the peace and a lord of the realm. The man enjoyed the painting for the last five years of his long and distinguished life. After his death at the age of 103, the painting was discovered and discretely returned to the gallery. The 'collector' had enjoyed the painting for the last years of his life; the gallery had enjoyed lots of free publicity, and made a small fortune selling books and postcards when the painting was eventually returned; and Nathaniel had made an undisclosed amount of cash. It was a win, win, win situation. Besides which, who actually owned what anyway? Just because you store your booty in a National Library or Gallery doesn't necessarily authorise your ownership of it. Take the Elgin Marbles, for example.

'Hmmm! Now there's a thought!' Thought Nathaniel, as he stepped off the train from London Euston, at Manchester Piccadilly. No, he didn't mind borrowing such things, from those that could afford to lose them, but in all this fiasco, there had been one or two innocent victims: It wasn't Arthur Pod's fault that his car had been stolen. Actually, Nathaniel realized it wasn't his own fault either; but that wasn't the point. It was a loose end, and Nathaniel hated loose ends. They had the habit of becoming frayed, and could be really annoying, dangerous even, something that might trip a person up at some point in the future. Then there were those bloody poodles. All enquiries had failed to unearth the Mattress twins, which was something of a blessing, except for the fact that they still had the dogs. Knowing the Mattress twins, Nathaniel was afraid about what could happen to the woman's poor pets. But he could never have guessed their true fate.

Nathaniel got out of the taxi outside Arthur's studio. As he pushed the door a small part of him hoped it would be locked, but it was open. Inside was a hallway; to the left was the door to the shop, which was locked; ahead were the stairs that led up to the studio. At the top of the stairs, he pushed the door open to the small reception area, causing a bell to ring in another room.

*

Arthur and Etta were two days into sifting through what had proved to be, not hundreds of pictures as Arthur had thought, but thousands.

'Arthur, this is amazing!' Etta had said, when she first saw the scale of the task that lay ahead. It took her only just a few minutes of random searching to know that there was very little 'rubbish'. 'There's some fantastic stuff here Arthur, how could you possibly think it was rubbish? Look at it!' She had pulled out the picture of a burnt-out scooter frame, covered in molten plastic, which looked like it had been carefully placed in a twisted hawthorn bush. 'I mean, this is so dark, so Gothic, and it says so much, but it's so, casual. What made you think of putting the two together?'

'What those? I didn't. They were like that. I just snapped them when I was out walking one day.'

'But Arthur, that's so poetic.'

'What do you mean?' Arthur couldn't see what it was that Etta obviously found so amazing, after all, he'd got hundreds of other pictures better than that one.

'I mean as in poetry. Poetry doesn't have to be about words. It can be visual, anything. It's a state.'

'I'm still not sure I know what you're on about. It was just something I saw, so I snapped it. That's all.'

'But Arthur, that's what makes it so special. That's why it's poetry. It's like when two completely unrelated things come together, and bring out some quality in each other. It can happen just for a moment, but it can be a beautiful thing, and often you can't capture it, because it's too momentary, and often you can't explain it to anyone because it only has the value of its own existence. But I'm looking through these, and already I'm finding this kind of poetry, time after time. Look here's another! And another! Arthur, these are just fantastic!'

'Well, I guess you should know, you're the artist.'

'Arthur, I'm not an artist, I'm an art lover. I may be a bit of a craftswoman, but certainly not an artist. I know what I like, and I like to think I know what's good, and these are very, very good.'

'Well, I don't know what to say really. I mean, thanks. I'm really, really please that you like them. But...'

'What?'

'Well, maybe you're just a bit biased?'

'Arthur! Credit me with some taste! It's not just me, I'm sure there are lots of people who would love them. In fact...'

'Uh oh! I thought there might be more to this than meets the eye!'

'Arthur, don't! Just trust me. I know what I'm doing.'

'What are you doing, exactly?'

'Can't you guess?'

'I suspect, but I don't want to say, just in case I'm right.' Arthur was getting increasingly worried.

'Well, come on, where's the new Arthur you were telling me about last night? What do you think?'

'An exhibition?' Arthur asked, tentatively.

'Not just an exhibition, but Arthur's coming out party!'

'But I'm not gay!' Arthur protested.

'Not that! You know what I mean, coming out as an

artist! I think it's time that you let everybody know what a talent you are, and I can't think of a better time or place to do it than on your fiftieth birthday.'

'But that's insane! That's in less than two weeks!'

'It's not as insane as you might think, Arthur. Look, you've printed everything the same size, A4, so we can buy a load of standard frames, all we need to do is mount them, and find somewhere to hang them—and have a party of course.'

'You make it all sound so easy! Who are we going to invite?'

'Everyone.'

'What do you mean everyone?' Arthur could feel anxiety beginning to twist.

'Everyone as in everyone. All your friends, family; as well as anyone who might be interested in your pictures.'

'Thank god for that! For a moment I thought you were talking about loads of people!'

'Arthur, I am talking loads of people. I know loads of people who would love your work. I've a friend who has a gallery, I'm sure she'd love to invite her clients. Also we've both worked for advertising agencies, they buy pictures for their offices, then there's the PR of course: magazines and newspapers. Like I said, loads of people.'

'But...'

'No buts! Don't be a wimp Arthur. You'll love it. The more the merrier, you'll see!'

So Etta's plans began to take shape. Her friend's gallery was out of the question because it was already booked, but she found an alternative space that she was very excited about, even though she wouldn't tell Arthur where it was. She made him focus and get together the contact details of all his friends, family and acquaintances and they invited them all; she organised invitations, food, entertainment, in fact she did everything—only getting Arthur involved when she felt he would like to give an opinion or decision, or when it was needed. Arthur was happy to let her get on with it all: she was obviously enjoying every minute.

They had been sifting through photos for several days, while Etta simultaneously made and took phone calls, faxes and email messages—when the office bell announced that someone was in reception. Arthur stood up, stretched his legs, which were stiff from kneeling on the floor, and went to investigate.

As he walked into the reception area, he vaguely recognized the man standing in front of him, but he couldn't remember from where. Nathaniel recognised Arthur also, and did remember he was in the bar on the ferry.

'Oh, hi. Erm, you're Arthur Pod? The photographer?' Nathan asked purely to be absolutely sure.

'Yes, what can I do for you?' Arthur liked to try and pre-empt his clients' requests. He thought the man didn't look as though he worked for an advertising agency, and he didn't look as though he was about to get married. Maybe he was the father of the bride?

'I wonder if you could spare a few minutes?'

'Salesman!' Arthur thought. 'Well to be honest. I'm very busy at the moment...was it a photo?'

'Oh no, no, I just wondered if you could spare a few minutes?'

'Definitely a salesman,' thought Arthur, 'Well, like I said, I'm…'

'My name's Nathaniel Smith. It's about your Munter.'

Arthur's train of thoughts screeched to a halt. 'I'm sorry?' He wasn't sure he'd heard what he'd heard.

'Your Munter Drophead, the one that was stolen?'

'You'd better come through, but be careful, there are pictures everywhere.' As he ushered Nathaniel through to the studio, Arthur's mind was racing as it tried to explore every possibility of what this man could possibly have to say about the Munter. Etta was sifting through photos, trying to decide which should go onto the already impossibly high 'Yes' pile. She looked up and smiled.

'Etta, this is Nathaniel, er…'

'Smith.' Nathaniel confirmed.

'Mr Smith has some information about the Munter.'

'Aah! I'm glad you're here as well Mrs Corbett, because there's also something I probably need to explain to you too.'

Arthur was even more confused, not only did this man know something about the Munter; he also seemed to know Etta. He cleared some photos from a chair and beckoned Nathaniel to sit down. After a couple of false starts while he searched for a place to begin, Nathaniel began to explain what had happened to the Munter and the poodles, making it clear that none of the events were actually directly due to his own actions: that he wasn't directly responsible for the Munter actually being stolen, or the 'dognapping' of the two poodles. He provided an address of where they might be:

'For all the good it will do you, we've tried enough times, but there's never anyone there.'

By way of reparation, Nathaniel asked if there was anything he could do to help the situation. He was shocked when Arthur replied:

'Thanks for taking the trouble to come and see us, but to be honest, there's not a lot anyone can do. As you've seen, the Munter is nothing more than a shell, I knew that already.'

'He went to Kiev,' Etta explained.

'Kiev?' Nathaniel asked, looking at Arthur while trying to sound casual, but hearing the strain in his own voice.

'Yes, great place by the way. That's where I found out about the car. I was told there was nothing left of it. Nothing that can be salvaged—there just aren't the parts in existence anymore to be able to rebuild it. So I'm afraid it will have to stay where it is. It's funny though…because the last time it disappeared it was discovered in a barn up in Orkney, that's where I had to collect it from, and now it's back in a barn again, it's kind of karma don't you think.' Arthur looked at Etta. 'I think I'm beginning to understand the poetry in things.'

Etta frowned: 'Well I'm very, very pissed off at these twins you mentioned. They broke into my house, stole my dogs and turned the place upside down. I'm not sure the end of a finger is enough justice.'

'There was also an earlobe,' Nathaniel added.

Arthur and Etta looked questioningly at Nathaniel.

'One of the brothers lost an earlobe.'

'We didn't find that!' Etta said.

'The dog swallowed it.' Nathaniel said, helpfully.

'Sounds to me like they have something in common these brothers and my dogs. I've always suspected they were slightly imbalanced—too tightly bred I guess.'

'Believe me Mrs Corbett, it's a match made in heaven.'

'Sounds more like a match made in hell to me. I'll leave it to the police to sort out, not that it will do much good—not if Laurel and Hardy are on the case,' Etta mused.

Nathaniel was puzzled about where Laurel and Hardy came into it all.

Arthur had been thinking: 'Hmmm!'

'What?' Etta asked.

'That strange message about 'the boyfriend's car', they definitely meant the Munter. That's why they didn't take the money. As we suspected, it wasn't just a simple dognapping. But why did they want the Munter? I mean what were they going to do with it?'

Nathaniel shifted uneasily, he had avoided mentioning the diamonds, but needed to quickly think of a reason: 'It was going to go to a 'private' collector—somebody interested in art and industrial design history. The twins didn't realise it, but while they were exchanging the money for the dogs, someone else was supposed to steal the Munter. This... person, had already tried on the ferry, it should have been towed off—taken from right under your nose, but you got it started again, and it appears that someone else stole it from under everyone's nose.' It wasn't the strongest explanation, but it was the best Nathaniel could come up with, and there was some truth in it. Inside, he was deeply grateful to his old instincts.

'Ahhh, that explains the missing starter motor cable. But who was going to steal it? You?' Arthur asked.

'No, not me I can promise you that. I've never been interested in cars!'

'Well you seem to know a lot about it all,' Etta asked. She could sense that they weren't getting the whole truth.

'No more than bits I've put together from here and there.'

'So where do you come in all this?' Etta asked, staring directly into Nathaniel's eyes. Arthur wished he'd asked the same question—it was the obvious one.

'Let's just say a friend of a friend of mine was closely involved. He feels bad that you've both suffered, and would like to compensate you if possible.'

'Hm!' Etta said: 'And that's supposed to make us happy?'

'What kind of compensation?' Arthur asked.

'Possibly a small sum of money?'

'Three-thousand!' Etta laughed, with a hint of sarcasm.

Nathaniel felt sheepish.

'It's not necessary from my point of view, I'll get the insurance money eventually,' Arthur said, 'but I can't speak for Etta though, those poodles were her livelihood.'

'I'll tell you what I'll do, leave me your details, and I'll think about it,' Etta said.

Nathaniel grinned: 'I can't exactly do that. Mainly because I currently don't have a permanent home, but my friend would be quite happy to compensate you…'

Etta shrugged: 'To be honest, I'm not interested. There's no telling where your friend's money will have come from anyway. I'll sort something out. I've got some ideas already, so tell your 'friend' thanks anyway. And thanks for taking the trouble to come and explain everything to us.'

Arthur looked questioningly at Etta, wondering what her 'ideas' were. Etta smiled and offered to make coffee. Nathaniel declined, he didn't want to face any more questions and felt it might be safer to leave.

'Here, at least take my mobile number, and if you change your mind, let me know,' Nathaniel offered, as he stood to leave. It wasn't exactly the conclusion he had hoped for. He'd come up to Manchester because he'd wanted to make sure that all loose ends were taken care of, and while he didn't think Etta and Arthur would create any kind of problems in the future, their matter-of-factness was disturbing. He'd also wanted to make himself feel better about the situation, which is why he'd offered the money. He wished they'd accepted it, because he still felt guilty about the whole business. He shook hands with Arthur, and was about to shake hands with Etta when she said:

'So you have friends who are art collectors?'

'Oh yes! I have lots of friends who collect pictures and sculptures, all kinds.'

'Aaah. Well in that case, we're having a little party in a few weeks, an exhibition. If you want to help us, why don't you come along, and bring some of your rich collector friends? I'll text you the details.' Etta was annoyed with Nathaniel, but pragmatic about business.

Nathaniel thought about it for a second or two, and didn't see any reason why not. It was the least he could do considering. 'Well all I can offer to do is to invite them.

What kind of exhibition?'

'Photography. They'll love it, I promise.'

And so Nathaniel left feeling slightly better.

'Strange lot these Northerners!' Nathaniel thought, as he sat in a taxi on the way back to the station. 'They get their car stolen and trashed; you kidnap their dogs and hold them to ransom, mess up their house, and they invite you to a party.' He reached into his pocket for his mobile, as he did so, a folded piece of paper fluttered to the floor. Nathaniel picked it up and unfolded it, on it was a phone number and a woman's name he didn't recognise. Out of curiosity he dialled. He sort of recognised the voice, and after a fumbled introduction, found himself talking, then flirting, with a certain very cute employee of Her Majesty's Customs.

40: The rope-making machine

'Where are we going?'

'Shush Arthur! Behave yourself. You'll see when we get there.'

'Awe! Give me a clue then?'

'No, because if you see where we're going then you'll guess and spoil it.'

Arthur and Etta were in a minicab, driving through the Derbyshire countryside from Etta's house to Arthur's fiftieth birthday party. They were both as excited as each other.

'I'm going to find out anyway, when we get there.'

'Well there's no point in me telling you then.'

'So, why do I have to wear this blindfold?'

'Because if you don't you'll see where we're going. Besides, it's sort of sexy.'

'OK, I'll save it for later then, and we'll see how you like it.'

'Tease!'

'I feel sick.'

'You don't! I'm not taking it off!'

'Are we there yet?'

'Arthur! Please just sit back and enjoy the ride!'

'Are we there yet?'

'Arthur!'

'Are we there yet?'

'Stop it! We'll be there soon!'

And they were.

*

The car stopped and after paying the driver Etta helped Arthur out. She turned him around. The cab drove off. It was quiet and the air was still and cold. Still blindfolded, Arthur didn't have a clue were he was, but it didn't feel like a party. He could smell the damp freshness that told him he was in the hills somewhere. He could also smell something else, beyond Etta's perfume, something familiar, but he couldn't quite bring it to mind.

'Come on Arthur, but be careful how you tread, just follow me.' Etta started to guide Arthur across a hard surface, then up what seemed to be track. He could feel something brushing against his body.

'How can I follow you if you're next to me?' Arthur asked, nervously.

'Stop being pedantic, you know exactly what I mean.'

Noise seemed to be coming from above him: the murmur of a crowd inside a building. They were definitely climbing up a track.

'There's a step up here, Arthur, be careful.'

Arthur lifted his foot and found the firm wooden decking underfoot. He stepped up.

'OK, that's it, just stop here a moment.' Etta removed

the blindfold.

It took Arthur's eyes a few second to focus. At first all he could see was a haze of purple, red, blue and green. Gradually everything came into focus.

'The rope-making machine!' Arthur said, almost in a whisper. He turned to Etta, who was smiling with delight, 'How on earth…'

'Ah ha! That's for me to know. Come on then! Let's go and party!' She held his hand and pulled him towards the door.

There was an almighty cheer as the pair entered the museum, followed by a rousing chorus of 'Happy Birthday'. Arthur looked around as he listened. He'd told Etta to invite everyone, and wasn't sure whether he'd actually meant it literally, but Etta had done exactly that: everyone seemed to be here. There must have been two hundred people or more in the room. With just a quick scan he could recognise his brother Gavin; there was Cedric MacNamara, holding up a bottle of something ominous; beside him were Jack and Geraldine; to one side was the London crowd around Lytton and Nancy; his eyes tracked the sound of some excruciatingly tone-deaf singing, and led him to Ronnie, hollering 'Happy Birthday' for all he was worth while his long-suffering wife Vix winced; Arthur could hear the lilt of a violin, and glanced over to see Uncle Joe, who winked at Arthur from the small stage, before closing his eyes and getting back to the business of playing; Arthur was almost shocked to see next to Joe was an electronic keyboard being played by the old parrot from the church (who Arthur would later find out was the very charming, very entertaining ex music-hall mezzo-soprano and piano comedy act, Wilhelmina Grossington-Stirrup: "She Carves Enchantment and Laughter Out of Ivory").

Soon after the cheers had subsided, Arthur had the first of many drinks in his hand, and was lost in a happy turmoil of greetings and congratulations, with Etta always by his side. There were congratulations, not just because of his birthday, but also because of his photos, which occupied just about every available spot on the walls, from which they attracted not just admiration, but—Arthur had noticed—a surprising number of small red dots. He had to admit that they didn't look half bad once they were framed and hung. 'Surprising really!' Etta heard him say to himself.

'That's not the only surprise! Follow me…' Etta took Arthur by the hand and they weaved their way gradually to the door—a slow process as Arthur paused almost every step to talk to someone, or to be introduced to friends of Etta's and friends of friends. Eventually they stepped out into the cool, dark night.

'This is amazing! How did you get it all arranged? I mean…I'm gob-smacked.

'Arthur, it was no problem, I can't think of anyone who didn't have the same reaction when I spoke to them. They were all up for it, and wouldn't have missed it for anything.'

'But it was such short notice?'

'It just goes to show then—that's how special you are.'

'I don't know…'

'Well I do! Now come on!' Etta grabbed Arthur's hand and dragged him back down the path towards the car park.

She pulled him to a halt just before they stepped around a corner of shrubs: 'Are you ready?'

'No.'

'Why not?'

'Well I don't know what I'm supposed to be ready for!'

'Oh come on you…' Etta pulled him into the car park.

Arthur's knees almost buckled as his heart skipped at least a single beat. Reality seemed to have shifted and left him standing slightly to one side. In front of him there appeared to be a Munter, and standing beside it, an apparition of Sergei with his arms wrapped around a cosy-looking Nadia. On seeing Arthur, Nadia unwound Sergei's arms from around her, and the pair walked towards him. Sergei then kissed Arthur and bear-hugged him. As the air was compressed out of his body Arthur realised this was very real.

'Happy Birthday Arthur! Finally we've made it to your beautiful country!'

Nadia had already stepped forward, and kissed Etta, before turning to Arthur.

'But how? I mean, what? I mean it's so…! It's wonderful to see you both!' Arthur kissed Nadia, tears were gathering in his eyes. The hairs on the back of his neck shivered with pleasure.

'Well, we had nothing to do, we got a call from Etta, and we decided to go for a drive!' Sergei said, as if it was the kind of thing he did every day.

Etta wiped away a tear.

'You drove here! From Kiev! In that!' Arthur pointed to the Munter.

'Yes! But of course! And it was wonderful' Nadia said, 'Sergei has always promised me a trip to the most romantic place in Europe, so...'

Arthur was still choked: 'How long did it take? I mean it's...'

'Well it's about two thousand kilometres, but we've done almost five thousand in ten days; without a problem: I tell you Arthur she is a beautiful motor, beautiful!' Sergei enthused.

'Five thousand! But where have you been?'

'To Spain, Grenada—the Alhambra Palace, have you been there? It's so beautiful, so romantic.' Nadia said, cuddling up into Sergei's warmth. 'And to France—a pretty little village called Florac, to visit my sister; and Paris of course...'

'Well you'll have to tell us all about it, but come on up and enjoy the party...'

'Wait! Before we go there's something we need to take with us.' Sergei beckoned Arthur over to the back of the Munter, then opened the boot; inside were four wooden crates: 'Forty-eight bottles of the finest Russian Champagne!' Sergei said, triumphantly; he then reached down and pulled out two bottles of vodka, '...and two makes fifty!' He yanked a crate out of the boot and gave it to Arthur, then another to carry himself. 'We can come back for the rest when we've finished these. They'll stay cool out here,' Sergei said, as he closed the boot.

'Well, that will make it lighter for you on the way home!' Arthur said, casually.

Sergei hoisted up the crate of champagne and the four

began to walk back towards the path: 'On the way home? We're not driving home Arthur, we're flying. Believe me, five thousand kilometers in that thing is more than enough at my age.'

Arthur looked at Sergei quizzically.

'No, I mean, we had a fantastic time! But drive back? No, no, no! Besides, that's not my Munter now, it's yours. I want you to have it.'

Arthur nearly dropped the crate of champagne: 'What!'

'It's yours Arthur. What am I going to do with it? I never drive it. No, you take care of it.' Sergei looked at Arthur and grinned, 'Happy Birthday Arthur. Just try not to lose this one eh?'

'But Sergei, I couldn't...'

'You already have Arthur. Besides, I need the space, I'm thinking of building a motorcycle. I have all these parts I've been storing since Brezhnev...'

Nadia was walking alongside Etta, behind the two men, she looked at Etta and shrugged: 'Men. They never stop being boys.'

'That's probably a good thing,' Etta replied.

'Aah, you women might laugh, but I have a theory about that...' Sergei said, as the four walked up to join the party.

…and finally

In the same car park, around half an hour or so later, a battered truck jolted to a halt. It had once been white, and had suffered considerably from being dragged all over Europe with various items of agricultural equipment in the back, including, at separate times, two tractors—one of which was still inside. The doors slowly opened and a large figure jumped down, beer bottle in hand: 'Well matey-boys, thaat were some do, some do indeed it were!'

Two more figures followed: the first, a lanky, stick-thin, hunched silhouette, who bit firmly into a cold bacon sandwich bought earlier that day as part of a bulk order from a van in a lay-by; The second, a considerably wider figure, straightened out his frock, and checked his makeup in the door mirror, before jumping down from the driver's side of the cab.

'Looks like a strange place tae bring a lassie tae'a party? What was the boy sayin'? I didnae get a word o' that?'

'Look! I've been translating for you two ever since we left Transdniester! I'm knackered! I don't know why you wanted to bring him anyway!'

'Don't be SO! Icarus. We only gave the laddie a wee lift home!'

'Two thousand, fucking kilometres on the history of the Thornbaarlocks of Meltingwherpe! Fuck me dude! Get me on 'Mastermind', I'm a fucking expert! Let's go and find Nathaniel and get drunk.'

Horatio stood a short distance away, peeing against a lamp post while looking at a parked car disapprovingly: 'Oi'll tell you whaat, matey boys, this is—without a shred-of-a-doubt, the ugliest caar oi've ever seen in moi entoyer loif! Whaat d'youz reckon on it?' He shouted over.

'What's the boy on about?'

'He says that car's the ugliest thing he's ever seen.'

'Aye, an' I've a mind tae thinkin' he's no' far wrong! What is it anyway?'

'It's a Munter Drophead,' Icarus replied, matter-of-factly. He was way past the stage when anything could surprise him. As the three men started to walk up the path that led to the party, Icarus threw the crusts of his sandwich into a rubbish bin, wiped the cold brown sauce from the corner of his mouth and muttered, to nobody in particular: 'What a trip!'

The Last Straw

Curtis Bollington

Shortly after Jack is made redundant from his mundane job, his girlfriend and best friend are killed in a car crash. With little motivation, diminishing redundancy money, and no prospects, he decides suicide is the only option. But a kitsch natural event makes him miss the train he'd so carefully planned to fall under. Afterwards he begins to suffer from flash insights into the thoughts of complete strangers, which leads to him into exploring the death and life of an anorexic woman—who has mysteriously left him an apparent suicide note containing nothing more than a username and password.

The Last Straw is a wry, humorous story about love, death, religion and eating disorders (the book's characters reserve the right to change the plot, the title, and themselves, completely at any time prior to publication).

Published 2012

Curtis Bollington is always open to comments and communication, especially the positive kind, and particularly those involving publicity opportunities, publishing contracts, paid work and creative projects.

Author's note: 'If you like my work even a little and want to help a struggling author, please help by recommending me, tagging my books and writing reviews whenever you can. Thanks.'

Contact the author online:

email: curtis.bollington@gmail.com

Facebook: http://on.fb.me/HidnGem

Twitter: curtisboll

blog: http://curtisbollington.wordpress.com